Nothing Disappears

Nothing Disappears

D. K. Smith

Cedar Point Press

rideau lakes   kansas city

FIRST CEDAR POINT HARDCOVER EDITION 2017

Published in the United States by Cedar Point Press
www.cedarpointpress.com

Smith, Donald Kimball
Nothing Disappears / D. K. Smith. –1st Cedar Point hardcover ed.

ISBN 978-0-9914737-5-5

cover photo: Lawrence Manning/Corbis/Gettyimages

for Annie
of course

"It is sufficiently agreed that all things change and that nothing disappears, but that the sum of matter remains exactly the same."
    --Sir Francis Bacon

"Now you see it. Now you don't."
    --Harry Blackstone (attributed)

Clown Day

In his more lucid moments Rudy used to say the only way to see something clearly was to make it disappear. In that instant just before it was gone you knew everything about it: the smooth sides, the awkward shape, the few rough edges where your fingers could find a grip. That was the only certain knowledge you'd ever have, and that was the difference, he said, between you and the audience: you knew what you were seeing, even as it vanished.

But it turns out old Rudy was wrong. I've made things disappear—scarves, rabbits, whole towns, in fact—and I know. It's not that instant before when you see most clearly, but the instant just after. Then you know things as well as you ever will because you know them by the empty space they leave behind. That's the moment of clarity—that and, if you're lucky, the moment when they reappear. The rest is just a blur of anticipation or loss. The longer you think about all that's gone, the less certain it grows, until memory itself becomes just another way of not seeing clearly.

Take this one town I used to know. In my memory it was a grey and overcast place huddled under lowering clouds. But on my first day back, fresh off the bus, finding my way down the familiarity of Main Street as if through someone else's dream, the sun was bright, and the whole town lay bathed in light as if giving the lie to all that I recalled.

Only one structure fit my memory. Wrapped in its own shadow, the Longfellow Building resisted even the warmth of early July. It was a crooked, slump-shouldered old pile, but it had always held a special place in the hearts of its neighbors. The tallest, grayest building on Main Street, it carried an air of gloom and ancient damp that was almost monumental, though its only real claim to fame was that it should have been knocked down twenty years ago. Over time that alone had turned it into a landmark. People noticed it. They admired it in the grudging, self-satisfied way of small towns everywhere. Growing up, children had it pointed out to them: the Longfellow Building, the ugliest building in Strawberry's Landing. The only structure in town with no redeeming architectural value.

At least that's what the Department of Housing and Urban Development had said when they'd sent a man out in the Eighties to advise local planners. The phrase was in his report, and it became a kind of watchword in town. No Redeeming Value. It should have come down. But it was saved because the town fathers used the last of their federal money to demolish three of the most beautiful buildings in all the Northeast.

The Landing was not a very progressive place, never in the forefront even by the conservative standards of Connecticut, and its first attempts at urban renewal came long after the rest of the country had all but given up on the idea. Town planners decided to make an example of one particular block in the south end of town where three beautiful brick buildings in the Federalist style stood across the second broadest Main Street in New England from an ancient hardware store, a diner, and the prepossessing gloom of the Longfellow Building. The plan was simple. Renovate the three beautiful buildings—the newly named Federalist Row—and clear out the shabbiness across the street to make way for something cheerier. This would revitalize the town, preserve its historic past, and make a name for the town fathers as champions of all that was good and beautiful.

The Mertel Construction Company was selected for the task. Although Mr. Mertel had no direct experience with historic renovation, he was the uncle of the town's then-mayor, which cloaked him in its own particular mantle of expertise. And the project, after all, was fairly straightforward. The delicate fabric of two-hundred-year-old masonry was to be reinforced: spidery strands of steel were to be laced through the walls. Then the bricks themselves were to be hand-scrubbed and sealed against the elements, and the windows re-glazed with a special thermo-pane that mimicked the faint purple tinge of ancient glass. Everyone agreed it was going to be a triumph of history.

But on that first day, less than eight hours into the project, history, like Elvis, left the building. No one knows exactly what happened. At least, no one would admit it. But the delicate brickwork that had outlasted two centuries, seven wars, and any number of smaller skirmishes, shrugged its broad shoulders and conceded defeat. In less than an afternoon, with all the vast array of construction equipment, supplies, and tools laid out before it, the facade of the middle building collapsed into rubble, taking a portion of the wall on either side along with it.

The entire town turned out to see the wreckage, poking through bricks and mortar mixed long before the Revolution, sidling up to the gaping front to peer in at the exposed shelves of floors and ceilings. The Mertels, uncle and mayor, were left with no choice but to complete the demolition, spending the town's entire budget of federal aid, while, across the street, the Longfellow Building remained exactly as it was.

Shortly thereafter, the younger Mertel decided to give up electoral politics. In a daring daylight escape, he named himself to the recently vacated post of Town Health Inspector, a lifetime appointment, and resigned from the mayor's office. Federalist Row was renamed the Federalist Lot, and the interim mayor, unable to find anyone with more serious plans, leased it to Buster Winfield, who preserved it in its fallow state and parked cars on it for $3 a day. The sole building raised on the lot was a small, plywood hut, only vaguely in the Federalist style, containing a chair, a space heater and a black-and-white TV.

As I stood now, on a Monday afternoon, in that cool and durable shadow I could still recall the sight of the ancient brick facade collapsing under the weight of everyone's expectations. It was almost twenty years ago. I'd been less than four, standing with my brother in the crowd, but the image was as clear as if the dust were still hanging in the air. It was my oldest memory, the first one to stay with me, and in the last seven years I'd never once thought about it. But now it came back, reappearing out of nowhere with the lingering smell of dust and disappointment, and I wondered if it was just coincidence that my earliest memory of home was of something collapsing. Standing there I realized: if I remembered that so clearly, then an entire town full of memories could be lying in wait for me in exactly the same way.

And with that notion came the thought of Kevin. I wanted to ask him what his earliest memories were—if he realized how treacherous and unreliable the past could be. But then, he didn't seem to have suffered from it. Quite the contrary. He seemed to have managed pretty well. Of all the differences between us, that was perhaps the biggest.

I gazed up at the grey façade, made even more gloomy by the streaks of soot washed into patterns just short of meaning. The windows stared out blankly over my head. From that first moment of its non-collapse, people had begun to develop a grudging respect for the building. It might be ugly, it might have no redeeming architectural value, but at least it didn't collapse. And if it wasn't going to fall down on its own, no one had the heart to tear it down. So it remained, growing shabbier with each season, and every few years some new public service group would move in until they could find a better place. It had held the Salvation Army for a while, then the Youth Service branch of the town welfare department, and, for the last few years, the Shortfellows Children's Theater.

Reflexively I straightened my jacket, patting pockets, checking props, shaking out my hands, all the jittery habits of opening night. I told myself it was nothing more than a strange new town, and we'd had our share of those. Except that it wasn't a new town. It was the oldest possible town, and it wasn't we anymore. It was just me. And I could feel the very familiarity of the place crowding in around me. I wanted to run to the bus station; I wanted to catch the first thing out of town. Don't worry, said Rudy the way he always did. His voice still a whisper in my ear.

Don't talk, don't think, don't worry... It's magic.

I pulled open the door and stepped in. The interior had been elegant once: oak wainscoting and high plaster walls, but now everything was scuffed and stained. Dust hung in the air with the stale, cedary smell of an attic only recently opened. There was no sign of life. No sound. Half a flight up stood a pair of broad doors, closed and locked. "Anybody home?" To the left a stairway rose, following my words out of sight.

A voice floated down. "Up here."

I climbed the steps all the way up to the eaves, ending at the only open doorway in the building. Beyond was a small room, brightly lit, crowded with furniture, hemmed in on all sides by the sloping roof. With a knock on the open door I stepped in.

On a high stool beside a desk a very young girl sat very still with her face raised patiently to the light. Before her stood a large and gaudy clown in orange overalls and a baggy white t-shirt, who was carefully smearing greasepaint over the child's forehead and cheeks. At my entrance they both looked up, the young girl with the tense expression of someone trying to maintain her balance on a narrow space, and the clown with a face of painted and inscrutable sadness. She wore a red sausage frown and black diamond eyes beneath a pink wig like a huge Brillo pad.

"Can I help you?" she asked.

I hesitated. "I'm a little underdressed."

"That's okay. We're very informal here."

"I called you earlier. My name's Charles."

"Then I must be Emily." She straightened up a little stiffly. "I'd shake hands, but you look so clean."

She had a low, warm voice, I'd noticed it that morning on the phone: like velvet brushed against the nap. But now it seemed so out of place emerging from the white, painted face that it might have been dubbed.

She held up a crumpled tube of makeup. "You don't mind if I keep working, do you? I'm a little behind."

"I could come back later."

"No, that's all right. I'm almost done." She squeezed a white blob onto her fingertips. "Have a seat. Anywhere you can find one." And she turned back to the young girl.

I looked around. There were several chairs, sagging and over-stuffed, and a long ragged sofa beneath a triptych of windows that overlooked Buster Winfield's parking lot, still operating af-ter all these years. Every surface was piled with bright scraps of clothing: gauzy dresses, coils of satin, a purple feathered boa. It looked as if a vintage clothing store had exploded. If colors were noise the place would have been deafening, but as it was the only sound was the whisper of traffic rising from the street below.

I shrugged off my jacket and looked around for some place to hang it. On the back of the door there was a hook, though it was already full. Black jeans, black turtleneck, black sweater. In that room full of bright colors they seemed out of place, though I suppose even a clown needs a break now and then. I hung up my jacket and turned back.

The girl was sitting like a statue slowly disappearing under a coat of whitewash.

"I think you missed a spot," I said.

Emily didn't answer. She wasn't, I noticed, a particularly friendly clown, but that didn't surprise me. I'd met a few in my travels, and as if carrying the weight of professional cheerful-ness like a sack of rocks on their backs, they tended to be a little grumpy on their own time. Or maybe she was just concentrat-ing. Her white fingers slipped over the girl's cheek, covering the last little trapezoid of pink skin.

I'd known a woman years ago, and the only way you could tell she was a pickpocket was by the way she handled her knife and fork at meals. She moved so lightly, with such precision, that it took no effort at all to imagine those same fingers dipping into a coat pocket as smoothly as a hand into water. Emily's hands were larger, long and muscled, but she had that same slippery dexterity. "I can see this isn't your first clown," I said.

"No indeed. Jill, here, makes twenty-nine."

"Twenty-nine?"

She glanced up, her expression impenetrable. "What's the matter? Don't you like clowns?"

"Well, sure. Everybody likes clowns."

"Okay, then."

"I was just wondering why you needed so many."

"Because," she said patiently, "today is Clown Day."

"Why did I think it was the Fourth of July?"

"It's a common mistake. We have a parade to lead...." She glanced at her wrist, where a large smiling watch face had been painted. "In about an hour."

"Is that the correct time?"

She shook her wrist. "It might be a little slow."

Her overalls were baggy and patched with as many different fabrics as there were holes. Polka dots. Paisleys. A large pink and white heart over the left breast. Rags dangled from her pockets as though spilling out. Just for an instant I thought I must have the wrong person. I had never, in my wildest dreams, envisioned her like this.

"Are you really engaged to the mayor?" I asked.

She looked up in surprise, pushing a few pink tendrils off her forehead with the back of her wrist, then almost reluctantly she smiled. At least I think she smiled. The painted frown shifted up slightly at the edges. "As far as I know. Why? Don't you approve of that either?"

"I think of mayors as being fairly serious people."

"That just shows what you know about clowns. Deep down inside, I'm a fairly serious person, myself."

Which I should have known, of course. Which I should have kept in mind.

"Is that what you called to talk to me about?" she asked.

"Your seriousness?"

"The engagement."

"Not exactly. I think I mentioned on the phone, I'm kind of

new in town."

"Of course you are." She gazed at me, as if expecting to find the date of my arrival like some stamp of freshness on my face. "How new?"

I checked my own watch. No smiling face. "Five hours, eleven minutes. More or less fresh off the bus. Before I set up shop I like to check with the local talent. You know, get a sort of clown's-eye view of the town."

"I can see how that would be useful," she said.

I was used to reading people's expressions. When you're performing, everything depends on knowing the audience: where they're looking, what they're thinking, what they're about to do next. But the white makeup was like a screen between us. At the time it didn't occur to me to wonder if it was just coincidence that she was so thoroughly masked for our first meeting, though I thought about it later.

"Are all clowns this suspicious?"

"It's the Fourth of July," she said.

"I thought it was Clown Day."

"The point is, it's a national holiday. And you climb off the bus, drop your bags, and head straight over here to talk to me?"

"Something like that."

She shook her head, gazing at me with her smooth, unreadable, sausage-frowned expression. "What exactly is it that makes me so interesting?"

In a town as small as Strawberry's Landing prominence is more a matter of personality than position, and Emily Burke had personality to spare. She'd come to college here because she'd wanted a small untroubled town, and when she discovered it was no more untroubled than the larger places she'd grown up in, she decided it was at least trouble on a scale she could manage. She'd been a gymnast in high school, and a dancer, but she didn't do either in college. College was a time to get serious, to give up childish pursuits and proms and parties, and devote herself to more important things. In her second month at Methodist University she and a group of friends broke into the main biology laboratory and released thirty-two monkeys and a hundred-and-twenty-one white rats from their cages. A few weeks later she was arrested for the first time when she chained herself, along with twenty-three others, to the gates of the Seabrook Nuclear Power Plant. But that was only the beginning.

Upon graduation she decided to stay on in town. She started the children's theater with the help of a federal block grant but continued to divide her time between putting on plays and getting arrested. She made several trips to Seabrook with Greenpeace, and down to New Haven with Citizens For a Clean Harbor. And one busy weekend she stayed right here in town with a performance of The Lost Treasure on Friday night and a full scale protest against toxic dumping at the Shapewell Metalworks factory on Saturday morning.

That was more or less how she met my brother. She and three others arrived at the plant wearing red and white coveralls with the Shapewell logo on the front, and with their faces made up into death's heads. They then proceeded to put on a sort of Morality Play. Climbing out onto a twelve-inch ledge outside the third floor of the building, they demonstrated how close to the brink of extinction Shapewell was taking the ecology of the Connecticut River. They tossed handfuls of metal shavings, rusty pipes, dead fish, and water fowl onto the parking lot below. They shouted down to the crowd that had gathered. They told them Shapewell was poisoning their drinking water. They told them Shapewell was killing them.

The television cameras arrived, and, as though connected by a kind of telepathic umbilical cord, so did Kevin. This was just a few months ago. He'd only recently become mayor, the youngest mayor in Connecticut since the Revolutionary War, and he was hot on the job. Perhaps he'd been in his office or in the middle of a Town Council meeting when he heard, because he arrived with several councilmen in tow. They stood in their shirt sleeves and loosened ties, as if preparing to wrestle with this latest municipal problem, but they proved ineffectual. Standing there amid a gathering crowd of police, they called up to the demonstrators to come down, to desist, to please be careful, but no one up on the ledge paid any attention.

And then there was a sudden hush in the crowd. I suppose it's possible that, even if the television cameras hadn't been there, my brother would have entered the building, climbed up three flights of stairs, and stepped out onto the ledge, but we'll never know for sure. All we know is what the cameras recorded: silence, then a whisper, and from a third floor window, high up the brick wall, a blonde head emerged. Moving very slowly Kevin braced himself against the window frame and drew himself out, setting his foot on the ledge. It took courage; I'll grant him that. He hated heights. To anyone who didn't know him he seemed merely to be moving in slow motion, but knowing how terrified he must have been, you could have seen that he was edging forward by sheer force of will. A twelve inch ledge two feet off the ground is plenty wide. You could jump around on it. You could dance. But thirty feet up with an asphalt parking lot underneath, it shrinks to the width of a fence post. Kevin moved slowly as if with every step he had to locate the ledge all over again.

Emily and her friends stopped throwing dead fish. They stopped shouting. They turned.

"I think you should all go inside," Kevin said slowly. Despite his fear, he spoke loudly enough for the cameras. "I think this performance is over. You've made your point. Now let's please stop before anyone gets hurt." As he spoke he continued to edge along toward the protesters until, with the word 'hurt', he could have reached out and touched them. It was then that Kevin realized he was the only one on the ledge not wearing a safety harness.

The realization startled him into one step too many. The edge of his foot caught on the building and very slowly he started to fall. He grabbed for the closest thing to him, which was Emily, and she grabbed him, and together they fell, the cable of the safety harness stretching taut, then miraculously holding. And gradually, two-and-a-half stories above a hard parking lot, twisting gently in the breeze, Kevin realized that the body he was gripping ever so tightly was female.

I thought it was strange, at first, that a moderate and politically ambitious mayor should become involved with someone so utterly immoderate. But Dewey Reynolds didn't seem surprised. Newspaper editors so seldom are. "You know small towns," he said. "They encourage eccentricity, as long as it's familiar. And Emily's a fixture. A popular fixture. Besides," said Dewey, "they're not all that different. Stepping out onto ledges. Chaining yourself to gates. It's all theater. But it's interesting theater. Worth keeping an eye on. Who knows? We might learn something."

He meant, I'm sure, we might learn something newsworthy, something that would make a good story for his paper. But my motives were much less pure than his. We were both curious about Emily, but I was curious for all the wrong reasons.

She gazed at me a moment longer, the greasepaint tube still clutched in her hand, but I just stood there, leaning against the edge of the desk with my stage-face on, smiling and blank. The little girl, just short of a clown now, with chalk white skin and her own blue eyes, sat there staring grimly ahead, pretending she was invisible, or that I was. That sort of determined seriousness is always hard to resist. It's like a large painted sign saying: kick me.

I leaned forward, snapping my fingers once in front of her face, just to get her attention, then with a little flourish I drew a yellow silk scarf from her buttonhole. As it grew longer and longer, her eyes grew rounder until finally I pulled it free and dropped it wispily into her lap.

She stared up at me without a word.

"Wait. Is this yours?" I reached out and plucked from her ear a tiny green frog and set it on the edge of the desk. The frog and the young girl both sat there, staring at each other, too surprised to move. "Maybe you should think about washing more often," I said. I was reaching for a silk rose when Emily laughed. Just like that. Gloomy frown and all. A laugh like a puff of smoke. She stood gazing down at the face of the girl staring down into the face of the frog. "How did he do that?" the little girl whispered.

Emily shrugged. "You'll have to ask Mr. Bentchley."

That caught me by surprise. I hesitated, then offered up a crooked smile. "I don't remember mentioning my last name."

"Didn't you?"

The girl reached out a cautious finger tip, not quite touching the frog's nose. It shifted its webbed feet and blinked. "What's his name?"

"He doesn't really have a name," I said. "He's new to the act. I just picked him up outside."

"Is he magic?"

"I wouldn't be surprised."

"Can I touch him?"

"Be careful of warts."

She snatched back her hand, but continued to eye him warily.

Emily, with a lingering smile, reached over beyond the frog and picked up a long, thin brush and an artist's palette dotted with paint, for all the world as if she were going to do the girl's portrait. "Okay, Jill. Let's get you finished up. We've got a parade to start. Eyes closed."

The girl obeyed. She sat up patiently. The frog stared. Emily dipped the brush in a smear of black paint and leaned closer.

"How did you know who I was?" I asked.

But Emily said nothing. She was all concentration now, leaning into her work. Delicately she traced a narrow diamond over each quivering eyelid and filled them in with feathery strokes. Then, dipping into the red, she gave the child a big, broad smile. I stood and watched. On her own face the makeup had dried some time ago, and the texture of skin showed through: thin creases at the corner of her eyes, and beneath the greasepaint on the upper lip the slightest crease of worry. Her eyes were warm and brown, and they looked out through the makeup as if through a mask.

After a moment she lowered the brush, then drew a rag from her back pocket and wiped a little smudge of stray paint from the corner of the girl's eye. Straightening up she stretched wearily and dropped the rag onto the desk. "That's it, Jill. Up the hill. Rachel's waiting."

The girl squirmed off the stool and turned, giving me a full look at her newly painted face. Despite the cheerful make-up the girl still looked very serious.

"Keep smiling," I said.

She glanced at the frog, still perched on the desktop.

"Go ahead. Take him. He loves a parade."

But instead she turned and raced down the steps, the slap of her footsteps echoing up the stairwell then fading away.

For a moment Emily stood there by the empty stool, looking slightly at a loss now that she'd run out of clowns to paint. "I should get going."

"I know. You've got a parade."

But then, reluctantly, she sat down on the stool. "You're not quite what I expected," she said. And not for the first time I wondered what Kevin might have told her. The eyes regarding me now were still warm, but distant again behind that bright, frowning face. It took a kind of double vision to keep her in focus, the chalk-white skin and sausage mouth beside those warm eyes and that soft, low voice. When she spoke her lips and the tip of her tongue showed like a quick, pink secret she was trying to keep. "Why didn't you tell me on the phone who you were?"

"I was undercover," I said. "I wanted to see what you were like. How did you know?"

"Your brother said you were coming back."

"What else did he say?"

She hesitated. "He warned me about you."

"He couldn't have. He doesn't know the first thing about me."

"He said you were kind of a screw-up."

I shrugged. "Okay. Maybe the first thing."

"Has he ever seen you perform?"

"Not for a long time. Why?"

She gestured at the frog, still sitting patiently on the desk. "You're better than he said you were."

I considered that for a moment. Then with a certain, pardonable ostentation I cracked my knuckles and pulled out the deck of cards from my pocket. I shuffled once to loosen them up, and fanned them out in my hand. "Pick a card. Any card."

Emily glanced over at me warily. "I thought you wanted to ask me about the town."

"I do. Take one. Go ahead. But don't show it to me."

With a serious expression not so different from the little girl's, she drew out a card and glanced at it.

I cut the deck. "Back it goes."

She replaced it in the middle of the pile. Under cover of straightening the deck I finessed her card to the top and cut it back under to the bottom. I was a little out of practice, but the cards were behaving well. The deck was smooth, and I couldn't help smiling. I shuffled again, feeling more comfortable now, feeling almost at home, slipping back into the familiar patter like an old suit of clothes. I could feel Rudy smiling over my shoulder. "Long ago, when I was a boy," I said, "I learned the secret of telling when someone was lying. I can listen to a voice and, just by the tone, I can tell."

"What sort of lies?"

"Any sort. All sorts."

I held out the deck. Emily shook her head. Her expression was impenetrable, shielded by the painted face.

"Guilty conscience?" I said.

"No more than the next clown."

"Well then..."

She held up her hands, smeared with greasepaint. "I've got to clean up."

"Then I'll show them to you. I want you to read each card. Read it out loud. And tell the truth. But when you come to the card you chose, I want you to lie. Make up another card. I'll know when you're lying."

She picked up the rag and began wiping her hands. "I've got a parade to lead." But she couldn't resist. Her eyes were on the cards.

I started lifting them up, holding them away from me.

"Seven of spades," she said.

"True."

"Five of clubs."

"True."

"Ten of clubs."

"True," I said. And then, "How does someone fall in love with my brother?"

"Is this part of the trick?"

"Tell the truth and you won't have to worry."

"How can someone not?" she said.

"Could you be more specific?"

From that white face her black diamond eyes gazed back at me as if it were obvious. "He's charming. He cares about people. He gets things done."

I held up the next card. "That's it? Cares about people?"

"You asked," she said. "Jack of Spades."

"Well, he does get things done. I'll grant you that."

"Six of hearts."

"True."

"Seven of hearts." She paused. "Why does someone run away from home?"

"This is my trick."

"Fair's fair. It seems an odd thing to do."

"Why does someone chain herself to a nuclear power plant?"

"I asked you first."

"I'm holding the card."

She shrugged. "Because it's important. Because someone needs to remind people what two tons of uranium can do to a state full of people. Or that ten thousand gallons of sulfuric acid poured into the river a little at a time is still ten thousand gallons. Five of Hearts," she said.

"People know that."

"Do they? I think people know what they want to know. If they don't want to hear it, they don't."

"And it's up to you to straighten them out?"

"Yes."

I paused, fingering the next card. "I'm not sure that's true."

"Of course it is. What else are we here for? If you're not doing something that changes the world, then you're wasting your time."

"You are a fairly serious clown."

"Didn't I say so? If you're not serious, what's the point? Six of diamonds."

"How serious?"

She shrugged, but she was leaning forward now, tensed with purpose. "If something absolutely has to be done, how serious is that?"

I stopped for a moment, weighing the cards in my hand. "I don't know. In my experience I can think of a few things that absolutely should not have been done, but I'm not so sure about the reverse."

She looked up at me. The painted frown was firmly in place, but her eyes held a glint of curiosity. "What shouldn't have been done?"

"Too much, even to think about."

"What about leaving town? Was that something?"

Without replying I raised the next card.

"Six of spades," she said. "Not a note. Not a telephone call. No warning at all. Your parents were frantic."

"Who said so?"

But it was her turn not to reply.

"I left a note," I said.

"That's not what I heard."

"Then you heard wrong."

"They thought you'd been kidnapped."

"They?"

"Your family."

I lowered the card. "No they didn't."

"They said you were traveling around with some old man named Weizman."

"Rudy. That's right."

"For seven years?"

"We were in touch. I wrote to them."

"How often?"

"As often as I could."

But she just looked at me, waiting. The cards were turning stiff in my hands. They seemed to be waiting, too.

"Not often," I said. "We traveled around. The northeast mostly. He had his circuit. Massachusetts, New York, Vermont."

"Was it fun?"

"Every so often."

"And the rest of the time?"

I shrugged.

"Then why do it?"

"What did Kevin say?"

"They thought you'd been brainwashed at first. Then they decided it was just the sort of thing you'd always done."

"You don't mean 'they'."

She shrugged. "He was worried about you." Emily glanced down at the card I was holding. It had drooped down toward the floor, forgotten. She reached out for it, turning it to see the face.

"Don't bother," I said. "It's the Jack of Hearts."

"True enough." But she held onto the card, looking down at it as if there were something more to be read in its face. "Why was it so hard?"

"Leaving home?"

"No. Coming back."

It wasn't a question I'd expected. Not from her, not from anyone. Though it was one I asked myself all the time.

I glanced down at the frog, who was staring at me now as though he couldn't believe what he saw. "Why does someone become a clown?" I asked.

"For fun."

"Remember," I said. "I'm still holding the cards."

"Do I need another reason?"

"I just thought maybe.... It's another face to hide behind. Someone else's smile. It's a little added protection."

She shrugged. "If you know the answer," she said, "why ask the question?"

"It was like that for me. Being on the road. It was like hiding in someone else's life. There was no past, no future. Just the moment. Or the afternoon. Or the evening. Nothing beyond."

"And that was fun?"

"No. Not fun, exactly." I thought about it, the long, long days of travel, the boredom, the occasional fear and excitement. "Actually, it scared the shit out of me, at least at first. I didn't really know what I was doing. But in an odd way I felt protected. Because it wasn't important. Because no one knew me. Because, in some fundamental way it just didn't matter."

She considered that for a long moment. "Your audience must have thought it mattered."

"Oh, that. Sure. You have to do the show well or people don't come. And then we wouldn't eat. That got to be pretty important. But on the level that most people live their lives...." I shrugged. "It didn't matter at all. You said a life ought to be important. Well, this wasn't. And you have no idea what a relief it was."

"It doesn't sound easy."

"Not easy, exactly. But all I had to worry about was discomfort: hunger, damp, a hard night's sleep, a night in jail. At the time it seemed manageable."

She regarded me closely. Behind the impenetrable makeup, her mind was turning something over. She hesitated.

"What?" I said.

"I've met your family."

"So?"

"They're wonderful."

"So?"

"They're smart. They're accomplished. They're nice."

"That's what I hear."

"And you just left."

"More or less."

"Why?"

I shrugged again. "Because I couldn't stay."

She shook her head. "Uh-uh. Now I've got the card." And she held up the Jack of Hearts. Funny that it should be that card out of all of them. After all this time. I felt as if I'd spent my whole life in the shadow of that card. But what could I say? I sat there. Even in a game of truth there's only so much you can tell.

"There was a girl," I said.

"I know. I heard."

"Did you?"

"Kevin told me."

"Then you didn't hear right."

"I heard she died."

"Yes," I said. "That's true enough."

I sat there watching my brother's fiancée, waiting to see if she might say something more. But clowns are undependable, they never talk when you want them to. They never tell you what you need to know.

She stood there looking down at the Jack of Hearts. "That's not enough." She said. "That's not an explanation."

"No." But what startled me was that I wanted to give her one. I wanted her to understand. I wanted to tell her, but I didn't know how.

In any magic trick you have to know what you're hiding as

well as what you show. You need to remember all the lies your trick is built on if you want to focus on that one, final truth. But I had lost track, somewhere in the last seven years, of all that I was hiding. When I'd made my life disappear all that time ago, everything had been sharp in my mind. But now the truth had grown blurry. I'd made it vanish, and I couldn't remember where. What could I tell her? That nobody just dies? Certainly not Gracie. That Kevin had killed her almost as surely as if he'd lit the fire himself?

I stood up, a little abruptly, perhaps, but a good magician knows when the show is over. "Thanks for your time. I know you've got some clowns waiting."

She hesitated. "I'm sorry."

"For what?'

She gave a wry smile. "I'm not sure yet. Maybe for all the wrong impressions I had."

"Don't be so sure."

"Come to the parade," she said.

I shook my head. Whatever plans I'd made on that long bus ride back, they didn't include this. I had planned to dislike her. I planned to hate her, if I could. But how do you hate a clown with a voice like that? "I don't think so," I said.

"I'm sure your family will be there."

"All the more reason. Though, I am sorry to miss Clown Day."

"Twenty-nine different shapes and sizes...."

But I was already turning to the door.

"So, tell me," called Emily. "If you wanted to leave so badly, why come back?"

I stopped and looked up. The white face, the eyes, and the steady, wide frown, all so coolly opaque. But then I noticed at the base of her neck, just above her collar, a narrow crescent where the greasepaint gave way to the warmth of her skin, a little curve of bare throat that had somehow been overlooked. It made me want to reach out a fingertip and touch that skin. Just the skin, not the woman herself, just that slight, exposed part. But I didn't.

Instead, I told her the truth, or most of it, as much as I could, addressing myself to that delicate hint of honesty beneath the clown's face.

"I heard you two were engaged."

She hesitated, caught between curiosity and surprise. "And you came back? Just like that? After all this time?"

"Of course. He's my brother. What was I going to do? Let him get married without me?"

And she just looked at me.

I slipped the cards back into my pocket before she could speak again. We'd had enough truth for one afternoon, and I was beginning to understand something. I had climbed onto the bus almost thirty-two hours before with only the vaguest of plans. But now I realized, almost in spite of myself, what it was that had brought me home, and I felt like the worst kind of magician: surprised by his own tricks.

Rudy had died, and I'd heard that Kevin was engaged, that he was mayor now and soon to be married, that things were still looking up for him. And I decided to return. I wanted to see his bride-to-be. But, more than that, I wanted to see what he'd built for himself in this town where our family had been living for two hundred years. I wanted to see for myself what his life looked like. And something else, something more.

As I gazed into the painted inscrutability of Emily's face I realized that I had come back in the spirit of fairness, in the belief that no one should have too much good fortune. I came back to make sure, if it was ever in my power, that Kevin wouldn't have everything exactly his own way.

Dorothy

So that was it. I was back. And now that I was, I tried to settle in. I told myself it was just another town and tried to cling to our usual routine. After seven years on the road it should have been second nature. I stored the trunks at the bus station and looked for a place to stay, but without Rudy the whole process seemed dark and unfamiliar. The two of us could stay anywhere. And had. Bus stations, YMCAs, boarding houses. I once slept under a highway overpass. But now I had trouble. I looked at a lot of places, but none seemed quite right. They were all too nice: cozy, comfortable, snug. They looked like college apartments, which they were. They looked like the sort of place I might have imagined staying seven years ago in some teen-aged fantasy of roughing it on my own for a while: all the comforts of home beneath a thin layer of grime. So I kept looking, and finally I found what I needed. Rudy would have been, if not pleased, at least grumpily satisfied. I watched the landlady's resigned expression blossom into furtive relief, though it really wasn't that bad. Definitely not the worst I'd had.

It was at the north edge of town beyond a cratered no-man's land of crumbling asphalt and abandoned warehouses. To get there you had to follow a curving ramp up onto the overpass that would put you on the bridge out of town, and then veer off at the last minute down a sudden side road, so that every time you drove home it felt as if you'd arrived by accident, as if you'd meant to leave town but hadn't quite managed to. The apartment itself was a crooked little caravan of three rooms on the second floor of an ancient duplex, and the only way in was up two half-flights of rickety brown stairs to what, in any more serious establishment, would have been the back door. I didn't take it for the price, which was cheap, or the bathtub which was ancient and enormous—apparently the only two things that even the landlady could think to say about the place. I took it for the crooked floors and the patches in the plaster and the water stains on the ceiling. I took it for the general air of sad disconsolation. I thought they would protect me. I bought a mattress for the floor and a table for the kitchen, and like any good traveler in uncertain times, I kept my bags packed.

What kind of a life does magic prepare you for? All that hard work and illusion, all those years on the road ... it should teach you something, if only how to climb off the bus in a strange town and not lose your way. It isn't easy. On the road each new town is its own little illusion, and each arrival, like any good trick, is founded on the threat of disaster.

There is always that moment, when you first arrive, when it could all go wrong. With the whole empty weight of the town pressing in around you—the bus station, the motel, whatever empty Elks Lodge or VFW Hall you could find to perform in— there is nothing to keep you from the realization that this is what you've come to. After all the miles and all the practice, this is where you've ended up, and of all the ways your life could have gone, this is where it went. It's a bad moment. And it takes both of you to keep it together, town after town. You have to cling to the surface of your life, like Wiley Coyote hanging in the air far beyond the edge of the cliff against all likelihood or possibility. Strangeness is the only comfort you have, and you need to hold onto that together, with jokes, with grumbling, with complaints or sudden, unlikely bursts of optimism. The town, you tell yourself, has nothing to do with you. It doesn't mean anything. You're just passing through.

It's the power of delusion; that pale filament of denial that runs through the heart of every kind of magic. Lose it and you've lost it all. But there's a problem with telling yourself you're just passing through. It only works if you are. The last thing a life on the road prepares you for is coming home.

For the first time I'd arrived in a town without any clear sense of what I was supposed to be doing. Putting up posters? Finding a stage? Rehearsing the act? I did none of these things. What I did was wait, twined in the soft strands of dread and anticipation, until finally on Friday morning the doorbell rang.

I was sitting on the floor of my living room eating breakfast with the rabbits, and I just sat there for a moment longer, stunned by the noise. I'd been so many years without a doorbell in places where almost nobody knew me and nobody at all came calling that the sound itself was odd and demanding. I glanced around at the rabbits, but none of them seemed bothered. Why should they? It wasn't their problem. They didn't know anyone in this town.

Despite what many people say, rabbits have a lot to recommend them. They're soft, they're quiet, they're good listeners, and for the most part they mind their own business. They don't ask for much in life, and they're happy with what they get. This morning I had Rex on my lap, scratching the spot just behind his ears that reduced him to catatonic bliss. His eyes were closed; his ears lay flat against his back. The others were all nose-down in the rabbit chow, pretty much at peace with the world, and following their example I sat perfectly still, moving only the fingers on Rex's neck, trying to blend invisibly into my surroundings. The bell sounded again, harsh and impatient. Reluctantly Rex and I climbed to my feet.

I stepped into the kitchen with a feeling of pale dread, as if all my vague uneasiness had suddenly materialized at my door. I gazed out through the curtains, and then, with a sudden awareness, at the curtains themselves. They'd been up when I moved in, and until now I had barely noticed them, certainly I hadn't bothered to put up anything in their place, but now I was sharply aware of them, hanging in every room. They were pink gingham and white eyelet lace, edged with a pink floral fabric that might have been part of a very young girl's favorite outfit. I thought wildly of ripping them down, and stood poised in a paroxysm of appalled indecision, but in the end I just opened the door.

"Goodness," said my mother. "So you are home."

In her arms she clasped a huge grocery bag, and as I stepped back she hurried in with a little breath of effort and set it down on the counter. Then turning, she reached up, with a bright, determined smile that resolutely ignored, among all the gathered and interposed circumstances of the last seven years, the fact that I was cradling in my arms a large, white rabbit, and gave me a brisk kiss on the cheek. I stared down at her, startled into silence. She looked utterly, inexplicably familiar, even across the distance of so many years. And more shocking still was the realization of how quickly that distance itself threatened to give way. Seven years away, seven years without an explanation, without a word spoken between us. And now this bright smile? This kiss on the cheek? Whatever else was true, you had to hand it to my mother. She knew what was important. "What a charming place," she said. "I knew it would it be."

"Of course," I said. "How could I live in a place that wasn't charming?"

"And those curtains. Really. They're too dear."

"I knew you'd like them. I got them especially for you."

Dorothy Bentchley was in her mid-fifties but looked ten years younger. She wasn't tall. When asked, she always gave her height as "in the low fives, darling" and she carried herself with an unshakeable conviction that good posture could make up for any lack of inches. She had a cap of thick blonde hair that had seen its share of highlighting, but never obviously so, and a round face. She'd been pretty as a girl but never beautiful, and as she'd grown older she had decided to settle for that with a kind of no-nonsense approach to grooming that drew as little attention to itself as possible. It wasn't that she didn't care, but that she didn't want to seem to care.

She'd gone straight from Methodist College into Methodist Law School and then, pausing barely long enough to fall in love with her Torts instructor and marry him a week after passing the Bar, she had gone to work for an insurance firm twenty-five miles north in Hartford. It was not the most prestigious position she'd been offered nor the best paid, but her family had lived in Connecticut since before the Revolution, and it couldn't have occurred to her to move. She may well have seen Ambrose Bentchley's newly won tenure as his greatest virtue since it forestalled any need for uncertainty or precariousness in the matter of where they would spend their lives. Dorothy was a woman who liked to have things settled.

Now she gazed around the room, taking in every detail: the walls, the industrial sink, the counters roughed out of two-by-fours. Three large rooms and a bathroom, lined up like a row of hostages.

As she looked around for something more to say I moved to forestall her. Hurriedly opening the fridge, I said. "What can I offer you? Orange juice? English muffin? Orange juice? I've got some coffee on. And I do have orange juice."

"Thank you, darling. No. Shouldn't you be at work?"

"What makes you think I'm not?"

She smiled, unruffled. "Or perhaps looking for a job?"

"I am currently what we of the stage call, at liberty. Are you sure about that orange juice?" There was a peculiarly sour smell emanating from the fridge which I had originally thought merely added to the apartment's charm, but about which I was now beginning to wonder. I closed the door.

"Thank you, darling. Maybe a little coffee, after all."

The coffeemaker was the one kitchen appliance I'd bought. It sat all alone on the uneven counter looking new, modern, and out of place. I poured her a mug. "I hope you take it black."

"Cream, two sugars, actually."

I handed it to her. "Sorry."

She took a tiny sip and wrinkled her nose delicately. "I wonder if you might have to clean that refrigerator soon, darling."

"I'll leave a note for the maid."

With a little nod she set her coffee down on the counter and turned to the grocery bag. "Well, you might want to see to it before you put these things away." And she started unpacking. Whole wheat bread, a narrow triangle of Brie, a quart of milk, a carton of orange juice. "I didn't realize you'd already have that, dear." Packages of cold cuts in white butcher paper, jars of mayonnaise and mustard, a head of lettuce, a bag of carrots, a box of Triscuits, and two cans of bean with bacon soup—my favorite when I was six. She set them all on the counter, arranged as if at the check-out aisle. "I'm not sure where they go," she said.

"Your guess is as good as mine." And then, despite my best efforts, "Thanks."

"You're welcome, dear. It's just a little something to help you settle in. I know it's difficult to find the time for everything at first." And I listened for the slightest hint of anger or disappointment or irritation, any suggestion that perhaps I should have called or stopped by in the four days I'd been home. Or perhaps that I might have ventured to call sometime in the last seven years. But her voice was unmarred.

She opened the milk and poured some into her coffee. "I don't know what I was thinking, not buying sugar. But I suppose it won't hurt to do without. I think I've put on a couple of pounds in the last little while."

There was, of course, no sign of it. She looked trim and understatedly athletic, like a cheerleader who'd found herself unexpected dressed for the Junior League.

"Maybe you'd like a sandwich? " I said. "I seem to have some cold cuts."

"Thank you, darling. You save those." She hovered for a moment at the counter, taking a sip of her coffee, balancing on her toes like a high-diver. "You know, I think maybe we should take care of that fridge right now. I'm a little concerned about that milk." And with a brisk concentration she slipped off her cardigan and started to roll up her sleeves.

"Don't do that," I said.

"I have time."

"I'll do it later."

"I can clean while we talk." And she gave a cheerful, inter-
rogative smile. "Where do we keep the cleanser?"

As it happens, we didn't keep it anywhere, but in the cavern-
ous gloom beneath the sink there was an ancient sponge, a bottle
of Lestoil, and half a box of SOS pads in the middle stages of de-
hydration, and with brisk determination my mother reached under and then straightened up, the fossilized sponge in one hand,
the ancient cleanser in the other.

I lifted them both from her hands. "Why don't I take care of
that later?"

"Well, at least let me put these things away." And without
waiting for an answer, she set about it. I watch with a kind of
bleak wonder as she wandered around, opening the all but empty cupboards, selecting the proper place for her new supplies,
talking all the while in a smiling, wandering voice with a quality like water slipping through your fingers. "...and you know
Marla Bankston? Jenny's daughter? You went to high school
with Marla, didn't you? Apparently she has some fabulous job
in Washington. The District, not the state. In marketing of all
things. At least I think it was marketing. Or advertising. Are
they the same thing? Anyway, I guess she's thrilled about it,
though I don't supposed I'd care to live in D.C. Though Kevin
liked it, didn't he? At least for a while. But those summers sound
so terrible, don't that? All that humidity and crime." She shook
her head, wondering at the prospect.

I don't know what I'd expected. Questions, of course. Criti-
cism, probably. A dark and suppressed anger that might glint
beneath the surface. But there was no hint of anything but easy
good cheer, as if we'd seen each other just last week, as if I'd
been away for only a few days. And I realized just how afraid
of this I'd been. I found myself slipping into that sense of easy
familiarity like a trap that had been laid. It was clear she had
simply decided to think of my whole time away in some blithe
and determined fashion all her own. And I could feel her trying

to reinsert me back into the present, as if to say nothing particularly important had happened during the last seven years. As if I'd been away on an extended field trip for a little longer than expected, or at some out of the way college without phones or regular mail.

I stepped back as she puttered, looking more at home in my kitchen than I'd ever feel myself, and I tried to consider her as if I'd never seen her before, as if she were a stranger, some elegant and well-dressed homeless woman who'd wandered in off the street. I watched her closely, as if there were nothing familiar about her, as if she were a new trick I was learning from scratch. My mother had always given the impression of being just a little scattered. Charming, but not altogether focused. A little fluttery and affectionate. But her greatest strength had always been that she simply couldn't imagine that anyone could really disagree with her, or that people, if they just understood, wouldn't see things exactly as she did. She was calmly, gracefully unshakeable. And as I stood watching, I realized that, despite everything, despite all my care, all my worry, I had completely underestimated her powers of determination.

With the last of the groceries tucked away she picked up her coffee and glanced at me expectantly. "Isn't that better?"

"God, yes," I said. "Why don't you come in and make yourself at home."

Gracious and smiling, she led the procession of two into the living room and abruptly stopped short. "Oh."

Growing up we had never had any pets. Dorothy's relationship to nature hadn't extended to a love of animals. She tended to see them in terms of dirt and disease, so that when I would periodically request a cat or a dog or even a goldfish, she would look gently scandalized, as if I'd asked to raise rats in my bedroom closet and for the next few days she'd point out newspaper stories and headlines of rabies alerts or young children savaged by the family dog.

Now, standing frozen in the doorway she managed a delicate

laugh. "I suppose I should have known."

"Of course. What's a magician without rabbits?"

"And you really need so many?"

"I'm afraid so. Union rules. Would you like to be introduced?"

"Not right away, dear. Maybe you'll just let us get used to one another."

"Of course."

She edged into the room, eyeing the rabbits warily, her hand brushing unconsciously at her skirt as if it had already picked up some spot.

"Have a seat," I said. "Anywhere."

There weren't many places to choose from. Rudy's two trunks were the only things approximating furniture, and they were overwhelmed by the space. One was shoved up against the wall like a bench at a bus station and the other was doing double duty as a coffee table in the middle of the room. The only other thing even approaching decor, not counting the rabbits themselves, was the low accordion fence that kept them confined to the back third of the room and a short pile of newspapers I'd been using as a breakfast tray and which now held the remains of my blueberry muffin.

Dorothy stood there a moment gazing around at all the possible places you could have put a chair if only you'd had one. Then she stepped over to the nearest trunk and settled onto it with a resolute smile. "So, dear, how are you managing? Settling in, I mean."

"Couldn't be better." I stepped over the low fence and eased back down with my coffee mug amid the rabbits. I lowered Rex to the ground, and he managed a few desultory hops before losing interest.

"Should you be eating off the floor like that?"

"I'm eating on the floor. It's completely different."

She gazed for a long moment at the expanse of scuffed wood imperfectly covered by newspapers and punctuated with a few damp puddles and a scattering of droppings. If you keep up with them rabbits are really pretty clean. I changed the papers every day and mopped the floor every other. I had a big nest of cedar chips for them to sleep on, which gave it the fresh, woodsy smell of a pet store. If you closed your eyes, you'd barely know they were there.

"Have you seen your brother's new house?" she asked.

"No. Is it nice?"

"Very nice. Three bedrooms. Beautiful furniture."

"And how many rabbits does he have?"

She hesitated. "Not as many, I think."

"Then how nice can it be?"

My mother valiantly sipped her unsweetened coffee.

"Their cage is too small for anything but traveling," I explained. "Besides, they like the company."

"How can you tell?"

Most of them were either napping in the wood chips or spread out over the newspaper chewing thoughtfully, lost in the headlines. Except for Rex. He'd abandoned the idea of food and was leaning, crouched, against my leg. I lifted him back onto my lap. "You should try it. It's actually kind of a comfort."

"Do you wash your hands?"

"Every so often."

"What does your landlord think of all this?"

"Strangely enough, she doesn't mind. It turns out she used to raise rabbits growing up back in Sicily. Of course, she thinks I'm planning to eat them."

Rex lifted his head at that and after a moment's reflection decided he was hungry after all. He scrambled down off my lap and sauntered over to the food dish. My mother and I watched him eat for a while. I've always admired rabbits. No matter what they're doing, they always seem to have nothing else on their minds.

"I don't mean to sound paranoid," I said finally, "but how did you know where I lived?"

"Your brother told me."

"And how did he know?"

She smiled. "I didn't think to ask."

"And how is he?"

"Kevin? Oh, that's right. You haven't seen him yet, have you. He's fine. Very well. He was elected mayor, you know."

"I know."

She smiled archly. "I thought you must. You've been back for how long?"

"Just a few days."

"And what have you been doing with yourself?"

"Oh," I said, "you know how it is. Tidying up. Getting the place organized."

She sipped her coffee and glanced around again. "You know, Charles, we have some extra furniture somewhere. You could have it if you wanted. Nothing fancy. Just a few little odds and ends up in the attic. They might make this place a little homier. A few chairs. Maybe a coffee table. Or, perhaps... You know, we do have those pieces of Nana's in storage."

I glanced up at her. Here I was thinking she couldn't do anything to surprise me.... "You're not serious."

And in fact, with an eye on the rabbits, she was obviously beginning to regret the offer, but she went on valiantly, "I'm sure she'd have wanted you to use them."

"I doubt it."

"Now, Charles. You probably don't even remember them."

But I did. Old and sturdy mahogany tables and sideboards and velvet upholstered chairs, heavy with years. My great great grandfather had sent away to England for them when he'd married, and they'd been passed down through more than a century. Shortly after Nana died, the enormous yellow moving van had pulled heavily into our driveway, as though it had arrived all the way from the other side of the world instead of just from the other side of town. As the movers lifted each piece down from the truck, unwrapping it and carrying it in, my mother went from chair to table to chair, dusting each in turn, though none of them were dirty, running her cloth over every smooth surface like a horse trainer calming his animal. A week later another van—it might even have been the same one—arrived to take them into storage.

They could have gone directly there. My parents must have known there was no room for them in the house. It was already jammed with generations of Bentchley furniture that had filtered down to my father. But Dorothy needed to see them. She needed to have them in her house, to acquaint them with their new home, their new owners, as if the furniture itself needed to be reassured about the passing of generations. She spent that week polishing every piece, showing them to us, pointing out the scratches, dents and discolorations that had accumulated over the years: the stain of a spilled tea cup, a tiny crack in a table leg.

"Do you see this?" she'd said as I stood watching her work. She poured a dribble of furniture polish onto her cloth and stroked it down the curving arm of a Queen Ann parlor chair, framed in carved mahogany with a seat and back cushioned in green velvet. The deep russet of the wood was marked by a scar on the outer edge of the arm about as long as my finger. It was blackened, like an old knot in a tree, and hollowed out slightly: an unsymmetrical curve added by the repairman who had tried to sand out the damage. Over time it had smoothed still further with rubbing and use, and the years had buried the injury under a warm glow of polish until the scar looked as if it were meant to be there, a noticeable but welcome blemish. "That was where your Great Grandpa Strawberry had his first stroke."

I was ten at the time. I tried to picture my grandfather somehow fitting into this narrow gouge which was much too small for his hand, much less his entire stroke, whatever that might be.

"He was sitting in the chair, smoking a cigar one evening, alone after dinner."

"Here?"

"No. Of course not," she said impatiently. "In the old house.

The one at the college now."

My grandfather, either tired of hand-me-downs, or reluctant to live in a house where three generations of his forebears had already lived and died, had donated the old house to Methodist College, where it now housed the anthropology department's offices and classrooms, leaving me at age ten trying to picture Great Grandpa Strawberry sitting in this chair, smoking his cigar late at night among the desks and dusty blackboards of a deserted classroom.

"He was sitting in his study, smoking, when the stroke came." My mother spoke in a low tone, making it seem as if the stroke had slipped into the room silently behind the old man's back, like an intruder in the house. "He couldn't move. He couldn't cry for help. He sat there, straight-backed and elegant in his evening clothes. And his cigar burned down along this groove. See?" She traced the cloth along the smooth, charred path of the burning ash. "By the time your great grandmother found him, his cigar had burned down all this way. She used to say he looked more patient than she'd ever seen him, waiting there, smoking, like a man lost in thought."

"Was he all right?" I asked.

"Yes, of course, darling. He was fine," she replied, a little brusquely. I'm sure she thought I was missing the point, and maybe I was. It didn't matter whether he was all right or not. Or that he'd died eventually from one stroke too many in the year the first automobile came to town. For my mother it wasn't the death that mattered. Or even the life. It was the fact of the chair itself—solid and tangible—and all that accumulated history preserved in the very smoothness of the wood. My mother wasn't one for abstractions.

At the time I'd reached out hesitantly and touched the scar as if it might have been old man Strawberry himself and not just his chair. I slowly stroked the dark indentation, thrilled and a little unnerved that it was still warm to the touch after all these years.

I know, I know. How could it not have been warm? My mother had been rubbing it like a determined boyscout trying to start a fire. But for me in that moment it still seemed to hold the eerie, claustrophobic heat of a body immobilized by some dark intruder while the ash burned closer and closer to his fingers.

We were not encouraged to use the furniture for the week that it filled our living room. But Kevin, of course, made it a point, and in truth, my mother didn't seem to mind. He sat in every chair as though trying each one on for size, and with a napkin he polished the surface of the old card table until he could see his reflection in the gleam.

"That was Aunt Dorothy's favorite table," my mother said. "She played bridge there every Tuesday and Friday for the last thirty years of her life."

Kevin called me over. "Do you see yourself?"

"No."

"Try it. Look down there."

But as I looked down into the dark wood where Kevin was peering cheerfully into his own smiling reflection, all I could see was the fine grain, swirling away into the depths.

"Do you see it?"

"Yes," I lied.

Though Kevin tried out all the furniture, he was drawn particularly to the stroke chair. Its history didn't seem to bother him. He was undeterred by ghosts. He sat there imagining himself in evening clothes smoking a cigar, sitting in the past dreaming about his future. He looked so comfortable I tried it myself once, settling gingerly onto the napped velvet. But as I leaned back all I could imagine was some sinister stranger slipping into the room behind me. The mahogany arms curved around like a threat, and all I could think of was what it must have been like to sit there, unable to move, trapped in a darkening room.

For that whole long week the entire living room seemed like that to me. All that old furniture. Even after polishing it seemed to fill the air with dust and made the whole room stuffy and close, as if too many people where trying to breath the same air.

Now I glanced around at my empty apartment. "I don't really think they'd fit in here, do you?"

"Well," said Dorothy, a little doubtfully, "they certainly wouldn't hurt."

"It's not exactly an antique sort of place."

"It isn't about antiques, darling." She spoke with a kind of smiling and light-hearted exasperation, as if it were all so obvious. "It's like family. I'd have thought it would be nice to have them around."

I nodded agreeably. "I'm just not sure the rabbits would like it."

"Charles. There's nothing that says you have to live like a hobo."

"Are you kidding? Most hobos could only dream about a place like this."

"Well, it isn't fair." She glanced around helplessly at the awful patchy walls and the terrible curtains. "What do you think people will say?"

"Don't worry. I won't invite anyone you know."

"That's not the point. This is our town."

"Still," I said. "There must be somebody you don't know."

"That's not what I meant."

"You're asking me to make a good impression."

"I'm asking you to be yourself."

"Then you're in luck. Here I am."

She shook her head like someone trying to get rid of an annoying buzz in her ear. It was another familiar gesture I'd almost forgotten. "All I'm saying," she said, "is, if you'd like to borrow a little money, or some furniture to get settled. Just something to help you start out..." But her voice died away as I shook my head.

What my mother didn't realize was that, as far as I was concerned, this wasn't starting out. I had already done that, seven years before, with a borrowed tuxedo and a silk rose up my sleeve. I wasn't just beginning now. I was six rabbits, two trunks, and seven years down the road, and the last thing I wanted was to start all over.

I reached out for Frankie, who had wandered over in a post-prandial daze. I picked him up and settled him on my lap. "Don't worry," I said. "If anyone sees this place, I'll tell them you did the best you could."

"Honestly, Charles. Is it so bad to want to be comfortable?"

"I am comfortable." And I looked down at Frankie, who had immediately fallen asleep without fuss or bother. With nothing at all on his mind. I wondered if I had the slightest idea what being comfortable meant. "Would you like some more coffee?" I asked.

"No," she said, and then caught herself. "No, thank you. I really should be going." She stood and, after a moment's reflexive search for a table, set the mug down on the trunk. "I just wanted to make sure you were settled in properly."

"The town welcome wagon."

She smiled. "Of course. And I wanted to mention that we're having a little cocktail party a week from Friday. Just a few friends. It's very informal. Though if you have a jacket...?"

"I think I can find one."

"Good. Then we'll see you there."

She turned as if that was that, as if everything had gone more or less as well as could be expected, and led the way into the kitchen. But at the door she hesitated. "I don't suppose you've met Emily yet?"

"As a matter of fact, I have. Yes." And as she waited expectantly, "I liked her, more or less. I was surprised. I didn't know Kevin had such good taste."

"She is a dear girl."

I waited. "But...?"

"I didn't say but."

"Of course you did."

"Well... You know she's a clown."

"Yes. But not all the time, I assume."

"No."

"I hear she's a force in this town. Dedicated, hard-working, public spirited. I'd have thought you'd be crazy about her."

"I am. Of course I am. We all are. She's a lovely girl."

I shrugged. "You don't have to say that on my account."

"And she's obviously very fond of Kevin."

"As are we all."

"I just wonder if your brother couldn't have found someone with more ordinary hobbies."

"I didn't know she had any hobbies at all."

"You weren't there for the parade the other day?"

"No," I said. "Sorry. How was it?"

"Excruciating. She was dressed in the most ridiculous outfit, dancing around, mugging for the cameras."

"Well. She is a clown, after all."

"Please. Even you never did that, Charles."

"Didn't I? Well. I probably just never thought of it."

"It was mortifying. Though Kevin handled it very well."

"Well. You know what they say about love."

"That's exactly my point," said Dorothy in a rush. "If your brother's a little blind about her, that's all the more reason why we shouldn't be."

"Mother, it was a parade. What are you worried about? You think she's going to wear that outfit to a town council meeting?"

"I don't know what she'll do. That's the whole problem. You've heard about these protests?"

"Some of them."

"Don't you think it's a little inappropriate?"

"Saving the earth?"

"Having the mayor's future wife chaining herself to some factory gate on the six o'clock news."

"I don't know. Maybe she's just got that show business bug."

Dorothy frowned. "Well. Someone needs to let her know how delicate her new position is."

"How about Kevin?"

"Your brother may not see her as clearly as we do. Please, dear. Just talk to her."

This caught me by surprise. "Me?"

"Of course."

"I've already talked to her."

My mother frowned impatiently. "Just mention our concerns."

"Our concerns? I'm not even sure what my concerns are."

"She'll listen to you, Charles."

"I don't know why in the world you think so."

"Because." Dorothy hesitated. "Well, you know. You have so much in common."

"What exactly? Our devotion to good works? Our seriousness of purpose?"

"You know what I mean. You're both…" She waved her hands a little vaguely, as if searching for the best way to suggest some unpleasant truth.

"…In show business?"

She smiled. "Besides, you said yourself you liked her."

"I said more or less. And what am I supposed to tell her, anyway? Quiet down and behave?"

"Is that such bad advice?" said Dorothy tartly.

"Well, I may not be the person to give it."

"Don't be silly. You've come home. Settled down. You've gotten it out of your system. We need to make the best of things. We need to learn from our mistakes."

"Don't worry. I've learned."

"Then just talk to her, Charles. Be nice to her. That's all I'm asking. What can it hurt?"

She took my silence for consent. "There. That's all," she said briskly. "I've had my say." She leaned forward and kissed me on the cheek again, then turned and opened the door. "It's nice to see you getting settled," she said. Then, stepping out onto the crooked landing, she glanced around.

There was a school yard next door, weedy and deserted. It spread out just beyond the fence with houses crowding in around it. Over the rooftops toward Main Street, the very tips of the tallest buildings were visible, grey slate and shingles and the hint of red brick. The streets, the buildings, the bricks themselves all so familiar they were no longer clearly visible except from a great distance. "It's a nice town, Charles. You must be glad to be back. In fact," she said, with a trace of impatience, but more than that, with something like genuine bewilderment. "I don't know how you could have left."

And as her footsteps sounded on the uneven steps descending from the little crow's nest of a porch, I felt the way Old Man Strawberry must have felt, sitting in the security of all that was familiar, in his own house, in his own study, in his favorite and most comfortable chair, and all but unable to breathe.

The Magnificent Rudy

When I was seven I saw my first magic trick. It was at school, and it must have been parents' day, family day, something like that, because they were all there: my mother and father and Kevin. I must have dragged them all along. I was at the age when I still thought if we just spent more time together we'd all be happier. I wasn't sure how the world worked, but I was casting about for something that might make sense of it all, and I was prepared to believe in magic.

The magician was billed as The Magnificent Rudy, a huge, impressive man who coalesced out of a puff of grey smoke into exquisite black and white: white hair, white gloves, white shirt and tie, black tails, tall black hat. He called for volunteers. At least, I assume he did, though I may not be remembering this exactly. It was a long time ago, and I may have the chronology slightly mixed. But I remember climbing the stairs to the stage with the fierce conviction that up there at least my family would have to pay attention.

I chose a card: the Jack of Hearts. At the time I was nervous about forgetting it, but even now I remember. It's a card I still use because it tends to stay in your mind, and whatever you do, you have to remember your card, even when you'd rather forget, or you're left holding nothing at all. So I use the card now, when I can, to remind myself of Rudy and of that young boy who vanished down the road, pursued by yet another puff of smoke and chasing after the sense of wonder and order and promise conjured up in that one distant moment when the Magnificent Rudy, gazing down at me, took the card, the Jack of Hearts, back into the deck, and gave me in its place an enormous watermelon.

I held it, transfixed, as he fanned out the deck of cards, then made them vanish in a handful of flame. From his empty fingers he drew rainbow-colored scarves, one after another, right under my nose, and dropped them into his hat. Then from my ear he drew a chicken's egg, and broke that into the hat. A mist of laughter rose from the audience. He plucked a bouquet of flowers from beneath my shirt, and pulled a single rose from my pants. Without any pain at all he drew from my mouth another long scarf. I could all but feel it dragging over my tongue.

And I could feel, as well, my eyes as wide as they could be. I could feel the dimensions of the world shifting and stretching, allowing room for more than I had ever imagined, even as I heard the laughter and the warm, scattered applause. It was for Rudy, of course. But also for me, for the both of us. And as I listened I wanted to look up, to make sure my family was watching, but I was still holding that melon, and I didn't dare take my eyes off his hands. He gathered everything into the hat, stuffed it all in, then raised the brim and tapped it against the top of my head, lightly despite the varied contents. Then, setting it down on a small table, he lifted out an enormous white rabbit.

The audience went wild. They applauded and laughed and whistled. The Magnificent Rudy bowed and smiled, and when the applause died down he turned away toward the next trick, leaving me standing alone and forgotten with the watermelon growing heavier and more awkward in my arms. I watched him anxiously, but he was examining a collection of props, deciding what to do next. He'd forgotten me completely. Nobody else seemed to notice; they were waiting for whatever came next; but I was left dangling. And I started to get mad. I stood there, a thin, dark-haired, pinched-faced seven-year-old holding a watermelon almost half my size with arms beginning to ache, and I started to get really pissed off. My whole family was watching, and he'd only given me half a trick.

It was very quiet in the auditorium. Somebody cleared his throat. A chair creaked. I took half a step forward. "Hey!" I said, "Hey! What about my card?"

And without a pause, without even waiting for the end of my

sentence, the Magnificent Rudy whirled around. A little tulip of flame flared in his hand, and then out of the naked air he plucked something and threw it straight at me. Open-mouthed I stared, frozen to the ground. And though I barely saw the card rifle through the air, I felt it hit with a solid, echoing thump and bury itself up to the Jack's smiling face in the thick rind of the melon.

That was the instant that ordered my life. It was that solid thump of something so thin and insubstantial that made sense of everything. It proved to me things were not always what they seemed, but more than that it showed me the underlying threat of even the simplest desire. There I was, only seven years old, but I had discovered a crucial truth: that while you sometimes get what you ask for, it's never what you expect. The most longed for object of your life might come to you out of thin air, but it comes with all the force of a knife burying itself between your ribs.

I remembered that lesson for a long time, though inevitably I lost track of it somehow—or took it for granted, which amounts to the same thing. But a week before my seventeenth birthday, I learned it all over again, and having committed it to memory for good, this time, I caught the first bus out of town. I climbed onto a Greyhound in the filtering light of 5 a.m. and climbed off when it wouldn't go any further. The trip must have been beautiful, through western Connecticut, Massachusetts, upstate New York, but I don't remember it. When the bus stopped for the night three-quarters of an hour south of Canada, I climbed down into the empty streets of a town so ramshackle, shabby, and out of the way that I was certain nobody ever arrived there on purpose.

I had only a single suitcase, packed hurriedly and badly balanced, that bumped against my knee as I walked. My mind was hunched with fatigue. I hadn't slept the night before, and for only seconds at a time on the bus, and now every sight and sound came to me from a long way off. As I walked, my gaze narrowed to the section of road just before me: old asphalt cracked and buckled under too many seasons of frost. There was a distant sound of traffic, but it bore no relation to the vacant streets around me or the blind and staring buildings.

I passed only one man, the only other soul in motion through the town. He wore a watch cap like an old sailor and layers of grimy plaid, and he carried a bottle in a crumpled paper bag. He was walking toward me down the middle of the street, and when he got within a few feet he stopped, we both stopped, and stared at one another as though at a mirage or some strange reflection in the mirror. He reached up and stroked the rough whiskers on the side of his chin. I rubbed my eyes. In the distance I heard a clock strike seven; it rang slowly, each bell clearing a space for itself, and we both waited, staring and uncertain, though what we were waiting for I have no idea. The last chime faded into the distant rush of traffic, and abruptly at the same instant we both started forward again, passed one another, and hurried away.

The YMCA was a large, grim building. The four red letters hung down the front, faded and old as if left there by accident. I stood for a moment, looking up at the sign, feeling myself float loose from the world, and I was sure that the first person I talked to would be able to see that I was in danger of simply drifting away or that the street cleaners, arriving early in the morning with their hoses and brushes, would just rinse me along the gutter and down out of sight. But at the front desk there was an ancient man who seemed not at all surprised when I spoke. He didn't appear startled by the sound of my voice asking for a bed. He took my eight dollars and gave me a small square of cardboard, bent and softened by use, with the number forty-five printed boldly in magic marker.

The cot had a similar cardboard sign wired to the foot of the steel frame. The beds filled the large room, lined up precisely, rough blankets folded and smoothed, pillows thin but centered: everything ordered against the coming night. A few of the beds were taken already, and the sprawled bodies looked like nothing so much as despair made flesh.

I lay down on the bed listening to their congested breathing. All the fatigue of the last twenty-four hours hovered around me. I tried to imagine tomorrow and the next day, the steady unfolding of hours and minutes, and it seemed impossible that I was there. Impossible that I couldn't just open my eyes again, and Gracie would be alive, and I would be back home.

I slid my suitcase under the bed and untucked the blanket to hang down almost to the floor. When I stood up the creak of springs was lost in the low murmur of breathing. I wandered out into the lobby, with no more clear idea of where I was going than of anything else, but at the front door, on a crowded bulletin board, I saw the poster. It showed a pair of sinister eyes peering out over a spread deck of playing cards. "The Magnificent Rudy Amazes and Entertains."

I was so tired it never occurred to me it might not be the same Magnificent Rudy. In my blurry brain, the distinctions between seven years old and almost seventeen had dissolved, and here he was again, brought back by popular demand. And talk about luck? As it happened, that night I was free.

It wasn't much of an auditorium. More a large meeting room with a scuffed wooden floor and a low platform stage framed by ancient drapes. There were rows of folding chairs, but only half were filled, and I wondered if this was it for the Magnificent Rudy: a series of bare auditoriums, a continuing blur of performances for collections of cub scouts and veterans and stunned, homeless young men on the lam from the dead.

I found a seat down near the front. The hall was warm and stuffy, and I was so tired that when the lights started to dim I didn't realize it at first; I thought I was just drifting off. But then, with a pre-recorded trumpet fanfare sounding as frayed and strained as the drapes and the hall, there was a puff of grey smoke, the stage lit up, and the Magnificent Rudy stepped forward through the swirling cloud and stood at the edge of the stage in white tie and tails with balls of fire rising from his fingers.

You have no idea. You can't imagine, sitting there, reading this. But the smudged walls, the seediness, the tacky auditorium, they all just disappeared. There was only a dark room, and at the center of it was magic. The Magnificent Rudy stepped out onto the stage and took care of me. He made my fatigue vanish, he stripped away the last twenty-four hours, and left me, for the sixty-five minutes he performed, free of everything but wonder.

A fan of cards bloomed in his hand, and he tossed them into a top hat upended on a brightly draped table. Then more cards burst out into the same hand. He threw them into the hat. Then both hands. The cards appeared from nowhere. He fanned them out smoothly, then scattered them into the upended hat. When finally the air itself was exhausted, he stretched out his hands over the black, silk brim, plucked it up, turned it over, and showed the audience just how empty a hat could be. Then out of that emptiness he drew a rainbow of scarves, piling them on the table, only to spread the pile apart and lift from its center a large white rabbit.

"Where did that come from?" a young boy cried somewhere in the dark, but nobody answered.

The magician set up a small box on a stand and lowered the rabbit into it. He closed the lid and locked it, then drew from beneath his coat an enormous Bowie Knife. The crowd hushed, leaning forward, agape. The first time he thrust it through the box there was a sharp squeak. He hesitated, startled, then gingerly pressed the knife through again. A thin squeal rose, then died away abruptly. The audience started shifting in its chairs. He thrust the knife through the box again, but as he removed it this time, there was a faint tinge of red, coloring the tip. From the back a young girl's voice rose in a wail, "Mommy! He's killed the bunny!"

Rudy dropped the knife, clattering onto the table, and fumbling with the key, unlocked the box and gingerly opened the top to peer in. His shoulders sagged. He looked heartsick. He started to close the top, then, whirling to face the audience, snapped his fingers, and with a sharp rap on the stand, collapsed the sides of the box to reveal nothing. Emptiness. And pushing back his sleeve, he reached into the top hat standing forgotten on the table and pulled out the rabbit. Just like that. Just like in the story books.

He made a series of scarves disappear, then recovered them from a block of ice; he made pigeons vanish; he did the Blackstone birdcage vanishing; he did Thurston's rising card trick; he did the Maskelyne & Davenant transportation, turning a rabbit into a pigeon into a duck into a stuffed bear.

And he did the trick with the watermelon.

He asked for volunteers, and I had to fight the urge to stand up. I was a boy gone back in time and, sitting in my chair, I watched as a youngster climbed uneasily onto the stage, looking a little anxious, glancing back at his father in the audience, then turning to look up at the dark-clad magician who towered above him. The father looked on, though it was difficult to see whether he was more pleased or impatient with the boy, urging him on. Or maybe that was just my memory playing tricks. It was his father, after all, not mine.

The young boy selected a card from the deck, showed it to his father, and stared at it, committing it to memory under the pressure of all those eyes in the audience, not realizing how little of the trick depended on him. And once again, for the second time in my life, I watched the Magnificent Rudy shuffle and cut; watched him draw scarves from the little boy's ears and a tiny live rabbit from the boy's pocket, which he transformed into a newspaper bunny and then tore open to reveal a chocolate version, which made the boy's face light up. And finally, when the watermelon was beginning to get heavy, when it was visibly shaking with the effort of keeping it steady, the Magnificent Rudy strode over to the table, picked up the cards, fanned them out and then tossed them into the air, where they vanished. And as they vanished he whirled around. I got to see him this time, got to watch as he made the deck disappear, then turned and threw the one remaining card. There wasn't much to see. He turned so precisely; the movement of his hands was so sharp, a lightning flick of the wrist. But this time I saw the card cutting through the air, saw it strike like an arrow into the green target of the melon. And I got to watch the spectrum of emotions flicker across the face of the boy: he looked pleased, startled, suddenly afraid, and then open-mouthed with wonder as if he felt the card embedded in his own chest.

As the lights came on and the room emptied, I stayed in my seat, looking at the closed drapes of the stage for one more piece of magic, even then hoping for some last trick to keep me a few more minutes from that hard, narrow cot. A janitor began to sweep the aisles, and a couple of young men began folding and stacking the chairs, but still I sat, until I heard a voice rising from behind the curtain.

"What the hell do you mean you're quitting?"

The reply was lost, muffled in the heavy curtain, but there was the scrape of furniture, a thump on the stage. The young men cleaning up ignored it. They'd doubtless heard much worse in shows past. But I stood up and wandered toward the stage.

"You can't just disappear on me in the middle of some nowhere town!"

"What's the matter?" said a child, mockingly. "Things can't disappear unless you want them to?" And I realized it was the voice from the back of the audience, the girl's voice that rose up during the performance, crying out that he had killed the bunny. "Well, I've got news for you," she said. "I'm out of here."

I crept up the steps to the edge of the curtain and peered behind. In the ordinary glare of the work lights backstage two men in shirtsleeves were packing props and supplies into two large trunks. I looked around for the little girl, but there was no sign of her. On the small magic table, bereft of its brightly colored cloth, stood an open bottle of whiskey. There were no glasses to be seen, but perhaps he had already made them disappear.

Without his white tie and vest, without his black tails, the Magnificent Rudy looked thin and old. He moved slowly, bending to pick up a tangled pile of scarves and rolling them into a ball to stuff them into a corner of the trunk. He had lost his assurance. Every movement seemed awkward. And from time to time he reached over and picked up the bottle and made a bit more of the whiskey vanish.

"I've had it with you." This time it was the voice of the young boy from the audience who had marveled at the first appearance of the rabbit. But I could see it was the second man speaking, gathering characters from the performance as he gathered up the loose and now unmagical elements that littered the stage. Bits of cloth, playing cards, boxes and scarves, and off to one side, on the floor, a small traveling cage with no fewer than half a dozen identical white rabbits. "Look at you," he said, this time in his own voice. "You can barely stand up!"

The Magnificent Rudy straightened, one supporting hand on the magic table. "Stand up? I don't need to stand up. I can levitate off the goddam stage."

"The only thing you can levitate is that bottle. You're getting embarrassing."

"Embarrassing? " He took a sudden step away from the table then seemed to think better of it, and stood there, balancing, as if uncertain whether he was going to turn around or fall right over. "Who do you think you're talking to? I was doing this act when you were still in diapers."

"Well, now you'll be doing it when I'm far away," he said. "I'm tired of holding you up. I'm out there doing cartwheels to keep their attention off your hands. Jesus. In the middle of that rabbit trick I thought you'd fallen asleep."

"I was building suspense you ignorant young parvenu. You're not giving ballroom dance lessons any more, counting it off under your breath. You have to feel it."

"You didn't look like you were feeling anything."

The Magnificent Rudy took a deep breath. "Sometimes,

Lennox, when I'm silent, I listen to the spirit of the great Robert-Houdin, that finest of modern illusionists. That master of the nineteenth century. He comes and whispers to me. And at this moment, Lennox, he's whispering to me that you should get the hell out of here! Finish packing up, and get the hell back to the hotel! I need to be alone."

"You know, Rudy," the man said. "I've got a few tricks of my own." He stepped over to a large trunk standing on end and open like a closet. He reached in and drew out an overcoat. "I bet this is one you haven't seen. I call it 'Getting a Life.'" He shrugged into the coat. "You still owe me two hundred dollars. So you don't mind if I keep tonight's receipts. They don't cover it, but I suppose this is one of those valuable life lessons that money can't buy." He straightened up and faced the magician. "I say the magic words: Rudolph Weizman is a drunken bum. And I vanish into the air."

He turned and strode out, and the Magnificent Rudy stood rooted to the spot, clutching the neck of the whiskey bottle like a strap-hanger on a subway train holding on over a rough patch of track. In the distance there was the muffled thump of a heavy door slamming, and then silence. He stood, balanced precariously, but as the shock waves of the sound finally reached him, he tottered and sank into the chair.

He sat there, staring around at the scattered props and equipment like a man who, startled in mid-journey, has seen his trunk burst open on the station platform with the train approaching in the distance. He tensed for a moment, as if with a single wild gesture he might sweep all the odds and ends magically back into their places, but instead, without turning, he reached back for the bottle. Though this time he didn't take a drink, he just cradled it in his lap.

I stepped out from behind the curtain. "Don't worry," I said. I have no idea why. Perhaps I was talking to myself as much as to him. But after the words were out I just stood there with no idea how to finish.

He turned in his chair. He was very drunk, but at the sound of my voice he sat up straighter, and when he turned it was with a controlled and precise air that suggested at any moment some decisive revelation. I half-expected him to produce a pigeon or a rabbit or a flash of light, but he just squinted at me as if peering through some wisp of smoke left over from my sudden appearance. "Next show's tomorrow," he said.

"I already saw the show. I saw it when I was seven. I saw you do that trick with the watermelon."

"You did?"

"You were great."

Bemused he reached up and brushed a lock of white hair back from his temple. "How old are you now?"

"Seventeen. Almost seventeen."

"Jesus," he muttered, more to himself than aloud. "Ten years. And ten years before that, and ten years before that." He took a long drink from the bottle. But having an audience, even an audience of one, helped. He reached down and picked up a couple of fluffy, white handkerchiefs from the floor. "And did you like it?" he asked.

"It changed my life."

"But did you like it?"

"Yes."

He nodded. He shook out the larger of the handkerchiefs and draped it over the hand that held the smaller. When he removed it, the hand was empty. "Have you ever been in such a shabby and depressing town?"

"I thought the show tonight was very good."

"Have you seen the bus station?"

"Yes."

He shook his head, marveling at the seediness of the bus station. "What did you like best?" he asked.

"The expression on the boy's face when the card stuck into the watermelon."

"Did you see the rabbit trick?"

"I didn't think you looked asleep."

"There's such a thing as a dramatic pause," he said. "A pause for effect."

"I liked it."

"You don't just race through an illusion. It's a performance, not a contest."

"It was dramatic," I said.

"Robert-Houdin's first performance lasted three hours. No, not his first performance. His first performance was a disaster." He shook his head, recalling a performance that had ended more than a hundred years earlier. Then, finding the thread of his argument again, "Because he had no sense of drama. That's right. He knew the tricks. Three hours worth of tricks ... in an hour. He raced through them. See, he didn't know how to perform." Rudy was concentrating on what he was saying, speaking in a low voice, but examining every word, nodding over some, flourishing others, as if working through an effect for the first time, fitting it all together. "It isn't about tricks. It's magic." He shook his head, but whether to disagree with himself, or to clear some lingering uncertainty, I didn't know. "That rabbit trick. Do you know how I did it?"

"How?"

"I'm not going to tell you. Do you know?"

"No."

"That's right. What do you think happened to the rabbit?"

"It disappeared."

"That's right. Vanished without a trace. I believe that," he said. He took another drink. The last of the whiskey drained away. He put down the empty bottle with a thump. "I believe it, and I was the one who did it. I'm the one with rabbit pee in the pocket of my jacket and in the bottom of my hat. I'm the one who has to feed the little fuckers, and stuff them into little black sacks and hide them, and I still believe that rabbit just disappeared into thin air. That's what makes me a great magician. And that's why you're just a punk, Lennox."

"My name's not Lennox."

He leaned to pick up one of his trick boxes from the floor, and lost his balance, spilling forward onto his hands and knees with a look of widening surprise. He stayed there for a long moment, staring down at the box just inches from his face. It was brightly colored, about twelve inches square, with four sides that fell open on command. It was a box that offered more than it showed, if you knew where to look, but at the moment the magician stared at it as though at a puzzle he'd forgotten.

I grabbed his arm and helped him to his feet. He was lighter than I'd expected, and shorter. The evening dress on stage had not only made him more imposing, but, as I was to learn, had provided plenty of room for hiding props. But here, in the stark, dim lights and clutter, with nothing to disguise him, not even the shadows, he seemed reduced to something less than the essentials. His arm felt thin and bony through the shirt. His face sagged; the skin was pale but warmed to a burnished pink by the blush of broken capillaries. His hair, white and fluffy, decorated like the feathers of a chick the back and sides of his head, but the smooth skin of the crown was bare and unprotected.

He stood, barely balancing within my grip. "Where are you staying tonight?" I asked.

"All this has to be picked up."

"Do you have a hotel?"

"I have two trunks."

"It's after midnight."

"God damn it! I have to feed the rabbits!"

I eased him back down onto the chair. He kept looking down at the box, as if trying to recollect where he'd seen it last. Then, with a look of concentration he reached down and hoisted it onto his lap. He stroked it, then turned it over, and with a twist, popped loose the bottom. Within the narrow recess another white rabbit lay dozing. "Hello, Frankie. Did you think I'd forgotten you?" He set the now truly empty box on the floor and sat, stroking the rabbit's head as I went in search of the night janitor.

I gathered up all the scattered equipment. There was no room to spare in the two trunks, and I couldn't figure out how some of the pieces folded or broke down, so I ended up standing everything in the back corner of a storage closet and piling the magic table and the boxes on top. "Not the rabbits," the janitor said. "No animals. They stink up the place."

He was about fifty with skin the same dusty color as the floor he was sweeping and a fat cigar butt gripped in his teeth. He seemed unsurprised by the old magician sitting, stroking Frankie the rabbit in the middle of the empty stage. "We get magicians," he said. "Jugglers and musicians, they're the worst. Dirty, noisy. At least he's quiet."

"I don't suppose you know where he's staying."

"All I know is, he ain't staying here. I gotta lock up."

Rudy was dozing in his chair, his hands loosely cradling the rabbit, who looked wide awake now, but disinclined to move. I checked the magician's pockets and the pockets of his coat, half-expecting to discover some unperformed trick waiting to go off, but the pockets were empty. "Did he have anything else with him?"

The janitor nudged a small canvas satchel with the toe of his shoe. "This ain't mine."

There wasn't much in it: clothes, toiletries. If this was his life, carried along on the road, then he had stripped it down to the bone. There was no room key, no reservation form, no glossy flier with photographs of laughing families splashing in the hotel pool. Nothing to indicate that there was at the very least a bed waiting for him somewhere in this town.

"You'll have to get him out of here." The janitor lifted the stumpy cigar from his mouth, and looked as if he were about to spit, then thought better of it. He pointed with the cigar. "There's a hotel, the Highlander, about three miles up South Street. They might have a room. Though they usually rent by the hour. Does he have any money?"

"No."

"Don't bother, then."

"I'll take him back to the Y."

He looked down at the soggy brown stub, as if wondering how he could put something so revolting into his mouth. "They fill up early."

"I've got a bed."

He looked at me calculatingly for a moment. I don't know what he saw there, what he could have seen, though I imagine he had seen everything over the years. But I was so green. An innocent. He shrugged, apparently coming to the same conclusion. "It's not like camp. They don't let you bunk up. One per bed is the rule."

"Well, then, what?"

This time he did spit, and brushed ruminatively at the moist mark with his broom. "Bus station's a couple of blocks north. It's open all night. Or the River Street overpass. At least it's covered, and there's a hot air vent from the power plant. Everybody usually minds their own business, I hear. But don't get too close. It's not all that cold tonight, and they might be feeling frisky."

"Frisky?" I stared at him, but the janitor just shrugged, as though he'd done all he could.

The Magnificent Rudy was not a heavy magician, but in that long walk, first to the Y and then to the bus station, he wasn't helping very much. I dragged his arm across my shoulders and got him to his feet, then managed to pick up his canvas bag and the little cage of rabbits. He was able to walk if kept in motion.

The night guard sitting in the registration window at the Y didn't hesitate. "We're full up."

"I've already got a bed."

"No you don't. Not for your type. We got none of that here. Get out."

"He's exhausted."

"Get out."

"He's drunk. He's an old man."

"I told you..."

"He hasn't anywhere to sleep."

"Read the sign." He jerked his thumb at the wall behind him: Young men's CHRISTIAN association. "Take him to the park, if that's what you want, but you're not gonna to stay here."

"Well, at least let me get my suitcase."

The night guard stood and picked up the telephone as if it were a club. "Who do you think you're dealing with, kid? Get the hell out of here, or I'll call the police!"

The Magnificent Rudy roused himself at this, peering around at the dimly lit lobby, settling on the now reddening face of the night guard. Then, slowly, he reached out and held his hand right before the man's startled expression. He held it there for a long moment without moving, then with a flick and a twist of his hand he snatched from the air and held out beneath the man's nose—nothing. Not a thing. An empty hand. Perhaps he'd used up his props without realizing it, perhaps he thought he had a flower or a scarf or a pigeon hidden somewhere to be retrieved. Or maybe not. The Magnificent Rudy held out his spread fingers as though holding something remarkable, and the night guard stared down for a moment, transfixed by the empty hand. Then he looked up and snarled. "Get out."

We stood on the steps of the Y for a long time, Rudy sagging against me, the rabbits huddled glumly in their cage. The night was warm, even for late June, but there was a foreboding of rain. The air was still, and as I listened, the small sounds making up the silence grew louder. The low rustle of traffic on the distant interstate, the hiss of steam from somewhere off in the darkness, a mumble of low voices that seemed to form themselves partially out of the hiss and rustle. My legs felt wooden.

The Highlander was three miles away, as out of reach as the moon. I thought of my room at home, my bed, and how, until this moment, I had taken sleep utterly for granted. It had never seemed any sort of achievement to lie down in the comfort of cool sheets, but now the whole prospect seemed miraculous. I thought of my parents finding my note, such as it was, and not comprehending it of course, but standing together over my un-rumpled bed reading that I had to leave, that I would call them when I had gotten where I was going. And, perhaps they even commented on how like me it was to leave such a short, cryptic note. No accusations, no explanations. Just articulated flight: the medium itself the message.

The Magnificent Rudy showed signs of settling. I managed to get us to our feet, and I started up the street, with Rudy falling into step only a little reluctantly. "Where are we going?" he de-manded.

"The bus station."

"Why the hell are we going to the god damned bus station? We just got to this hell-forsaken town."

"It's going to rain."

"What the hell does that have to do with anything? You think we're going to leave town just because it's raining? Are you in-sane, Lennox?" He turned his head, examining me suspiciously. "Have you been drinking again?"

"I'm not Lennox."

He shook his head. "You have been drinking. I should have known."

He had a wonderful voice, I should mention that now. Low and resonant, it hung on the air like some beautiful shape. Over the years, that was the one thing that made it easier to listen to the inevitable cursing: the voice itself was so beautiful, the enunciation so perfect, the tone so sculpted, that sometimes I would listen to the most obscene and insulting diatribe just for the pleasure of the sound.

We stepped through the heavy glass doors into the bright, fluorescent glare of the bus station, and he stopped, looking like some small, clawed creature pulled out from under a rock. Squinting and grimacing at the light, he straightened up, drag-ging against my weight. "You stupid ass, Lennox. You've forgotten the trunks."

"No, no. We're not leaving town. We're just going to sit down and take a little nap."

But I wasn't accustomed yet to talking to Rudy drunk. He caught the wheedling, simple-minded tone. Drawing himself up to his full, if modest, height, he glared at me haughtily. "Who the hell do you think you're talking to?"

But I didn't loosen my grip. I'm sure I thought if I could just get him sitting down the whiskey would take over and he'd be quiet for the night. But I didn't know him, then. I didn't know who I was dealing with. "How about over there?" I said.

He relaxed, and took a step in the right direction, the first bit of misdirection crucial to any sleight. Then, with perfect timing, as I turned, he tripped me. "Police! Police!" he cried in a high-pitched voice. "That man stole my purse." And then, because it was perfect for the moment, or because he'd discovered one last prop in his pocket after all and just couldn't resist the effect, he threw a smoke pellet to the floor and stepped back behind the sudden white cloud.

The bus station at three in the morning was not swarming with policemen, but there was one, a slow-moving and doughy man, pale in the harsh light, who was sitting at the snack-bar. He looked up, distracted and more than a little peevish at the sudden fuss, and glanced around for the woman who had called out. Seeing no one, he might conceivably have turned back to his coffee, except that there I was, sprawled on my hands and knees in the middle of a thinning cloud of white smoke, and he must have realized that wasn't the norm even for a bus station at three a.m. He stood up and started toward me, hesitantly at first, drawing his gun as he approached. A couple of concerned citizens took an uncertain step toward me, searching for the source of the cry, but he gestured them away. I climbed slowly to my feet. By that time, of course, the Magnificent Rudy had vanished, along with his canvas bag and every one of his rabbits.

"What's going on?" the policeman demanded. The revolver

drooped in his hand, prodding the air in my direction.

"Nothing officer. I slipped."

"Where's the woman?"

"What woman?"

"Where's the purse?"

"What purse?"

He glanced around, but nobody replied, nobody even met his eyes. Everybody had settled back into the dazed self-absorption of 3 am. The late hour and the silence weakened his resolve. After a moment he slipped the gun reluctantly into his holster and glared suspiciously, fingers tapping the worn black leather of his belt.

I smiled. I felt a rising tide of exuberance: part nervousness, part fatigue, partly the dawning realization that I was so entirely on my own I could even go to jail and I wouldn't have to answer to anybody. The policeman took half a step toward me, still hesitating, and I just left. I turned and walked out, stepping from the bus station into a cool, persistent rain.

I spent the night under the River Street overpass, lying on concrete, listening to the water gulping through drain pipes overhead. At first I kept a wary eye on the other half dozen bodies curled indifferently in the darkness, but after a while I fell asleep, trying to calm my nervousness by imagining the stories I'd eventually tell about this night.

The next morning I discovered my wallet was gone. I stood up, stiff and aching, and looked around in the gathering light. The piles of rags and filthy blankets were resolving into sleeping bodies. They appeared not to have moved all night. I glanced around the ground where I had slept. Then cautiously I circled each of the dozing figures, hoping that, if one of them had taken it, there would be some clue. But there was nothing. I set out to retrace my steps, glancing in garbage cans, under bushes, searching the ground without any conviction. I checked the lost and found at the bus station, then finally traced my way, along streets that looked utterly unfamiliar in the daylight, back at last to the VFW Hall.

The auditorium was empty and dark. The chairs had all been put away. The curtain was drawn. I searched the floor then wandered up the steps to the stage. The floor was scuffed and dusty, scoured by years of traffic, but it was quite bare.

I stood there, half-formed thoughts slipping through my mind, wondering how you wired money, what my parents would say, whether it was still possible, as in the old movies, to work for your breakfast. I was thinking about finding the janitor and asking if I could sweep up for the cost of a meal when the stage door opened, and the Magnificent Rudy strolled in, looking neat, rested, and cheerfully well fed.

He nodded at me carelessly, without recognition, then strolled around the edges of the stage, a little aimlessly at first, but with an increasing sense of purpose. He kept glancing up, wondering no doubt why I was observing him so closely, but after a while he forgot me in the growing panic of his search. He turned and crashed through the stage door out into the hall, and an instant later returned and began to make the rounds of the stage again, looking paler now.

I walked over to where the janitor had left his equipment, overturned the empty bucket, and sat down. In the daylight, sober, Rudy had filled out. He looked broader, more in focus, and he moved with a desperate energy. When he stopped and stood before the empty corner, drumming his fingers on the air, I said, "They're in the store room. We locked them away last night."

He turned. "Pardon?" And perhaps he wasn't quite as precise and collected as he looked. He wavered a little.

"Your trunks," I said. "They're locked away for safe keeping."

"How can they be?"

"It's magic."

He stopped and regarded me more closely. The momentary relief gave way to wariness. "Who are you?"

"I'm not Lennox."

"And where is Lennox?"

"He vanished without a trace."

He gazed at me, concerned and unsettled, until finally the mists parted, his expression cleared. He straightened up.

"Not another word," he said imperiously. "The Magnificent Rudy will read your thoughts. Now concentrate."

I sat there wondering when the shift changed at the YMCA so I could get my suitcase; perhaps even take a shower. My skin felt stiff and coated with dirt. My eyes felt gritty. I would have to get up in a moment and walk, but the thought made me want to cry.

The Magnificent Rudy held a hand to his temple. "I'm receiving something. Concentrate," he said. "You are sixteen. But you won't be for long. You are on a journey. Fleeing heartache and sadness, but you cannot escape."

The words caught me. I stared up at him. "You can't read minds."

"You have loved and lost. Your love has been snatched from you."

"You were falling-down drunk last night."

"She was taken from you by someone you loved. Someone who betrayed your trust."

I rubbed my face, trying to loosen the skin to distract myself from the sudden possibility of tears. You have to realize, I was tired. I felt about eighty years old, worn out and frail. And he had that great voice. "So," I said. "Can you read my future?"

"Just your thoughts."

"Well, can you tell what I've eaten in the last twenty-four hours?"

He bought me breakfast. We went around the corner to a place called the Ritz Diner, an old Airstream trailer hunched up on blocks. He ordered coffee for himself, then, looking at me, reading my mind, he ordered a cheese omelet with home fries and extra toast and a large glass of milk.

"I thought you didn't have any money," I said.

He hesitated, considering that for a moment, then without

any flourish at all he laid something on the table before me. "It's your treat," he said.

It was my wallet. "Where did you find it?"

"You should carry it in your front pocket. The world is full of unscrupulous people."

"You took it?"

He shrugged sheepishly. "Force of habit."

I stared at it for a moment, then put it away. "Thanks."

He took a slow sip of coffee. "So, Lennox is gone?"

"You don't remember?"

"I said I could read your mind, not mine. What exactly are you doing here?"

"You said it yourself. Fleeing heartache and sadness."

"Almost always a good guess," he said, "but never as easy as it sounds. How long are you in town?"

The food arrived. The eggs were leathery and the cheese no kind I could identify, but it tasted just fine. "My plans are in flux at the moment," I said.

Rudy added a little avalanche of sugar to his coffee and stirred it thoughtfully. "I don't suppose you have any useful skills?"

Still chewing on that nameless cheese I pulled my practice deck out of a pocket and shuffled it. He smiled in surprise. I fanned them out a little clumsily, and forced the King of Diamonds on him, all the time aware of how smoothly the cards had flowered in his hands the night before. Cutting the deck, I brought the card to the top and false shuffled twice. "Spell out the name of your card," I said, and as he spelled King of Diamonds, I dealt out a card for each letter from the top of the deck, then, with the final "s", stole the King from the bottom and dropped it face up on the pile.

He barely glanced at it. He was no longer smiling. Looking intently at my hands still curled around the remainder of the deck, he reached out and turned them over. He had a light touch, firm, with the suggestion of strength, but delicate as a spider. "Your fingers are too short," he said, "that could be a problem. But your palms are good. Lots of room. You've got to work on your pass, though. You can't expect to do it right under my nose like that if you aren't a lot smoother. Not faster. You were fast enough. But smoother. You can move as slowly as you like, as long as you don't look like you're doing anything. And you need to change your grip." He shifted my thumb along the side of the deck and lined up the other fingers along the opposite edge. "Okay. Now try it again. Slowly."

I did the trick again.

"Hold the deck further forward in your fingers. It gives you more flexibility. More room to move. Again."

I did it again.

"Good," he said. "Practice that an hour every day."

He picked up his coffee again and was about to take a sip when he stiffened slightly and caught his breath. He was no longer interested in the cards or my hands. He hunched over the table staring down into his coffee, brow furrowed in sudden concentration. His face was pale. His lips were a thin line. After a moment he drew out a brown plastic vial, shook out a tiny lozenge and slipped it under his tongue.

I watched , the cards held uselessly in my hand. "Are you okay?"

He nodded, but it was a moment before he spoke. He took a deep breath and let it out slowly. "So," he said finally, his voice sounding thin and wispy, "are you running toward something or away from it?"

"Why don't you read my mind?"

"I have two more shows in town here, then Lake Placid for a week, and the summer in Saratoga Springs."

I stuffed the deck back into my pocket and picked up my fork to scrape at the cheese glued to the edge of my plate. "And you need someone to carry you home at night and watch your trunks?"

"I've watched them before. I can do it again."

"So?"

He drew his hand, empty, from his pocket and right under my nose flicked out a wide and perfect fan of cards. "Pick one."

I did.

He collapsed the fan, shuffled, then cut my card back into the deck. His fingers moved with such precision that at every moment each card was exactly in its proper place. He slipped the deck into his pocket and brought out a white handkerchief, which he spread in his lap like a napkin. Then, with an empty hand, he plucked cards out of the air, speaking their names an instant before they appeared, as though calling them into being: "Two of clubs, three of diamonds, four of hearts, five of spades. Six of clubs." As they appeared, he dropped them below the edge of the table onto his lap, onto the spread handkerchief. Then he reached down and gathered the four corners of the white cloth, knotting them, and brought up the bulky little bundle of cards, holding it suspended like the pack a hobo hangs from his stick. "What was your card?"

"Seven of diamonds."

He set the packet down before me. I untied the knot. There was only one card there, lying in the folds of white linen.

"If I practice," I said, "I could do that in about a hundred years."

"You'll have it by the time we get to Saratoga Springs."

The secret to spontaneous, effortless magic is hours of preparation. Rudy had what was essentially a play list, a choreographed arrangement of all the tricks in his show, and a script to go with it. A thick sheaf of papers, dog-eared from handling. That afternoon, backstage at the VFW Hall, I pored over it. And as I read, he puttered, sorting out his equipment, arranging it, fitting together all the parts he would magically take apart later, nesting the scarves and balls and numerous rabbits within their hidden spaces in all the boxes, hats, and pockets. Rex in the left pocket, Waldo in the hat, Frankie in the magic box because he preferred the feel of a firm floor under his feet and being in a pocket made him nervous. Each trick was choreographed down to the movement of hands and eyes and the lines of patter. When he performed, Rudy looked as if he were making it all up as he went along, as if each trick had only just occurred to him, but here in the script every gesture was planned.

I studied it until my eyes crossed, until my brain grew mossy, and as the evening approached I began to get so nervous I couldn't stand still. I paced the stage, reading the book, trying to trace the tricks on the air before me, trying to memorize the correct moment when a voice from the audience is supposed to say "He's killed the bunny!" or when an unidentified person should cough repeatedly or fall off his chair. But I noticed these directions were all handwritten in the margins.

"Forget that stuff," Rudy said. "Lennox was a clumsy ass. And the one before him, too. Neither could walk across the stage without tripping." He nodded at the scrawled notes. "That was all they could manage." Then he paused, holding Waldo in one hand, the big hat in the other. "Do you have any good clothes?"

I shook my head. I had returned to the Y that morning for my suitcase, and I'd learned why you never leave anything in a room full of men who have nothing at all.

From the first trunk he drew out his second best tux. It was a little small, but, Rudy said, it would do for now.

I sat at the door and sold tickets. Then, when the time came I put on my deepest voice and over the speakers read the short intro from the first page of the script. "All the way from the stages of Europe and the Far East...." Then I eased the lights up on the stage, from darkness through red to blue and finally, with a burst of smoke, to a sudden, single pin spot, shining off Rudy's white shirt and hair.

The lights were my idea. Lennox had thought there were only two positions for a light switch, on and off. In addition to being clumsy, and never having worked in high school theater, he obviously had no soul for magic.

I was nervous as a boy on his first date, but the evening went well. I handed things over, I carried things away, moving like an altar boy through the church service. The too-small costume went over well with the audience. There was a little ripple of laughter as I stepped onto the stage. Rudy noticed it, of course, and incorporated it effortlessly into the act. And I played it up, too, elaborating on my own hesitancy and clumsiness, providing all the necessary misdirection, without coughing or shouting or falling off my chair once. I felt like another Blackstone.

That night we slept in a motel. It was a cheap, low building with a bright yellow sign out front and walls made of cardboard, but it seemed luxurious. Lying in bed, in the darkness tinged yellow by the glow from the sign, listening to the deep, regular breathing of the Magnificent Rudy in the darkness across the room, I felt for the first time since I'd packed my suitcase that I was no longer traveling, that I'd finally arrived wherever it was I was going.

But I should have known. You never really arrive. After all the miles, all the hours and nights on the road, it all turns out to be just one long return home.

No Place Like Home

In what, at times, seemed like a second lifetime on the road I met a number of people I'd consider experts on the subject of seedy out-of-the-way bars, and most of them were waiting at bus stations. I don't know what it is about that particular locale—the unvaryingly bleak fluorescence, or the plastic seats molded to make sleep impossible, or the fact that everyone in the world is driving away except you—but it breeds a kind of shimmering desperation among its citizens. So if you're looking for a nice place to drink—cheap, noisy, and not too fancy, but with a little something to take your mind off things—you could do worse than talk to one of the regulars. I asked an old man named Driscoll.

He'd been a fixture in the Landing for as long as I could remember. Thin, grey-haired, with unshaven cheeks and a belly like a basketball, he was the grey and shambling manifestation of the town's collective unconscious. It was said he'd been a pressman at the newspaper years ago, and the roaring of the big machines had driven him into a lifetime of trying to quiet his nerves. But for whatever reason, I used to see him now and then, sleeping on a park bench or bending intently over a shopping cart of empty soda cans. And with all the bleak portentousness of five a.m. on a desperate morning, his had been the last face I'd seen on my way out of town. I had glanced out through the smeared bus window, and there he was standing lost in hunched and febrile thought before an empty street corner.

So it seemed like fate when I ran across him again while stopping at the bus station to pick up the trunks, and on impulse I sat down. He was slouched by the broken video game in that prime corner away from the draft and the faint, miasmic sourness of the lavatories, waiting for a ride that was never going to come.

I bought him a cup of coffee and a doughnut in the middle of the afternoon, and though he smelled like the unwashed exhalations of a brewery he regarded me shrewdly.

"Well," he said. "Well now." And he considered the matter a moment longer. "If you really want down and dirty...?" and his voice trailed off. He took a noisy sip of his coffee.

"How down and dirty?" I asked.

"Oh..." And he just waved his hand, as if there weren't sufficient words.

"So, where?"

"The Anchor. Definitely. And O'Loughlin's. That's a nice little hole, not too fancy. Or the Barnacle down by the...by the... whatchamacallit, the bridge there. But...," he said and looked me over with sudden slyness. "A young guy like you. You pro'ly want somethin' with a little more ooh-la-la." He gave me a loose, wet grin. "Dontcha? A little more of that oom-pa-pa?"

"Could be," I said cautiously.

"I thought so. I could tell. No question. Then definitely. What you want... The Eagle. Oh, sure. It's a little shee-shee. Little paper napkins. Fancy glasses and shit. Everything but those little umbrellas in your drinks." He laughed again. "But it ain't like you don't just piss it all away anyhow."

I thanked him. I told him I'd take it all under advisement, though in the end there seemed only one choice. If there really were a bar that even Driscoll thought was down and dirty, I decided I didn't want to see it. At the same time I was confident that, going for the shee-shee, for that little bit of oom-pa-pa, I wasn't going to be drinking too far up the food chain. I was pretty sure I wouldn't run into anybody I knew.

The White Eagle Tavern was half a block from the river, slouching on the hillside among the last of the old maritime warehouses in a part of town that had been slowly subsiding for more than a century. It was a short building and squat, like a marker put down to reserve a space and then forgotten. On either side the old clapboard warehouses loomed above it, three or four stories tall and improbably narrow, with lofts facing out over the water as if still waiting for a ship to dock. All together they stood in a wavering line like the last few drunken onlookers who hadn't yet been told the parade had already passed.

To get to the bar you had to walk behind the whole row of buildings. The street was too narrow for cars, so you slipped past the blank walls along a dark cobblestone alley lit only by the dim blue and yellow neon of a Old Style sign in the window up ahead, so that, though you finally stepped in through the front door, it felt as if the only way to enter was to sneak in.

When I got there the place was almost deserted, with the startled look of a popular restaurant just moments after a bomb scare. It was a single, narrow room, made smaller by the hot glow of lamplight against red walls, red ceiling, red-painted trim. The thick light filled the air, softening all the edges, as if designed like the lights of a submarine to protect your eyes and keep your night vision sharp for the moment when you stepped back into the darkness.

It could have been any time of day, any season. Certainly there were no concessions to the recent Fourth of July. No red, white, and blue banners. No fireworks. Half a dozen booths like short, paired church pews were lined up along one wall, and a row of round tables the size of garbage can lids crowded into the middle of the room. And over the bar the television was tuned to what looked like a home exercise program, with a hostess, smiling in spandex, leaping about mouthing silent encouragement.

Two men and a woman sat hunched and evenly spaced along the length of the bar, while in one of the booths three young college students in baseball caps and windbreakers sat laughing among themselves and smoking as if it were something new for them and more fun than they'd expected. The rest of the place seemed to be waiting for something to happen.

I sat down at the bar. It was genuine wood-grained formica, and behind it a section of the wall was papered with a red and gold velveteen pattern that wouldn't have been out of place in a New Orleans bordello. Perhaps this was part of the ooh-la-la Driscoll had mentioned. Or maybe he had in mind the painting that hung on the wall between the popcorn machine and the rows of bottles. Given the name of the bar it was a little surprising that such pride of place was given to a picture that included not a single image of an eagle. Instead there was a raven-haired woman reclining naked in her boudoir. I'm not quite sure what it was that made her naked rather than nude. Perhaps it was the artist's exuberant sense of volume or his scrupulous attention to the wealth of pubic hair. In any event, she stared out with dark eyes and a teasing smile, obviously quite pleased with the effect, while beneath her the bartender sat on a high stool reading a book. The bartender, too, had dark hair and pale skin, and her face looked just enough like the woman's in the painting to encourage speculation among at least the less sober patrons. Something in the stiffness of her posture suggested she got asked about it a lot.

After a moment she slipped a swizzle stick into her book and wandered over. She was dressed in keeping with the decor: red sleeveless t-shirt, black pants. Her hair was thick, chopped off at the earlobes and frizzing violently as if from the shock. Her eyebrows were thick, and beneath her eyes there were echoing smudges of fatigue or make-up, dark as bruises that gave her a rumpled and distrustful look.

"What'll you have?" she said.

"I don't know. Lately I've had this recurring dream about a very large scotch. No ice. Soda on the side."

"Been dreaming about any particular kind?"

"I don't know. I'm pretty open minded."

She reached back for the Dewars and poured without another word.

I took a sip. The scotch caught in my throat, all rough edges and fumes. Just like old times. I looked up half-expecting to see Rudy sitting there beside me raising his glass.

"Okay?" she said.

"This tastes vaguely familiar."

"You want to run a tab?"

"Definitely."

Turning to the cash register she rang a ticket through and laid it to the side. Then, with a slow, surveying glance of the place she perched back up on her stool.

"Is this place always so lively?"

She shrugged and opened her book. "It picks up after eleven."

I glanced up at the clock. It was in keeping with the painting. Two long legs in stiletto heels were splayed wide, pointing at 10:25. "You know. I'll bet that's exactly the sort of clock my mother would like."

She didn't even glance up. "I'll tell her when she comes in."

I sat for a while drinking my scotch and thinking of all the bars I'd been in over the years. Rudy had a weakness for bars that matched and complemented his weakness for the stage, and in each case we tended towards the cheap and weather-beaten. Between the two they formed the only fixed and reliable points in our travels. To step out onto a stage, no matter where, no matter what kind, was to sink into a routine as orderly and reliable as breathing. And each bar—no matter how seedy or raucous—was a warm bubble of comfort and familiarity on a changing road.

We would come in after a show and take our seats, pretending to be normal, chatting with anybody who'd chat with us. We'd drink and sit and take in the sights. I liked every bar we ever went. I liked them because they were cozy and dark—warm in the winter, cool in the summer. I liked them because they were nothing like anything I had left behind. And I liked them because somewhere in the dimness, in the air of waiting that hangs over every such place, there was a humming sense of possibility.

Nothing magical. We always made it a point to check the act

at the door. Even Rudy needed a place that was ordinary once in a while. If people asked what we did we said insurance adjusters or taxi drivers or traveling salesmen, though what we were selling depended on the night and how much we'd had to drink.

Once it was ladies' corsets. I don't know why. We'd been drinking for a while that night, after a particularly thin turnout at the show, and some woman asked us what we did, and Rudy said, "Ladies corsets." And in the silence that followed she asked to see our stock. I started to laugh but Rudy didn't miss a beat. He said we didn't have them with us. Sorry. They were back in our motel room. And the woman said, "Well, where is this motel room?" She was neither particularly young nor particularly thin. In fact, she might genuinely have been interested in a lady's corset. But she had a wonderful smile, and Rudy sat there for a moment, nonplussed. I'm not sure this had ever happened to him before, but he was a man of great resources. He volunteered, a little hesitantly perhaps, to show her, and they left together. I'm not sure what he said to her, or how he explained the complete absence of ladies' undergarments back in our room, but they returned a couple of hours later, laughing about something, so I guess there were no hard feelings.

"Ready for another?" The bartender kept her voice flat and business-like, but I was a connoisseur of rudeness, and there was a crystalline note of solicitude that, in a place this seedy at this time of night, amounted almost to friendliness.
"Good heavens, yes," I said and watched as she poured. "If I told you I was a traveling salesman in ladies' corsets, would you believe me?"

"Is it true?"

"It's a hypothetical question."

She looked me over. "Ladies' corsets? "

"Corsets, lingerie. That sort of thing.

"Do people still wear that shit?"

"I guess some do."

"You mean like bustiers and shit? All that black lace?"

I agreed as how that might qualify, and asked if she'd like to see my stock.

"Listen," she growled. "Do I look like the lingerie type to you?"

"It's hard to be sure, of course. But it seems like a definite possibility."

"Is that right?" she said with that flat, business-like voice, but there was something not altogether unlike a smile on her face as she turned to replace the scotch.

At the clink of the bottle in the rack one of my companions down the bar perked up and began to show some interest. He glanced around, his eye falling on the empty beer mug beside his hand, comparing it, perhaps, with the small glass newly filled before me. With very slow movements, so as not to startle it, he reached down and drew the wallet from his hip pocket and spread it open. Then, with increasing concern, he searched through all the little pockets and folds. "Hey!" he said with a note of rising wonder. "I been robbed."

"Charlie," said the bartender tiredly.

I glanced up in surprise, but she was talking to the drunk.

"No, really," he said. "I had it."

He was dressed in pants that had once been clean and an ancient shirt that hung down below the uneven hem of an old hunting jacket. None of the clothes looked new, and none were the same size, as if he had dressed from the closets of three different strangers.

"I think it's time to go home, Charlie."

"But, my money.... " He showed her the wallet, opening it wide. It couldn't have been more empty. "Look."

And just for a moment he reminded me of Rudy, on one of his really bad nights, sloppy, despairing—too drunk to realize he'd neglected to hide the string of scarves up his sleeve. The man glanced up from his wallet, and reflexively I smiled.

"Hey!" His voice was blurry, and a little out of sync with his movements like a movie soundtrack starting to slow down.

"Hey, you! What's going on?"

"Not much," I said. "My brother's marrying a clown. My mother's not too happy about it."

He shook his head angrily. "No, dipshit! I mean, where the hell's my money?"

"Sorry. Can't help you there."

He frowned and glanced back at the bar, noticing again his empty glass.

"Goddam!" he said. "Now my beer's gone!"

"Take it easy, Charlie," said the bartender patiently.

"Bull Shit! ...take it easy. It's my goddam beer's been stolen."

"It's right there," she said. "He didn't touch it."

"That's a fuckin' empty. He can steal all the fuckin' empties he wants. I can walk down the fuckin' street and trip over fuckin' empties. It's my goddam beer I'm after."

"You drank it, Charlie."

"The hell I did!" His voice kept rising. "You think I wouldn't know it if I drank my own goddam beer?"

The man further down the bar was nursing a boilermaker and talking quietly with the woman a couple of stools down, but at the rise in volume he glanced over. "Wendy?"

"It's all right," said the bartender.

But my companion was glaring at me again. He glanced down at my drink. "What the hell's that?" he demanded.

"Lemonade."

"Bull Shit! Where'd you get it?"

"I found it."

Stricken with the unfairness of it all, he turned to the bartender. "You hear that? Fuckin' A! You hear what he said?"

Beyond him the man and the woman got up from their separate stools and with a glance at Charlie pulled on their jackets. "See you, Wendy," the man said. His companion just smiled. They walked out keeping the same distance—about the width of an empty barstool—between them.

"See, Charlie?" Wendy said. "You're driving people away."

"But, didn't you hear him? He found it."

"You want me to call the police again?"

But he was so outraged he was almost weeping. "He steals my money. He steals my fuckin' beer, and you're callin' the police on me?" He turned and glared furiously, then abruptly he lunged. It took him a moment. He wasn't sitting very securely on his stool, and he didn't get much of a push-off, so in the end he only teetered across the six feet separating us and managed to grab hold of my shirt as he started to slip.

"Charlie!" The bartender took half a step toward me, but unless she was prepared to vault the bar, I didn't know what she could do. She had a little aerosol can in one hand, but she seemed undecided where to apply it.

Charlie was gritting his teeth. "You son of a bitch." He had a fierce grip on my shirt and he was twisting the fabric, but his expression was melting into a look of uncertainty as if having come this far he didn't know what else to do. He was breathing hard.

"Hey," I said, "Charlie. That's my name, too."

"What?"

"It's true."

"Bullshit."

"Tell you what, Charlie. What if I buy you a beer? How about that? One Charlie to another. We'll toast to my brother's engagement. What do you say?"

"Really?" His fist was still tangled in my shirt, but he was standing up a little straighter now, considering the matter. He glanced back toward his seat. Wendy was already there. She set the beer down where his empty glass had been and stepped back.

"Okay," he said nodding. "Okay." He released his grip and, stepping carefully, made his way back to his seat. He picked up the beer and took a long drink, then sighed. "Fuckin' A. There ain't nothing like it, is there?" Then, gazing up at the TV screen where the exercise program was bouncing into high gear, he shook his head and murmured, "Look at the tits on that one."

I took a sip of my own drink. My heart was pounding, but it was starting to slow down again, and I could feel the beginnings of a smile.

Wendy was looking concerned. "You okay?"

"Sure."

"I'm really sorry."

"Don't be. I've met worse. In fact, I was a little afraid nothing like this would happen. I thought you said it didn't start jumping until later."

"Must be a full moon." She still had the little can of pepper spray in one hand. She reached over and set it on the bar.

Her arm was pale as unpainted plaster, and I noticed, in the little twist of movement, the dark hint of hair beneath her arm, which carried, in that sudden wispy glimpse, the faint, electrical charge of something inadvertently exposed. And in that momentary and sheepish little thrill I realized how long it had been since I'd seen the less public places of a woman's body. And that thought, alone, put a little nervous lump in my throat.

"It's probably," I said, "all the recent excitement. The fireworks and everything. I don't suppose you went to the parade?"

"There was a parade?"

"I hear the mayor was there. And twenty-nine clowns."

"No shit." She didn't sound much impressed.

"Yeah. I'm kind of sorry I missed it, too."

"I get all the clowns I need in here."

"But what about the mayor? I'll bet you don't get His Honor in here very often."

"Not very. No."

I nodded. "I knew there was a reason I liked this place."

Across the room one of the young men eased out from his booth and wove his way up to the counter, keeping a careful eye on Charlie. His baseball cap was green and he wore a Hartford Whalers warm-up jacket. His face looked tan even in this terrible light and he smiled like someone who'd been told all through high school how good looking he was. He leaned against the bar, not quite vertically. "Hi. How you doin'?"

Wendy turned to him. "Just peachy."

He glanced up at the painting and back at her, but all he said was, "Nice picture."

"What can I get you?"

"Three more."

"Old Style?"

"No. Uh-uh. Change of plans. We want a, um, a kamikaze, a planter's punch, and, uh..." He turned back toward the booth. "What was that last shit?"

"A sloe gin fizz," one of his friends called. They were laughing.

He turned back to Wendy. "That's right. A sloe gin--"

"I heard."

He grinned. "You know how to make 'em?"

"I'll manage."

He regarded her a moment longer, waiting for some further reassurance.

"I'll bring them over," she said.

"You're the man." He turned and wandered unevenly back to his table.

"Anybody card those guys?" I asked.

"Sure," she said. "The one on the left is twenty-eight. The other two are both thirty." She reached over to gather up a handful of bottles from the rack, then turned and started pouring. As she worked, the sleeve of her t-shirt gapped open on a glimpse of black bra strap. It caught my eye like that little movement of misdirection in any good sleight of hand, the sort of gesture that tells you something's going on, even if you don't know exactly what.

"You get many college students here?" I asked.

"Not too many. Every so often we get a few in slumming, but it's kind of a long way for the little dears to walk." She glanced up at me measuringly.

"I work for a living."

"I figured. Are you new in town?"

"Trying to be."

She shrugged. "It's not a bad place. Not all that exciting, but not bad."

"Are you from around here?"

"Born and raised."

"Ever think about getting away?"

She shrugged. "From what? One place is as good as another. The stuff I'd want to get away from is probably the stuff I'm carrying around, anyway. I don't know how far I'd get from that."

She gave the cocktail shaker a compact, wristy twist, and turned to gaze back at the array of glasses. They were stacked on a glass counter and glowing from below with a pale, electric-blue light. "What do you think?" she said.

"I don't suppose they'll know the difference."

She took down a tall, tulip glass, and poured in a froth of pink.

On impulse I asked, "Have you got any of those little umbrellas?"

Wendy gave me a quick measuring glance, bruised eyes and stiff, electric hair, as if she could go either way with it. Then she bent down, sifting through the shelves under the bar, and straightened up with a little pink umbrella. She popped it open and dropped it into the drink.

"That's it," I said.

The planter's punch took shape more swiftly: two bottles of rum in one hand, fruit juice in the other, poured to some unvoiced count. She shook it, poured, and then, as if it were all part of the same trick, she picked up a pack of Marlboros and plucked one out. She lit it and swallowed the smoke as if sucking it through a straw. "So," she said gaspily in little grey wisps. "Fruit?"

"Beats me. Oranges?"

She glanced over at the booth. "Cherries all around, I'd say." She spiked the fruit on little plastic swords and dropped them into the drinks, then arranged them on a tray.

"A thing of beauty is a joy forever."

"Yeah," she said. "It's a fucking party." She tucked the cigarette into a corner of the ashtray. "How about you? Ready for another?"

"I could be convinced."

She picked up the bottle that I was beginning to think of as my own, and filled my glass. "Your name really Charlie?"

"Charles," I said. "Occasionally Charlie. Never Chuck."

She reached down behind the bar and brought up another little umbrella, purple with red stripes. She slid it open and dropped it into my glass. "Go wild," she said.

Wendy carried the tray of drinks around the bar, and behind me I heard the three caballeros cheer as they arrived. One voice chimed up: "Which is which?"

I lifted out the little purple and red umbrella and sipped the scotch. Go wild, I thought. I shook my head. Returning to your childhood home is like creeping back into a dream you once had. It's familiar. You seem to know you're way around. But there's a vague and insubstantial feeling that beneath the outward appearances everything is shifting before your eyes, as if you can see it all clearly but have lost all sense of what it means. I thought of what Wendy had said, that what you're running away from is the same as what you're carrying. But that didn't seem quite right. Because what I'd been carrying on the road with me was nothing I'd brought along. From the start, with Rudy, I was inventing a new past, a new childhood, building it from scratch. And now that I was back, I felt the danger of losing it, of having it usurped by the memories and history of someone I no longer was. So I looked around the bar, trying to see it all as just another stop on the road, trying to hold onto the jumpy instability of a new place and the soft, woolly comfort of the scotch.

After a moment she wandered back and retrieved her cigarette. The red light brought out the depth of eyes. She looked like
someone with dark secrets.

"So," she said after a moment. "Lady's corsets."

"Well, not just corsets. Underwear, stockings. Lingerie in general."

"How long have you been doing that?"

"Oh, I've always been interested. But turning professional...?
That's been pretty recent."

"Sounds interesting. I suppose you do a lot of traveling?"

"That's a fact. At least I used to." I hesitated. "Let me ask you
a question."

"Maybe," she said.

"Do you have a mother?"

"That's the question?"

"Don't answer if you don't want to."

"Yeah. I've got a mother."

"Look at me," I said. "Examine me closely from every angle."
I spoke as clearly as I could, but this was my third scotch, and
the words were getting a little soft around the edges. "Do I look
like someone who's settling down?"

"Well," she said doubtfully. "You look comfortable."

"Okay. Sure. But that's not the same thing, right? I mean, settling in a downward motion and settling down are two completely different things. Wouldn't you say?"

"I might."

"I mean, you'd have to, wouldn't you?"

"Maybe."

"Can I buy you a drink?" I said.

"No."

I nodded. The scotch was slipping its long, soft fingers back
behind my eyes. "You've got a nice smile," I said.

She regarded me with an expression of bland consideration,
just beginning to soften at the eyes. "How would you know?"

"Just a guess. Do you think it's possible to live in a town all your life, and still find some part of it untouched by who you were before?"

"I think maybe you've had enough to drink," she said kindly

"My brother's engaged to a clown."

"Is that right?"

"Right here in this town. She has pink hair, a big red nose."

"Too bad."

"No. See. That's the thing. It's more than he deserves."

I was, perhaps, a little drunker than usual. Normally I stopped drinking at some point, and switched to club soda. It had become a sort of habit with me: start strong to keep Rudy company, then ease off to make sure I was in shape to get us home at the end of the night. But tonight there seemed no need. Rudy was beyond my help, and I wasn't all that keen on getting home. The rabbits were fine without me. And the sooner I went to sleep the sooner I'd have to wake up again, so I sat there, watching Wendy work—it really did pick up around eleven—and let the smoke and the noise swirl around me like some long and leisurely magic trick whose ending got lost amid all the effects.

From the row of booths behind us there came a little bubbling of laughter, and one of the three students, a different one this time, unwedged himself from behind the table and stood up a little unsteadily. He leaned down to gather up the three empty glasses.

"I'll get those," Wendy called.

But he just shook his head, laughing at the difficulty of holding the three large tulips in his hands. "I can do it. It's just a matter of--"

He turned with them cradled precariously in his arm, but as he took that first step, one slipped and with a quick, unlikely bounce on the carpet shattered with a sudden popping sound. His two friends cheered, and after the first look of almost comic shock he burst out laughing.

"Shit," Wendy muttered. "It's like fucking babysitting."

"God, those little puppies are slippery," the guy said, arriving at the bar. "Here, let me get that."

Wendy was coming around with a dustpan and broom, and the guy held out his hand for it. Wendy just shook her head, and the laughter back at the table bubbled up again. Mr. Personality glanced back and grinned, raising the two remaining glasses in a toast, then turned to the bar. He looked at me. He was bigger than I'd thought. On his t-shirt in big red letters it said Methodist Football. "Those little puppies are slippery," he repeated

"Is that right?"

"Hey. At least it wasn't full."

Wendy was just stepping back behind the bar, emptying the shards of glass into a wastebasket in the corner. "Say there, good-looking," he said. "Could we have a bowl of popcorn and three more of these killers." He set the glasses on the bar.

"I'll send them over."

"Nah. I'll wait. I want to see what goes in them. Besides, I kind of like the view." He leaned on the bar and grinned up at the painting behind her. "Is that you up there? You're looking pretty good."

Wendy ignored him. She began setting up the drinks. She had the two rum bottles in one hand and the punch mix in the other. The guy watched with interest as she started to pour. "Whoa. Easy on that fruit juice, babe." He reached out and caught the end of one of the bottles, tilting it up for an extra splash.

She jerked the bottles away. "Hey!"

"Attaway, Randy!" one of his friends called out. "Self-serve!"

"I'll do the pouring," Wendy snapped,

"Just trying to be helpful."

"Well, don't."

He held up both hands, grinning. "Okay, okay. Don't bust a bra strap."

As though that were a signal his two friends started edging out of their booth. With a glance at them she thumped the bottles angrily back into the rack. "Just keep your hands on that side of the bar."

"Hey. I don't see what you're getting so pissed off for. You're supposed to be taking care of us." He glanced around at the other customers. "I mean, that's your job, right?" A few stools down Charlie didn't answer, but with an instinct for these things he was already easing down off his seat and sidling away.

"Yeah," said the kid in the Whalers jacket. "That's right. You should be serving our every need."

Wendy straightened up. "Then maybe what you need is to leave."

"What'd she say? Leave?" The third kid was swaying gently, and seemed to be having trouble following the action.

"How can we leave?" said Randy. "We haven't even finished our drinks." By now the three vividly colored cocktails were lined up along the set-up shelf just behind the bar. He started to reach for them, but quickly, without ceremony, Wendy snatched them up and poured them into her sink. Pink and then white and then caramel fluids swirled and drained away.

"Hey! She's dumping 'em out!"

Randy stared down at the sink as the last of the color slid off the stainless steel and down the drain. "You can't do that."

"Want to bet?"

Our third contestant was still struggling to make sense of it all. "Didn't we pay for those?"

"They're on the house," said Wendy. "Now it's time to go home."

"Hey! What do you think?" demanded Randy. "We're just gonna leave?"

"That's it."

"What's going on? You think we're lowering the tone or something?"

"I think you're causing a scene."

"What the fuck?" Randy stared at her. "A shithole like this? And you think we're causing a scene? What about that drunken piece of shit, there?" By this time Charlie had made it to the back door. He didn't even turn his head as he pushed it open and slipped outside. "He yells his head off all he wants, and we're the ones causing a scene?"

"Are you going to make me call the cops?" she said tensely.

Number three stopped swaying. He seemed suddenly to have no trouble following the conversation. "Cops?"

"Oh, right," said Randy. "Like the cops would bother with a dump like this. What are they going to do? Come and clean it up for you?" He snatched up the open jar of maraschino cherries, and for a moment I thought he was going to throw it at her or smash it against the wall, and I tensed, ready to make a grab at him, but instead he just shook it out, scattering the red fruit across the floor. They bounced like soft, little BBS in a mist of sugar syrup. "Aw, shit," he said. "Now look what you made me do."

This struck all three of them as extremely funny.

Wendy picked up the phone. "Last chance."

"I'm shakin'. I'm shakin'," said the one in the Whalers jacket, and as though he'd learned a new trick he was reaching for the jar of olives.

Sometimes, in some of our less refined venues, Rudy and I used to run into the occasional heckler. Usually they stayed out in the audience and yelled, shouting out rude advice or offering their own obscene solutions to the tricks. We tried not to let them interfere, but if a heckler didn't shut up, Rudy invited him on stage. In the spotlight, with an array of bright silk scarves blossoming out of his unzipped fly, or a raw egg materializing out of nowhere to dribble down his back, even the toughest of them didn't last long.

Once, however, at a state fair in Agawam, Massachusetts, we had a drunk who was unswayed by magic. The scarves, the egg, the silk flowers blooming out of the top of his pants, nothing stopped him. In fact, he capped off one trick by turning and taking a swing at Rudy, and the show ended abruptly as I frantically tried to make his face disappear through the packed earth of the fairgrounds.

Now I stood up. "You heard the lady. Didn't anyone ever tell you not to play with your food?"

They all turned, measuring what sort of threat I might be. It took them half a second to decide. "Hey, man," said Randy. "This isn't our food." He grabbed a handful of orange slices and scattered them toward the back of the bar. But he was beginning to realize how silly that was, and he started looking around for something more substantial to break.

I grabbed him by the sleeve. I don't know why. Maybe I was planning to get him in a headlock, or something, or intimidate him with the steadiness of my gaze and the firm tenor of my voice, but I guess we'll never know for sure because, as soon as I gave his arm that first, sharp tug, he punched me.

I fell backwards by awkward and bumpy degrees into the row of barstools, sprawling among a little forest of upturned legs and cushions. Randy stood over me, looking startled but not displeased, while his two friends stared down with open mouths.

You should always be thinking, Rudy used to say, you should always be preparing. You should always know exactly what you're going to do next. Except, at that point I hadn't a clue. In fact, I was a little surprised to discover, quite abruptly, that I had somehow leapt onto this huge, smooth-cheeked, corn-fed jock and was trying to twist his head off and bang it against the bar.

Anger is a wonderful thing. The Whalers jacket and his no-longer-swaying companion had taken an interest and were trying to peel me off their friend, but I wasn't having any. And that was my advantage. They may have been only a few years younger, but these guys were kids. They'd been playing games their whole lives. But after seven years on the road, I didn't play anything anymore. I had this guy's blood on my hands. It was drooling out of his nose, smearing all over the red letters on his shirt. One of his friends made a startled sound as my elbow connected with something, but I couldn't be sure what. Things were moving pretty quickly then. Randy couldn't keep still. He was bouncing off the bar, and staggering back, trying to do something about the arm I had locked around his throat.

Then I looked up, and there was Wendy, out from behind the bar, looking much shorter than expected, and waving that little aerosol can. She shouted at me, something about my eyes, and without a moment's hesitation she gave old Randy two seconds of pepper spray right in the face. The only sound he made was a loud gulp, the sound a bathtub makes with that last gurgle of water going down the drain, then he reared back and dropped like a large, stricken stone.

I don't know if that's what Wendy had it mind. It isn't what I would have chosen. He landed more or less directly on top of me, and since I hadn't reacted quite in time, the pepper spray was clawing at my throat, and tears poured down my cheeks. I could barely see Randy's two friends dragging him to his feet.

"Come on, man!" But Randy was just coughing and weeping and bleeding all over his shirt.

"Now, get the hell out of here!" Wendy's voice seemed loud and effortless. She, at least, had no trouble breathing.

The Whaler's fan sneered. "You couldn't pay us to stay." But his heart wasn't in it. They had Randy walking now. He was bent over with the force of his coughing, but he managed to make it to the door. They staggered out together and slammed it shut.

I lay there for a moment longer, coughing up the last of the pepper spray. Then I felt a strong pair of hands on my bicep. "Can you get up?" With her help I dragged myself upright, and got a grip on the edge of the bar. My cheek was throbbing; my ribs felt soft and dented. "Are you okay?" she said.

"Peachy." My arm was sticky with the pulp of maraschino cherries. There were stains on my shirt that were either juice or blood. Wendy let go of my arm. She turned.

"Whoo-hoo! Hey, bitch!" The voices were muffled. They were lined up outside, the three of them, hunched in front of the broad picture window, even Randy, whose face looked puffy and mottled in the neon glow. "This is for you, honey! Thanks for the drinks!"

I stared at the little chorus line, trying to focus. It took me a moment to realize they had unzipped their pants and were waving their little pink companions in our direction. In the dim light I could make out the faint splash beneath the glass as they emptied an evening's worth of beer and cocktails against the side of the building.

"Jesus Christ," Wendy muttered. She was shaking her head. "Just another goddam Wednesday night."

But I was smiling. I couldn't help it. I thought of my father, my mother, I thought of Kevin, and I knew this could never have happened to any of them. Not in a million years. I wondered if they even knew this went on in their very own town. I tried to imagine what they'd say, but couldn't think of a word. There was no question about it. This wasn't the town I'd left, and here was the proof of it: I was standing in a bar with no one I knew, with bruised ribs, and a black eye, and my own, personal little three-gun salute. My official welcome home.

Breaking In

I found myself on the street. I wasn't sure how I'd gotten there. There had been a drink to kill the pain of my injuries, and then another, less antiseptic in nature, to celebrate my valor, and then I wandered out the door, worrying that perhaps this wasn't exactly what I had meant to do. That perhaps I should have stayed, lingering at the bar until closing time to see if Wendy needed a lift home—an idea that seemed untenable, not simply because I lacked a car or, on a more fundamental level, was much too drunk to drive, but because I had suddenly been struck by an unaccustomed feeling of nervousness.

In the past, having tucked Rudy safely into bed, I would on occasion slip out with a bartender, or a waitress, or an usherette from the theater. But it wasn't something that happened frequently, and when it did it tended to unfold with the awkward, accidental urgency of an impending mistake that could always be corrected by simply boarding a bus. But this was different.

I glanced around. In the darkness all the buildings of Main Street seemed to have subsided into themselves, as if lost in their large, brickish dreams. The storefronts and the parking lots looked empty and distracted, draped in the soft and dusty cloak of their new strangeness. The whole town was like one of those little, frozen scenes in a snow globe, but when you shook it, instead of tiny plastic flakes filtering down, a whole shimmering sense of loneliness settled over the street.

I thought of Rudy. I suddenly wanted just to hear his voice, cursing or muttering or complaining about something, or working his way smoothly through a trick, bringing the whole complicated story of disappearance and recovery alive, again and again. Standing on the street there, I wished, just for a moment, that I was one of those deranged street people who could paint the world with their private hallucinations, holding entire conversations with friends from their past. Even that much of Rudy would have been a comfort.

And then, out of the corner of my eye I caught sight of something, a little flash of blue light, and I had the momentary image of the little puffs of flash paper flame that Rudy used to like to scatter throughout the act—little exclamation marks for the eyes. I was pretty drunk. And I had the sudden, disorienting sense of being caught unprepared, like one of those nightmares from childhood where you're suddenly standing naked and at a loss in front of a blackboard full of strange runic scratches or up on stage with nothing up your sleeve. The lights made no sense. But then gradually they coalesced from the glint of magic into the more pedestrian jumble of blue police flashers, skittering through the trees at the south edge of town. And because I've always liked a good police story, and because I was already tired of being alone, I wandered toward it.

Two police cruisers had pulled up in front of the huge dinosaur bulk of the Shapewell factory. Their lights gesticulated wildly over the brick facade and danced through the trees across the street, turning the whole scene jumpy and strange. Even the breeze from the river felt uneasy. One of the officers was standing by his car murmuring into the radio while the other was talking to a balding, rumpled man in corduroys and a windbreaker just inside the heavy glass doors. I hesitated, conscious of the rolling imbalance the night's drinks had leant me, but then I shook out my hands and straightened my jacket, letting the strangeness of the situation carry me along.

The cop at the door looked me over, taking in the bruises, the smell of scotch, and the mismatched stains of maraschino and blood.

"What's going on?" I said.

"This is a crime scene," he said. "Just move along."

"I know the owner."

"Good for you." And he was already turning away, one hand

brushing idly at his nightstick, when Hugh glanced out the door and stared for a moment. Then with the thin, restrained eagerness of a man intent on finding out more than he wants to know, he pushed open the door and stepped outside. "Charles? Is that you? My God. It is you. What in the world has happened?" As if he weren't the one talking to a cop in the middle of the night in the middle of a crime scene. As if he had simply come to expect the lurk of disaster in the merest sight of me.

He'd been the last person I'd talked to before I left, before I climbed onto the bus; the last friendly voice at four in the morning after a long, dreadful night. And now the sight of him was all the proof I needed of how long I'd been away. He had always been bald, ever since I could remember, but now he looked old. The fringe of brown hair had turned dull grey and ragged over his ears, and the warm, familiar face looked shrunken, all creases and folds. I'd heard he'd starting drinking again.

My left cheek throbbed, and I could almost feel the bruise spreading into a sunset of reds and purples. As I shook his hand I tried to hold onto the pain of it and onto the strangeness of the scene, but his smile, startled and familiar, drew me back against the current of all the years.

"Hey, Uncle Hugh. How are you doing?"

He started to hug me, hesitated, then settled for a pat on the shoulder. "You look fine. A little older." He glanced at the black eye without a word. "But fine," he said.

"You, too. How's Aunt Mary?"

"She's fine. We're both...." He made a vague little gesture of the hands. Fine. "So... you're back?"

"Apparently so."

"Come on in." He glanced at the policeman, who grudgingly stepped aside.

The glass door wasn't as heavy as I remembered. The hallway wasn't as wide. In fact, the whole factory seemed to have shrunk. But as I moved deeper into the building I recognized all the old familiar scents. The air conditioning had been shut off overnight, and in the closed stillness I picked up the tang of acid, the lingering blur of hot metal, the oil and grease oozing from the joints of the machines. I'd lost track of this particular jumble of smells, and for more than seven years I hadn't given them as much as a thought. If someone had asked me, I wouldn't have known what they were talking about, but now I took one unthinking breath and felt my entire childhood crowding around: all the hours I'd spent racing through the hallways, playing among the machines on the shop floor while my father and Hugh nodded over chess in the quiet of the office and Gracie waited around the next corner for me to catch up. I reached up and pressed my cheek, welcoming the dull, blooming ache as if that alone were the only durable evidence of all the difference seven years could make.

I glanced up. "The cop said something about a break-in?"

"The alarm went off. Sergeant Williams and I got here about the same time. Someone had been through the office."

"What do you mean, been through?"

"It looks as though they tried the safe."

"You're kidding. Did they get it open?"

"No," he said, then glanced over, irritation and surprise crimping his expression. "What's funny?"

I could feel my smile spreading with all the sly, boisterous underhanded pride of a childhood badly spent. "The safe."

"Oh." His face relaxed, as if too tired even to hold onto its anger. "That's right. I forgot." And reluctantly he smiled. "That was a long time ago."

As a boy I had been fascinated by Hugh's safe. It was a wonderful old thing, an antique, black and solid like something out of an old gangster movie, and I had spent hours trying to get it open. It was set into the wall behind the reproduction of an old Wyeth painting of a woman alone on a broad prairie. Gracie had loved the painting for itself, but I had liked it only for what it covered. I'd swing back the frame and step up to it like a safe cracker and, with Gracie acting as lookout, spinning slowly in her father's chair, I would twirl the dial, pressing my ear to the cool iron as if I might actually hear the tumblers fall. Occasionally Hugh would come in while we were playing, and he'd open it up with a few deft twirls and take out some papers and a handful of caramels from the bag he kept there. He'd hand the candies around, then carefully lock it up again.

"Do you still hide candy in there?" I asked.

"No. I just keep it in the desk, now. It's easier."

"I finally got it open, you know."

"The safe?"

"Years ago."

"You were always a determined little boy."

I smiled at that, though I didn't admit there'd been no real skill to it. Hugh had a terrible memory, and he had long ago penciled the combination onto the bottom of his desk drawer. I'd stumbled onto it one day, and without telling anyone, memorized it. So I could impress Gracie, I suppose. Or Kevin. Though that seems like a very long time ago.

Hugh turned. "Come on in. Make yourself at home. But watch your step."

I followed him through the door, and almost tripped over a pile of file folders. "Jesus!"

Hugh had always been disorganized, his office messy as a child's closet, but never like this. The oak desk looked as if someone had tried to turn it inside out. The drawers were yanked open, papers spilled and scattered on the floor; pencils, files, paper clips littered the floor.

"Who did it?"

Hugh just shrugged.

"What did they want?"

"I don't know. Maybe they were looking for candy." But he wasn't smiling now.

I glanced over at the far wall. The painting was still there, pretty and familiar, but it was hanging ajar, and behind it the old and friendly safe was gone. I looked again. In its place was a shiny steel door, thick and heavy and brand new. It looked as if it wouldn't put up with a bunch of young kids playing burglar. It looked as if you couldn't open it with high explosives.

A young red-haired policeman with three stripes on his sleeve stood in the middle of the mess. He held a small black notebook still closed in one hand as he prodded a fallen ashtray half-heartedly with his toe. He glanced up at me suspiciously.

"Friend of the family," I said.

"Keep out of the way."

Hands in my pockets I sidled through the clutter, stepping carefully toward the desk. It had been pried open. The top drawer lolled out. On the dark and dusty wood inside all the old scratches and stains were still visible. Pencil marks, childhood hieroglyphs, the dark puddle where Gracie had knocked over the ink bottle, now as ancient and permanent as the wood itself. And back in one corner out of sight, the long penciled number which, if you could remember where to break it, would give you the combination to a safe no longer there.

"Looking for this?" the policeman said.

He was holding a grey steel cash box, battered and familiar. I'd almost forgotten it.

"No," I said. "Just looking."

He regarded me skeptically. The box hung open and empty. He held it carefully in one hand, and I wondered if even now after fifteen years my fingerprints were still on it, buried beneath layers of use.

"It was on the floor here," he said.

"It's usually in the desk."

I remembered it well. Hugh kept it locked away in the bottom drawer most of the time, but occasionally he left it open. Years ago, when we tired of the safe, we would open the drawer and take turns peering down at the heavy piles of quarters and nickels, the fine, thin dimes that poured from hand to hand, the pile of bills, wrinkled and dirty, but thick as a phone book to our greedy eyes. We'd stare at it marveling at how well Uncle

Hugh's factory must be doing if he could have this much money just sitting around. One night we counted it; the night of our burglary. We snuck in at the deepest dark hour and opened the box. Ninety-three dollars and change. Divided three ways it was a fortune.

I looked at the box now. The lock had been pried apart. "I take it they didn't find the key."

The policeman regarded me more closely, noticing the bruises now. "Who did you say you were?"

"It's all right, sergeant," said Hugh. "He's with me."

The policeman looked unconvinced, still trying to find a place for me in his suspicions, but he glanced down and scraped the toe of one shoe across the floor by the edge of the desk. "Kids. That's all." He was nudging what might have been the residue of a little camping trip: a scattered pile of ashes and cigarette butts, a couple of half-finished joints, empty beer cans tumbled and abandoned. "Looking for a place to party. Looks like they snuck in, had some fun, and left." He glanced at Hugh, who was still staring down at his desk, concentrating on other things. "They tripped the door alarm on their way out."

"How much did they take?"

Hugh shrugged. "There wasn't much. Seventy-five, eighty dollars."

"How old do you think they were?" I asked.

The policeman glanced around. "How old? Hard to say. Teenagers, probably. Why?"

"No reason."

After a moment the policeman slipped the little black notebook into his pocket. He looked like that last faithful guest at a bad party, calculating the earliest polite opportunity to leave. If Hugh hadn't been one of the town's more prominent citizens he wouldn't have been there now; a quick look around, and then file the report in the morning. But the owner of the town's last remaining factory deserved at least the pretense of interest. "I'm afraid there's not much more we can do, Mr. Barker. We see this sort of vandalism all the time."

Hugh glanced up. "I suppose it's not much of a crime."

I looked at the sergeant. He shrugged his agreement.

It was so quiet. I hadn't remembered the quiet. There had always been at least the air-conditioner, but with all the machinery shut down the whole building was silent. And along with the silence there was something more, an unremembered sweetness to the air. The other odors of the factory didn't carry into the office, and somehow, though the air in the office was heavy and still, it had a light floral scent, as if the fresh summer night had found its way inside with the burglars. I glanced over, expecting to find the windows open, but they were closed up tight.

The cop from the front door poked his head into the office. "Wake up, Jeff," he said cheerily. "The mayor's here."

"The mayor? What the hell for? What's he want?"

"Driving by. Checking up. Who knows? On your toes."

As the sergeant turned and hurried from the room I caught Hugh's look: curious, thoughtful, not altogether pleased at the unexpected state visit. With a final look around at the mess he followed the sergeant out. I followed in turn, though more slowly. I'd already met the mayor. Granted, it was some time ago, but I didn't really expect him to have changed.

Out into the parking lot, in the midst of the police flashers, shone the headlights of an official black car. Sergeant Williams and his partner were standing on the sidewalk at what doubtless was meant to be attention, talking to a tall youngish man in flawless formal wear. At the time I wondered if he wasn't going a bit too far, dressing up like a diplomat on a visit of inspection, though I later learned he'd been out to the ballet. He was blonde and slender in his tuxedo, though prone to a little softness around the waist. He didn't tend to exercise much; he'd always been too busy. But he looked graceful, elegant and utterly at ease. Even in the darkness that was clear—in the way he stood, in the soft gleam of his shoes in the stark lights. He looked like a man unsurprised by good fortune. Which, I suppose, was itself unsurprising.

After his four years at Methodist College, Kevin had broken with family tradition and journeyed a hundred miles north to Harvard Law School. After that a clerkship in Hartford for the connections and one in Washington for the experience. Then, at the ripe, old age of twenty-seven, he returned home to take up a teaching position down the hall from his father. There must have been great joy in the land. Great rejoicing. But within a few days of the appointment, certainly within hours of unloading his books onto the office shelves, the whole situation must have seemed so settled and proper as to be all but inevitable.

The chances of so convenient an opening on the faculty of the Methodist Law College were, of course, astronomical. It's a fairly good law school, and the faculty who come tend not to leave. A stranger could be forgiven for thinking it unlikely that Kevin could so quickly segue into the only teaching job he really wanted. But in retrospect, there was no room for doubt. The whole course of my brother's life had that kind of smooth, inevitable curve, all certainty and expectation.

Now the mayor was smiling, shaking hands. "So, Jeff, still on the graveyard shift? You must like the excitement."

"Not much excitement here, Mr. Mayor," though the sergeant was smiling back gratefully. Everyone likes to be remembered. "It's just a little vandalism. Some kids breaking in. Pete and I were just finishing up."

"Well, good," said the mayor cheerfully. "Maybe I'll just tag along. You know I've got a weakness for crime scenes. If you don't mind."

Sergeant Williams smiled. "You're the boss." But as he turned, he spotted Hugh. "Oh, Mr. Barker's here." He lowered his voice slightly, "And some vagrant, says he's a friend of the family."

His Honor spotted me and grinned. "Well, I'll be damned." He stepped forward, all bonhomie and easy good cheer. "I heard you were back in town." And he reached out and took my hand—no hesitation about a hug or a pat on the shoulder—and shook it with warm and brisk precision. Then he noticed my eye. "What the hell happened to you?"

"I got into a fight with a drunken football player over a jar of maraschino cherries."

He shook his head. "You do lead the most interesting life."

I shrugged. "What are you doing up so late?"

"We were just headed home and caught it on the police radio. But, hey." He stepped forward and, reducing to its essence a lifetime of being the older brother, gave me a sharp little shove, friendly but a little too pronounced, less like someone who doesn't know his own strength than like someone who does. "You know where the office is. Why didn't you stop by?"

"I've been pretty busy."

"So I hear. Sources close to the mayor's office tell me you've been performing without a license. Entertaining small children and frogs."

"Something like that."

At that moment there was the muffled thump that only very expensive car doors make, and an already familiar voice said, "It's okay. I'm with him."

Kevin smiled. "I understand you've already met Emily."

I turned and stopped. I hadn't really expected her to be in greasepaint. I mean, regardless of my mother's concerns, I didn't suppose she dressed like that all the time. But the image of her—painted face, baggy overalls, pink Brillo hair—was still fresh in my mind so that, even though she was standing right in front of me, it took me a moment to locate her.

She was still tall, but whatever bulk those orange overalls had given her was gone tonight. She wore a black dress that began in a thin band around her neck and flowed like dark water around and down to her ankles, leaving pale and bare her shoulders and arms and a narrow wedge of cleavage. The fabric glinted in the reflected glare of the headlights, and though it certainly wasn't hiding anything, in the darkness it seemed to reduce her in size, blurring the boundary between her body and the night. She wasn't pretty, exactly. She had a long, determined nose and lips that lapsed in spite of themselves into a thin, judgmental curve. And even without the white greasepaint there was a suggestion of inscrutability, as if most of her expression was being held in reserve. But her hair was the color of a two-year-old penny, hanging thickly to her shoulders, and when she moved there was a faint glint, a single diamond stud in one ear, understated and elegant.

Kevin stepped up. "Emily Burke. My long lost brother Charles."

A light breeze carried the hint of perfume. It wasn't anything I was accustomed to. The women I'd met in the last seven years didn't tend to wear perfume, or if they did it was more than you wanted to smell, but this was as fresh as the night.

"Nice eye," she said.

"It's just a little something I'm trying. I'm not sure I'll keep it."

"It suits you."

"Thanks. You know, I'd swear there was something different about you. I just can't put my finger on it."

"It's probably the earrings," she said and she held her hands jauntily up to each ear like a game show hostess displaying some new prize.

"That must be it. How was Clown Day?"

"Huge. One girl's mother called to say she refused to wash her face ever again. And your brother made yet another wonderful speech."

"I decided to come down firmly on the side of patriotism, good citizenship, and the family," Kevin said cheerfully. "Stick with what you know. That's what I always say."

He was grinning as he turned, one hand on her elbow, still working the introductions. "And you know Hugh, of course. And our guardians of justice."

I stepped back. And as I watched her smoothly greeting Hugh and the policemen in turn, I realized how misleading first impressions could be. When I'd first met her, I couldn't imagine a more ill-suited pair, but now, sleek, well-dressed, and impenetrably elegant, they looked like two of a kind.

"So, what's the story, Hugh?" said Kevin. "Everything all right?"

"A little messy. And some money stolen."

"How much?"

"Petty cash," I said. "Apparently some kids broke in and just helped themselves. Can you believe it?"

Kevin glanced at me, but he just nodded sympathetically at the news. I couldn't tell whether he remembered or not. "Mind if I take a look?" he said.

"There's not that much to see." But after a moment of the mayor's expectant silence Hugh shrugged. "Come on in."

"I've seen it," I said.

"Come anyway," said Kevin. "We haven't had a chance to talk."

His Honor strolled ahead with Hugh and the sergeant, who had his little black notebook out again and seemed to be referring to his notes. Emily and I followed. She was gazing intently around at the building. I was watching her. In the brightness of the corridor she seemed to have altered slightly, as if she'd grown more substantial in moving from darkness into light. She looked larger, now, more solid, with deep breasts and broad shoulders. It was unsettling how changeable she seemed, as if shifting before my eyes. I found myself watching her closely, waiting for the next transformation.

Feeling my gaze, she glanced over.

"Fasteners," I said.

"Pardon?"

"Metal fasteners. That's what they make here. Paper clips, molly bolts. And a peculiar little collapsible screw thing Hugh invented about fifteen years ago that carpenters use to anchor onto plasterboard. Incredibly useful, I'm told."

"I know," she said.

"Oh. Right. Of course you do." I'd forgotten the early protest. And now the picture of her in coveralls and a skull's mask,
swinging in Kevin's arms above the asphalt was yet another separate image to add to the mix. "Have you been inside, or just
standing out on the window ledge throwing fish?"

"Just on the ledge." She glanced around. "It's a great old
building."

"Hugh's grandfather added onto it back at the turn of the century, but the main part's been around since the Civil War."

"And it was his daughter? The one who died?"

"Grace," I said, and waited for that familiar little sliver of
grief, now dulled to a soft and burnished sadness. The memory
was like a stone picked up as a memento and carried so long that
it was the act of carrying, rather than the stone itself, which now
evoked the past.

"Kevin told me," she said. "It sounded so sad. She died in a
fire?"

"In her house. It was just a small fire, but there was a lot of
smoke. It caught her before she could get out. And before anyone
could get in."

"How old was she?"

"Fifteen," I said.

"That's so young."

I could think of nothing to add to that. I glanced up at Kevin,
smiling and chatting with Hugh and the police. He strolled with
a kind of slow formality, as if any group he walked in was a procession. "Exactly how long have you known each other?"

"Not all that long," she said. "A little more than six months."

"Do you always get engaged so quickly?"

She laughed. It was a nice sound, surprising, like a pair of
doves bursting out of a hat. "What can I say? We're impulsive. "

I didn't bother to tell her that Kevin was the least impulsive
person I knew. Who knows? He may have changed. "Have you
set a date?"

"Not yet. We'll have to make time for it. And things look pretty busy for a while."

"More gates to be chained to? More ledges to stand on?"

She glanced at me, as if measuring my tone. "Maybe. And your brother's got some plans of his own."

"He was always a big one for plans."

"And there's something wrong with that?"

"I don't know. I suppose it depends on the plan."

"Oh, you'll like this one," said Kevin, appearing suddenly between us. "It's right up your alley. It's kind of a magic trick. We're going to take a perfectly ordinary and nearly invisible small Connecticut town, and put it on the map."

"I don't think I've seen this one."

"Well, you will." He slipped one arm snugly through mine as though I might wander away, and slipped his other hand into Emily's, easing us into formation. I had the sudden image of a synchronized swimming routine, and I wondered what shape we were about to form, but he just stood there for emphasis, glancing around the familiar corridor. "It's a great old building, isn't it?" And I wondered if he'd been eavesdropping. "But, definitely getting a little seedy."

"I've seen seedy," I said. "This could be a lot worse."

"But it's not going to be. That's the whole point. Look around," he said, slipping into the smooth and practiced rhythms of a speech. "Cities can't go on like this: populations bleeding away, superstructure rotting, crime taking over."

"Is crime taking over?"

"It's worse than it's been. Look at tonight. Oh, sure, it's not the South Bronx, but that's our advantage. We can make a real change here. Keep the past, and build for the future."

"Sounds like a campaign slogan."

"It was," he said cheerfully. "And will be again."

"Then shouldn't you be telling all this to someone who cares?"

But Kevin was unbothered. Up ahead Hugh and Sergeant Williams stood, waiting for us to catch up. "Uh-oh," he said. "Falling behind." And with a wink, he released us both and hurried forward. It made me think of an act I'd scene years before where a juggler kept a row of plates spinning on these tall sticks, moving back and forth from stick to stick, keeping everything in motion.

"My God," I said. "I feel this overwhelming desire to vote for that man."

Emily ignored me. Her gaze was still following Kevin, and she looked as if she'd rather be up ahead spinning some other plate than mine.

"Does he always give so many speeches?"

"He says what he believes."

"And that is?"

She shrugged. "Something's going wrong today. You don't have to be a rocket scientist to see that. And not just here. Have you looked at statistics for the cancer rate in this country over the last thirty years?"

"You know. I meant to..." It somehow came out snider than I'd intended, but I just let it hang.

Those thin, judgmental lips clamped shut. "You can joke all you want, but the facts are there. People are getting sick. Cities are getting sick. How can they not be related? You can't screw with the environment, let the cities go to hell, and expect it not to affect people. Take this place. This is Norman Rockwell land. It's small town America, and it's still scary."

"Have you ever spent the night under a highway overpass because you were too broke to find a room?"

She shrugged impatiently. "Okay, so it's not a war zone. But parents are still afraid to let their kids stand out in front of the theater at night. We have to keep them inside till they get picked up. Is that any way to live?"

"I'm guessing no. Right?"

"People have to stop being cruel," she said, "to each other, to the earth, to the cities. And this is as good a place as any to start."

"So, what exactly is it you're going to start?"

"It's what Kevin's going to start. Don't worry. He'll tell you. He likes telling people."

"It's not going to be another Colonial Williamsburg, is it? I mean, we won't have to wear costumes, will we?"

"Maybe just you," she said curtly and hurried forward to re-join the group.

Sergeant Williams stopped the tour at the end of the corridor and stood looking up at a row of windows set high in the wall. What was now Hugh's office had been built onto the old build-ing as a one-story addition, and these windows, eight inches high and wide as gun ports, peeked out over the low office roof, offering a view of the dark sky. One of them, third from the left, hung slightly ajar. Kevin was gazing up at it with a look of con-cern, but without any glimmer of recognition, as if that particu-lar window, which had never closed properly, meant nothing at all to him.

"The lock doesn't quite catch," the sergeant was saying. "Looks like they just popped it open with a screwdriver."

Hugh squinted up at the narrow frame. "Impossible. How could anyone squeeze through there?"

I waited for Kevin to laugh, or explain just how it could be done, but he said nothing. Maybe it wasn't something he wanted to recall. He was mayor now, and it might not be for the best to dig up his old life of crime. Or maybe he really didn't remember; I suppose that was always possible. It had been a long time ago, and perhaps it wasn't as clear in his mind as mine.

It was a summer night, dark and moonless, which may be why every aspect of it still glows in my memory with its own bright phosphorescence. A very young nine-year-old snuck out of his house long after bedtime, with his older brother. Together they collected Gracie at her house. The boy insisted on that. He refused to go without her.

It was eleven o'clock on a Friday, and even then, all those years ago, the area around the factory was dark and abandoned.

They wore black clothing, t-shirts and jeans, and only Gracie's reluctance to smear charcoal on her face kept them from doing the whole midnight commando thing. They'd scouted it out that afternoon—at least, Kevin had—so when they came back at night they knew where to find the drain pipe. It wasn't as easy as it looked on TV, but there were braces all the way up, and our heroes were fearless with excitement. At least, most of them were. Clambering to the low roof of the office they scrambled back over the asphalt and gravel. Around them the whole countryside spread out, invisible in the darkness.

They knew which window to try: the lock didn't fit, and if you pressed firmly with the tip of a penknife the tongue of the latch lifted and the window eased open. Kevin was so clever. He was six years older and the brains of the gang, so he went first, dropping loudly to the floor. It was a long way down. That was the one fear: to fall so far. But they were commandos. They were fearless.

Still, when the moment arrived it seemed that for every foot they had crept up the drainpipe they now had to drop two. Once Kevin had jumped down, there was nothing to do except follow, but for a long time the young boy and girl crouched in the darkness overlooking the countryside, whispering urgently. He was telling her it was much too far, certainly too far for her, and she was telling him to jump or get out of the way. So, there he was, scared out of his mind, but trapped between his older brother and his best friend.

Hanging for as long as he could, he dropped, landing like a sack of washers, and lay there with the dawning realization that he had survived. He was lying there still, marveling at his good fortune, as Gracie landed and rebounded beside him. Then Kevin helped him to his feet, and together they crept through the corridor and the dim glow of security lights to the office.

It seems remarkable now. There was an alarm on the doors, and on the factory floor, but nothing on the windows. Why would there be? Who in the world could squeeze through an eight-inch window. So there they were, three children, alive with nervousness and excitement, strolling right into the office.

Gracie stood anxiously as Kevin held the flashlight and said, "Okay, kiddo. Do your stuff." And the boy climbed onto a chair before the safe. The numbers from the drawer were fresh in his mind. He recited them under his breath as he turned the dial, too nervous even to pretend that he was listening for the tumblers. Then, deft as a burglar, he swung open the door, and turned with satisfaction to see Kevin's smile.

There was a full bag of caramels. The boy spilled them out onto the desk, dribbled them like gold through his fingers, divvied them up. Each burglar got five. And that was that, he thought.

But Kevin wasn't through. He was still standing by the open safe. "Just one more thing," he said, and shone the flashlight in. "Ah. Here we go."

"What is it?"

He withdrew from the safe a silver key ring, gleaming in the light. "I'll show you."

"What are you doing?"

But without answering he stepped to the desk and unlocked it. Then, opening the bottom drawer he drew out the cash box and set it on top.

"You can't do that," the boy whispered, appalled.

"We're burglars, aren't we?"

"But, what if we get caught?"

"We won't."

"What if we do?"

He smiled down at the young boy and girl. "Do you want to have an adventure, or not?"

Wide-eyed and speechless they watched as he scooped out the money, ninety-three dollars, more than any of them had ever seen at one time, and stuffed it into his pocket. Then hurriedly they retraced their steps, fearful of every creak and whisper in that old deserted building. But, at the wall beneath the window, they realized their mistake. Dropping ten feet from a window was one thing; leaping back up was another. What could we have been thinking?

But we were frantic, Gracie and I. I still remember that. The sudden rush of terror as we stared up at the open window. We raced back into Hugh's office and dragged a heavy wooden chair the length of the corridor, but it was too short. Even Kevin couldn't reach. Gracie started to cry. I was glad of that, glad that she beat me to it, but it made me even more crazy. I looked around for some solution, some way to stop her tears. Kevin was smiling. I remember that, too. Maybe that's what made me so mad. Maybe it wasn't just Gracie's tears. But, between the two of them, I was determined to save the day. I grabbed her hand. "Come on."

"Where? We can't reach."

"We'll go out the door."

She stared at me. It seems obvious now, but in all the panic of the moment we had forgotten the door. "What about the alarm?"

"Never mind! Let's go!"

Ah, young love. I still remember her expression. It comes to me in odd moments of panic or relief. She looked as if I had saved her life, as if I'd done all that she could have wished, as if I'd produced a miracle.

"We can't," Kevin said. "They'll see us."

But I had Gracie by the hand. We rushed to the door, shoved hard on the bar and pushed it open. Then we ran, all of us, Kevin, too, racing across the deserted parking lot with the money burning a hole in his pocket.

Now I stared up at the open window as if all my riotous childhood was crowded around on the other side of it. "We suspect kids," I said gravely to Kevin.

The sergeant glanced over in irritation. "It opens onto a low roof, on the side of the building. Back from the street. We think they must have climbed a drainpipe, then popped the window.

Climbed in here, then went out the front door. It's all gravel. There won't be any footprints."

"So you don't know who it was?" asked Kevin. "I suppose it could have been anybody. Kids out for a little fun. Just picking a place at random."

The sergeant shrugged. "I'd be lying if I said we had a clue."

"And nothing's missing, Hugh? Besides the money, I mean."

Hugh glanced at him, measuring the statement, and I caught a brief flicker of some invisible effort just beneath the surface. "No," he said finally. "Just the money."

"It's mostly vandalism," said the sergeant. "They messed up the place pretty good. Left some cigarette ashes. A few beer cans. Looks like there was some pot, too. You want to see?"

Kevin glanced back at us. "Emily? You want to see an actual crime scene?"

"I'm not really dressed for it."

"I guess not, then, Jeff. I'm sure you've got it under control."

"Oh, sure. No worry about that."

Kevin turned and shook Hugh's hand. "Good to see you, Hugh. Sorry about all the fuss."

He nodded stiffly. "My best to your father."

Kevin smiled. "And Charles," he added, turning, "don't be a stranger. Stop by the office, and I'll take you out to lunch." He shook my hand again and clapped me on the shoulder. It felt like a photo op, though there wasn't a camera to be scene. Maybe he was just rehearsing. Then, he slipped a hand through Emily's arm.

With a thin, no doubt relieved, smile Emily nodded good-bye to me and they strolled out in a little swirl of perfume and satin. Her hair fell thickly, flaring with static or irritation or just a desire to be somewhere else. The warm color glowed in the bright lights. The fabric of her dress gleamed, shifting like an optical illusion. I watched until the heavy glass door eased shut behind them. They were laughing together as he helped her into the car.

"Nice guy for a mayor," Sergeant Williams said.

The other cop nodded. "Really takes an interest."

"Yeah, he's got a real feel for the little people," I said. "You mind if I just look around?"

The cop turned to glare at me. "Weren't you listening? There's nothing here."

"Just for old time's sake."

The sergeant shrugged. "We're just about through."

I wandered back into Hugh's office, and found him staring dazedly around at the chaos. He looked beat. "You okay?" I asked.

He shook his head. "What a mess."

I bent and started picking up the empty beer cans, dropping them one by one into the waste basket. "So that's our new mayor."

"That's him," he agreed. "Never too busy to stop by."

"What do you know about her?"

"Not much. The only time I met her she was standing on my ledge throwing garbage into my parking lot and calling me names. Still. She seems nice enough. Why?"

"Just curious. She doesn't seem like Kevin's usual choice, exactly."

"I don't know. She seemed pretty enough."

"I suppose." I glanced down at the pile of cigarette butts and ashes on the floor. "Have you got a broom?"

He nodded toward a closet in the corner.

"Still," I said, opening the door, "she's not exactly a load of laughs."

"No?"

"Takes herself a little seriously, don't you think?"

Hugh shrugged. "You should have seen her the other day. She was dressed like a clown."

"Even clowns can be too serious."

He looked doubtfully over at me, as if to say I was giving it an awful lot of thought.

I took out the broom and dustpan, and turned back to the pile of ashes. But as I looked down at them, I was aware again of the silence and the ancient familiarity of the place. I marveled that some random group of kids unraveling the puzzle of their own childhood should have stumbled so precisely onto mine. And I thought about Kevin, about Gracie. I thought about the burglary, our burglary, and all that had led from it, more or less directly. I tried to see it as a lark, an adventure, but all I could see was the three of us: Gracie in tears, Kevin smiling, and me on the edge of panic. The future in miniature. And I thought of Emily Burke. The sound of her voice. The color of her hair. The pallor of her shoulders almost as white as greasepaint but warm against the dark dress. The details were vivid, but I somehow couldn't see her clearly. Her image kept shifting. The more I thought of her the more out of focus she seemed.

And as I continued cleaning, sweeping up the litter and ashes, I realized it was even worse than that. My senses themselves were distorted. I picked up the dustpan full of cigarette butts and blackened roach ends smoked in this office less than an hour before, but I could barely smell them. They gave off only the faintest hint of stale ash. Instead, what I noticed was the fresh scent of Emily's perfume, still lingering in a room she'd never entered.

Not good, I thought. Not good at all. A trick of the air currents, perhaps. A trick of the mind. I didn't want to think about what it might mean, but how could it possibly be a good sign, after all the miles and all the years on the road, that I'd been back in town less than a week and I couldn't get the scent of my brother's fiancée out of my nose?

Then, looking down, I realized my other senses were playing tricks on me as well. In the dull smear of ashes piled in the dustpan I saw a little gleam, like a tiny shred of cellophane catching the light. I brushed through with a finger tip, turning the ashes to powder, searching for that flicker in the dust, not even sure it was there. An optical illusion. Then it emerged as a little seed under my finger tip, a piece of ash that wouldn't crumble. Not cellophane. No longer shiny, coated in grey dust, but there like a little prize, appearing as if by magic. A tiny, dull, sharp-edged diamond on its thin gold post.

There's This Trick I Learned...

Once long ago, while a ragtag assortment of disgruntled Indians and irate French trappers traded shots with a gradually increasing posse of English soldiers out on the distant frontier of what would someday become Canada, Thomas Wetherford Strawberry stepped out of a rented skiff and sank up to his knees in the mud of the New World. Grabbing onto a stand of cattails, he dragged and clambered his way up the bank to firmer ground and stood panting from the effort. As water oozed out of his shoes, and the swampy smell of river mud rose from his stockings, he gazed around at the settlement he had come so far to see. He wasn't pleased. It had been a long, rough trip from England, and Thomas had weathered the late spring gales by keeping his mind firmly fixed on the bright and bustling community to which he was bringing his talents. He imagined his glowing future and looked forward to the chance of building a whole new life in a society untouched by past mistakes. And then he arrived. He trudged out of the mud into an outpost of perhaps two hundred souls on a rocky bend of the Connecticut River in the raw and muddy heart of the country and sat down on a rock. Contemplating his damp and ruined shoes, no muddier than his hopes, he wondered if it was too late to catch the ship back to England.

But when he looked up again, later, after his stockings had dried and his shoes had been cleaned, Thomas saw what he had come so far to reach: two hundred people gathered in one place and hundreds more in the rich surrounding countryside, who were dressed in skins or old wool and patched felt, wearing the same shoes they'd worn since they'd arrived in the country, carrying much-mended farm tools and traps, who hadn't seen a dry goods store closer than a five-day ride in as long as they could remember. In other words, Thomas Strawberry, the self-styled adventurer, burgeoning entrepreneur and, let's face it, something of a show-off, had found that most attractive of quantities: a captive audience.

He pulled from the rented boat the first of his bundles and carried it up the path to an empty lot, and there he set up his tent and raised the elegantly carved wooden sign he had brought all the way from Bond Street in London: Strawberry's. It was a serendipitous choice for a sign. People who hadn't seen any fruit more exotic than an apple or a pear for years began to wander in, only to discover that, not only did he have no berries, he had no fruit of any kind. What he did have was the most captivating array of brand new tools, fabrics, household gadgets, and knick knacks they had ever seen. He had shirts and dresses, corkscrews and biscuits, eggbeaters and spoons, gunpowder and sugar, sacks of beans and fine white flour. The populace looked in, poked among the household gadgets, held up the clothes, argued about the need for things they'd gone so long without, muttered at the prices, and left. But they returned.

By the end of the summer Thomas had a wooden building on the site and his own boat making regular runs down the coast to New Haven and back. He had not been a success back in Stratford. He hadn't enjoyed working in his uncle's shop, hadn't enjoyed the closed, established feel of somebody else's account books going back seventy years. Or, so I imagine. Maybe he just didn't fit in. But the newness of America gleamed like a prize before him, and he worked very hard.

He was not a good bargainer. In fact he almost never got as much as he wanted for anything. But, he was a magician of sorts. He told stories, entertained people, listened to their troubles, made them laugh. And he never let a customer leave dissatisfied. Word spread that his merchandise was good, that he always had news from New Haven and beyond, that there was always a barrel of hardtack and a pitcher of cider for those who stopped in, and that, when it came right down to it, he was a soft touch.

That was his talent. People came to chat, to eat the man's free biscuit and beat his price down on some not quite crucial piece of merchandise, something they wouldn't have bought but for the satisfaction of getting it for less than they should. And often as not they bought just a little more than they'd intended.

He wrote glowing accounts to his sister and her family back in Stratford, and word got around that there was money to be made by the man with the right approach. The following spring, up the river, in Thomas's own boat, loaded down with the year's first run of fresh supplies, appeared C. K. Bentchley, with a fine, determined light in his eye, and the confident conviction that if a soft and lazy simp like Strawberry could make a go of it here, he himself would have the town eating out of his hand in a season.

No one really remembers what it was that first sparked the enmity between the two men. Maybe it was a woman. From what little I know of C. K. Bentchley, that seems more than likely. Or maybe it was something less defined: a vague but natural antipathy of opposites, distaste on the one hand, impatience on the other. But whatever it was, like the physical laws of positive and negative, it continued to bring these two together.

Bentchley was a solicitor, but when he got to Connecticut he found the legal needs of two hundred farmers and trappers insufficient for his purposes. And besides, he had larger things on his mind. It was said that in the course of his first two years in the country he opened and closed a tavern, a hotel, a blacksmith shop and a dry-goods store. Nothing seemed to last. It turned out he just didn't have the right personality for an inn keeper, and this was a time when most people did their own blacksmithing. The town didn't really need a second dry-goods store, though Bentchley nearly stuck it out just to draw business away from Thomas. But in the end even the overseeing of a shop proved too close to manual labor.

This was not to say he actually worked in any of these establishments, beyond, perhaps, a little light supervision. Bentchley thought of himself as a doer, and so preferred to supervise, to give himself a larger perspective from which to make plans. His method was to find the right idea and the right person with the talent to implement his plan, and to bring together these two forces like an alchemist combining elements. But he expected fast results. That was both his strength and his greatest flaw: the impatience that drove him forward sometimes drove him beyond his target, and he would simply continue past, flying onward to the next goal. He always had bigger plans in mind.

The fact of the matter was, as Bentchley himself admitted frequently, he just wasn't suited to the scale of a small frontier town. He was a man ready to meet the needs of a much larger community. And so, after a couple of years, he settled into an occupation that would sustain him for the ten or fifteen years it took the town to grow into his plans. He met a woman who could provide the talent, and with the last of his original capital they went into business together. He maintained his law office on the main street, just a couple of blocks down from Thomas' store, though that was mostly for appearances. The address of the other business, of which he remained a secret partner, was just outside of town, beyond the range of puritanical eyes, but still within easy reach.

In retrospect it's remarkable that, in a town so small, anything could remain a secret, and that an upstanding citizen like Charles Kevin Bentchley, great-great-great-great-grandfather Charles, that pillar of the community, who grew to be one of the largest property owners, organizer of the town militia, First Selectman, and eventually the town's first mayor, could have owned a brothel for ten years without anyone being the wiser. Though, in retrospect, perhaps some were. The wiser, that is. Or maybe there really is some balance in the world that repays diligence and hard word and friendliness, and doesn't allow ambition to have everything its own way. I'd certainly like to think so.

In any event, when the time came to formally inscribe the name of the settlement in the land records of the colonial capital, when it had grown into a town and not just a collection of shacks and tents, C.K. put it about that Bentchleyburg or Bentchleytown, or just plain Bentchley had a nice, substantial ring to it. But the citizens disagreed. Tacitly, informally, without apparently having decided anything at all, they continued to refer to it as they had since some ship's captain, mooring his boat, had peered around for some identifying characteristic to apprise his passengers of their destination, and had spotted the sign on Thomas' store and the well-worn path down to the jetty, and had told the latest crop of settlers, farmers, and fur trappers, "Welcome, everyone, to Strawberry's Landing."

In later years the two men continued as they had begun. Thomas maintained his store, and expanded with the town, riding the swell of the developing country, into a nice, modest property and the largest shop on what was now most definitely the Main Street. Bentchley, too, thrived, though never quite as much as he would have liked. Their progeny continued on in more or less the same spirit, with a degree of antipathy that rose and fell with the times, until finally, six generations later, the breach was healed when Ambrose Bentchley married Dorothy Wells, whose mother was a Strawberry, and with the naming of their two sons, Thomas Kevin and Charles Wentworth, they blurred together the last of the feud, and mixed up all the elements of that first family history so that, in some fashion, we've been struggling ever since to sort it out.

Now, as I turned onto Main Street to the sound of the noon whistle down at the factory, I saw Kevin waiting for me on a street corner about two hundred and fifty years and the same number of yards from where Thomas Strawberry first came ashore. And it occurred to me that in a landscape as charged as this one, there was no place where the past had no claim. And if on some level I was still running from it, which I most assuredly was, this was the last place in the world I should have run to.

Kevin stood in the middle of the sidewalk looking as relaxed as he would have in the comfort of his own house—the one my mother had been so obviously pleased about. He was communing with his constituents, immersed in conversation with a small group of silver-haired women and a slender young man in a baseball cap, and I didn't have to hear him to see the smooth, eager, certainty in every gesture and look.

It seemed odd that he should be standing there, so much himself and yet so unlike how I remembered him. Now I heard little snippets wafting out, afloat on a ribbon of talk—"tax base," "crucial growth," "moment of truth"—and just seeing him made me feel out of place and uneasy. I had thought of him so much over the years, planning how I would make him sorry, how I would make him pay. I imagined him undone by guilt and by the inescapable knowledge of his own responsibility that would make even a man of Kevin's glib confidence squirm. But now here he was, unshadowed by all the memories and associations that should have crowded around him. For so long, now, when I'd conjured up his face, it had been overlaid with the image of Gracie on that last day, crying and stricken, and the images had been bound so closely that now, to see Kevin, smiling, charming, and untroubled, was as unnerving as if I'd looked into the mirror and found some stranger.

Neither Kevin nor the woman seemed to notice my approach, but the young man looked up and nodded. It took me an instant, even after seeing her face, to recognize Emily. Her hair was tied back, she wore a work shirt and jeans, and the baseball cap was pulled low over her eyes. No make-up. No jewelry. No earrings. Not even one. "Fancy meeting you here," she said.

I was surprised by the easy tone. Last time we'd met she'd seemed more than a little distracted, but I suppose in retrospect that was understandable. At the time she must have had a lot on her mind. Now I marveled at how relaxed and friendly she seemed in the sunlight, as if her conscience were clear as the sky.

"His Honor's in conference, I see."

"Always," she said. "How's the eye?"

"Colorful. I think it's beginning to clash with my clothes."

Reluctantly, as if against her better judgment, she smiled.

"You can never have too much color."

"Yeah, but you're a clown. What kind of taste are we talking about here? I mean, look at that outfit. No greasepaint. No evening gown. What are people supposed to think?"

She laughed. "They'll think I have to work for a living."

"Well, it definitely needs a little something to liven it up."

She considered that for a moment. "I do have that pink wig at home."

"Nothing so extreme. I was thinking maybe just a little jewelry. Those earrings, say. From the other night? That should do it."

She glanced down at her shirt and jeans. "With this outfit?"

"Why not?" In my pocket I could feel the diamond like a small, hard seed between my fingers. "I understand they're wearing diamonds with everything this year."

I said it lightly, but there must have been something in my tone. She glanced up, her smile fading, her eyes turning vague with caution. "Not me," she said. "I'm not that crazy about jewelry."

"Afraid of losing it?"

This time she said nothing at all. The last of the smile slipped away. Her mouth opened, but she seemed to have forgotten what it was she planned to reply.

"No, Helen. That's not my point." His Honor's voice rose suddenly out of the silence, and with a look of relief Emily turned and resolutely bestowed the remnant of her attention on Kevin. "What we need is more, not less," he said. "That's the whole issue."

"More cars? More smog? More run-off into the river?"

"More jobs," he said patiently. "A larger tax base."

But she just shook her head. She was tall and severely dressed in a dark skirt and blouse. She carried a Bonwit Teller shopping bag, though the nearest Bonwit's was in Boston, and she spoke with the crisp finality of a grade-school science teacher, which is what she'd been for more years than I'd been alive. "Mr. Mayor. I have to say, you have no idea what you're talking about."

I leaned closer to Emily. "He certainly has a way with the voters." She didn't reply, didn't glance up. "Maybe he should just agree with her. That's what I always did."

"Not Kevin," she said. "He can go on all day. This is his favorite part."

"What about you?" I asked. "What's your favorite part?"

"What I'm talking about, Helen, is resuscitating this town. Before it's too late."

"It's already too late," she snapped. "We should be restricting growth, not encouraging it."

"If it were any more restricted, we'd be going backwards."

"Mr. Mayor, we are going backwards." Helen glanced around. "Look at this place. The river was pristine before we arrived. The land was beautiful. And now look." She gestured around at the town as if it were all some terrible scar on the land. "What we don't want are more businesses coming in here, bringing their filth. We're guardians of the land, Mr. Mayor, and we can't afford to foul our own nest."

"But, Helen…," Kevin said, his voice rising again, and he was off.

I'd never been sure what a mayor did in a town this small, but I'd always suspected it was a position so lean and inconsequential—the occasional Mertel construction disaster aside—as to be all but honorary. But what struck me now was how busy Kevin seemed, even just standing there, as if his ideas alone, dressed up in a display of earnest conscientiousness, took up a world of space and effort.

When the women finally gathered themselves up, a little excitation of bags and shoes, and headed off down the street, Kevin turned with a wry smile.

"And she's one of my supporters." He shook his head. "If I hear about the 'guardians of the earth' and the dangers of development one more time…"

"The thing is," said Emily, "she's not entirely wrong."

"What she is," Kevin said, grinning at me, "is a nut."

Emily shrugged. "She makes a certain amount of sense."

"You don't think she's a tad extreme?" Kevin asked. And I wondered for the first time, though not the last, if he had any idea of Emily Burke's sense of the extreme.

Now she frowned, as if they'd had this conversation before. "There's run-off along the whole length of the town. That's what you get when you build at the edge of a river. Everything we do, every poison we make, gets washed right in, and every new company adds its share. It doesn't matter how many businesses you bring to town, if no one can drink the water."

The mayor smiled patiently. "People have been living alongside this river for a thousand years."

"And look at it," she said. "Would you want to drink that water?"

"It's improving."

"Bullshit!"

Kevin looked a little taken aback, but then his startled expression hardened into annoyance. He turned to me. "So, what do you think, Charles? Was that the voice of reason?"

With some people, just that first glance of ruffled irritation is its own reward. "If something absolutely has to be done," I said, "then you have to be willing to do it."

"What the hell does that mean?" he said peevishly, as Emily gave me a quizzical glance. "Because that's exactly the problem. Something definitely needs to be done. But what? That's the issue."

"No," said Emily. "Survival is the issue. If you can't breathe, if you can't find a drink of water that won't kill you, then it doesn't matter what else you have. Wouldn't you say?"

"Maybe," he said cautiously. "Yes, of course. But you know as well as I do, it's no good campaigning on clean drinking water and all the air you can breathe. People want more than they have."

"That is more than they have."

"They don't believe that."

"It's still true."

"Well, the truth never got anyone elected. Not all by itself."

Emily looked grim. "Even an elected politician dies if he drinks too much hydrogen sulfide."

Kevin sighed and offered up his most resigned smile. "Look. I'm not saying we don't pay attention to it. I'm saying we have to give them more. It's not enough to take something away, even something bad. You have to give them what they didn't have before."

"Clean water," Emily repeated.

"Enough, already."

She started to speak.

"Please?" he said, holding up his hands.

She bit back her reply. Can't we all just get along, I thought with a grim and slender satisfaction, as I watched the heat rising in her cheeks. It looked, I noticed in a distant corner of my brain, surprisingly attractive.

"Be reasonable," said Kevin.

"I am reasonable."

I thought of the mess in Hugh's office, the desk emptied, files overturned, and I wondered how far her definition of reasonable extended. But the mayor had his smile in place again, and he turned back to me. "The problem is that Emily isn't quite under-handed enough to be a politician. She's just a little too straight-forward."

And I suppose that's right. I suppose you could say that nothing was more straightforward than breaking and entering, though that raised its own questions.

"Fortunately," he said, "I'm sneaky enough for both of us." He slipped his arm through hers and turned, glancing around at the town, as if to reassure himself that everything was as he'd left it. "So. Who's got lunch?"

Emily regarded him for a moment longer, then almost re-luctantly she reached down behind her and picked up a large, white deli bag.

"I thought you were taking me out," I said.

"I am," said His Honor. "To the newest spot in town."

We headed up Main Street, pausing now and then for the mayor to greet his public. Some of them just smiled or said hello, but most had questions or a word of advice they wanted to drop in his ear. He strolled along, picking up one conversation after another, greeting each person in turn as Emily walked, silent and a little stiff, beside him.

At the southern end of town we crossed to a large oblong of manicured grass, cradled within the curving tail of Main Street. It was less a park than a large, bucolic traffic circle with a grey stone obelisk in the center, honoring the dead of four different wars, but there was a brand new picnic table perched on the grass. Kevin sat down and, taking the bag from Emily, began to set out the food. Three sandwiches wrapped in butcher paper, bags of potato chips, three small bottles of apple juice.

I glanced around. "This is the newest place in town?"

"Does it look familiar?"

"Not very."

"Have a seat."

I sat down on the bench opposite as Emily slipped in beside him. Main Street stretched away before us, broad and busy with the lunchtime traffic: a long double row of shops and office buildings lined up as if for inspection.

"All that time you were gone," he asked, "did you ever miss this place?"

"Not much."

"I don't know that I believe you."

"I don't know that it matters."

He laughed and turned to his sandwich, unwrapping the white paper. "You know what most people see when they drive through this town? Nothing. Not a thing. It's just a place in be-tween. Not quite scenic, but too small to be anything more. They drive through and think: Something's not quite right. Something's missing. That's if they notice the town all. Most people just forget about it ten minutes after they leave. They remember the trees and the reservoir as they come in, and the river road as they leave, but the town itself is just some vague sense of shabbiness in between." He made it sound like a personal grievance, as if every driver through town was deliberately putting him out of their minds.

"Don't worry. I'm sure it's nothing you've done."

"Not yet. But, you know. I've learned a few things in this job." He picked up the sandwich, turning it over in his hands as if looking for flaws. "It turns out people don't mind inconvenience. In fact they like it. Nothing gives that sense of safe reassurance about a place like inconvenience and a little bit of shabbiness."

"Well, it is their town. If they like it that way--"

"Well, it's my town, too. And I don't." He took a sudden big bite, crunching down through the lettuce and meat, leaning forward to protect his suit against drips or spills. Then he wiped his fingers on a napkin, taking his time chewing and swallowing, gazing around as if the whole town were his room and he were deciding how to rearrange the furniture. "Do you remember this park from before?"

"No."

"That's because it wasn't here before. Picture an empty lot full of weeds and old coke cans. Half an old picnic table. And now look. A little money, a little effort. People love it. They go out of their way to tell me how much they love it."

"I suppose there's a moral to this story?"

He laughed. "Sometimes you just have to show people what they want."

"I thought you had to ask them."

"Sometimes. But there are different ways of asking."

"And what if you show them what they want and they still don't care?"

He shook his head impatiently, as if I were missing the point. "There are people willing to invest in a town like this. And God knows we need them. Companies. Ones you'd actually want to have around. But they have to want you, too. People in this town don't recognize that."

"Some people just don't know what's good for them."

"You think you're joking. But most of the people here don't even see the town, anymore. They don't notice the weeds and old tin cans. They walk right past them. And that old factory of Hugh's? They think it's some sort of natural formation. Run-down, maybe. Ugly, for sure. But it's always been there and it always will be. They don't want any changes. It's not just that they're cheap, though God knows they are. It's that they genuinely don't see the need. But that doesn't mean they don't want to change. It just means they don't know how."

"And you're going to show them the error of their ways?"

"Is that such a bad thing?" He took another huge bite of his sandwich, chewing slowly, swallowing. "Have you ever noticed what happens if you let your house go to seed, then paint the front door? Just the front door?"

"I can't say that I have."

He wiped a thin smear of mustard from the corner of his mouth. "It looks so good you have to paint the front porch to match. And then the windows and the shutters. And then you can't stop until the whole thing is done."

"It's been so long since I've painted my door."

"Well, you should try it some time. Or you could just watch me. Because that's all I need to do. Get that front door painted. After that, they'll be clamoring for more."

I glanced around at the park, all neat grass and tidy edges. "Is this the front door?"

He shook his head, smiling. "Too small. This was just for practice. I've got something else in mind."

I waited. I looked down at my sandwich and realized I wasn't that hungry. His conversation annoyed me. Sliding between earnestness and a kind of zesty irrepressibility, he just assumed that all action was simply a matter of desire. Assumed, with the inherited certainty of Dorothy's great gift, that everyone would agree. And I marveled at his attitude. That he could look at a town, which embodied everything that was most intransigent and unforgiving about the past, and see only some blank and boundless opportunity.

"The trick," he said, "is to start small enough so you can do a good job, but big enough to make an impression. You don't have to do everything. You just have to show them what could be done if they gave you just a little more opportunity. Then you have to make sure they do."

"How long did you say it was till the next election?"

Emily leaned forward, the irritation still lingering in her voice. "A little over three years."

His smile turned a little cool, but he didn't hesitate. "All the more reason to start early. It's all about that first project. You've got to be focused and thorough. Start jumping from one thing to another, and people will think you don't know what you're doing. You're allowed to fail later, but not that first time. It has to go perfectly. Old Buddy Mertel can hide for the rest of his life in the Health Inspector's office, but people are never going to forget the way those buildings fell."

"You'll just have to hope for stronger walls."

"It's not about hoping," he said. "You've got to make sure. Screw up that first time and you might just as well retire."

"Are you sure you're taking this seriously enough?"

He frowned. "This isn't a game, Charles."

"Not even a little?"

"This town needs some serious help."

"And you're going to provide it?"

"Your damn right."

"Well, good for you."

He leaned forward over the table. "Think about it. What does this town need? More than anything?"

"An ambitious mayor?"

"Energy, Charles. Vitality. That's what brings companies. And companies bring people. But look at this place. After seven o'clock the whole town is dead. Hell, you saw it the other night."

"That was more like midnight."

"Take my word for it. It looks the same. No one's around. The town center used to be the place to hang out, to play. Now it's become an empty shell. We need to develop ways to bring people downtown and keep them there, for shopping, for fun, for living."

I turned to Emily. "You two should talk more often. You've got a lot of the same ideas."

But that first flush of irritation was finally fading from her cheeks, leaving a splotchy memory of it behind. "That's because they're good ideas," she said quietly. "You should listen."

"Think about it, Charles. What has this town got that makes it special?"

"You know, I've been wondering that my entire life."

He pointed across the street to where the roof of Hugh's factory showed above the trees. "There's a river out there, and we're ignoring it. Picture it. A beautiful park right along the river. Apartments looking out over it. A grocery store, maybe a doctor's office, a community theater. Who knows what? A little oasis two blocks from the center of town and right on the river."

"And that's going to give the town energy?"

"What do you think?"

"I think it's pretty crowded along the river. Where exactly are you planning to put this little oasis?"

"Well," he said, "hypothetically, suppose you had a factory you didn't need."

I glanced up sharply. "That who didn't need?"

"Suppose it was unproductive, an eyesore, taking up space. Valuable space."

"There aren't too many factories in town any more."

"Not too many. No." I watched the smile feathering out on his face: the smile of a kid who has gotten used to surprising people, and enjoys the effect a little too much.

"Does Hugh know about this plan of yours?"

Kevin hesitated. "We've been discussing it. Off and on."

I considered the utter lack of enthusiasm with which Hugh had greeted the mayor's arrival the other night. "And how does he feel about it?"

"He's coming around. And think about it. What could be more perfect? A little transformation. You should appreciate that, Charles. A little sleight of hand? You think you're the only magician in the family? I'm going to make an old eyesore disappear. And in its place...Abracadabra. A brand new town."

"Nobody says abracadabra anymore."

He laughed. "They will now."

Over a lifetime an older brother can be many things. I know there were times when I loved him, when I wanted nothing more than to be exactly like him, but now all the intricate clockwork of our relationship seemed composed of nothing but irritation. "You know," I said slowly, "even magic doesn't always work the way you want it to."

"I guess that depends who's doing it."

I shook my head. Magic is supposed to teach you control and assurance. It's supposed to give you the certainty that even those small, slight gestures of insignificance and chance are all under your control. But over the years it's had the opposite effect on me. Perhaps I was too amazed by it, my thinking too muddled by wonder and delight. Or perhaps I just lacked the confidence. But for me, every trick was shrouded in uncertainty, and even when I was the one pulling the scarves out of my sleeve, or making the pass or the feint, or rigging the deck, I always waited with my heart pounding and a knot of doubt in my throat as the trick unwound to its wondrous conclusion. And the pleasure I felt at the end was the same as the audience's: a marveling relief and excitement that a few more loose and frantic pieces of the world had once more, against all odds, fallen into place.

But Kevin was nothing if not confident. It was a feeling that spilled out over the boundaries of his own doing to include all that revolved around him. As if the rightness of events and their dependability were confirmed by a kind of magnetic field radiating out from his own, unshifting center.

I could only stare at him for a moment. He seemed so untrammeled by events, so certain of his plans and his just desserts. I wondered if he remembered great-great-great-great-grandfather Charles, a man with so many plans he'd had to wait for the town itself to catch up, and then, when it finally did, he had nothing to do but stand around and watch them name it after somebody else. I wondered if Kevin realized how undependable plans could be, if he realized that it was never your plans that stayed with you, never your triumphs, but always your worst mistakes reaching out to you from the past. And with that, out of the blue, I thought of Gracie and her plans, which had been much more modest, but none the less out of her reach. And I thought of all the mistakes that had followed me for years like some homeless dog.

I reached into my pocket and drew out a quarter. "Do you see this? Solid as a rock." I tapped it on the table. "You know it's solid. I know it's solid. That doesn't depend on anything." I laid it down flat in front of me. "What would you say if I told you it was going to sink right down through this table and come out the other side?"

The mayor picked up his sandwich. "I'd say someone had a trick up his sleeve."

I looked around. No one had touched the apple juice. I picked up one of the small bottles and set it on top of the coin. "The secret's in the weight," I said. "It needs that little extra pressure. And one more thing. It needs complete darkness." I took my paper napkin and draped it over the bottle, wrapping it, molding it around. "And now, just a little concentration. A little magic. And presto." I lifted the bottle, still wrapped in its napkin. But there was the quarter, exactly as I'd left it.

"My God," said Emily, smiling. "You've actually transformed a quarter into a quarter."

I peered down at the coin. "Something's wrong."

His Honor was smiling.

"Wait. I know. This should be heads." I turned the coin over and replaced the bottle on top. Then I made a magical pass with my hands. "Oh mighty quarter. In the face of all this certainty, please demonstrate that even cold hard cash is nothing more than we believe it to be." I lifted the bottle again, and there was the coin, as solid and unchanged as my brother's smile.

"Too bad, kiddo," he said. "Looks like you've gotten a little rusty."

Frowning darkly, I replaced the bottle for the third and final time.

Emily leaned forward in sudden sympathy. "Don't worry, Charles. Even a magician can have a bad--."

But then I raised my hand and slammed it down on the napkin-wrapped bottle. And with a bang it collapsed, smashed into the table, flat as a piece of paper. I whisked away the napkin, and there was the quarter, exactly as it had always been, round and solid as metal can be, but the apple juice had vanished.

Emily stared. And as I drew the undamaged bottle from beneath the table and placed it beside the coin, a smile began to dawn across her face. I picked up the quarter and tapped it on the table, then tossed it to Kevin. "I guess I am getting rusty." She laughed.

But Kevin was frowning grimly. "Do that again." He stared down at my hands and the bottle and the table before me, and I remembered why I'd stopped performing in front of him years before. "There were two bottles, weren't there?" he demanded.

"You bought them. How many did you buy?"

"Let's see your hand."

Emily laughed. "Forget it, Kevin. You can't explain a miracle."

"Do it one more time, and I'll tell you exactly how it's done. Go ahead. As fast as you want."

But I only smoothed out the napkin and laid it in my lap. "It's magic, Your Honor. Even I don't know how it's done."

He shook his head and brushed his fingers across the hard

surface of the table. "Well," he said. "It's not a bad little trick..."

"You're too kind."

"...but, Charles?" He leaned forward, with a smile that had turned brittle and sharp. "Don't you ever tell me again that I'm the one playing games."

He stood up and stepped over the bench. "Now, if you'll excuse me, I have some work to do." And with a curt nod to both of us he strode out of the park, crossing the street with a careless glance at the traffic that parted smoothly before him. He was, as I said, nothing if not confident.

And sitting there watching him hurry away, I wondered if there wasn't something, in the deepest heart of hatred, that holds us in a state of uncertainty, as if the very thing that drives us to revenge, distracts us from it. Because, hate never exists on its own, without all the linked fragments of love, envy, and the low and sneaking burn of admiration. There is always something appealing in the fact that others can do what seems so impossible to us. And worst of all, beneath everything, there lurks the fear that all the differences, all the sharp distinctions we make to separate ourselves from those we despise, may at base be no more than chance and illusion.

Emily was watching him too with an expression I couldn't read, part annoyance, perhaps, part something else. She turned to me. "Do you have to give him such a hard time?"

"Me?"

"His job's tough enough already."

"I doubt it."

Then she smiled again, a slow, reluctant smile. "But that was a good trick."

"Thanks."

"Got any others?"

I looked at her. Her eyes were wide and clear. Clear eyes, clear conscience. And even though I had long ago learned that appearances were never less than deceiving, the thought came to me that I was simply wrong. That I was jumping to conclusions.

That what you want isn't always what's true. In fact, it almost never is. I said, "Actually. I do. You might be interested."

"Bring it on."

"It's bigger than anything I usually do. And a little tricky. It needs a volunteer from the audience."

"Like me, for instance?"

"That's what I was wondering. It calls for some pretty fancy footwork. I need you to get all dressed up. Lipstick, perfume, diamond earrings. Two earrings. One in each ear."

"You don't say?" She was no longer smiling.

"Then I need you to sneak away from something, some performance. A ballet, say. Not for long. It shouldn't take long. Maybe half an hour. During intermission, say. Pretend you're going to talk to a friend, go to the Lady's Room, something like that, and then you just keep going."

She was looking hard at me now.

"Tell me if you've heard this one before," I said.

But she just shook her head.

"Okay. See. You change your clothes. Something black, but informal. Like that outfit hanging on the back of your office door. But you don't change your earrings. I mean, why bother? Or your perfume."

"My perfume?"

"Then you drive to a large brick building and let yourself in through a window. A window your fiancé might have mentioned at one time or another. You break in, lower yourself down, then disappear out the front door. When the lights come up, there isn't a sign of you. By the time the police arrive you're back at the ballet."

"That's ridiculous."

"You don't think it's a good trick?"

"It's impossible."

"Of course. If it weren't, it wouldn't be much of a trick."

"But it doesn't make sense."

"See, that's why I mention it. Because it doesn't. Not really. I mean, it seems like a lot of trouble to go to."

"A lot," she agreed.

"So why would you do it?"

She considered that for a moment, her jaw set at a new, more stubborn angle. "It's your trick. You tell me. It sounds a little risky."

"Do you think? I'd say it was a pretty safe bet using His Honor as an alibi. He's so self-absorbed he wouldn't know if you were gone for a minute or for thirty."

At that she turned. Kevin was almost out of sight now, and Emily gave him one last, quick glance as he vanished down a side street. "And why, exactly? If you're so smart. Why bother?"

"That's what I'm asking."

"How much was stolen? Eighty dollars? Well, I've got news for you, Charles. I've already got eighty dollars."

"Maybe you thought there'd be more."

"Maybe I was just enjoying the ballet."

"What does it cost to put on a demonstration, these days? How much are mailings?"

"We don't do mailings."

"Is stealing for a good cause still stealing?"

"This is ridiculous." But she was still staring at me, her eyes warm and brown, her lips a slender curve of doubt and worry.

I laid my hand on the table before her, a closed fist. "Say the magic words."

She looked down at it, as if it might turn into a dove and fly away, but when I opened my fingers the diamond earring just lay there. "Guess where I found it."

She made no move to touch it. She just gazed down as if it were an idea that was just now taking shape. "It's funny," she said after a moment. "I almost never wear jewelry."

"You should. It looks great on you."

"It's just an earring, Charles."

"Is that what you're going to say?"

"That's what it is."

"You know, my mother's a little nervous about you. She's afraid you don't know how delicate your position is. She's afraid you might damage her son's career."

"And what do you think?"

"I think his honor spends his time trying to turn strangers into votes, and this is exactly the sort of thing likely to turn votes back into strangers."

"Tell me you're worried."

"Not worried, exactly."

"Give it back."

"No."

"Your brother's right, Charles. You're just playing games."

"And what are you doing?"

"This is real, Charles. There's too much at stake for games."

"So, tell me what's at stake."

But she said nothing.

I rolled the diamond between my fingers. It was sharp, unyielding. "At least tell me what you were thinking. Breaking in like that."

"Why?"

I shrugged. I wasn't sure. But it seemed suddenly important to know why she'd done it.

"What do you want, Charles?"

"I want Kevin to lose his job and live unhappily ever after."

"So, what are you going to do? Are you going to turn me in?"

"Maybe. Maybe I'll just take this over to the newspaper and see what Dewey Reynolds can make of it. He can get a quote from the mayor. What's it likely to be, do you think? After all that work. All his plans, his career, his big improvements up in smoke? What's Kevin likely to say?"

Emily sat there for a moment longer, then slowly she leaned across the table, so close we were nearly touching, and whispered almost into my ear, "Why don't you ask him?"

If Something Absolutely Has to Be Done

So, why didn't I ask him? I could have. I could have walked right over to his office and confronted him on the spot. I wanted to, if for no other reason than Emily's sharp-eyed and angry assurance that I wouldn't. And I could already imagine the satisfying glint of doubt and anxiety that would bloom in Kevin's eye. Wasn't this what I'd been waiting for, off and on, all this time? If I wanted to make sure that everything didn't go his way, that he would somehow lose all that I had lost, this seemed a pretty good way to begin.

But I didn't. I didn't say a word. And even now I'm not quite sure why. There is always one good, solid justification for doing almost anything, and a host of vague, equivocal reasons for not.

Maybe it's because there was some dark assertion in Emily's eyes, an assumption that we had something in common if only our vague and mutual dislike, which turned her challenge into a kind of plea. Or maybe it was simply that to ask Kevin, straight out and honestly, was just too obvious a path. I don't know whether I had always been drawn to the underhanded, or if it was something I had learned from all those performances of trickery and magic, but whatever the reason, I carried in my heart the certainty that the full meaning of something could never be expressed in the most straightforward terms. The world is nothing if not complicated. And ultimately, I suppose, I wasn't really sure, even then, what I wanted. You need to know how the trick ends if you want to begin it correctly. And at that moment there was no way I could have foreseen how it was going to turn out.

So I did nothing. And as if to signal the degrees of complexity lurking in even the most inconsequential aspects of coming home, a letter arrived that afternoon from my mother: a formal invitation to the party on Friday. She gave the time and the date. And in a display of thoroughness that was almost endearing she wrote the address on the bottom. Perhaps she had written a number of these and had, in simple adherence to Emily Post, included all the information normally reserved for a formal invitation. Or perhaps she really thought I might have forgotten where she lived. But it made me realize, in a way only the most obvious and unsurprising things can, the intricate gravitation of attraction and complexity that goes by the name of home.

So I went out looking for simplicity and got to the White Eagle around midnight. Just as Wendy had promised, the place was rocking out. All the booths and tables were full, and people were milling around in inadvertent little clumps as if they'd gotten stuck on their way to or from the bar and decided to make the best of it,. They stood, gesturing and shouting to be heard while, from the jukebox, early Led Zeppelin shook them like a passing train. My former seat was taken, but there was room at the end of the bar, and I squeezed in.

There was a dusting of ashes sprinkled over the bar and a crushed napkin blotted with a perfect lipstick kiss. Beside me a very thin woman with pale, permed hair and a peacock smear of blue above each eye glanced over, annoyed. "Hey! Is your name Frank?"

"What?"

She leaned toward me, raising her voice above the music. "Frank!?"

"No. Sorry."

"Fucking hell." She glared at me. "You sure?"

"Yeah. Pretty sure."

"What?"

But I just shook my head.

She turned back to her drink and gave the ice cubes an angry stir. And in that moment I felt that startled glint of recognition that comes when you catch sight of yourself unexpectedly in a store window, and a stranger's face becomes suddenly your own.

On the road I might have been Frank. Or if I wasn't when I came in, I would have been by the time she'd asked the second time. It would have been the kind of opportunity I wouldn't have resisted. To step into another man's shoes, another man's name, and conduct the whole night's elaborate negotiation of chitchat, laughter, and persuasion in someone else's place. Knowing that I was leaving in the morning, or if not that morning, the next. Knowing that nothing I did could follow me back onto the road. I could put on Frank, whoever he was, like a coat for the night, and whatever happened I'd be myself in the morning. It was magic. A life of second chances.

But now I realized, glancing over at the woman, who was so clearly resigned to the knowledge that all the mistakes she'd ever made were following her everywhere, that I wasn't on the road any more. And I looked around at the bar with a little banner of uneasiness unfurling in my chest.

There were two bar tenders tonight, a tall, skinny man with a pony tail and more mustache than chin, and Wendy. They were both busy. She had her hair tucked into a black leather cap pulled backwards and low, and she wore a lavender bowling shirt unbuttoned almost to the black satin V of her bra. The name Ralph was embroidered over her left breast and the words Mid-Town Concrete angled across the back in letters rendered pink by the light. In the middle of drawing a pitcher of Old Style she glanced up and spotted me. "Scotch, no ice," she said. "Soda back."

"It's nice to be remembered."

She flipped off the tap and hoisted the pitcher. "Three seventy-five."

As a burly man in a black t-shirt and a biker beard dug into his jeans, she turned and set a shot glass before me and filled it until the surface of the scotch shivered at the very rim.

I picked up the napkin with its luscious imprint. "Is this your shade?"

She took it without a word and crumpled it into the garbage, then turned to ring up the biker, whose wadded bills looked as crumpled as the napkin, though without any obvious lipstick.

My namesake wasn't on his stool, but in his place a round-shouldered man with well-combed hair frowned up at the television where a spokes model for the Playboy Channel was selling a video cassette of her erotic fantasies for nine-nine-ty-five, ten dollars off the regular price with absolutely no obligation, while across the room in the corner booth I spotted a familiar face. Driscoll, apparently following his own advice, had abandoned the bus station in search of a little ooh-la-la.

I reached into my pocket and laid the diamond earring on the bar. It looked tiny and almost invisible against the wood-grained swirls and shadings. The gold post gleamed, but the stone itself remained dull as ashes. I tried to make sense of its being there, but the longer I stared at it, lying out of all context alone on the bar, the less it seemed to mean anything at all.

I had stopped by Dewey Reynold's office that afternoon, wandering in on a delicious knife edge of irritation and uncertainty, carrying the possibility of telling him everything right up to the very moment I didn't. I'd always liked Dewey. He had an outsider's affectionate antipathy toward the town and, more important, he seemed to be one of the few people uncharmed by Kevin's success. I had worked for him one summer in high school, running errands, writing some stories, enjoying the behind-the-scenes whir of a newspaper. It had that same magician's sense of peering into the back of things at the gears and levers of daily events.

"So what can you tell me," I asked, "about the break-in last night?"

Dewey just shook his head. He had great powers of silence surprising in a newspaperman. Leaning back in his chair, coaxing a thin creak out of the springs, he could let the moments pile up indefinitely, gazing out through his office's big bay window. He always seemed so pleased with the view.

When he'd first bought the paper maybe ten years before, the facade of the old building had been plain as a cliff face with narrow windows like gun ports down the front. But he'd found this baroque confection of mullions and glass at an estate sale in East Haddam and he'd snagged it on the spot. The rest of the building remained as it was: peeling paint, battered furniture, and a dungeon in the basement for the presses, but his office had been completely redone with this great window built out over the sidewalk, so that now, sitting amid the stacks of old newspapers and a cloud of smoke from the Lucky Strike always burning in his ashtray, he could lean back in his chair and survey the whole sweep of Main Street, from the thick stone tower of All Saints' in the south to the sharp, brick steeple of St. Mary's. He spent part of each afternoon sitting there, high above the street, reading the day's paper and gazing out at what a newcomer could be excused for imagining was the entire town. He was a northern New Hampshire boy originally, but he'd lived in eighteen states in fifty-three years, and all that travel had given his judgment a hyperopic quality which he interpreted as clarity of vision.

"Poor Hugh," he said finally. "He's had a lot of bad luck lately."

"Is that what you call it? Losing a daughter? Bad luck?"

"It's certainly not good. But, no, I wasn't thinking of that, exactly. This break-in...."

"It's not that bad," I said. "A mess to clean up and eighty dollars missing. It could have been worse." And hearing the tone of my own voice I wondered at this sudden desire to apologize for Emily without ever having mentioned her name.

Dewey shrugged. He tapped his cigarette in the general direction of the ashtray and watched as a little cloud of ash drifted down onto the carpet. "I was just thinking about luck."

"What about it?"

"How it works. Some people go from one thing to the next. Each one bigger than the last. No false steps. No mistakes. One happy chance after another. And other people," he waved at the grey smoke, "they attract their share of bad chances and more."

"You're saying Hugh?"

"This break in. His daughter. That fire. A few fires, actually."

"A few?"

"Have you noticed how sometimes bad luck falls into patterns?"

"No one's unlucky on purpose," I said.

"I know. I'm not saying that. But maybe it's karma. Think about it. Boating accidents, say. Some people might have a string of them; one shipwreck after another. Wasn't there some survivor of the Titanic? He'd been in something like a dozen of them. Or car accidents. You've seen the people. They always drive cars with dents and scratches, but it's nothing they've done themselves. They just seem to attract them."

"And Hugh?"

"Fires. Small fires—that don't quite burn anything down. That fire where his daughter died. There was some smoke in the rest of the house, but most of it was in that one room, and, when you think about it, there wasn't much actual damage. The waste basket and the corner where it started."

"And Gracie, of course."

"Yeah," he agreed somberly. "Smoke's the killer. Catches you by surprise. But then a few months ago there was a fire at his factory. A small fire on the shop floor. Apparently the wiring just got old and frayed. Might have done some serious damage, burning all by itself late at night, but a police car happened to be driving past." He looked up at me, as if inviting me to wonder at the coincidence.

"Two fires in seven years?" I said. "That doesn't sound so mysterious."

"Four actually." He appeared not to be paying attention to what he said, as if the news just popped up by accident between us. He was frowning at the tiny stub of his cigarette, wondering if he could get one more drag out of it, then apparently decided not and crushed it out. "Last month there was a second one at the factory. No one knows how it started. Then, about a week before you got back, another. Just a little one. They're always little fires. This one at his home. Upstairs in his study. It seems a cigar flipped out of the ashtray and landed on some papers in the wastebasket."

"It could happen."

"Of course."

"Things do happen."

"I said they did."

"But...?" I waited.

He brushed ruminatively at the fine dusting of ashes on his grey pants. "Three in two months? Doesn't that sound odd to you? A bit out of the ordinary?"

"Why would anyone start just a little fire?"

"Apparently the fire department arrived before it got to be a big one. The house has smoke detectors now. And an alarm system."

"So?"

"It's just that I'd have thought fire wasn't something Hugh would be careless about. Not after all that's happened."

"Getting an alarm installed doesn't sound careless."

Dewey drew another cigarette out of his pack, but he didn't light it. He held it like a piece of chalk as if about to draw something in the air. "It's just that he seemed a little confused about it afterwards. The most recent time. He claimed someone else had set the fire. He claimed he'd been burglarized."

"I thought you said he had an alarm."

"He tends to keep the upstairs switched off. He gets forgetful, he said. Walks in his sleep."

"Then there could have been a burglar."

"Later he said it was an accident. The burning cigar. His story changed a couple of times."

I hesitated. "I hear he's been distracted lately."

Dewey peered up at me and smiled with the weariness of one who's made a business out of other people's secrets. "A man's entitled to a few drinks. That's not what I'm saying. But he claims he woke up one morning and his study was a mess. Someone had gone through his papers, searched the room. Then they went out the way they'd come, silently, down a twenty foot brick wall, to the patio, without ever making a sound."

"He can be a very sound sleeper."

"The point is, have you seen his study?"

"No. Not lately."

"Could you tell if it had been ransacked?"

I shrugged and followed his gaze out the window. It wasn't a big town. Three churches, twenty-five stores, thirteen bars, two diners, five restaurants. You might be forgiven for thinking you could see it all from any one place. But small towns can be more complicated than larger ones. Hugh Barker used to give me rides on his shoulders. He used to tell me that bad grades in school didn't mean anything about a man, that my father had always been way ahead of him in college. He used to say that in the end it didn't matter. In the end it would all work out.

"Was there any money taken?" I asked.

Dewey shook his head. "In the end he decided not. Not this time."

"Did he put in for the insurance?"

"No."

"So," I said. "No robbery. No insurance fraud. Nobody hurt. Just a small, accidental fire."

"I know he's a friend of yours," said Dewey.

"A series of unrelated accidents."

"An old family friend."

I watched him squinting up at the designs the smoke made. "You're not accusing Hugh," I said.

"Certainly not. He's a pillar of the community. You know, rumor has it, Community Savings is looking for a new president. They're looking at Hugh."

That caught me by surprise. "What does Hugh know about banking?"

"Enough to be president. What a bank wants is a symbol of

forthrightness and upstanding citizenry. It's one of the last places where pedigree and sheer honesty are more important than skill. Banks are one of those inherently profitable things, but they're delicate as a soap bubble. The president's main role is to inspire confidence."

"Well, they couldn't do better than Hugh."

"Exactly what I said. But it does seem a bit awkward, all these little problems."

"You said it yourself. Bad luck."

"That's what I said." He waved away the last remnants of smoke. "I just think it's interesting."

Wendy had hit a lull and was standing uncertainly, balanced in the middle of all that noise. She looked younger with her hair tucked away: a bruised looking twenty-five in the low, reddish light. The jukebox faded out with a long, plaintive cry, and in the comparative silence she glanced over at me.

"You happy with that empty glass, or do you want a refill?"

"I could be convinced. Thanks."

She poured a fresh drink and set it down. "That's a hell of an eye."

"People tell me it suits me."

"Well, you can't believe everything you hear."

I handed her the empty glass. "I see you found another jar of cherries."

"Nah. I just picked 'em up off the floor. It seemed a waste to throw them away."

I paused and peered up at her. "Don't you ever smile?"

"Are you kidding? All the time. I'm smiling now."

She took the glass and washed it quickly in the sink, stacking it to dry. Then, with another glance around the bar, she reached down into the open neck of her bowling shirt, her fingers rustling like a mouse beneath the fabric. She caught my glance. "Something on your mind?"

"Not a thing."

When she drew her hand out she was holding her cigarettes. She tucked one between her lips but as she reached for her lighter I held up my empty fingers and with a flick of the wrist offered her a book of matches. "Allow me."

"Aren't you the tricky one."

I lit a match, and she bent to bring her cigarette to the flame. The bowling shirt was meant for someone a good bit larger. It gapped open as she leaned forward. In contrast the black bra fit very snugly, but the smooth, opaque satin, so deliberately revealed, looked almost demure.

She exhaled out of the corner of her mouth. "I can see I'm going to have to keep an eye on you."

I dropped the match into the ashtray. "Let me ask you a question."

She shrugged.

"Do you ever drink with the customers?"

"Sometimes. Was that the question?"

"No."

She pointed her cigarette at the earring on the bar. "Is that a cubic zirconium?"

"I don't think so." I gave it a little flick. It made a tiny skittering motion—silent in all the noise—and lay still, giving off the feeblest of glints.

"Needs to be cleaned," she said.

"I wouldn't be surprised."

"Is it yours?"

"Not exactly."

"So, what are you doing with it?"

"That's the problem," I said, and after a moment glanced up. "Have you ever stolen anything?"

She looked more interested at that. "You stole it?"

"No."

"You mean like shoplifting lipstick and stuff?"

"I mean like breaking in somewhere and stealing money."

"No, thanks."

"Would you do it if you had to?"

She looked at me appraisingly. "What do you mean, 'Had to'?"

I shook my head. "It beats the hell out of me."

If something absolutely has to be done, how serious is that? When I first heard that, I'd taken it as a figure of speech, a sign that there was more on a clown's mind than parades and grease-paint, but now I wondered. If a group of kids could break in and steal ninety-three dollars, then why not one adult? After all, if you've already spent an afternoon on a narrow ledge thirty feet in the air, maybe a little burglary doesn't sound so tough… If it absolutely had to be done. And if it were even possible.

I thought of those high, narrow windows in Hugh's factory. Too small for anyone but a child. And I thought of the way she looked in that dress: solid, broad shoulders, deep breasts. Whatever else she was, Emily Burke was certainly not a child.

But there was a trick Harry Blackstone used to do. It was busy and convoluted, as all his tricks were, but it reached its climax when he fired his wife out of a cannon over the heads of the audience. The smoke cleared, and a box was lowered from the ceiling where it had been hanging all along unnoticed. It was taken on stage and opened, and inside was a smaller box. This opened in turn to reveal a box no larger than a broad-brimmed hat. It was set alone on the stage and opened, and Mrs. Blackstone unfolded out of it like a flower to the applause and wonder of the audience. She was a pretty woman, tall and slender. Maybe as tall as Emily. But her chief attraction to Harry Blackstone was that she could fold herself into a space thirteen inches square. A very useful skill, when escaping from the back of a canon or squeezing through the smallest of openings.

I flicked at the earring again, wondering about Dewey Reynolds and his faith in bad luck. What would he make of the story if I told him? Mayor's Fiancé Burglarizes Factory. One man's bad luck is another man's good. It was certainly the last thing in the world Kevin wanted or expected, and therefore it was everything I should have desired. But, sitting there, flicking at the earring, thinking of Emily, I remembered that watermelon trick from all those years ago and the hard, solid sound of the card I'd demanded burying itself just over my heart. And I thought about all the potential problems of getting what you ask for.

"How despicable is it," I said, "to try to get back at someone through his girlfriend?"

Wendy glanced at me, the smoke rising from her cigarette in a thin, grey string. "Why ask me?"

"I can't think of anyone else to ask."

She shrugged. "I don't know. Maybe not despicable. But it sounds a little indirect."

"Would you do it?"

"I guess it depends on the girlfriend. Is this the clown?"

I looked up, startled, as Wendy gazed at me with the bland superiority of a bartender who's actually been listening all this time.

"The one your brother doesn't deserve."

"Maybe," I said.

"So, what'd she do?"

"I'm not sure. I think she broke in and tried to rob a place."

Wendy looked impressed. She picked up the diamond and turned it in her fingers. "So, she's what? Some kind of jewel thief?"

"No. She just left that behind by mistake."

"And you're keeping it as a souvenir?"

"I'm keeping it as evidence. I guess." And I suddenly wondered. "It is evidence, isn't it?"

"Probably not any more." She regarded me with the cool and ruminative cynicism that is the stock and trade of bartenders everywhere. "So have you got a thing for this girl?"

I frowned. "Hardly. She's self-righteous, superior, and annoying."

"That sounds attractive."

"And did I mention she's a burglar?"

Wendy handed back the. "So, now you're holding out for someone without a criminal record? That's kind of snobbish, isn't it?"

"Maybe. Have you got a criminal record?"

She glanced up with feigned surprise. "What? We're talking about me all of a sudden? You're kind of jumping around a little, aren't you?"

"Are you always this critical?"

"Me? Nah. Sometimes I'm a real pussycat."

I was sitting, considering that, when a rough hand slapped my shoulder. "Attaway! Didn't I tell you? Not a bad little hole!"

Driscoll had obviously found his niche in the world. I had never seen him look better. His face had filled out, or perhaps it was just the dim light of the bar that smoothed his whiskery cheeks. His shirt was a print of tropical foliage, dulled out to oranges and reds by the light, and smudged under one arm with a grey smear of grease. He set an empty pitcher on the bar and leaned past me toward Wendy. "You see this guy? You take good care of him."

"I take good care of everybody," Wendy said.

His mouth gaped with silent laughter. He nudged me on the arm. "D'you hear that? She does, too. Didn't I tell you?"

"Are you having a good time?" I said.

"Hell, yes." He gave the pitcher a little shove. "Fill 'er up, sweet thing."

She set the pitcher under the spigot and slapped the lever down. "Three seventy-five."

But Driscoll already had a ten out and laid it the bar. "What'cha drinkin' there?" he demanded.

"Thanks," I said. "I'm fine."

"Damn right, you're fine. And you know what? She's fine, too. Aren't you, sweet thing?"

"Hell yes," said Wendy. She set the full pitcher down and picked up the bill.

"And another drink for my friend, here," Driscoll said.

"He says he's fine."

"What the hell does he know?" He burst out laughing again and, hoisting up the pitcher, surged back toward the corner booth.

Wendy dropped a damp cloth onto the Formica and started to wipe it clean, pausing for me to pick up the earring. "Friend of yours?" she asked.

"We're almost like brothers."

"You sure about that drink?"

"I haven't finished this one."

She hesitated, then turning back to the bottles, poured a second scotch and set it down beside the first one. "First rule of the house. Never pass it up when it's offered."

"Good rule," I said.

"That applies to drinks, too," she said.

I glanced up. "What was that?"

She finished with the damp cloth and dropped it behind the bar. "You're a grown-up. You figure it out."

I sat up a little straighter. "What makes you think I'm a grown-up?" But she was turning away and didn't seem to hear.

"So," I said. "What do you do when you're not tending bar?"

"The usual. I eat. I sleep."

"Alone?"

"What?"

"Do you always eat alone?"

She reached up in back, tugging the brim of her hat snugly down over her neck with something very near to a smile. "Not always. Why?"

"No reason. I just thought maybe you'd like to try it with me sometime."

"Eating?"

"That's what we're talking about, isn't it?"

She shook her head in wonder. "My, my. Aren't you the smoothy."

It got busy again, and she moved up the bar, mixing drinks and filling pitchers. Over by the television the round-shouldered man got tired of the sales pitch for strawberry flavored massage oil and turned the channel to basketball. There were a few isolated shouts from the back of the room, but most people just perked up and watched the game. It went on for a while. I had about half my second drink left when Wendy squeezed past the other bartender. She looked at me. Or maybe she just glanced around the bar at the moment I happened to be looking at her, but her glance snagged on mine for an instant before she headed down the narrow hallway past the bathrooms and out the back door. It eased shut behind her.

Kobe Bryant picked off a pass, then pranced up to the basket and stuffed it through, knocking a man over in the process. The referee came by. They had a long and very animated discussion about it. I glanced up at the back door. It was still closed. The crowd was cheering. Bryant was giving them the high sign and urging them on. I tried to think of what I would have done if I were still on the road, but somehow it seemed a long way away. I was nervous. I hadn't been nervous in a long time, and gazing toward the back of the bar I tried to consider what that might mean.

The door was heavy steel, thickly painted, with a deadbolt and a big red sign that said Emergency Exit Only. I pushed it open and stepped out into the cool air. After the smoke and noise, the night seemed almost painfully clear. There was a small courtyard between the bar and the next warehouse and a narrow alley leading back along the building to the street. Wendy stood smoking, staring up along the high warehouse wall, but at the sound of the door she turned.

"Nice night," I said.

She eyed me speculatively. "I'm on my break."

"Me, too." I glanced around. "It's quiet out here."

"Used to be," she said, but she didn't really seem to mind.

She was shorter than I'd thought. Her cap was at the level of my nose. The dark circles under her eyes were lost in the general shadows. Her face and throat were pale blurs, marked by dark lips and eyes. The heavy door shut behind me with an unexpected thump that made me twitch.

"Jumpy?" she asked, exhaling a little wisp of smoke along with the word.

"No more than usual. Can I bum a cigarette?"

"You know how much these things cost?"

"I'll buy one."

She reached inside her shirt and brought out the pack again.

"No pockets?" I said.

"You got a problem with that?"

"Actually I like it."

"So do I. Need a light?"

"Sure. Well. No, actually. I don't smoke."

She drew thoughtfully on her cigarette and gazed at me for a moment, the smoke feathering over her lips "In that case you're sure taking a long time to get to the poin--"

I bent and kissed her. Her eyes opened wide, and she stopped talking, but with the tail end of that final word I got the last unexpected breath of smoke as she exhaled, and it caught in my throat. I drew back, making thin, croaking sounds, and then burst out coughing. She shoved me away. "What the hell are you doing? Cut it out!" And then, when I couldn't, "Are you all right?"

I managed to nod.

"Then stop it."

"I'm trying." I was wheezing now, leaning next to her, struggling to catch my breath. "Do you know CPR?"

"No. Do you need it?"

"No." I kissed her again. Her teeth were hard and smooth against my tongue, but only for an instant, a moment of surprise. Then her hands came up, wrapping themselves in two handfuls of my shirt, and her mouth, tasting of smoke and coffee, opened so eagerly I might have been that very thing she'd been craving all night. Through the thin fabric of the bowling shirt her waist felt thick and solid. My fingers, wandering up her arm, searching for an entrance, slipped inside one baggy sleeve to feel the feathery tickle of hair and the soft and silky ridge at the tight boundary of her bra.

"Is that it?" she whispered right up against my mouth. "Is that what you want?"

I didn't know if she expected an answer, but my throat was too tight for any chance of speech. Behind me the muffled sound of the juke box was like a warning, but too distant to matter. Her grip on my shirt tightened. My legs were already unsteady, I felt off balance just standing there, and now we started to topple those last few inches against the wall behind her. Reflexively I reached out to catch us, but my hand was still trapped in her sleeve and it pulled the fabric taut, pinning her back, while the grip on my shirt left no room to move. We seemed bound together. But my other hand, unfazed by the sudden confinement, was searching on its own. Her shorts were baggy and loose around her legs, and I found my way up under the fabric to where the smooth, dry curve of her thigh gave way, not to another layer of fabric, but to the feathery surprise of pubic hair.

Her mouth was locked on mine again, but I could feel her smiling under my lips. "Uh-oh. What have you got there?"

But it was all I could do to breathe. I pressed upward. She was overflowing my open hand. The hair now rough against my palm and the humid flesh parted beneath my fingers. Her voice was low in her throat, a deep rustle of sound. "What are you going to do?" she said. "You going to fuck me right here?"

Her voice startled me. "Here?"

Up the alley there was a scrape of movement. A small sound in the darkness. I froze.

But her breath was hot against my ear. Her hand, drifting under my t-shirt across my bare stomach, began toying with the puzzle of my belt buckle. "That's the way," she said. "You feel that?" She was moving against my hand, marking the rhythm with the low murmur of her voice. "Do you?"

There was a flicker of movement at the corner of my eye.

"What was that?" I said.

"Shhh."

"Listen..."

The sound of footsteps echoed up the alley beside the bar, hesitated, then continued on into the darkness.

"Forget it," she murmured. "It's nothing."

"Wait."

Wendy stood motionless, catching her breath, staring up at me, with her grip tight on my shirt and her wet flesh pressed against my open hand. "You're kind of nervous," she said.

"I didn't used to be."

"So, what do you want to do?"

My voice was tight. "My place? It's not far. I have a bed."

I could hear her smile, though it was too dark to see. "I'm working. Remember?"

"When do you get off?"

"Late."

"How late?"

She kissed me again, her lush lips blooming like a flower in the darkness, then she let go of my shirt, and reluctantly I withdrew my hands. She stood, briskly tugging her clothes back into order. "Where are my cigarettes?"

The pack was lying forgotten at my feet. I bent and picked them up and held them out. She took them, then reached up to take hold of my hand. For a moment I thought she was going to shake it, but instead she raised it to her face and breathed deeply. Her scent was thick on the air between us. She bobbed her head down in a quick nod and drew the full length of two fingers into her mouth, sucking gently before easing her lips away. She looked up. "Scaredy cat," she whispered, and released my hand. Then she turned toward the door.

"Wait."

She turned, smiling now.

"Do you want to come to a party?" I blurted.

"When? Now?"

"No. Later. Next Friday."

"I don't know," she said. "You think it'll be fun?"

"Maybe. If you're there."

"Okay. I'll pencil you in." And still smiling, she paused at the door." Don't go back in there," she said. "I'd hate for anybody to get the wrong idea."

She said it as if there were a right idea that should have been obvious to everybody, but I had no notion what it was. Then she pulled open the heavy steel door and slipped inside without a backward glance.

Nothing Up My Sleeve

We traveled at night, Rudy and I, to save money, to save time, to be gone just ahead of the law or an angry audience, or sometimes just because Rudy would get so drunk, so fiercely afraid of having no place to go, that we would get on the first bus leaving town and travel to the end of the line. I'd be dozing fitfully, with an eye out the window at every stop to make sure our trunks stayed on the bus, getting out periodically to check on the rabbits, while Rudy slept like the dead, his skin clammy, his breathing fitful and shallow, fluttering on the verge of silence.

The bus rides became an entire past in themselves. They carried us, wrapped in darkness and the straining roar of the engine, through a realm indistinguishable from dream. When I think of traveling with Rudy I think of racing headlights bent by rain, drifting street signs, the ghostly glow of store fronts closed and forgotten, and a long immersion into darkness. We passed through towns without people, towns reduced in my mind to a single sprawling structure so fallen into decay that it now stood open to the elements. It was a world unconnected to the bright daylight into which we'd open our eyes and emerge from the bus station. The two seemed antithetical, one the negative image of the other, all light and dark reversed, all rules of order and expectation changed.

Occasionally Rudy would wake up. He would reach out and grip my wrist and, too weak or distracted or drunk to raise his head, would whisper fiercely, "I told you to be more careful!" or "Don't leave me!" or "I dreamt you were dead!" Speaking from the depths of some murky past he would claw his way out to grab my arm, asking me to save him from something that had long ago come and gone.

One morning I woke from an uneasy sleep to the moan of

brakes and the first hint of grey in the dark morning sky. We were the last two on the bus, and the driver didn't give us a glance as he stood, gathered up his hat and jacket, and stiffly descended to the street. I shook Rudy awake and together we trudged in step, like two long-paired prisoners just released from irons, up the aisle and down the steep steps to the parking lot. I didn't bother to look at our tickets. We were at the end of the line. That was all we needed to know.

In the bus station I asked a bored dispatcher for the nearest bed, and, taking up a trunk in each hand, started up a narrow side street through the morning gloom, with Rudy clutching the rabbits and shambling along beside. After a night on a bus the trunks felt impossibly heavy, and Rudy, gradually waking up as we walked, wasn't cheerful. I concentrated on each step forward and on the beds that were waiting for us. I knew better than to think too far ahead; early morning was too sad a time to think about the future. So I was concentrating only on the possibility of sleep, and of waking up to breakfast, reducing my concerns to those I could feel, trying not to think at all. I was utterly unprepared to reach the rooming house, a seedy mustard colored saltbox on a narrow street, and find it dark as the morning.

I stared at it for a moment, willing the lights to come on, determined by hope and disappointment alone to open it up. But the door stayed locked. I walked along the crooked porch, to where a row of old lawn chairs lined the railing, and sank into a seat.

"Well, this is nice," said Rudy, cranky and stiff from the long ride. "We might as well still be on the bus."

"At least we're not vibrating. Now watch. I'm going to perform a little magic trick for you. I'm going to make the sun appear."

"Oh, nice. The sun," he said. "How about something more useful? Let's see you make a bagel appear. Or a boiled egg and some toast. Now that would be magic."

"First the sun."

"Or a cup of coffee," he said almost dreamily. "Wouldn't that be something? Or tea? A nice hot cup of tea?" Then he winced and, raising one long and graceful hand, meditatively stoked his breastbone.

"Are you okay?"

"Just tired," he said.

"Well, sit down, for God's sake." I helped him into the lawn chair, then stood there for a moment. My legs were filled with sand. "Have you got your pills?"

"I don't need my pills."

"Well, there's aspirin in your pocket. Why don't you take a couple of those. I'll go find us some breakfast. That should pick you up."

"I'll come with you."

"No. You stay here."

"Where's here?" He glanced around at the ratty porch furniture, and beyond at the sparse and careworn lawn just emerging from the greying darkness.

"I have no idea. I'll surprise you."

"I don't like surprises."

"You're a magician. That's what you do."

"I surprise other people. There's a big difference."

And it's true. A magician should never be surprised by what happens. All the work, all the preparation and practice, are designed to prevent surprises. I know that now. But back then I'd only been on the road for a year-and-a-half; I'd woken up in every sort of town, and snuck out of more than I like to remember, and I hadn't been surprised by one.

So that morning I picked up my coat and started up the street. The air was warm for September even without the sun, and I walked along quietly, enjoying the disorientation that came with being in an unknown place. It was a game I played with myself on those early mornings to keep my mind busy. It reminded me of moments as a boy when I'd woken up abruptly from a sound sleep with no idea where I was. I would lie in bed and know that the world had shifted while I slept, that the shape and direction of basic things had altered. Walls were in new places; the sounds of traffic came from unexpected directions; in the darkness I could not even picture my own familiar room. I used to lie there, sure that it would all come back to me, that my whole life would slip back into place whether I wanted it to or not, but for those few uncertain seconds I could enjoy the utter freedom of not knowing.

Now, off to my left a dog began barking, and the sound of a car engine hung on the air. In the rising dawn houses and trees coalesced around me. Lights were coming on, windows glowing like lanterns. I was in no rush to find a coffee shop, no rush to get back to the rooming house. The morning air was perfumed with grass and some faint, sweet scent I couldn't name but which made me think of school starting up and the end of summer vacation. I took streets at random, not looking carefully around, but just walking and letting the low, ordinary noises of the morning wash over me. There were no demands, nothing needing to be done. I was out of sync here, and the strangeness of it all comforted me with the protection of a foreign place.

But then, like that moment after waking when, with a sudden shifting turn, the world becomes familiar again, I noticed a stand of willow trees grouped together in a way that made so much sense I knew I must have seen them before. I looked at them, looked around, and as I walked down the street like a man coming slowly out of a dream, I saw the patterns of houses and driveways and trees gradually taking on more and more meaning.

I thought about turning back, retracing my steps to the run-down porch where Rudy would be dozing over the trunks, twitching like one of the rabbits in the grip of an uneasy dream. I thought of all the miles we'd driven, nights and nights of driving, miles piled on miles. How many nights is enough to travel? How many miles before your nightmares can't find you?

But your nightmares are yours because you need them.

They're as much a part of you as anything you've ever done. I followed the curve of the street as it climbed a shallow hill, and stopped before a white wooden fence. A row of rhododendrons grew up behind it, but there was a narrow gap where, years before, young children used to sneak through in their games. Crouching down, I eased between the wooden slats and slipped past stiff branches into the yard.

A broad picture window stood off to the side, lit up faintly from within. I edged up to it like a burglar, creeping forward to steal a look. Inside, the living room was laid out carefully: old family portraits hung on the walls with a carefully planned casualness, elegant furniture arranged on a vast oriental rug as if for a photograph. It was a room that didn't look much used, but beyond it, the dining room opened up, wrapped in a warm glow of lamplight.

Standing in the cool of the morning, with the damp smell of grass and earth rising around me, with the familiar light of yet another day catching me out in the open, I peered in through the window at the man and woman sitting down to breakfast. In the golden glow they looked so cozy: a pot of coffee between them, a basket of toast. They were reading the newspaper, leafing through the pages, not speaking, not even looking up at one another, but there was such a sense of comfort and self-sufficiency, of rootedness, that for an instant I longed to be at the table with them; I wanted to have some part of that scene. But I knew that was out of the question.

So I just stood there, staring in, no longer sneaking, oblivious to the possibility of being noticed. If they had looked out, what would they have seen? Some stranger peering in hungrily after a long night on the road; some vagabond. For how could they have recognized me? I was transformed beyond their knowing. Ambrose and Dorothy Bentchley, looking up from their papers to glance out the window would only have seen a vacancy where their son used to be. Just as I, looking in, saw only a scene that was familiar the way dreams are familiar, but no more real than that.

I told myself this was only what I might have imagined. I told myself it didn't matter, that out of all the towns I might have arrived in, this was merely one. It was an illusion; it didn't erase what had happened; it didn't change anything. It didn't mean that I'd come home.

But there was some part of me that wanted, more than anything else, to be eating toast, drinking coffee, sitting there bolstered by the silence. More than that, I wanted my childhood back. I wanted to take up my old place at that table, to slip back into that image of certainty and warmth, and drag the years around me like a blanket. I wanted to come back even as I realized it was no longer mine to come back to. What would they say, if I walked in? What would I say? What would have changed?

So I just stood there, marveling at the warmth of the scene, marveling at how attractive it looked, how attractive they looked, Dorothy and Ambrose: a handsome couple, prosperous and satisfied. And the more I looked, the harder it was to recognize them, though the details that had grown vague in my memory now stood out so sharply. His face was longer than I remembered, his nose narrower. She looked shorter, broader, with a stubborn jaw. But the more I stared, the more like strangers they grew, changing before my eyes. I reached up and touched the cold glass. The morning chill was soaking into my clothes and skin. All the warm lamplight and the imagined aroma of hot coffee was nothing more than appearance, and I felt, as I gazed into where my parents were sitting, that I could no more join them than I could climb in through the screen of a television set.

I picked up coffee on the way back to the rooming house, and we drank it waiting in the bus station for the first ride out of town. We were on the road for another five years, until Rudy became too sick to travel, and in that time I always made sure to check our tickets for the destination. But I never forgot that image of two handsome strangers sitting together in their dining room just out of my reach

"Darling," said Dorothy, opening the door. "I'm so glad you could come. Don't worry, you're only a little late. Please come in." She reached up and pressed her smooth cheek against mine, wafting the familiar, no-nonsense scent of soap and powder. "And you've brought someone. How nice."

I turned. "Dorothy Bentchley...This is Wendy..." As an introduction after all this time it must have sounded incomplete, because as my voice trailed off we all waited for a moment until the two women, realizing that was the end of it, reluctantly nodded to one another.

Wendy was looking uneasy, glancing from Dorothy to me and then around at the rugs and the pictures on the walls and the well-dressed crowd just visible through the living room doorway. Maybe she was wondering what she'd gotten herself into, or maybe she was just thinking it all looked as boring as she'd feared. Though in that regard, at least, she had done her bit. She wore a silver baby-doll camisole with spaghetti straps and a hem that rode across the top of her thighs, ready to billow up at the slightest breeze. It was thin, almost translucent, and beneath it a black bra showed through, while what looked like black lace bicycling shorts encasing her thighs to just above the knee. I wore Rudy's second-best tuxedo over a t-shirt and jeans, and together we made the perfect couple.

Dorothy cast her eyes over us with a glance of consternation—a brief faltering, no more—then, smile resolutely back in place, she led the way. As we stepped into the living room, most of the faces turned toward us, and after a long moment of startled stillness Ambrose strode over, cradling a drink in his hands. "Charles," he said jovially. "Better late than never." He reached out and took my hand, gave it a friendly shake. "And I don't believe I know this young lady." He held out his hand to her, and Wendy took it, a little gingerly. "Ambrose Bentchley," he said.

My mother smiled between them like a referee determined,

regardless of the circumstances, to do her part. "This is Wendy."

"Nice to meet you, Wendy. Please come in. The bar is in the next room. Hors d'oeuvres on the tables. What can I get you to drink?"

You had to hand it to Ambrose. He was impressive. In many ways, he was not unlike his hair. It was the color of dark honey and he wore it just a touch long, always on the verge of shaggy, as if he couldn't be bothered to think about it, though in fact it was painstakingly arranged. He'd found a barber who could give him the appearance of casual disarray, even as he made certain there was always a perfect part down the left side. He wore half-glasses perpetually on the end of his nose, red frames that seemed so bright beside his usually quiet colors that they seemed accidental and perhaps just a little out of character—that slight touch of eccentricity, so pleasing in an otherwise staid academic. But in the proper light the frames blended perfectly with the blush of his skin and the warm highlights in his hair, and in those moments they could be seen for what they were: the last careful detail that tied his features together.

As he and Dorothy led the way into the dining room, where a crowd of bottles stood arrayed on the old mahogany sideboard, I watched them. It was the first time in a long time that I'd seen them standing together like that, and I was surprised by how young they looked. I gazed at them in all their blonde cleanliness, in their earnestness, in their careful politeness and comfortable air, and I thought how little they knew of anything that could go seriously wrong. Implicit in every gesture was the conviction that nothing was more natural than to be smiling and drinking with a group of their friends in an elegant house lit by the warmth of the late summer twilight. I wondered what Rudy would say to all of this. I wondered what he'd think. And I tried to conjure him up in all his gruff and grumpy kindness as a kind of protection, because I realized as I looked around, how beautiful everything seemed.

Ambrose fixed our drinks with puttering efficiency, then

handed them out. "Come on in. You know everybody here."

Wendy looked doubtful, but as I gazed around I saw it was true. Friends of my parents, neighbors, colleagues from the law school. I'd grown up aware of them all in a kind of distant, peripheral way. But that seemed a long time ago, and now it was odd to see them gathered together, to be introduced and reintroduced. It was like being ushered into an alternative life, a guided tour of what I might have been if only I'd played my cards right, if only I hadn't proved such a mystery and a disappointment. It was as if here in one room my parents had assembled a large and collective recrimination for all the time I'd spent away. They were all very nice, of course, very polite and even friendly. But there was a question hidden in everything they said, and with every look they were appraising me, as if I were a form of currency they hadn't come across before. I felt like the only one in the room who didn't know the secret handshake.

Or rather, not quite the only one.

"Get a look at these people," whispered Wendy grimly. "It's like a Rotary Club meeting."

"I know what you mean."

"And what about that Ambrose and Dorothy? Are they scary, or what? Could he possibly have a bigger stick up his butt?" We had made a few trips to the sideboard to refill our glasses by this time, and she had begun to loosen up. "How exactly do you know them?"

"Oh..." I shrugged vaguely. "Friends of friends... of friends. I don't really know them that well."

"And they thought you'd like this?"

"Free food, free drinks, free entertainment," I said. "What's not to like?"

"I guess," she said doubtfully and took a sip of her drink. Then, reaching up, she draped an arm around my neck and drew me down. "We'd better stick together," she whispered. "It's our only chance."

"Good idea."

She smiled and peered around with a look of scornful wonder, as I followed her gaze. I was trying to see everything through Wendy's eyes, trying to borrow a sense of derisive disinterest, but the essential pleasantness of the scene kept creeping in on me. Ambrose was laughing across the room, chatting with some colleague, and he seemed so at ease, so handsome and attractive and pleased with things, that he gave off an air of grace that hung on the air around him like an invitation to join in. And Dorothy, looking elegant and considerate, passed a tray of cheese and crackers with an expression of teasing thoughtfulness as if she could tell, with her hostess' intuition, that you'd been secretly longing for just one more. I had to fight the urge to be charmed.

"Danger, danger," whispered Wendy. "Alien approaching."

I glanced up. Fred Bonner was a tall, stork-like man who was something of an authority on Constitutional Law, though locally he was better known for his large collection of expensive pens and a tendency to awkward silence. Now he stood, hesitating in mid-stride, caught between the subtle undertow wafting the crowd toward the hors d'oeuvres table, and the need to refill his glass at the bar directly behind us. He wore a grey suit that might have been cut for somebody much shorter and a heavy black fountain pen clipped to his breast pocket. He stood there fiddling with his glass, half-listening to the conversation behind him and glancing occasionally in our direction. He seemed unnerved by Wendy's dress.

I caught his eye, and reluctantly he stepped forward. "So, Charles," he said heartily. "So. How are things?"

"Things?" I said. "Why, things are great. Things could not be more delightful." I gave him a big smile.

It seemed to take him aback. "Good... I'm glad to hear it. So... welcome back."

"Thank you. It's really great to be back."

Wendy was still draped against me, her arm looped around my neck, her eyes fixed gravely on our visitor, but at that she turned. "You're back? I thought you just arrived."

"I've been on tour."

"Really? And how was it?"

"Great. It was really great."

Bonner was frowning, fingering his glass. He might have taken the occasion to slip past us to the bar, but at Wendy's movement his eyes caught again on her dress. He licked his thin lips. "I don't know how you managed," he said. "Traveling all the time. No mail, no phone. Or why you'd bother, for that matter. I could never do it... All that time..." He hesitated. The fabric of the shift was just opaque enough to suggest that only an accident of the light allowed such a clear view of her underwear, and he glanced over and away with the nervous stealth of a shoplifter.

Wendy smiled sweetly. "So, tell me, Mr...?"

"Bonner," he said hurriedly. "Frederick Bonner."

"So, Fred. How do you like my outfit?"

"Oh..." The faintest pink, like the glow of a little sunset, crept up his cheeks. "It's very nice. Very charming," he said with a stiff little effort at gallantry.

Wendy smiled demurely. "Thank you." And in a low, conspiratorial whisper. "It's not that comfortable. This bra's really a bitch. It's so tight it keeps squashing my boobs together."

Fred stiffened, and made an obvious effort not to glance at the boobs in question.

"And these shorts," she added relentlessly. "God. Every time I take a step they creep right up my ass. You know? It's like somebody's hand sliding right up there." And she shook her head ruefully. "But what can you do? I mean, anything for fashion. Right?"

He opened his mouth, and closed it. "I suppose...," he said and, clearing his throat, offered a sudden tight and paralyzed smile. I smiled back for a long moment, nodding benignly, as if we were both marveling at the mysteries of women's fashion. But then in spite of myself, I felt a little tremor of sympathy. I knew what it was like to feel out of your depth, and it wasn't all that funny. I nodded at his empty glass. "Looks like you could use a drink."

"Yes," he said quickly. "Yes, thank you. Well… It's nice to see you, Charles. And nice to meet…" He gave a quick nod in the direction of Wendy's breasts. Then, waving his glass goodbye, he hurried past, making a beeline for the bar.

Wendy laid her head against my shoulder and sighed contently. "I just love your friends," she said. "I'd like to meet them all." Then she turned, glancing around. "I need a the ladies' room Do you have any idea where it is?"

I told her where it was.

"Hold this." She handed me her drink, and gave me a quick kiss on the lips. "If I'm not back in an hour, send out the search party."

I watched her go with a wild and sinking sensation, part relief and partly the sudden exposed feeling of an antelope left alone on the plain. And sure enough, a moment later, with a sense of almost dreamlike immobility I watched as Dorothy approached with a tray of newly replenished crab puffs. She held them out with a wry and knowing smile that seemed automatically to suggest that we were both somehow in on the same joke. "Having fun, darling?"

"It's very nice," I said. I tried to think of something tough and snappy to say, something ironic, but Wendy seemed to have carried our shared store of disdain away with her. I shrugged. "It's kind of odd to see everybody."

"It has been a while," she agreed, glancing around the room. "Do they all look more or less the same?"

"Actually, they do. I feel like Rip Van Winkle waking up old and grey-haired to find everyone around him completely unchanged."

She laughed, and against my will I felt a little answering flush of pleasure. When I was growing up, my mother had laughed and smiled a great deal, but always with a sort of premeditation, as if it were something she 'd meant to do anyway, regardless of what was being said. But every so often I would surprise her into a laugh, through some joke, some trick, some bit of inadvertent foolishness, and I'd feel as if I had given her something extra she hadn't anticipated. As if here was a laugh she wouldn't have had without me. And then I would plan and scheme how to surprise her again, how to catch her off guard, as if each joke were an ambush I was setting. And now, all these years later, I found myself revisiting, with a sense inextricable from my childhood memories, that little wiry flush of satisfaction, and in that same instant felt an answering spark of irritation at how little I had learned.

"You're friend is certainly very interesting," Dorothy said dryly.

"Isn't she? I knew you'd like her."

"She has a very distinctive sense of style."

I nodded. "We get a lot of compliments." But looking at Dorothy, elegant and unerring in a pale blue dress, I felt the slow gnawing of embarrassment. I thought of Wendy's outfit, and it seemed like a serious error in judgment. Even my jacket and jeans were like a costume, and I had the sudden image of that man in the commercial who gets the wrong package from the dry cleaner and comes to the black tie event dressed as a penguin.

"Does she always dress like that?"

"I don't know. I could ask." But then, in the grip of that cool and knowing smile on my mother's face I found myself admitting, "I don't really know her that well." I flushed.

"Well, she certainly seems very interesting."

"You said that already." I was beginning to feel angry, and I was grateful for it. "She has nothing but nice things to say about you."

"I'm sorry, darling. I just don't like to see you not being yourself."

"I am myself. I'm always myself." I didn't bother to tell her that was part of the problem.

"Charles." She was frowning gently now. "I didn't mean to

make you angry."

"Don't worry. I'm not angry." I smiled coldly. "I just need another drink." I turned and headed for the bar. And though I tried to maintain an attitude of righteous annoyance as I stalked off, it still felt, as it always did with my mother, like a tactical retreat.

By the time Wendy returned I was three scotches ahead of her, but she didn't seem to notice. She slipped her hand through my arm. "That bathroom is so charming. There are little soaps in the shape of flowers. If only I hadn't knocked them all into the toilet."

I handed her drink back. "What do you say we leave and go have some real fun somewhere?"

"Are you kidding? I'm having a great time. It's like a field trip to Geeksville." She stood glancing around the room. "Look at that. Can you believe it? We've been sucked into a fucking Talbot's ad. You want to wander around and make fun of them to their faces?"

"You don't want to just leave?"

"In a sec." She took a hefty sip of her drink, and swallowed hurriedly. "Uh-oh. Watch out. Don't tell me you know those guys, too?"

I glanced over and hesitated. "I think I've run across them somewhere."

On the other side of the room Kevin raised his glass, and Emily, in the middle of some heated discussion, glanced up and said something smilingly to him. Then they started to make their way toward us through the crowd, pausing now and then to greet people and shake their hands.

Kevin was doing his best to look casual in a pale suit so sharply pressed it could have been made out of cardboard. But Emily wore a smooth, copper-colored dress that exactly matched the shade of her hair. It was a long way from her clown costume; and a long way from a burglar's basic black. I watched her, expecting to see some hint of those other incarnations in her face or movements, but there was no trace. I suppose I'd expected her to lurk, to be more uneasy in her guilt, but in profile her face was clear and guileless, and thief or not, she looked so elegant strolling across the old familiar room that, when they stood beside us and I turned to make the introductions, the bright vulgarity of Wendy's outfit startled me as if I'd never seen it before.

"Kevin Bentchley. Emily Burke," I said. "This is Wendy..." And my voice trailed off, almost against its will. "I'm sorry. I just realized I don't know your last name."

"Kamisky," she said coolly.

"Wendy was just admiring your outfit."

Emily smiled cheerfully. "Thanks. It's my second-best dress. If we meet at one more party, you'll have seen them all."

"And nice earrings, too," I said.

Her smile seemed to catch on something and reflexively she reached up to touch the pair of plain, gold posts, as if double-checking that they were still there. "I'm glad you like them. "

Kevin was running his eyes over Wendy's outfit. "My brother's told us so much about you."

Wendy frowned. "Your brother?"

"He's just teasing," said Emily. "He hasn't mentioned you at all."

"Hold on a sec. Who's your brother? Do I know him?"

Kevin looked smoothly amused. "Apparently not. Charles?"

Wendy turned, not altogether pleased, and drew her hand out of my arm. "Tell me you're brothers," she said flatly.

"In a manner of speaking."

"You said you were a stranger in town."

"I said I was trying to be."

And Kevin laughed. "Well, they don't come much stranger than Charles."

Wendy was frowning, and I felt my cheeks flush. I'd like to say, at that instant, I had a premonition of disaster, but it isn't so.

Or if I did it was indistinct from the general grip of irritation and embarrassment. All I was aware of suddenly was Dorothy slipping in beside me with a glass in her hand and an air of vigilant courtesy. "How is everybody here? There's mountains of food, you know. Please help yourselves."

"We're fine," said Kevin. "It's a nice little party."

She glanced around with a contented air. "It's not so bad, is it?"

"It's wonderful," said Emily. "What a beautiful house."

"Thank you, dear. It is a nice old wreck. Are you finding everything all right, Wendy?"

"Hell, yes," she said, raising her glass.

"Charles?"

"Hell, yes."

A tiny crease marred her forehead for an instant, and then was instantly erased. "Good. I'm glad to hear it. And glad to see you've all met. But, Emily, dear. What's this I hear about the theatre? I do hope you're not in any trouble."

If the tone irritated her, Emily didn't let on. "No worse than usual," she said. "It's just a little fund-raiser. We're just trying to bring in a little something extra. To keep ahead of the repo men."

"Emily runs the Children's Theatre...," Dorothy explained.

"Gosh," said Wendy. "How darling."

"...It's called Shortfellows."

"Because they're always just a little short," said Kevin.

Wendy nodded. "Isn't that cute."

I took a sip of my drink. "This isn't going to be one of those Jerry Lewis telethon things, is it? Volunteers standing by to take your calls?"

Emily gave a wan smile. "I wish. It's just a little show we're putting on. Next month, in fact. So don't forget, everybody. Mark your calendars. We'll have clowns, juggling, a play, the usual. We may even have the mayor hosting it, if I can swing it."

"That's right," said Kevin. "Entertainment for the whole family. So bring your checkbooks."

"Or, better yet..." Emily turned to me. "Bring yourself."

Wendy glanced up at me coolly. "Is that right?"

I swallowed. "I don't know. I'm not even sure I have a check-book."

"Then bring your rabbits."

"His rabbits?" said Wendy.

"I'm not sure they have a checkbook either," I said.

But Emily was eyeing me appraisingly. "I've been meaning to ask you for a while. Ever since that little demonstration at lunch. I thought you might help us out. Maybe perform a little."

That took me aback. I stared at her for a moment, trying to read her bland and smiling expression. After my earlier crack about the earrings I was half expecting some sharp-edged joke, but she seemed to be serious.

"Perform?" Wendy was glancing back and forth now, the irritation rising in her face.

"How about it?" said Emily. "A little magic? A little hocus pocus? It wouldn't have to be much."

"I don't think so."

"It's for a good cause. You could walk on stage and make our deficit disappear."

"I have this thing about amateur theatricals."

"Don't think of it as amateur. Think of it as pre-professional."

I shook my head. "You know what they say. Never work with children or animals."

"I'll tell you what," said Emily generously. "If they get out of hand you have my permission to make them disappear."

"Or saw them in half," said Kevin.

I stopped and turned, but he was smiling cheerfully. Reminiscently, even. "God, Charles," he said. "Do you remember that last magic show?"

"I remember."

"When was this?" Wendy demanded.

"Some time ago. I was in high school."

"Not exactly David Copperfield," said Kevin with a laugh.

"No. Not exactly."

"But, hey. You've got a month to practice. You should be able to smooth out all the rough edges by then."

I was holding my drink a little too tightly. "You think?"

"Definitely," he said. "In fact, it could be fun. Here's your chance to make a comeback. I'm sure we'd all like to see that." And smoothly, still smiling, as if that settled it, he raised his empty glass and strolled off toward the bar.

Emily was frowning. "Just ignore him," she said.

"I always do."

"It would actually be a really big help. Will you at least think about it?"

"Probably not."

"Please."

I shrugged. "I'll ask the rabbits."

And with a quick nod and a smile she turned and hurried off after Kevin.

Wendy watched her go. "Well," she said. "Wasn't that exciting."

Dorothy was still standing there with an uncertain expression, like a referee at the end of the match trying to decide who'd won. "I'm sorry, Charles. It's too bad of her to put you on the spot like that. Now that you've put all that behind you... Well, you certainly mustn't feel obliged."

"You know," I said. "I think I'd like to have another drink."

Wendy followed me back to the sideboard. "So, how do you know her?"

"Her?"

"Miss Second Best Dress."

"Oh. She's engaged to him."

"That's the clown?"

"That's her."

"She looks like she's got a stick up her ass."

"Does she?"

I filled my glass and splashed a little more into hers.

"So you're a magician?"

"Used to be."

"How did she know that?"

"I may have mentioned it."

"At lunch the other day."

"It's not what it sounds like." But what did I know?

Wendy took a big gulp of her drink and glowered up at me. "So," she said. "Do something magical, why don't you?"

For the rest of the evening, as I moved around the room, I was aware of Emily standing in her second-best dress, beside but not too close to my brother. More often than not she was frowning, shaking her head, gesturing sharply with her hands, deep in one fervid conversation or another. At one point, Kevin passed her a plate of hors d'oeuvres; perhaps he was hoping to distract her. She took one, continuing whatever point she was making. But then glancing up she caught my eye. With a sudden wry smile she held up the cracker, then popped it into her mouth and showed me her empty hand, front and back. Nothing up her sleeve.

In the mean time Wendy drank and looked around, making comments under her breath, peering up at me. At one point she slipped her hand under my jacket, tucking her thumb into my belt. "You having fun?" she said.

"Hell, yes."

"You glad I came?"

"You think I could do this alone?"

She pulled me closer so her breath was warm against my neck. "Say something nice."

I gazed down at her. "You look really nice tonight."

"Really?"

I hesitated, trying to recall the feel of her in the alley behind the bar, trying to recapture that undistracted moment.

"--No! That's not the point!" A voice rose sharply across the room. "It's not a matter of how nice it would be if you could."

I glanced over, and Wendy, frowning, tightened her grip on my belt. "Well, shit," she said. "It must be show time."

"You have to," said Emily. "That's all there is to it."

She was standing in a little knot of people, squaring off against a compact, balding man named Roger Bean. Usually he divided his considerable powers of confrontation between the law school and the chairmanship of the County Democratic Party, but now his focus was closer at hand.

"I'm not saying it's unimportant," said Bean. "I'm saying we just might not be able to fix every flaw in the entire free world right away. And saying 'yes, we can,' over and over again isn't going to change that."

"Maybe that depends how you say it," Emily snapped.

Kevin was there at once, his voice low, his hands raised in some vague, calming gesture. "Roger's point," he said soothingly, "is that there are practical limits to what we can do."

Emily turned on him, and even I was surprised he didn't stay out of it. "I know what his point is. And my point is that limits aren't about practicality. They're perception."

"Your perception," said Kevin. And it occurred to me to wonder who's side he'd have been on if Roger Bean had chosen some hobby other than the Democratic Committee.

Emily glared at him. "You're goddam right. And it'd be yours too if you were honest with yourself."

"Jesus Christ," Wendy muttered. "Can you say 'Drama Queen'?"

I hesitated. "Maybe she thinks it's important."

"God, yes." She tilted her glass back and started crunching on one of the ice cubes. "Oh, goody. Here comes the referee."

Across the room Dorothy was edging into view, a concerned look on her face, though I don't know what she thought she could do. The mayor had an audience, and he was already hitting his stride. "You want honesty?" he said. "Then be honest. Deal with the facts."

"What do you think I'm doing?"

"The way they are. Not the way you want them."

"Well, screw you, too," Emily snapped.

"Oh, my," murmured Wendy. "Somebody's had a little too much to drink."

Dorothy glanced around, spotted me, and after a moment's indecision hurried over. "For heaven's sake," she whispered. "Can't she make it through one party without a scene?"

"That's exactly what I was saying," said Wendy sweetly.

Dorothy's glass was half-empty, and mine much more so. I reached back to the sideboard and picked up the scotch.

"What? Oh. Just a touch, dear." She held her glass up absently, her eyes still glued to the brewing argument, and I topped it up, then filled my own. With a look of irritation Wendy nudged her empty glass against my arm and I reached again for the bottle.

Shaking her head, Dorothy took a sip of her drink, and looked startled. "Is this scotch, dear?"

I didn't answer.

"I deal with the facts!" Emily was saying.

"Not the political facts."

"There aren't any political facts! Political conveniences, maybe."

Kevin was smiling coolly, glancing up at the other men. "Idealism. I remember that."

I thought she was going to slap him.

"For heaven's sake," Dorothy murmured. "Why do they have to argue?" She took another anxious sip, scotch or no.

"It's probably instead of sex," said Wendy.

My mother looked startled, and seemed about to speak.

"Don't worry," I said hurriedly. "I'm sure it's not."

Across the room Kevin was still on a roll. "Maybe it's time you just face it. Idealism is fine, but this is real life. Sometimes you have to be practical."

I wondered if he had any idea how practical she could be. I could see Emily gritting her teeth from all the way across the room. "I though you were supposed to be on my side," she said.

"I am on your side."

"It's a little hard to tell."

"You've got to realize," observed Roger Bean. "Those 'conveniences' you're talking about are crucial. This town wouldn't run for a week without them."

"I don't care how damned 'crucial' they are. They're not going to do a thing to keep the groundwater clean. Your facts and conveniences are going to let anyone with any clout in this town do whatever he damn well pleases!"

"Language, please." Dorothy whispered half under her breath.

"The law says they have ten years to comply," said Green.

"Ten years! Ten months is too long! God damn it! In ten years the aquifer will be so polluted you wouldn't want to use it to water your lawn! You have to stop them now."

"You can't. Not just like that."

"Of course you can!" Emily snapped. "Just like that!"

"Too loud," murmured Dorothy. "Too loud."

Much too loud, I thought. I was willing her to be quiet, willing everyone else not to listen. I thought of the shambles in Hugh's factory, the fires, the burglary at his house. Everything Emily said seemed like a confession, now. Everything she was willing to do was like an announcement of what she'd already done.

"For God's sake," Wendy muttered to no one in particular. She rattled the ice cubes in her glass. "Bar tender."

But I was staring with Dorothy across the room. It was like watching a balloon blown up, breath by breath, and just waiting for the pop.

"You do what you can," Kevin was saying.

"You do what you have to! Whatever you have to! Everything else is just bullshit."

But this was too much for Ambrose. He stepped up beside Kevin. "That's all well and good, young lady," he said sternly. "But some things are against the law."

"Oh, dear," murmured Dorothy.

Emily turned like a boxer, outnumbered but still game. It was like one of those childhood battles on the playground: all that yelling and swinging, but this time in that beautiful, shimmering dress. She was standing, glaring at the circle around her. She looked cornered and furious. Hell. She looked beautiful. "Then, change the law!" she demanded.

"Just like that? Don't be ridiculous."

"Then maybe you should break it!"

I held my breath, looking around to see if anyone else had heard. I was marveling that they didn't get it right away, that they didn't all make the same sudden connection.

"Maybe it's more important," she said, "that people can drink the water without dying, than that some law-abiding greedhead can squeeze out one last dime."

"Young lady--" Ambrose began.

Dorothy was gripping my arm. "Charles. Stop them."

"Are you kidding?" said Wendy. "It's just getting good."

"Charles--?!"

I'm not sure quite what she expected, maybe she didn't know either. But her voice was pleading, and God help me, I took a step forward. "Ladies and gentlemen!"

I was drunk. Much too drunk. I could tell that right away. My tongue was thick, my hands uncooperative. But I had a few props tucked into my pockets, and I was hoping something would occur to me. "As unaccustomed as I am to public speaking..." With a broad gesture I threw a spray of flash power into the candle flame—a little too much—and it went up with a bright and blinding whoosh, leaving a halo of smoke rising toward the ceiling. People were staring, now, dumbfounded. At least I had their attention.

There was a big crystal punchbowl in the middle of the table. It had belonged to my grandmother. Flanking it were two sprawling bouquets of cut flowers and a tray of canapés, while around them stood arcs of matching glasses and an array of napkins and condiments, spoons and forks. It all looked perfect and delicate.

I picked up one of the glasses and threw it in the air. In the instant it landed back in my cupped hands, it burst into a fluffy bouquet of silk roses. I waved them through the air and tossed them to Wendy, who was staring so blank-faced and startled that in reaching for the flowers she dropped her glass. It bounced on the rug, scattering ice cubes, and in the confusion she bobbled the flowers, which fell in a bunch at her feet.

It was perfect, really. It might have been choreographed. Dorothy turned, appalled at all the flying glassware, and in that moment I loaded the wind-up goldfish into the pocket under the left hem of my jacket and slipped the roll of silks up my cuff. It was like old times, performing for my family. It had that same air of desperate showmanship. Now, at least, I'd had some practice. "Ladies and gentlemen. Whenever I hear loud voices raised in anger, it always makes me uncomfortable. I can't help thinking all that attention should be directed at me." I had a little more flash powder ready, but I wasn't judging amounts very well. The fireball nearly took off my eyebrows, and the whoosh was like a truck going by.

Too much flash. The sure sign of an amateur. Rudy would have hated it. The art, he always said, was in distracting them without their ever knowing it. But I'd been drinking scotch for an hour-and-a-half, and I couldn't take any chances. "Now I'd like you all to notice I have nothing up my sleeve." I drew back my right cuff.

It's a little risky, but they do expect it, and if you show them the right, they usually forget afterwards that you didn't show them the left as well. I turned three empty glasses upside down. The cut crystal was translucent. The white tablecloth showed indistinctly through. I arranged them in a line, then re-arranged them, then straightened the line. It isn't always important what you do, so much as how you do it. A quick, precise movement draws the eye.

People were starting to gather around the table, not sure quite

what was happening, but gazing down sharp-eyed and expectant. Emily, the anger cooling in her face, turned half-shrugging,
like a good sport willing to be entertained, though Kevin, frowning, was looking anywhere but at me.

"Now if you want to argue, argue about this," I said. "Why do
these glasses look so empty when they're really so full?" I tilted
up the first glass and ran my finger around the inside, then set it
upside down on my empty hand. Reaching up between spread
fingers I drew out a string of silk scarves: blue, then yellow, then
red.

There was silence. "Feel free to gasp," I said, but no one said a
word. They stood, staring, caught between embarrassment and
a kind of speculative suspicion.

All except Emily, who had started to smile. "God damn," she
said. "It must be magic."

I picked up the second glass, holding it by the handle. "You
know, they feel so solid." I rapped it a couple of times on the table.

"Charles, please!" cried Dorothy. "The crystal!"

"But sometimes they just don't hold up under stress." I shook
out a linen napkin and draped it over the glass. "Now, a little
help from the audience." I held out my covered hand. "If one of
you would just take hold of the napkin."

Emily started to reach for it, but Kevin stepped in. "Allow
me," he said, grabbing one dangling corner.

"Not yet," I said. "Timing is everything." I turned to Emily.
"And you, Miss. If you'll just blow on it." I held my covered hand
up before her face. Kevin was already tugging on the napkin.
"Not yet, sir. Please be patient."

Emily started to lean forward but Kevin wasn't going to wait.
With a tight smile he jerked the napkin away, but I was ready. I
spread my fingers. The hand was empty. Kevin stared down at it,
startled, disappointed. There was a little gurgle of laughter from
Emily, but from the rest there was only the slightest of murmurs.

It was a nightmare crowd. The audience from hell. But what

did I expect? I turned immediately. You can't give them time to think. I plucked up the last glass, holding it again by the handle. "Well, that's a little disturbing," I said, "having it just disappear like that. Maybe we need to weigh it down with something." I picked up the ladle and half-filled the glass with punch. The mixture was pale pink, frothy with sherbet. It sloshed onto the table cloth. I was moving too quickly, getting careless. I took a sip. Cloying and sweet, the punch coated my tongue. I looked up at Emily. "Let's try it again. But this time without the napkin. Now, pay attention. Don't drop it!"

I tossed it into the crowd.

It wasn't, perhaps, the smartest thing to do, but this group was really starting to annoy me. There was a sudden crackle of voices, Oh's! and Ahs! The people closest to the table jerked back to avoid the spill, and my mother's sudden cry rose like a tearing cloth: "Charles!"

But Emily, bless her heart, braced herself, beautiful new dress or not, and caught it, face blanching, jaw tensed, clutching it out of the air. And she held it up, surprised and smiling as she realized that what she'd caught was a large, silk gardenia.

I stood there, waiting for something, a gasp, a sound of some sort, wondering what the hell they were waiting for.

"Jesus," my father muttered. My mother just stared, her own stiffened face gradually thawing, her outstretched hand sinking to her side. Nobody else said a word.

My hands were shaking. I'd almost bobbled the switch, and I felt an angry flush rising into my face that wasn't helped at all by the cold, clinging dampness of the punch soaking into the leg of my jeans. I looked around. Wendy stood staring, uncomprehendingly, as if she'd wandered into a play without her script. Others were shaking their heads and a few guests ironically applauded with the very tips of their fingers. Only Emily stood, grinning down at the clean white blossom in her hands.

Dorothy stepped up. "I think that's wonderful, dear. Now, don't you think--?"

"Just one more," I said, turning. I glared at the crowd. "All this talk about the water table, the river. I mean, what the hell is the fuss?"

Emily's smile started to fade. She narrowed her eyes. "Don't you start on me, now."

But I ignored her. "Seriously," I said. "What's it all about? What are we talking about here?" I shook out another napkin and wrapped it over the front of the punch bowl like a stiff, linen screen. "So you dump a little something into the water table." I pulled a fistful of daisy petals from the bouquet and dropped them into the punch.

My mother's voice was thin and brittle. "Dear? What are you doing?"

"It's just a little bit, here and there." I picked up a couple of crackers and crumbled them into the bowl. "I mean, what does it matter?" I picked up the tiny bowl of mustard and poured it, thick and viscous, into the mix. "After all. It's not as if you're not going to want to drink the water, just because you've filled it with a lot of other shit."

"I think that's about enough," my father said sharply.

"Not quite," I said.

Emily was staring with something between amazement and dawning appreciation while off to the side Wendy watched without expression, glancing back and forth from Emily to me as if waiting for the worst.

"There's one last step. We have to say the magic words. Does anyone here know magic words?"

Wendy glared at me and at Emily and around at all the well-dressed, staring people. "I've got some," she said fiercely. "Who the hell cares?!"

I used the last of the flash powder. Too much. Way too much. I threw it toward the candle at the same moment I whisked away the napkin, with the thin sheet of plastic I had draped over the surface of the punch, and dropped the wind-up goldfish into the bowl. My timing was perfect. The whole switch was smooth and flawless. But nobody noticed because when the powder exploded with a shivering whoosh it sent little tracers scattering through the room, and when people finally uncovered their eyes, all they noticed was that one of the large bouquets was burning like a torch.

I looked around. Voices were rising. Shouts seemed to be bouncing off the walls. Dorothy stood frozen to the carpet, staring wide-eyed at the flames, and Ambrose's mouth was drooping into a perfect, gaping oval.

"The flowers!" someone cried.

"Jesus Christ!"

It wasn't exactly what I had planned. People were shouting. The place was burning. Sparks were flying. But I ask you, what else could I do? In a scotch-soaked haze of anger and desperation I hoisted the priceless, cut glass punch bowl that Grandma Strawberry had imported all the way from England, and doused the flames with a tidal wave of pink lemonade, curacao and a froth of half-melted raspberry sherbet.

Standing There Looking at Emily

I reached the top of the stairs, tucked high under the eaves of the Longfellow Building, and stood there by the open door, still breathing from the climb and the heat of late July. I didn't bother to knock. Emily was sitting on the battered sofa in a clutter of bright scraps and costumes reading the morning's paper, but she glanced up like someone who has seen her share of pitiful and has just remembered what it looks like. "Well," she said.

"No clowns today?"

"I gave them the afternoon off." She wore baggy white shorts and an orange t-shirt, patchy with sweat. The thick copper hair was tied back. There was the faint gleam of perspiration along her hairline. The room seemed to concentrate the heat of the day in a little cocoon around us. "I was just looking for a news update. I understand there was a fire last night at the Bentchley residence. Sources say they managed to get it under control, with only minor structural damage, but somehow the perpetrator escaped. He's thought to be still at large, hiding somewhere in the area."

I nodded. "Is there a number to call if I have news of his whereabouts?"

"Better just keep it to yourself," she said. "I understand the owners are thinking about pressing charges."

"It's a family of lawyers. You really think they won't?"

Emily leaned back, stretching her legs out comfortably, and waved me toward the end of the sofa. "At least it was a good show."

"You know, it's funny..." I eased myself down beside a red feather boa, "...but that last trick has never gone so well. Except for the fire, of course. I don't suppose you noticed the goldfish in the punch."

"I did. It was a nice touch."

"I usually save it for children's parties, but it was all I had with me."

"I think it was a big hit."

I nodded gloomily. "Yeah. Me, too."

She sat there, smiling down at her shoes for a while, a pair of old canvas sneakers dotted with paint. She had the pale distracted air of someone with something on her mind. That was okay. I had something on mine as well. "So," she said. "Who was the babe?"

"That was no babe. That was my mother."

"No. The other one." Then she seemed to change her mind. "Is she really angry?"

"Wendy?"

"Your mother."

"Oh, I think so. When I left last night she still wasn't speaking to me."

"Don't worry. It'll pass."

"It's not like we've done all that much talking lately as it is. But still..."

"She'll get over it."

"I suppose anything's possible."

She glanced over with a sly smile. "So, her name's Wendy."

"Who?"

"Don't be coy."

"She's a bartender."

"That was a great outfit."

"She has no fear."

"I was thinking the same about you." Though there was something in the tone that made it unclear whether it was a compliment or not. "Did she enjoy the party?"

I considered that for a long moment. "That's a little hard to say."

We had left the party in a tense halo of scotch, adrenaline, and banked anger. Wendy drove, her silence unreadable, though steeped in discomfort. We hadn't really settled on where we were going, but she didn't ask for directions, so I assumed it wasn't my place. She just kept turning and snaking her way angrily through the twisting back roads, headed toward Main Street and the highway out of town.

After all the excitement at the end, my head felt surprisingly clear, for better or worse. I glanced over, trying to concentrate on the remembered feel of her lips in the alley behind the bar, trying to recall the dark and musky scent of her that had lingered on my fingers. But squinting against the occasional headlights and the darkness of the road, all I could smell was the clinging smoke of too much flash powder and the sharp tang of singed cuffs. For an instant I wondered if we were just going to spend the night driving, letting the road unfold like the view through a bus window, and it seemed, just for the moment, that even after all this time I hadn't come very far.

"Well, that was fun," I said finally.

And as if she'd been waiting for just that sound, she turned. "Shit! What was that? What the hell were you were doing? Jesus Christ. What is wrong with you?"

"I thought you'd be impressed. That's not an easy trick."

"Yeah, well. It was fabulous. You nearly started a forest fire! And what was going on back there with that what's-her-name? Miss Let's-put-on-a-show, in her second best dress? Why didn't you just drool all over her while you were at it?"

"What are you talking about?"

"I'm talking about you just stepping in there, all that talk about dumping shit into the river. What was that? A public service announcement? Is that something you worked out between you? You were supposed to be there with me, remember?"

"I was there with you. But you saw them. Everybody was jumping all over her. I thought she could use a little help, that's all."

"So it was up to you?"

"Somebody had to do something. Besides, what do you care? The whole place could have burned down, as far as you're concerned. You never have to see any of those people again. At least you're not related to them."

"And what was that about?" she said with sharpened outrage. "Your family? Why the hell didn't you tell me?"

"Okay. I should have."

"Well, no duh! What's the matter. Are you ashamed of me?"

"No," I said firmly. "Of course not." Though that very possibility gleamed like a thin vein of silver through the back of my mind. "I invited you, didn't I? I was afraid you wouldn't come if I told you. Hell, I wouldn't have come if I'd known. And I sure as hell didn't want to go to that party alone."

"Jesus," she muttered, annoyed still, though not perhaps completely unmollified. After all, she didn't pulled over and tell me to get out. So somehow, even with all the anger and jealousy, we were still in the same car, still heading, presumably, to her house. And after a moment she glanced over. "Are you glad I came?"

"Yes."

"Do you want to come back to my place?"

There was something so sweetly unguarded about the question after all the anger, after that stiff and appalling party, after driving so long in silence, that it cloaked the whole moment in a soft and comforting vulnerability that made me smile. "What a good idea."

"Did you like my outfit? You never said."

"You look beautiful."

"Tell me again."

But, as we drove across the bare, floodlit bridge and south past a miniature golf course and a series of identical brick apartment buildings so drab and impersonal they might have been lined up in some sort of protest, I was thinking about Emily. Her fierceness and commitment. Her willingness to face off against everyone in that room. And for what? She must have known she wasn't going to convince anybody. But to expend all that energy, all that rage and passion... as if the very futility was part of what drove her. It had no point, no lasting effect. Nobody's mind was changed. If anything, the whole party of calm and moderate citizens was left feeling reassured that passion and commitment were, at the very least, embarrassing and a little too obvious. But I couldn't help admiring it, nonetheless. It wasn't personal, I told myself. It was just admiration: a magician's appreciation for showmanship in all its most unbridled forms.

We hit the commercial strip just outside of town. The street lights seemed too bright after the dim glow of the back roads, and the scenery looked blank under that flat, inquisitorial glare. But almost immediately Wendy turned down a side street between a muffler shop and a Seven-Eleven, and we were back in the mysterious darkness of side streets and sleeping houses. Then she pulled into the driveway of a low, dark house and doused her headlights.

She sat there, stiff and hesitant behind the wheel. "This is the place."

There was no breeze. The night was empty except for the low background hum of a whole neighborhood of air conditioners, thrumming together like some vast insect swarm.

"Do you hear that?" I said.

She cocked her head, listening, but she was distracted now, tentative, as if all her assurance were leaking away into the night. When she climbed out of the car it was almost reluctantly.

"Come on," she whispered. "Don't slam it."

We all but tiptoed up the driveway. Between the darkness and the stillness, whatever remained of the scotch seemed to be reasserting itself. I slipped my arm around her waist and she glanced up at me as if it hadn't occurred to her I might try that. I bent and kissed her. Her lips parted, but grudgingly. She seemed more than a little preoccupied. "What's wrong?" I asked.

"Nothing." Hurriedly she unlocked the back door, and beckoned me in. It was a narrow kitchen, with a big table at one end and dark cabinets crowded over the counters. "Do you want something to drink?"

"Why are we whispering?" I said.

"I just like it quiet."

"Maybe I should go home."

"What about your drink?"

She moved hurriedly in the darkness, opening a cupboard and lifting down a bottle and two glasses, opening the refrigerator for ice cubes. The fridge spilled its milky light over the floor and cupboards, lighting up the fatigue in her face. She wore a weary, puzzled expression as if once more she'd come up against some nagging, familiar problem. It made me tired just to see her. She fished out the ice cubes and dropped them into the glasses with a series of sharp, brittle sounds, then closed the door.

In the darkness I stepped up beside her. "It's getting late."

"Don't you want to stay?"

When I didn't reply she turned, hovering in the darkness, a hesitant shadow, then she reached up. Her lips were dry and insistent. "You can't go now," she whispered. "You've kissed me."

"Is that the rule?"

"You can't leave until you fuck me," she said. But the word had lost something in the translation from the alley to this prim and tidy kitchen. Her voice sounded thinner. She held me by the jacket, but her grip was more tentative now, her fingers tangled in the fabric. "Don't you want to?" she whispered.

The house was silent around us, a small dark box within the larger darkness beyond. Too small, too dark, and too quiet. It occurred to me once more that there was no bus waiting in the morning to carry me away, and with that knowledge the whole situation took on a kind of pale foreboding. "You said something about a drink?"

She picked up one of the glasses, and I expected her to hand it to me, but instead she took a long sip from it. As I reached for the other she stopped me and, rising on tiptoe, pressed her mouth against mine. Her lips were cool and tightly closed, but as they warmed and softened the scotch trickled, cold and burning, over my tongue. It took me by surprise, dribbling down my chin. I wiped at it with my fingers. "Sorry," I said, embarrassed. "I wasn't ready."

"Are you ready now?" she whispered.

She drained the glass and raised her face. This time, on the trickling tail end of the scotch came her tongue, cool but warming. And her hands, one warm and one still cold and damp from the glass. They slipped under my jacket, grazing my ribs through the thin t-shirt, and continued up to my shoulders, easing the tuxedo off and down my arms. I caught it and hung it on a chair. She was already tugging the t-shirt out of my waistband with a kind of silent, workmanlike determination. I raised my arms and she dragged it up over my head.

The silver camisole was so light and loose that lifting it felt like undraping a statue. Her arms slipped easily from the fabric, and she ducked her head as I drew it off. Even in the darkness, the deeper blur of her bra showed clearly against the pale shadow of skin. My fingertips traced down the full curve of her shoulders to the smooth, frictionless satin.

"Behind," she whispered.

The bra felt armor-stiff and smooth, with thin edges of stitching along the boundary between fabric and the soft pucker of flesh. I traced the wide strap all the way around to the rough conclusion of a hook and eye, then with a tiny, unheard click the satin loosened like a shedding skin. My hands slid up, pushing the fabric into a tangled necklace and cupping the shallow breasts as if to protect them modestly from sight.

"That's nice," she murmured.

"Do you want to show me the upstairs?"

"There's nothing up there."

"I was thinking maybe a bed."

"Do you really want to climb all those stairs?"

Her breasts slid away from beneath my hands as she sank to her knees. Her hands traced over my stomach to my waist and began with fierce proficiency to unsnap and unbuckle. The refrigerator thrummed behind me, working very hard. I leaned back against the edge of the counter. With a slow mechanical purr the zipper loosened, and as if it were all part of the same movement somewhere over our heads a footstep creaked, and a lamp came on in the stairwell just beyond the kitchen.

"Wendy, honey?" The voice was thin and hesitant, echoing down the stairway.

I started up, but Wendy hooked her fingers into my waistband and hissed, "She won't come down. She's afraid of the dark."

"Wendy?" The footsteps started down the stairs with a creaking as if the whole house were resettling, but they lost momentum and slowed into a long hesitation. "Is that you, honey?"

I stood stiffly upright, barely breathing. Before me Wendy knelt, her bra a black tangle, her breasts sagging, naked and neglected, as she stared back over her shoulder.

"It's just me, mom. It's okay."

"Honey, you startled me. Are you just getting home? Is everything all right?" The stairs creaked again, as the nervous woman tried to make up her mind whether to risk the trip down.

Hurriedly I tried to refasten my jeans, but Wendy caught my hands. "Everything's fine, mom," she called. "Go back to bed."

"Would you like a snack? I could fix you something."

"No. Really. That's okay."

But now, gaining courage from the sound of Wendy's voice, the footsteps were slipping down the stairs. I snatched at the open waistband of my jeans and hurriedly started buckling as Wendy clambered to her feet, fumbling with the tangle of her bra. Then her mother turned the corner and stood silhouetted against the hall light. Just for an instant her shadow darkened the kitchen again before she reached for a switch, and the fluorescents jumped and flickered. Then we were all standing there frozen in the light.

I snatched up my t-shirt and the crumpled ball of her camisole, as if I had a plan for them, and stared up at her. Wendy, frantically struggling to fit the crumpled bra back into place, tried to yank the straps clear, but they had gotten too tangled, and finally she just gave up. She stood glaring, the perfect image of outraged dishevelment, while her mother, frozen and appalled in a pink chenille robe and a wild confusion of hair-rollers, could only stare. "Oh, dear God."

"Jesus, mom! Will you turn off the goddam light!"

In a flustered rush the woman turned and fumbled at the switch. Darkness fell. "Oh, dear... Good gracious..." Once more in silhouette her hands were busy adjusting her robe, fluttering about the rollers adorning her head. "Why didn't you tell me, sweetie? I didn't realize you had company. Oh, dear. I must look a sight."

Beside me Wendy was reaching awkwardly behind to re-hook herself, muttering under her breath. "Jesus fucking Christ." Then she snatched the camisole from my hands. "Mom, this is Charles. Charles," even in the darkness I could tell she was glaring up at me, "this is my mom."

"I'm very pleased to meet you, Charles," her mother said primly.

"You, too," I said, faintly, then turning to Wendy. "Well. Thank you for the nice evening...." And, coward that I am, I fled.

It was a three hour walk home, and I didn't see a taxi until I was halfway over the bridge within a few blocks of my apartment, and even then it didn't stop. I tried hitching, but there were few cars at that time of night, and there must have been something about a man in half a tuxedo, with a long stain of sherbet down one leg and an expression of exhaustion, that dissuaded anyone from stopping. And for whatever reason, when I woke up in the early afternoon, with a headache and a rage of guilt and embarrassment, instead of calling Wendy as any decent man would have, I wandered into town.

I didn't have a plan. At least I don't remember one. But sometimes our most intricate schemes are the ones we keep hidden even from ourselves. And now I sat there on the sofa, while Emily hesitated, as if she, too, were sorting through an arcane catalogue of conflicting feelings, glancing around at the cluttered room.

"I've got something for you," she said.

She leaned over and grabbed it off the desk, then held it out to me. It was a reproduction of an old vaudeville flier advertising one of Robert-Houdin's extravaganzas from the glory days of Victorian magic. It must have been an early photo before he'd really found his legs, before he'd nailed his timing down, when he was all grim-eyed efficiency and no flourish, when he'd compress three hours of tricks into one unrelenting hour, leaving audience after audience stunned and depressed. There was a top hat on the floor in front of him, and a rabbit poking it's little nose out. And the magician was smiling so grimly for the camera that he was obviously having a terrible time. He was in the process of doing something dramatic, though it wasn't clear exactly what. I suppose he could have been making some sort of magical pass over the hat, or casting some spell, but mostly he seemed to be struggling to disentangle himself from his own voluminous cape. It reminded me a little too much of last night.

"Where did you find this?"

"On the internet. Kevin said you used to like this guy."

"Thanks. You wouldn't know it to look at him, but eventually he turns out to be the greatest magician of the nineteenth century." I glanced up. "Is that what I looked like last night?"

"No."

"That wild gleam of desperation?"

She smiled. "No."

"What's the occasion?"

She hesitated. It looked as if there were more on her mind than she knew what to do with.   "I wanted to thank you."

"For what? Making a fool of myself? No need. It's the sort of thing I do for free."

"It wasn't that bad."

"It was terrible."

"Actually, it was pretty good."

I shook my head. "Rudy and I had a few audiences like that, but not in a long time. I'd forgotten what they were like."

"I think they enjoyed it."

"No, you don't."

"Well. They should have. And thanks," she said, "for jumping in like that." She hesitated. "I was starting to lose my temper."

"I noticed."

"I appreciate the support. There aren't too many people in this town..." She shrugged. "It's like I'm talking to myself most of the time." And she gave me a warm smile.

"I was just getting a little worried," I said.

"You were?"

"I thought you might say more than you meant to."

She considered that for a moment. "No one was really listening all that closely."

"I was afraid they might be."

"And then what?" She smiled wryly, but a little touched. "Did you think they were going to drag me off to the pokey right there?"

"Something like that."

"I'm not sure His Honor would have let them."

"I don't know. Last night he seemed to be leading the charge."

"Yeah." She shook her head. "He can be kind of a jerk when there's an audience around. Still, I usually try not to make such a scene in front of the voters. It just makes things harder for him in the end."

"Tell me," I said abruptly. "What exactly do you love about him?"

"You asked me that already."

"I mean, what is it you love right now? Right at this moment?"

She hesitated, then leaned back into the sofa. "I have a theory," she said. "I think love is all about opposites. All the little things you love are exactly the things that drive you crazy."

"I don't buy that. I think there are things you love, and there are things that drive you crazy. And nothing will drive you crazy faster than deciding they're the same thing."

She shrugged. "Maybe. But what can you do? When you love 'em, you love 'em. When you hate 'em, you still love 'em."

"So, what do you love?"

"About Kevin?"

"For a start."

"His hair."

"What else?"

"His shoes."

"His shoes?"

"Have you seen them?"

"What else?"

She thought for a moment. "Right now? At this moment? After last night? That's about it." The corners of her eyes crinkled. Her hair, I noticed, grew straight back from the temples, and there was a faint downy hint of sideburns, pale against her cheek. "So, what about you? And what's her name."

"Wendy."

"I know," she said. "Wendy."

"It's hard to say."

"That's not a good sign. You're not giving up already? If it were easy," she said, "anyone could do it." Then she seemed to consider that for a moment. She was glancing around the room again, looking for some clue amid all the wildly colored props and costumes. "You know the problem with people who think they're always right? They almost never apologize."

"I thought love meant never having to say you're sorry."

"No," she said. "It doesn't." And she turned to me. "You look like you want to say something."

"It's about the factory."

"Yeah?"

"Why?"

"Why are you asking?"

She was gazing up with careful eyes. No trace of greasepaint now. But once a clown, always a clown. And who can ever tell what a clown is thinking? I drew the earring out of my pocket and held it up. The last of the ashes and dirt had long since rubbed off, though the diamond was still dull. Up close the four tiny prongs gripped it like little claws, but the setting was clogged and grey. "You really should have them cleaned. They'll look a lot better."

"I told you," she said. "I don't wear them very often."

"Maybe you should."

I dropped it onto her lap. It rolled into a little fold in her shorts. Slowly she reached down and picked it up, turning it in her fingers. "So?"

"That's all."

She looked at it thoughtfully for a moment longer, then dropped it into her shirt pocket and, after an instant's hesitation, as if wondering if there were something else she was supposed to do, she leaned back on the sofa. "You're full of surprises, aren't you?"

"I try to be. How about you?"

"I'm just a simple, small-town girl."

"Why Hugh's office?"

"Why do you think? It was dark, deserted. I knew he kept money there."

"But not much."

"You said so yourself. There might have been more."

"I don't think so."

She said nothing. She picked up the red feathered boa and ran it slowly through her fingers as if it were a pet she was calming.

"There was fire there recently," I said. "At the factory. Two, actually, over the last few months. You wouldn't know anything about those, would you?"

She considered that, as well. I watched her, counting off the seconds in the rise and fall of her breathing. "I think I may have read something in the paper about it," she said.

"Dewey Reynolds thinks Hugh's just unlucky. What do you think?"

"Are you asking me if I tried to burn down Hugh's factory?"

"I'm asking if you think it's just bad luck."

"Charles. Tell me what you think of your brother's plan?"

"The urban oasis? I think it sounds good for my brother."

"Come on. Admit it. If anyone else were doing it, you'd love the idea. I mean what's not to love? A new park downtown, a new river front, new apartments, shops."

"And His Honor getting to play Santa Claus?"

"But what do you lose? What do we lose? An outdated factory that's a lot more trouble than it's worth." Her fingers stopped smoothing the red feathers. She looked at me. A neck that was slightly too long, and a nose slightly too broad, and the warm clown's eyes. "Tell me," she said. "What would you do if you saw a crime being committed? Right in front of you? Would you try to stop it?"

"What sort of crime?"

"Any sort."

"Like breaking and entering, for instance?"

She brushed that away impatiently. "More important than that. Something more dangerous. What if you saw someone being poisoned, say. Right in front of you. What would you do?"

"Depends on who it was."

"Say it's anyone except Kevin."

"Okay. I'd try to stop them. So?"

"So, how slowly do you have to be poisoning someone before it doesn't count as murder?"

I hesitated. "Is this a trick question?"

"It's not that complicated. If you kill someone slowly is it any better than killing them fast?"

"We were talking about Hugh's factory."

"That's right."

"Is that still what we're talking about?"

"Let's just say we are. What would you do?"

"What does Kevin say about it?"

"Let's say, just for fun, he doesn't know."

"I thought you were a simple, small-town girl."

"You already answered, Charles. You'd try to stop them. Anybody would. You couldn't just stand by and watch someone being killed."

"So what, exactly? What are you saying?"

"I'm saying, if someone's dumping a hundred thousand gallons of poison into your drinking water, even if he's your very best friend, then it's not so different from just pulling out a gun and shooting you."

"Maybe," I said. "But he is my very best friend. And I don't see any gun."

"Why is that, do you suppose?" she said.

"Maybe because there isn't one."

"Or maybe you're just not looking."

I stared at her in vague surprise. But in the back of my mind I was thinking how it's possible to be talking round and round, and yet never touch on the one true point. I wanted to shake my head. I wanted to tell her she didn't understand. I didn't particularly care about things—about the water table or run-off or the greed of the town's leading citizens. I didn't care any more than any of the people at the party last night. It wasn't her ideas that I cared about. But Emily sat there, staring at me in a rage of earnestness, and I said not a word. I was thinking about all the growing complications gathering around me and where I fit in among them. I was thinking about Hugh's bad luck and about my own. And I was thinking about Kevin and his plans, and Hugh and his fires, and about Wendy. But all the time it was Emily I was looking at.

The Smell of Smoke

When I knocked on the familiar front door and Aunt Mary let me in, I was startled by the sharp smell of smoke still hanging on the air. I remembered, of course, what Dewey Reynolds had said about the recent fire in Hugh's office, but this was so acrid and sharp, so immediate, it was like an old memory made suddenly real. The simple act of stepping inside felt like an unexpected risk. As if to say that nothing could be put behind you forever, that the worst moments were always lying in wait. But when I looked around I was surprised by how cheerful and pretty the house looked. It had been so closely linked to fire in my mind for such a long time it was strange to see it all clean and undamaged.

Mary was thinner than I remembered, but still pretty, with Gracie's pale blonde hair grown darker now and greying. She looked older, but instead of sagging like Hugh she seemed to have tightened with the years, and she had a look of faint but constant concern that gave her eyes a haunted, reminiscent depth.

"Charles! You look so grown up. And thin. You've dwindled away. Come along. Hugh's upstairs in his study." She turned and led the way.

I didn't remember a study upstairs, but it was a large house, and there had been plenty of time for changes. As I climbed, the acrid smell grew sharper and my memory along with it, so that at the top of the stairs I turned automatically and ended up following not the most recent trail of smoke, but a much older one.

Hugh's new study had been built from what was left of the family room, though transformed, of course. It was filled now with the dark, heavy furniture I had always associated with Hugh: the big oak desk, the filing cabinets, bookcases against one wall, and the big wingback chair with the worn patch on one arm where, many years ago for no reason at all, Gracie and I had idly sanded the dark leather down to a pale suede.

The room was larger than his old study, but somehow the furniture seemed even more crowded. All the spaces between were filled with a welter of papers and files and books, a disarray so widespread and thorough it might almost have been deliberate: all that clutter trying to crowd out older memories of the room. But the smell of smoke was still strong, and there was a recent dark smudge on the ceiling that made it hard to tell where the layers of past and present left off.

Hugh was sitting at his desk. He stood up and reached across to grasp my hand. "Charles. Sit down, boy. Sit down."

"Wait," I said. "I've got a new one." I had the cards ready.

When I was a boy Hugh and Mary had always been my first, and best, audience after Gracie. My parents had always greeted my tricks with expressions of patient interest, but the Barkers actually enjoyed them. They didn't know how they were done, and they didn't care. They always played their part, shuffling or choosing or cutting the deck, diligently but without too much scrutiny, and one or the other of them inevitably said, "It must be magic," which at the time was all in the world I could have asked for.

Now I fanned out the deck and let Mary choose, then cut her card back into the middle and brought it to the top. I false shuffled a couple of times, and handed back the deck. She took it, but awkwardly now, with none of her old dexterity. Perhaps just for an instant she was waiting for Gracie to laugh, or take the cards, or wave the magic wand over the deck. Gracie had always been crucial to the performance. Her nervous giggling had balanced my frowning concentration, and together we'd made a complete magician. Over the last seven years I'd refined my showmanship. Thousands of hours spent practicing and performing. But I could see now that neither of them cared about my new technique. They noticed only what was missing.

I took the cards from Mary, wrapped them in a handkerchief, and magically drew the selected card out through the fabric. I showed it to her, but it meant almost nothing. She smiled. "It's magic." But the smile didn't reach within a hundred miles of her eyes. "I'll see if I can't find you boys a couple of cold drinks."

When she left I settled gingerly into the leather chair. It was harder than I remembered, and smaller. As a boy I'd had to sit far forward, struggling to touch my feet to the ground, though that was a long time ago. Certainly in the more recent years before I left I'd been sitting it in much as I was now, but the mind always goes back to a certain past, as if only those memories were the ones that formed you.

"You remember this old place?" said Hugh, glancing around.

"Not this room, exactly."

"No. But I remember you in that chair. Both of you. Do you remember? When you could both sit there at once? I have a photo of that somewhere." He turned and sifted absently through the piles on the bookshelf behind him before giving up, his attention petering away. "I'll find it later."

"That'd be fine," I said. I brushed a finger over the pale patch of sanded leather. After all these years it still felt rough. "Hugh. I need to ask you some questions."

"Questions?"

Just at that moment Mary walked back in carrying a tray. She cleared a space on the desk and set it down: two glasses of ice and a pitcher of lemonade. It looked so wholesome, like a little bit of Norman Rockwell brought to life.

"You boys have fun," she said—I don't know what she thought we were going to do, something fun and cheerful; or maybe that, too, was just left over from the past—and slipped out of the room. Hugh peered vaguely down at the tray for a moment, then with a glance up at the closed door, drew an open bottle of gin from his desk. "Are you a drinking man, Charles?"

"It's been known to happen."

"Attaboy." He poured it high over the ice cubes, then slipped the bottle back into the drawer and topped the glasses up with lemonade, though there wasn't much room. "What sort of questions, Charles?"

"I don't know." I picked up my glass. "How's business?"

"Business? Hell. Business is great. Business is booming. The world needs paper clips and fasteners and little twisted bits of steel that sit on your desk and organize your papers. Can't you see?" He waved his glass over the clutter on his desk. "I don't know where I'd be without them." He took a long and thirsty drink. "You know," he said, "I hadn't noticed it before, but you sound a lot like your brother."

"You don't mean that."

"Just something in the tone of voice."

"I'll try to watch it."

He nodded. Then he glanced around at the newly painted walls and the clutter of furniture that couldn't quite crowd out his memory, and the sudden irritation died away like a light going out. "The world's a strange place, Charles. Have you had a chance to notice that, yet?"

"Oh, yes."

He took another long drink almost draining his glass, then gave the ice a little shake. "Are you a planner, Charles?"

"A planner?"

"Do you make plans? Because that's what they tell you. All your life. Make plans. Prepare for the future. And then what? A little spark in a wastebasket. A cigarette butt. An old match. Anything. Right there. Over there in that corner." I glanced up at the recent smudge of smoke on the ceiling, but Hugh was looking elsewhere. He stared across the room at the clean, white wall as though he could still see the marks of that first fire showing through the paint. But they were all gone, by now.

The room was still, as still as that distant, calm, and windless day all those years ago. And through that ancient stillness the smoke had risen straight up into the air. I tried to picture it now, seven years after the fact, but all I could imagine was some solid, puffy column, like a narrow thundercloud or an illustration from some children's book that shows smoke rising like cotton from a chimney. Though it would have been darker and much wispier than that: more like a mist than a thundercloud. It wasn't a big fire. But even at the time, forced to imagine it, I gave it more substance than it actually had.

If I'd really seen it, perhaps it would have been easier. Perhaps then it would have become only a cloud of smoke, which the fire department rushed to deal with, which they did deal with in less than three minutes once they arrived. But I didn't see it. No one saw it. Which, of course, was the whole problem. Late on a Wednesday afternoon the neighborhood had been deserted. Parents not yet home from work, children inside playing. Eventually, the Sri Lankan nanny in the house across the street had noticed, and had decided that, even in such a strange country as this, smoke should not be drifting out of a second floor window. She called the police with an urgent: It smokes! There is a burning here!

And so the firemen came and put it out. But by that time the smoke had filled the room, billowing up on the draft from an open window and a door left ajar, filling the rest of the house, seeping into the walls and the floors, into the fabric and carpets, so that, when I had finally arrived on the scene, when the firemen were already putting their equipment away, when Gracie had already been taken away in an ambulance with the siren blaring, more as a gesture of hope than urgency, and the neighbors had begun to assemble now that they were no longer needed, the acrid smell was like a damp and heavy sorrow.

"I was going to give it to you, Charles," said Hugh. "You and Gracie. Did you know that?" He was squinting at me now, as if the smoke were still in his eyes.

"Give it to us?"

"The factory."

"Oh."

The ice was melting into a thin wash at the bottom of his glass. He looked at it, shook it. "A wedding present."

"We were just kids, Hugh."

"It didn't seem like such a long shot."

"I don't know much about making paper clips."

"There's not that much to know. I thought it would be good for you to have something to do. You always seemed a little lost to me."

"A little."

"Do you know how long that factory has been in my family, Charles?"

"A hundred and fifty years."

"Building toward this." He shook his head again, and laughed, though not much of a laugh. "Have you noticed, Charles, how many different ways things can go wrong?" He reached into his drawer for the gin again and added it to his glass, holding up the bottle to me.

I shook my head. "I need to ask you about that, Hugh."

"Don't worry. You won't be getting it now, Charles. You wouldn't want it now."

"Hugh? About those fires."

He shook his head, raising his glass. "Don't ask me about fires."

"I know who broke in, Hugh. Into the factory."

"You do?"

"But she didn't set the fires, did she?"

He glanced up, puzzled. "She?"

"I went up to Hartford, Hugh. To Environmental Protection. I've looked at your emission reports."

"What are you talking about? My reports?"

"They're fine."

"What?"

"They're well within legal limits."

"What are you talking about, Charles? Are you checking up on me?"

I leaned forward in my chair. The glass in my hands was cold and slippery. "Tell me about the fires, Hugh. Please."

But he was still staring at what was long gone, shaking his head wonderingly. "How has it come to this?"

"Come to what?"

"All of this. You... Gracie... God damned paper clips. I spend my life making goddam paper clips, Charles!"

"People need paper clips."

"No."

"Aren't they buying them?"

"Hell, yes. They're buying them by the truckload. So what?" He peered at me as if I weren't quite in focus. "We were ship-builders, once. That was something, wasn't it? In my father's day people worked our boats up and down the Atlantic. All the way out along the Shelf. Good boats. Tough, strong. Solid in a storm. I would have liked to build ships. Wouldn't you, Charles? There's something great about a ship. It touches the heart. But people don't need ships anymore. People need paper clips. Clever me." He swirled the last of the ice in his glass, watching it melt. "Fifteen years ago I could have walked away, free as a kite. I could have just let it go. I had enough to retire. I could have sold it. But no. I had to move into paper clips."

"Sometimes you change with the times. You have to."

"Do you know what you get if you borrow two million dollars, Charles? New machines, new products. A new business altogether. You mortgage your future. And then the past creeps up and snaps your back."

"What past?"

He stared at me, a little blearily, now. "Have you ever made a mistake, Charles? One that follows you around for the rest of your life?"

I felt his words like a sudden pain. At first I thought he was talking about Gracie. At first I thought he meant me. I said, "It wasn't your fault, Hugh."

But he wasn't listening. "I built a whole new factory with the money from my future. What a joke. I borrowed it, a whole shit-load of money, to build a future for my daughter, and now look." He drained his glass, and sat there, leaning back in his chair, looking down at it cradled in his hand. "Do you remember her?" He could have been talking to anybody, and for a moment I won-dered if he knew who I was.

"It's me, Hugh."

He glanced up, startled. "What?"

"Of course I remember."

"You remember how she used to laugh? How she used to fol-low you around everywhere? Just tagging along."

"I remember."

"She used to ask me years ago, if we could adopt you. At night, when I'd read to her in bed, she'd lie back, eyes closed, al-most asleep, and she'd say, 'Can we have Charles come live with us?'"

The tears were like little sparks at the corners of my eyes. I blinked them away. "That would have been good."

"Do you remember? Once, as a boy, you asked if you were ad-opted. You said, 'Uncle Hugh, who are my real parents?' It was a little sad and sweet. Just like you, Charles, a sad and sweet little boy."

"I was never very bright."

"You're the magician, Charles. Tell me how it could all have disappeared? That she's gone, and nobody's fault? Do you know what that means, Charles? An accident. A little spark, that's all. Where does that leave me? No explanation, no reason at all? Just bad luck?"

I rubbed my fingers over the pale, sanded scar on the arm of the chair that all the years hadn't erased.

"And what about you?" he said, looking up. "Seven years without a word, and now suddenly here you are?"

"It doesn't feel suddenly."

"Seven years, Charles."

"I know."

"You didn't write."

"No."

"You could have called."

I didn't want to tell him that was the one thing I couldn't do. I thought about that night seven years ago, standing just outside this room on the patio below, sobbing against his shoulder, marveling even then that he could be so still when I felt myself being shaken to pieces.

"I can think of a hundred reasons why you came back," Hugh said. "But I'm damned if I can think of even one why you left." He held up the glass, as if it were a lens through which the whole scene could be made to focus again. "The next morning, I waited for you. Here, in this room, down there on the patio, out in the yard. I walked up to your house. I waited all day for you to come back. I had visions of you wandering around the town all night, exhausted and lost." He shook his head. "Your parents were worried sick. We all were...."

"I left a note."

Hugh stopped and looked at me as if what I'd said made no sense at all.

"I couldn't stay, Hugh."

He lifted the gin bottle and stared at it, then set it down again. There was only a little left in the bottom, and it hardly seemed worth while. "You couldn't say good bye?"

"I couldn't."

"What about Gracie? Your parents were there. Kevin came down for the funeral. We were all there. Where the hell were you?"

What could I tell him? That I was in Watertown, New York? That it was precisely because everyone else was here that I couldn't be?

If there had been no one else, if it had just been Hugh and Gracie, I might have come back, but not with my whole life standing around the grave site like that. Not with Kevin coming all the way from Washington, D.C. just three days after he'd left, to make the fine, caring gesture, to stand, sad and grief-stricken by the open grave as if it were all just a terrible accident, a stroke of fierce but unavoidable fate. That's what undid me. The thought that Kevin could stand on the smooth grass of that hillside without a flicker of guilt, and think only that here was another piece of the world's puzzle fitting snugly and mysteriously into place.

I'm sure he never thought for a moment that he was responsible. I'm sure it never occurred to him to wonder whether, if he had only done things differently, he could have kept her alive.

"I wasn't mistaken in you, was I, Charles?" Hugh turned his nearly empty glass on the desk, watching the condensation drip down into a wet, turning circle. "People change. I know that. God knows, things change. But were you always the sort of person who would just run away?"

And I couldn't answer that. But suddenly I could see Hugh, waiting all these last seven years for it to make sense, thinking that the piece that would solve the puzzle was somehow always the missing one, wondering if I had taken the truth away with me. And I realized, after all that had happened, that I owed him something.

"Listen, Hugh," I said. "Let me tell you a story."

Gracie

Growing up, it had been just the two of us, Gracie and me, until after our late-night burglary at the factory, when it became the two of us plus Kevin. He joined us only now and then, when he felt like it, when he had a plan that needed our help, or maybe just when he was bored, but in retrospect those adventures provided the vivid center around which the rest of my childhood assembled. They were more exciting, more lively than what came before, though they brought with them their own anxiety.

I began to worry that Gracie would become bored with the games we played on our own, that somehow she'd grow up faster than I would. I tried to come up with my own adventures, but more and more of our time seemed to be spent waiting for Kevin. I began to feel as if we were trapped on two of those moving walkways at airports, and I could see Gracie speeding up, ever-so-gradually pulling ahead, out of my reach.

Then Kevin began spending less and less time with us. He'd moved on to other audiences, and there was now a steady trickle of girlfriends, whom Gracie and I would watch from the upstairs window. I got tired of the game pretty quickly, but Gracie didn't. I would practice my magic tricks, making cards disappear or, my favorite of the time, picking a card and making it appear magically sticking to the ceiling, but I had more and more trouble keeping her attention. I'd be doing my tricks, and Gracie would be peering down through my bedroom window at Kevin and his latest girl, dressed up for a prom or a party or an evening out. I began to long for the time when he would go to college, and when he finally did, albeit just a few miles up the hill, I had Gracie to myself at last. But things never quite returned to the way they were.

Love is a slow transition. I don't know that I would have said I loved Gracie at all until that final year, and even then the feeling had built so slowly and imperceptibly it was hard to differentiate from what you'd feel for a brother or a sister or for one of your own limbs. It was only afterwards I could put a name to it, but by then it didn't matter.

Kevin was away at college, and then at law school. He came back for visits but never stayed long, and his attention was always elsewhere. Then one summer he returned for an entire month. It was after his first clerkship, when he was preparing for the move to Washington, and he came home to rest. Perhaps he was bored or just between girlfriends. Or perhaps he hadn't been paying attention to Gracie as I had. Certainly she was different than he remembered. Though I suppose he must have seemed exactly the same to her.

He was sitting in the kitchen over a late cup of coffee when she came in, and although it would be too much to say he didn't recognize her, certainly he looked twice. She wore a t-shirt and shorts, her face already shining with the heat of the day. It's impossible to say if she was beautiful. At least impossible for me. Short nose, limp blonde hair, a round face transformed only by her laughter. She's too much a part of my memory to be seen clearly, too close and familiar. But when Kevin looked at her that morning, he must have seen a brand new girl, one he'd never seen before. And for Kevin, every new girl was a new possibility.

"Grace?" He smiled and set down his coffee cup. "How many years have I been gone?"

"About five-and-a-half months," she said, with a hesitant smile I'd never seen before. "You saw me at Christmas."

"You didn't look like this at Christmas."

"I didn't? How did I look?"

"Different," he said. "Definitely different."

She blushed.

"So," he glanced at me, "what are you two up to today?"

"There's a magic show at the summer school. We're rehearsing."

"Charles is going to saw me in half."

"Oh, now that would be a pity," Kevin said, with a sly smile that I had seen before, though never in this context. "I'm home for a while. I hope I don't miss the show."

"You can come if you want," she said.

"But definitely. Do you wear sequins or feathers or anything?"

"It's a magic show," I said coldly, "not a striptease."

"Too bad," Kevin replied, and Gracie giggled. Even then I wanted to protest, to tell them to stop it, but I knew they wouldn't know what I meant.

That afternoon Kevin made the long hike up to the attic where we were rehearsing. Ours was a big old house, built by my grandfather at the turn of the century, with a third floor attic that amounted to a single huge room under the eaves. It was cold in the winter and too hot in the summer, and there were two or three nests of wasps that made their homes up there, but I didn't mind. At an early age I learned what Old Thomas Strawberry had discovered in setting sail for America: when you can't find a place for yourself at home, you have to go in search of one. I claimed the attic as my own.

I spent my childhood making gradually more substantial changes: cleaning, insulating, painting. I started out by covering the stud walls with scraps of ancient, grandmotherly wallpaper that had been in an old trunk for years. But there wasn't enough of any one paper to do more than a portion of a wall, so by the time I had run through my supplies the attic looked like an ancient patchwork quilt in stripes and florals and a large patch of red-jacketed men on horseback riding to hounds across a green background. About then I discovered wallboard.

By the time Kevin's footsteps climbed heavily up the uncarpeted stairs for the first time in years, the attic had become a large white room with smooth walls and a painted floor, anchored by the massive brick chimney rising through the center. There were still some piles of abandoned furniture and junk up there, but I'd pushed them all into one end under the eaves, and the rest was mine. Part workshop, part rehearsal space, it was a place where the world obeyed my rules, where objects disappeared, albeit a little clumsily, where anything, given enough work and practice, was possible. It was a place where, if Kevin had been a different sort of person, he would have felt like an intruder.

"Is everybody still in one piece up here? I haven't heard any screams."

"We're not ready yet," Gracie cried, but she didn't seem disappointed to see him.

"Don't I get a private showing? I'm a friend of the artist."

Gracie was lying in the magic cabinet while I was taking some measurements for the final adjustments. Her head and hands protruded from the top, her feet from the bottom, held in place with stock-like slats that kept her steady and gave her leverage to bend the rest of her body down and activate the spring on the false bottom. Even under the best of circumstances there wasn't much room to spare, and at the moment it wasn't going well. It looked as if the whole bottom would have to be removed and realigned.

At Kevin's entrance Gracie started to climb out of the box, and I snapped, "Don't move!"

She laughed again, for Kevin's benefit. "Sorry. I guess I'm a little tied up now." She wiggled her fingers and toes in greeting.

"So, how does this work?" he asked.

"It doesn't," I said.

"Well, how is it supposed to work?"

"I lie like this," Gracie said, straightening out like a heroine on the railroad tracks, "and when he starts to saw, I scream and struggle. Oh! Oh! That hurts!"

"No," I said. "Not 'That hurts.' You say, 'Careful.' 'Not so fast.' 'Stop.' We don't want to frightened them. We just want to amaze them."

She took it from the top. "Not so fast! Stop!" She struggled against the stocks holding her wrists and feet, then grinned. "Don't you think I should be an actress?"

"You are," said Kevin smiling. "I assume there's a false bottom."

"No," I said. "That's where this trick is different. I really do cut her in half."

"We're even going to use fake blood," she said.

"Okay," I said snappishly. "Climb out. I've got to re-do the whole thing."

"Well, that's not my fault."

And although it was perfectly true, the coquettish tone of her voice, so entirely for Kevin's benefit, made me even more angry. "If you didn't squirm around so much you wouldn't have bent the springs."

"I didn't!"

"Get out. I have to fix it."

"Allow me," said Kevin, stepping forward. He raised the slat holding her feet, then, utterly unnecessarily, reached in and lifted her out of the box like a rescued damsel.

In retrospect, it's hard to blame her for what happened. Maybe I should have done that, should have lifted her out, swept her off her feet. It wasn't that I didn't want to. It's just that I had no practice in such things. She knew me too well, knew how far short of suave and sophisticated I fell, in spite of all I would have wished. We'd grown up together. How could I sweep her up in my arms in the face of such unnerving friendship and knowledge? But Kevin, of course, had no hesitation. He stood there laughing, with Gracie in his arms half embarrassed, half thrilled. She blushed and glanced at me, daring me to laugh. And perhaps I should have, perhaps that would have changed everything. But of course I didn't. There was nothing funny about it. In that instant, with Kevin tall and handsome as a movie star, and Gracie lost in the moment like a woman swept away, I saw them both clearly for the first time in years.

He lowered her to the ground. "Well, if the maestro, here, needs to fiddle with his equipment, how about taking a stroll with me. I'll buy you an ice cream cone. You've got to keep your strength up if you're going to be sawn in half."

And that was that. Away they went, marching down the stairs, leaving me standing there with what had suddenly become nothing more than an empty plywood box.

I didn't see much of her for the next few days. And when she did finally come back to the attic, once I had the box finished, once we were ready to rehearse, she brought only half her attention.

"But she loved you," Hugh said. "And you loved her."

"I was sixteen. What did I know about love?"

"We all saw it."

"We grew up together. How could we possibly fall in love? We were standing too close even to see each other clearly."

She stopped coming so often to the attic after that, and I ended up rehearsing most days by myself. And then she'd suddenly show up. I'd be standing over the top hat, or the deck of cards, or the long plywood box, speaking to an imagined audience, moving smoothly through the trick, when a creak of the stairs or the sound of the door down below would break the spell, and Gracie would be standing there with a faint reminiscent smile on her face for whatever adventure she had just been engaged in.

I didn't ask where she'd been. I tried not to imagine what they were doing. But as I practiced, I couldn't help conjuring up the sight of them together.

"We thought she was with you all that time," said Hugh.

"No."

"She told us she was going to rehearse."

"Did you see that magic show?"

"Of course," he said. "It was very good."

"It was terrible."

As the summer continued I didn't say anything. I didn't tell anyone. I rehearsed my tricks as if that might save me, repeating them over and over, but no. I didn't see Gracie for days on end, and when I did, she would arrive in the early evening only to leave a few minutes later when a low whistle rose to the window. She would smile, shrug, and hurry down the stairs.

In magic there is something called a "shell." It's when you retain the shape of an object beneath a sheet or a napkin while the object itself is no longer there. You pretend that something remains when there is only the illusion of its shape.

It took me a while to realize I was being used as an alibi.

Then, one evening, I followed them. When Gracie had come and gone, and I could no longer face the sound of my own voice, I traced her route down the stairs and out into the back yard. And I followed them both, a long way through the darkening twilight, down to the river bank.

In sleight of hand so much is a matter of suggestion, of convincing the audience to believe in something that isn't quite there. The hint of a movement, a sound, a flicker of the hand is enough to create a finished image. You don't always have to see something to know that it's happened. In the darkness of the river bank, there was little chance of seeing all that unfolded, but the small sounds of whispering, the low catch in her voice, faint glimmers of movement, and the pale gleam of her skin, white as a flag in the dark, showed much more than I needed to see. And more than I could walk away from. Long after they'd left I stayed, sitting alone in the darkness on the grass listening to the sounds of the water, which, that late at night, amounted almost to silence.

The night of the magic show arrived. Hugh helped load the equipment, all painted and finished, into the back of his station wagon and carried it to the high school auditorium. I told him Gracie was resting up, though in fact, I had no idea where she was. So perhaps, in this as well, I was to blame. I was an accomplice in my own unhappiness.

I wasn't sure Gracie would show up, but there she was, in a costume I had never seen before: all sparkles and sequins. A gift, it turned out, from an admirer. She was giddy and excited, laughing and fidgeting in the wings of the stage as we waited to go on. I usually get nervous before a performance, but I wasn't that night. I remember it so clearly: I didn't feel anything at all.

It was our turn. We walked on stage. And it was terrible.

Her timing was off. Her concentration wasn't there. And neither, of course, was mine. She fumbled the cards, she dropped her cues, and made up for it by posturing and vamping for the audience, who loved it. They laughed, they applauded. But they weren't applauding the magic. If anything, they were cheering the beautiful sparkling costume that Kevin had provided, that fit her so well, and perhaps they were applauding this new Gracie, who had lost all her shyness. When the time came for the finale, I sawed through the box viciously as if I were actually cutting through wood and flesh, and when she screamed, quite convincingly, and the mixture of caro syrup and food coloring oozed out of the box, I stared down at it, wishing it were real.

Hugh looked down at his glass of gin, as though half expecting to see a bead of fake blood dribbling down the side. "So, what are you saying, Charles?"

I shrugged. I wasn't even sure. Maybe just that love is a killer. It lifts you up, carries you along, and then vanishes. It covers your eyes with a fine white cloth, and leaves you there, waiting for the magic, when the trick is already over.

I don't know what it was like for Kevin: fun, harmless, exciting. I sometimes think other people weren't quite real to him, or they were real only as long as he chose to pay attention. He left the week after the magic show, on a Wednesday, in the early morning, to take up his new and prestigious clerkship in Washington. He didn't tell her he was leaving until the night before, and even then he didn't say what time, so that she must have thought he was still there, in the house just up the hill, in the bedroom window just visible through the trees. She must have thought he was still in his room, packing, glancing repeatedly out the window in case she might wave or gesture good-bye.

"What?" Hugh whispered hoarsely. "What was that?"
"She thought he was there. In his room, packing for the trip."
"So?"
"It's a five minute run down the hill to this house. He'd see the smoke. He'd run and save her."
"It was an accident, Charles. A spark in a waste basket."
"She thought he was there, looking out his window. She wanted to get his attention."
"No," he said desperately. "She was a child. A child doesn't kill herself for love."

And she hadn't. Not really. Not for love. For anger, maybe, for sadness, for desperation. She was so young. She wasn't thinking clearly. She was hurt and angry and desperate. And also, as it happens, pregnant.

She lit a very small fire in a wastebasket in the second story family room of her large and beautiful house, to make Kevin sorry he had broken her heart, to give him a chance to come racing down the slight incline of Arbutus Street to rescue her, to fling open the door, which was left unlocked and slightly ajar in anticipation.

That was a mistake. The open door let in a draft that filled the room with smoke in an instant. But Gracie wanted to make sure there would be no barrier to Kevin, no reason for him not to save her, no reason at all, except he wasn't there.

Gracie lit the fire, waited, and nothing happened. There was no panic. No startled cry. No one even noticed. Certainly, no one at our house, which was less than a block away, with a perfect view of the Barker family home framed through the trees. The smoke, rising all on its own without benefit of fireplace, should have been a clear warning of disaster, but there was no one to be warned.

"She couldn't have known how fast the smoke would fill the room."

"Charles," he said. "Pregnant?"

"She was desperate."

"I don't believe you."

"She didn't know what to do." And even after seven years, her voice was still locked in my brain, the sound of her grief like the sound of a piece of fabric tearing. "She said he was leaving her all alone."

"Alone?" Hugh whispered. "What about me? Or her mother? What about you?"

What about me? I thought but couldn't say. Did she think about me at all? I loved her all her life, and she left me just like that.

"We would have done anything for her," said Hugh. "We loved her. How could she do this?"

He spoke as if it had just happened, as if we were having to go through it all a second time, and I wondered what the point of knowing the truth was if it gave you nothing more than the pain all over again.

"Oh, Charles." His gaze dropped to his lap. "I missed you, boy. I needed you here."

"It was more than I could do."

"How?" Hugh shook his head wonderingly. Then he looked up at me, eyes clouded with gin and memory and something like amazement. "How could he? How could he just leave? Did he know?"

"I don't know."

"And he walked away? How?"

I used to ask myself that. How could he just walk away. But, what else did I do?

I never wanted to see him again. Or anybody else. I wanted

to make everybody disappear, but I couldn't. So I made myself vanish instead. But that didn't solve anything. I should have known that nothing ever really vanishes. Despite all appearances, despite the most convincing of your senses, everything that disappears is simply waiting in the wings.

"How could he leave her like that?"

"He didn't know what would happen," I said. "None of us did." And that was true, I told myself. That was the only comfort.

"All this time," Hugh muttered abruptly. "And now he thinks he's got me."

I glanced up. "Got you?"

But he wasn't listening any more. "My daughter," he muttered, "and a child?"

I leaned forward. "How has he got you?"

"What?"

"How?"

"The factory. He wants it for his little project."

"I know. So?"

"So, maybe he's not going to get it. In spite of all his little games."

"What games, Hugh?"

He turned, reaching for the last of the gin, and as he did he glanced up at the ceiling where the newest smudge of soot remained, darker than ever. The latest in a series. The smell of smoke seemed even thicker on the invisible air.

I followed his gaze up to the ceiling. "Hugh," I said. "Tell me. Who set the fire?"

He raised his glass and drained it. Then looked dully up at me, as if he were a stranger, an old man I'd never met before, hunched in his chair against all the events that crowded in around him. "Oh, the fire," he said, as if it were obvious, as if it were a very old trick indeed and he was surprised I hadn't seen through it. "I set that myself."

Water, Water Everywhere

In one of the more gracious and shady corners of what is a particularly gracious and shady campus stand a series of three brownstone mansions on a little cul-de-sac at the bottom of Observatory Hill. They're large and solid, built from identical dark stone but in three distinct styles. And though together they represented almost a hundred years of varying architectural taste, they had been joined together with additional walls and corridors into a single complex structure. Together they gave a pleasing sense of age and accretion, each era building on the next. It was only if you looked closely that you realized the three houses had been designed from the beginning as a single building. Built in the early nineteen thirties, it had incorporated all the conveniences of modern architecture along with the pleasing impression of great age so that it stood as a kind of pre-fab emblem of ancient and decorous wealth, while avoiding any suggestion of modern vulgarity. The architectural equivalent of having your cake and eating it, too. It seemed only fitting that a building of such ingrained duplicity and complex vanity should house the law school.

I entered through a side door and climbed the narrow, slate stairs to the second floor. There were still a few students around, plowing their way through the summer session, and the sound of lecturing voices, dulled by the masonry walls, thickened the air. I hesitated at his office door, feeling the vague uneasiness that lingers in any school during the summer time: familiarity tinged with the nagging awareness that you weren't supposed to be there. I knocked and stepped in.

He was sitting behind his immaculate desk in shirt sleeves and tie, with his reading glasses perched primly on the end of his nose and a pen in his hand. He glanced up over the top of the red rims, and then after a moment lowered the pen and leaned back in his chair, tilting his head down slightly to see over his glasses. "Charles." He gave it a kind of neutral sound, as if he hadn't yet decided what it meant.

"You busy?"

"Not too. Have a seat."

He had an old Barcalounger in one corner, with a heating pad pinned to the cushion for the days when his back was acting up. The wire trailed off into the corner over a pile of Connecticut Statutes. "Nice place you've got here."

"Don't make anything disappear, all right? I'm not sure we're covered for fire."

"I'll try to control myself."

"Oh. Your mother asked me to give you this." He reached into his desk drawer and drew out the little wind-up goldfish. He reached out and handed it to me. There was a pink scum of raspberry sherbet dried under one fin.

"What makes you think it's mine?"

He gave a faint and weary shake of his head, then gestured at the chair. "Have a seat."

The Barcalounger was too soft, designed to make you much more comfortable than I was prepared to be. I looked up at him. "Have you ever had one of those days when nothing went quite right?"

"Sure," he said. "Many times. Though I don't ever remember setting anyone's dining room on fire."

"No. I suppose you wouldn't."

"But then, I've always been a kind of old-fashioned guy."

I sat there, sunk too deep in the soft cushions of my childhood, feeling like a youngster in a grown-up's chair. I took a deep breath. "You know, I didn't actually intend to ruin your party."

"I'd like to believe that."

"Do you know how hard it is to do that trick? I mean, without the fire. It takes years of practice. I worked like a dog on that trick."

"And was it worth it?"

This wasn't quite the direction I'd meant this conversation to take. I'd come in with the best of intentions, but there was something steely in Ambrose's simmering manner that kept pushing me off track. "Believe it or not, I'm sorry for the mess."

"Well, that's more your mother's department than mine. Maybe you should mention it to her."

"I did, but I'm not sure she heard me."

"Then maybe you should mention it again." He looked coolly over his glasses, a man who knew without a doubt how reasonable he was being in the face of every obstacle.

"You know," I protested, "if you hadn't started arguing, none of this would have happened. That's why she asked me to do something. To break up your argument."

"And you think that was what she had in mind?"

I was stung by that. I managed to struggle up out of the chair. "The thing is, I've never really been sure what she had in mind," I said curtly, all irritation and sharp-edged embarrassment. "Or you, for that matter. But even you've got to admit, it certainly livened things up. It gave the party a real boffo finish."

"Is that what you call it?"

"It's a term we magicians use."

"Charles," he said grimly. "What is your problem? Is it us? This town? You know, it's not such a bad place. It hasn't treated you badly. The world is full of kids who'd love to have grown up just the way you did."

"You think so? How many?"

"Well, if you hate it so much, then why bother coming back? I mean, what's the point? You were free of us. You could have just stayed away. I mean, if you want to screw up, you can screw up anywhere."

"It's not as easy as that," I said. "It doesn't really count unless you screw up at home."

Ambrose sighed and rubbed his eyes. I didn't remember ever

seeing him look so tired before. "Charles… I'm trying to under-stand."

"So am I."

"Then maybe you should start making sense."

But that had always been more his line than mine. "Home is where, when you don't have to go there, they don't have to take you back," I said.

"What does that mean? Does that mean you're going to leave again?"

"Do you want me to? Would that make things easier?"

My father stared at me for a moment, then he took off his glasses and dropped them on the desk. His face looked un-finished without them, unfixed and malleable, as if some new change or detail might make him into a completely different per-son. "You can leave any time," he said quietly.

"Great," I said. "Okay." I started to turn away.

"So, why rush into it?"

I hesitated, turned back to him again, this time taking in the tired eyes, the hair, not just artfully mussed now but genuinely disarrayed as if he'd been running his hands through it with-out regard for the careful part. His shirt was still beautifully pressed, of course, and his tie tightly knotted. If he'd been any-one else he would have looked perfectly groomed, but for Am-brose it amounted to a kind of all but general unraveling.

He sighed. "Families are tough," he said.

And even now I'm not sure whether he meant they were du-rable or just difficult. Maybe he didn't know either. "Is that sup-posed to be a comfort?"

"Maybe. I hope so."

After a moment I shook my head, "I'm not going anywhere."

"Well," he said. "That's something."

I walked to the door, then hesitated again and turned. Am-brose had his glasses back on and he'd picked up his pen. "Dad?"

He looked up.

"Have you talked to Hugh lately?"

"Hugh? Why?"

"No reason. I didn't see him at the party the other night."

"No. He was a little under the weather. He's been having a tough time lately."

"That's what I hear."

"Don't worry. Things are turning around for him. I imagine he'll like being a bank president."

"Is that definite?"

"All but signed and sealed, I think. Certainly, there's no one better for the job. So, unless the world ends or there's some major disaster, I imagine we'll all be moving our accounts to Community Savings by the fall."

"Then I'd better start saving my money."

"I guess you'd better."

I nodded. "One last thing. Do you remember any problems Hugh might have had with the factory? Anything unexpected that might have come up?"

"Problems? Why? What sort of thing?"

"I don't know. I talked to him yesterday. He seemed a little preoccupied. I thought maybe something was on his mind."

"Not that I know of. Why? What's going on?"

"He mentioned something, some problem from years ago."

"Something in particular?"

"I don't know."

"Well." He leaned back in his chair. He drew his glasses off again, tapping them meditatively against his lips. "There were all those renovations, of course. When he converted the factory. All those new machines. That building's so old, I think there was some settling before he got it all reinforced. But he took care of it. That would have been, I don't know, fifteen years ago. God," he murmured, "fifteen years. You'd have been, what? eight?"

"About that."

He shook his head, smiling thinly. "You were less complicated at eight, Charles."

"The world was less complicated. I was probably exactly the

same."

"Maybe."

"Was there anything else? Anything you remember?"

"Nothing."

"I have these vague memories as a kid. Great piles of dirt. Big holes in the ground. I remember playing on them, wondering at the time if they were trying to bury something."

"Bury something? You mean like treasure?" He chuckled. "That might be a problem. I'm not sure the bank would want to hear that he was keeping his money in the back yard."

"So maybe not treasure. Piles of dirt, big holes in the ground. Lots of machinery."

My father looked puzzled for a moment, and even a little disconcerted. Though maybe it was me. Maybe I was looking at him through disconcerted eyes. After a moment, though, his face cleared. "I know what you're talking about. But it wasn't Hugh. It was the city. Back when they were doing it everywhere. Putting in city water. That's all. Laying pipes. Connecting the factory up. Nothing too remarkable, I'm afraid."

"Fifteen years ago?" I said.

Ambrose shrugged. "More like eight or ten."

"Big piles of dirt?"

"They dug up the whole parking lot."

"Just for water."

He laughed. "Sorry it wasn't more mysterious."

"But, why then? What was he doing for water before?"

"He had his own, I imagine. All those old factories did. Private wells. That's all there was a hundred years ago, or they just pumped it out of the river. But not that factory. The river's pretty silty, there, and they'd have needed clear water. Just pump it out of a well."

"So why go to all the trouble for city water?"

"I don't know. Maybe it was easier. More efficient."

"All that digging? It seems like a lot of trouble to go through for more of the same."

"Maybe he wanted fluoride in his water."

"Maybe."

"Or...." Ambrose looked thoughtful. "Wait a minute. There was something else. He mentioned it, but it wasn't a big deal. He didn't want any of his workers to be concerned, but it turned out he had to get on city water."

"Had to?"

"Apparently his well had gone bad."

At Least Tell Me Before You Do

Fire, by itself, has no substance, neither solid, liquid, nor gas. It's a state of flux, hovering in that moment between spark and cinder. And if it can be said to have a meaning, apart from the many separate meanings that we ourselves provide, it lies only in the fierceness of its irreversibility. It can never be unlit, only put out, which is not at all the same thing.

If Hugh had lit that one little fire in his study, one in a series of fires that seemed drawn to him like his own bad luck, then simply having put it out was no solution and no explanation. But he wouldn't tell me any more. And though he had invited me to stay for lunch, suggested another drink, offered to open a second bottle he had tucked in the cupboard in the kitchen, he had closed the door on any further revelations, which left me with nothing but a sharp and tickling awareness of other people's secrets. And as a magician I hated all secrets but my own.

So I took a cab to the Longfellow building. And as if I were just arriving, new in town and settling in for an extended show, I climbed all the way up the narrow stairs carrying two large trunks. I moved slowly, lifting one ahead of me, dragging the other along behind. I'd forgotten how heavy they were. By the final flight my legs were spongy, my arms ached, and there was a stitch in my back from carrying the weight. It was just like old times.

At the top I set them down on the landing and pushed open the door. "Honey? I'm home."

Emily was there, standing behind her desk, but she wasn't alone. Beside her a thin young man in a work shirt and jeans was frowning over a ragged pile of papers, tracing something with his finger, while, in the corner, a very thin woman in a Save the Rain Forest sweatshirt bent over a hotplate making a cup of tea.

They all looked up, almost comically startled, as if I'd stepped out through a sudden cloud of smoke.

"Who the hell are you?" The young man snapped, grabbing at his papers and shuffling them all together.

"I'm the health inspector," I said. "Did somebody here call about a rat problem?"

He glanced anxiously over at Emily, whose first startled expression was easing into a smile, though behind them the very thin woman was casting about nervously into the darker corners of the room. "It's okay," said Emily. "He's just kidding."

The woman offered up a weak smile, as if to say she'd known it all along, though her friend at the desk just kept frowning. He had the papers more or less in order now. "We're in the middle of something, bud. Now get the hell out of here."

"That's not very friendly."

"Maybe if you tried knocking," said Emily gently.

"I didn't know you had company."

"Charles, this is Tina and--"

"No names," snapped the young man.

"--Richard," she finished.

Richard looked disgusted. "Jesus Christ! Why don't we just take out an ad in the paper?" He bent and began stuffing the pile into a battered leather briefcase. A xeroxed portion of a street map lingered enticingly in view for a moment before disappearing with the rest.

"It's okay," said Emily. "He's a friend."

But Richard seemed unconvinced. He gave her a long and eloquent glare, and after a moment she shrugged. "Maybe this isn't such a great time, Charles."

"It's too late. I've just carried those things up four flights of stairs."

"What things?" She stood and poked her head out the doorway, quailing at the sight of the trunks, looking huge and immovable on the narrow landing. "How much did you bring?"

"Everything. Well, not the rabbits. They're still at home,

though they're very excited about it."

"It's a little more than I expected."

I nudged one of the trunks with my foot. It was very heavy, but then, it had every right to be, considering how much of a man's life it held. "I wasn't sure how big a show you needed."

She glanced back at her two companions. "Well. Now's probably not a good time to..."

"Don't worry," I said. "We can figure it out as we go."

Richard had straightened up and was standing with his arms crossed menacingly. "Don't you get it? She doesn't want you here."

"Of course she does. She invited me."

"Well, you've just been de-invited."

"Oh, come on. I'm not even sure that's a real word." I glanced back at Tina, who had reached down and turned off the hot plate, and now stood with the steaming kettle in her hand. "If you're making tea, I'll have a cup."

She looked even more uncertain. "It's anise," she said doubtfully, but after another long moment she set about making it.

Emily leaned back against the desk. "I bet you didn't realize running a children's theater was so mysterious."

"Is he leaving, or not?" With a scornful look Richard snapped the brief case shut. Tina stepped up cautiously and set a mug on the corner of the desk. The scent of warm licorice wafted up on the steam.

"We've got just a few more things to talk about," Emily said to me.

"Hey. I can take a hint. But what am I supposed to do with my stuff? It's a lot to carry home again."

"You can put it downstairs. Anywhere in the auditorium."

I picked up the mug of tea. "I'll need some help."

"You brought it up here."

"But now I've got my hands full."

She smiled wryly. "I'll carry the tea."

"No, that's all right. I've got it." I nudged the smaller of the two trunks. "That one's pretty light."

With an easy shrug she glanced back at her friends. "I'll just be a sec." She reached down to pick it up. "Jeeze! It weighs a ton."

"Lift with your knees, not your back."

She edged her way to the stairs and worked her way down slowly, thumping the trunk on every other step. I followed, careful not to spill the tea. At the bottom she led the way through the double oak doors into an enormous, dusty room, with a low wooden platform at one end. It could have been any one of a hundred bleak and silent stages, summoned from my past. At least I was on familiar ground.

"You can just shove them off to one side for now," said Emily.

"That Richard sure is a load of laughs, isn't he?"

"Some of what we do isn't all that funny."

"But there's no rule that says you can't have a sense of humor and save the planet at the same time, is there?"

"I have a sense of humor," she said "Lucky for you."

I bent and shoved the heavier trunk against the wall and then, with a glance at Emily, sat down on it. "So, tell me. What are you doing with a map of Hugh's neighborhood?"

She frowned. "You've got quick eyes."

"That's not an answer."

"You're right. Ask me no questions, and I'll tell you no lies."

I thought of what Dewey had said: a burglar climbing up a twenty-foot brick wall into Hugh's office and out again. You've seen his office. Could you tell if it had been burglarized? Just because he'd set his own fire didn't mean he'd robbed his own office. I thought of all the possible things she could be planning, but what I said was, "You know you could get into serious trouble. You could go to jail."

"Are you going to tell me again how your mother would disapprove, or what a blow it would be for Kevin if he found out?"

I thought about that. I thought about the bill I'd been adding up all these years that I'd been waiting for Kevin to pay. And I tried to recall the point at which Emily had ceased to be a means for collecting on it. "No," I said. "I'm not worried about Kevin."

"Charles--"

"I just want to know what you're doing."

"I've got to go." She said, but at the door she stopped. "If you want to unpack that stuff you can go ahead."

"Will it be safe?"

"We'll lock up." Then she stood, still hovering between leaving and staying. "I can give you a hand in a bit."

"You don't need to."

"I don't mind."

"Okay then. I'll try not to disappear."

"You're a magician," she said. "You're supposed to disappear." And she closed the door.

It was almost an hour before she returned. By that time I had the boxes and tables set up and loaded with everything but the rabbits, and I was leafing through Rudy's playbook for a little inspiration.

She strolled in as if there were nothing on her mind. "Sorry I took so long."

"Planning anything interesting?"

She ignored the question and, walking over to the first of the magic tables, she blithely opened a box. "This one's empty."

"It must be broken." I hefted the playbook. "What do you think? Is half an hour long enough? I've got a half-hour, an hour, and a ninety minute version."

"Half an hour sounds good. It might be hard to keep the troops quiet for an hour."

I nodded, weighing the playbook in my hand, as if somehow that might have all the answers I needed. "I spoke to Hugh," I said abruptly.

"Did you?"

"He's got a clean bill of health. I checked the EPA."

Emily eyed at me carefully. "So?"

"But his wells went bad. At the factory. Did you know that?

Maybe ten years ago."

"So?"

"So, he lit a fire in his office at home a few weeks ago. And probably one at the factory."

She sank down onto the empty trunk. "So?" she repeated calmly, though her hands, I noticed, were knotted together in her lap.

"So, tell me what it means."

"Why don't you ask him."

"I'm asking you, Emily. What is going on? What are you doing?"

She shook her head tautly, her hands pulling at each other as if they wanted nothing more than to be free. "I'm not going to tell you, Charles."

"I need to know."

"Why?"

"Because you could get into some serious trouble."

"You said that already."

"So just tell me where it ends. What are you trying to do to Hugh?"

"Nothing bad. Honest."

And there was something so disarming about that last, childishly earnest promise. I had a sudden sense of her as a young girl, crossing her heart and hoping to die, and I had the sudden urge to wrap her in whatever wild and hapless protection I could offer. "I just want to understand. That's all. I want to understand what you're doing."

"Why?"

But to that I said nothing. The truth, like everything crucial, like magic, like love, is a balance of disguise and revelation. A fragile equation that depends, as often as not, on hiding all that is most important.

After a moment she reached over and lifted Rudy's playbook from my hands. She sat leafing through it. The old typed sheets, the careful handwritten notes that had added up over the years like miles on an odometer. "What was it like on the road?"

"Lonely," I said. It surprised me. All that time with Rudy, tired, exhilarated, gloomy, exhausted, riding a wave of adrenaline and desperation from town to town, I had never thought of myself as lonely. We were alone, yes, but there was nothing wrong with that, was there? Nothing until now.

But Emily just nodded, gazing up at me, her eyes warm. "You look like a man who'd get lonely."

"How can you tell?"

"You look lonely now."

She closed the book. Every effect, every trick was there, laid out with all the necessary set-up, all the dialogue and choreography. Everything Rudy had put together in the course of his life. I used to think it was all I needed. She dropped it onto the floor. The slap it made echoed in the empty room.

"Do you know what happens to wood if you leave it in water all the time?" she said.

"Jesus Christ!" I was scowling furiously. "Do you even know what I'm trying to say here? I don't want you to get hurt!"

"What happens, Charles?"

I shook my head impatiently. "I don't know. What? It floats?"

"It rots. Not all at once. But eventually."

"For God's sake, Emily..."

"Think about it. You have to treat it, to keep it from rotting. You have to soak it in something. Creosote, say."

"Okay. Fine. So you soak it in creosote."

"Now, think about a factory that makes ships. That's made ships for a hundred and fifty years. Wooden ships. For a hundred and fifty years they were soaking their lumber in creosote, preserving it, keeping it shipshape. And for a hundred and fifty years, do you know what they did with that creosote afterwards?"

She had my attention now.

"They poured it out on the ground. Just like that. Dumping it out, to let it evaporate."

"And did it?"

"Some. But most of it just got washed down into the ground with the first rain. Out of sight, out of mind."

"Is that legal?"

"A hundred and fifty years ago who knew from legal? But now? No. Not any more. Now they definitely frown on it. But Hugh's father did it, his grandfather, his great-grandfather. And when the federal government decided it was illegal, Hugh asked them for an exemption. A kind of great-grandfather clause. And he got it."

"How?"

"You'll like this," said Emily. She was leaning forward in a fever of earnestness. "This is right up your alley. He told them to test the water. Just like that. If they were worried about it, test it."

"How do you know?"

"I've seen the reports."

I shook my head helplessly. "So what does this have to do with being up my alley?"

"Do you know what they found when they tested it? Nothing. They checked the groundwater under that factory every year for ten years. Up until he went out of the shipbuilding business and voluntarily stopped dumping. And each year it came up perfect. Pure as rainwater."

"But how?"

"It was magic," she said dryly. "Nothing up his sleeve. Thousands of gallons a year for a hundred and fifty years, and you know what? It just disappeared. Vanished without a trace."

"And they really tested the water?"

"Every year."

"How did he do that?"

"You tell me," she said. "You're the magician. How would you have done it, if it were your trick?"

"I haven't got a clue."

She spread her hands as if revealing the simplest of solutions. "There's a secret compartment."

"The hell there is."

"It's called a sub-porous impermeability. A layer of rock, in this case granite, deep underground. It sits just above the water table and keeps anything from soaking through. It's like a huge holding tank. Generations of creosote have been settling down onto this layer of granite, and just sitting there. The water was fine. They could test it to their heart's content."

"So?"

"So fifteen years ago Hugh got a loan. He completely refurbished his factory. He needed a new foundation and he brought in a pile driver. It was pretty hard on that sub-porous impermeability. It cracked. And that holding tank of creosote started to leak."

"His well," I said.

She spread out her hands. "Ta da."

"Okay. But, so what? I mean, it's bad, but it's not his fault. He couldn't have known."

"Where did he think it had gone?" she said quietly. "A hundred and fifty years of creosote?"

"Maybe he didn't know."

"Bullshit, Charles. You're the magician. When something disappears, do you know where it's gone?"

I sat for a while, staring down at the dusty floor and the book of magic tricks that was most of what remained of Rudy's life. I thought of how easily everything a man could build might just disappear. But at the same time I thought, That was it? A crack in the granite? Poisoned well water? That didn't seem enough. The physical facts seemed insufficient, because somehow the simple, mechanical explanation didn't begin to account for the anxiety I felt, or for the level of urgency in the room. The explanation of stone cracking and chemicals leaking didn't do justice to the passion that Emily felt for it, or the fear that was absorbing me at the prospect of all it might entail. But then, it's never the mechanics of a trick that define it. The effect is always far beyond the facts. The movements of a hand, the secret pockets and compartments, that's what it all devolves to in the end, but they're only a rough platform for all the heart's most complex yearnings.

"What exactly is it you want?" I said.

"I want someone to be responsible."

"Hugh?"

"For a start."

"But what can he do?"

She looked at me for a long moment, trying to decide how I was going to like the rest of the story. "The city wants the factory."

I stared, feeling something escaping like air from a tire. A kind of bitter, settling disappointment. "You mean Kevin wants it."

"For the city."

"For his master plan?"

"So he can clean it up," she said.

"Or so he can be governor some day."

"That's not the point."

I leaned back and gazed bleakly over at her. "Why are you doing this?"

"I've told you why."

"Does Kevin know? About your sub-porous impermeability?"

"He knows. He knows we need to clean it up, and the only way that's going to happen is if the city owns it."

I felt a sudden knot of anger tightening in my chest, as if I'd been taken advantage of, as if all my worrying about Emily had been tricked out of me, and I'd been duped into a concern for Kevin against my will. "Isn't that convenient? What a great team you make. Here's His Honor, all high-minded and virtuous, trying to pull Hugh into this deal, and all the time you're pushing from behind."

"There's no other way," she said. "I didn't ask your friend to dump poison in his back yard. But now that he has, he's got two choices. He can lose his factory, his reputation, and all his friends. Or he can sell it to the city for a dollar. He gets it off his back. The city cleans it up. Everybody wins."

"Is that your plan?"

"What do you mean?"

"It sounds like something Kevin might have come up with."

"What does it matter who thought it up?"

"It matters to me."

"The results are the same."

I shook my head. "Was Kevin in it from the beginning?"

"You said you wanted to understand."

"I said I wanted to understand you. I already understand him."

She stared hard at me. The serious eyes, the warm mouth. "Then you understand me."

"I don't think so. Did he tell you to break in to Hugh's factory, into his house? Was that part of his plan? Does something absolutely have to be done, just because Kevin tells you to do it?"

She stood up. "I've got to get going."

I tried not to care. It wasn't my problem. It was Kevin's problem, just like it was Kevin's fiancé. But I found myself saying, "Another meeting?"

"That's none of your business."

"I'm curious."

"Don't be."

"What are you planning?"

"I'm going home, Charles."

"And then?"

"Just home."

"You're not going to do anything? Nothing risky? Nothing illegal?"

But she wouldn't say. "Turn off the light on your way out, will you?"

"At least tell me before you do."

She turned and looked at me with those deep, serious eyes. "Why? What's it to you?"

But I didn't answer. The only reason I could think of was too complicated, too foolish and self-defeating, to explain. I'd come all this way to get even with my brother, to make him face all that he'd done. But more than that I'd come back to extricate myself from a lifetime of bobbing like a cork in the wake of his plans and desires. And here I was, after all that had happened, against all my better judgment, right back where I started.

"Good night, Charles," she said quietly, and closed the door.

Right Before My Eyes

I waited in that empty room, listening to her footsteps echo up the stairs to her office. Then, in that long, attenuated moment of silence, I turned off the light and slipped outside. The evening was warm, the sky slipping into the first deep blue of summer twilight. I'd seen so many towns at exactly this moment over the last seven years—every one of them easing into darkness in exactly the same way, all the strangeness disappearing into an identical, enshrouding blue. In even the most alien of places the twilight brought its own comfort, and every town became more welcoming with all the hard, shabby edges, the potholes and the patches and the vacant, staring windows, hidden in darkness. And now, even the town I was born in was changing before my eyes. The streets and buildings that might have been drawn from an old dream were settling into that general crouching vagueness of the world at night.

In all the other towns I'd have known exactly what to do. At this point, late in the evening, I'd be packing up the show, or putting it in storage if we were staying for a couple of days. I'd be looking for a place to sleep, or going to a bar with Rudy, or back to our motel to drink in our room. Every day reduced to its essentials. But now each moment was new and uncertain.

Out on the sidewalk I stood, looking up at the grey, blank-faced building. A single light showed at the very top under the eves, and before my eyes it winked out. I hurried across the street and found a bench tucked behind a pair of shabby looking ginkgo trees, one of His Honor's recent improvements to the town. I was sitting there when she came out. Above my head the leaves looked jade bright in the streetlights and beyond them the sky had turned black. The heavy door of the Playhouse opened. Emily glanced around, taking in the air, and I waited, dark and

unmoving, in the shadow of the trees. She descended to the sidewalk and turned the corner, walking quickly up the side street
to the little parking lot behind her building.

As she turned the corner I ran toward the municipal lot. I had
a car now, though it wasn't exactly a thing of beauty. I'd bought
it shortly after that long walk home from Wendy's, more for its
price than its good looks, and so far, despite the more or less constant impression of impending collapse, it hadn't let me down.

I climbed in just as Emily, in an ancient and sagging Pontiac station wagon, lumbered past heading south. By the time
I coaxed the engine into life and pulled out onto Main Street
her tail lights were already making the distant, swooping curve
around Union Park. But there wasn't much traffic, and I hurried
after. As we left town, passing through the last gauntlet of gas
stations, fast-food chains, and the sprawling fluorescent extravagance of Shop'n'Save lit up like an airport, the road narrowed
and the darkness closed in. Along that curving road the silhouette of her car melted into the darkness. The only thing left was
that pair of red tail lights, and driving became a matter of just
keeping them in sight. I concentrated, leaning forward over the
wheel as if locked in a staring contest with those two red lights,
and when they vanished at every curve I peered ahead, unanchored and drifting, until they swung back into view.

This went on for miles. I wasn't sure what my reasons were.
I wasn't making plans. I was just consumed by a kind of dark
and rising anxiety, and if I was seeing anything besides those
unblinking taillights it was a vision of Richard, Tina, and Emily, dressed black as the night, creeping one more time over the
rooftop of Hugh's factory, but this time with a row of police cars
waiting in the darkness below. She spoke so coolly of the risks,
but I wondered if she really believed in them anymore. You can
get too comfortable standing on a ledge. As I drove I had some
half-considered notion that Emily Burke needed someone to remind her how far she might fall. It didn't occur to me how close
to falling I was myself.

We drove for what seemed hours, but which must have been no more than forty minutes. And after the endless recurring loop of swoops and curves, the sudden brighter flare of brake lights caught me by surprise. I slowed, peering ahead, and saw the car, with a little wobble in the darkness, vanish. I coasted along, wide-eyed and astonished, looking for some clue. The woods grew thickly along the edge of the road, and for a moment Emily seemed simply to have disappeared into them. But then a sudden gap opened in the trees, and the narrow, gravel track of her driveway led off toward the faint glow of house lights. I drove past, pulling onto the shoulder, and as I stepped out into silence and the scent of dry leaves, I noticed my shirt was sticking damply to my skin. I didn't know, hadn't even considered, what I would do when I found them: follow them, reason with them, or just leap out and tell them to give it up for God's sake. But now the darkness itself drew me on.

I followed the gravel back through the trees, listening to the crunch of my own footsteps, feeling my way. The lights were growing brighter as the house came into sight. It was small and white, more a cabin than anything: two bare stories with a tin roof painted bright blue. There was a dirt yard in front where the Pontiac stood parked, and in the back, a porch looked out over a sloping hillside. I stopped, hesitating at the broad expanse. A single bare bulb on the porch lit up the center of the clearing, throwing the trees into deeper darkness.

As I watched, a light came on downstairs. A moment later a window on the second floor lit up, and a shadow moved behind glowing pink curtains. I stepped gingerly out from the cover of the trees and eased my way toward the station wagon. Peering in through the dark windshield I could see almost nothing; the inside was crowded with sinister, uncertain shapes, but I couldn't make them out. I stepped to the back hatch and very gently tried the handle. It was unlocked, but the hinges were stiff, and every creak seemed loud as an alarm bell. Slowly I pried it open. What did I expect? A grappling hook? Burglar's tools? Though, at that point I had only the vaguest notion what tools a burglar might use. I leaned in, groping. My hands brushed over a cardboard box, dusty-sided and smooth, and I fumbled it open to find a jumble of old clothing and costumes. I felt through it all, but it was soft fabric down to the bottom. Beside it there was a long pile of lumber and a roll of canvas, and two bulky spotlights, heavy as anchors. Nothing more. Nothing sinister. I eased back out onto the ground and stood, at a loss.

Then came the sound of a slamming door sharp as a firecracker. I drew back, crouching against the side of the car. Emily stepped off the porch onto the hillside. She was dressed in a dark shirt and dark overalls, with a thick parcel tucked under one arm and a camping lantern in the other, and without a glance in my direction she headed off across the clearing.

I gave her a moment, then backed away toward the edge of the woods and, sticking to the darkest shadows, eased along after her, picking my way carefully through the twigs and old leaves. The clearing spread out down the long, shallow hillside. Dirt turned to grass under my feet, and I had to leave the trees behind, but by then we were beyond the reach of the porch light, and I could give her plenty of room. Carrying that lantern, she walked through the low grass within her own small, shifting dome of light.

I was nervous; I was tired; I wasn't thinking clearly. But still I kept following. Having started I could only continue. She slowed down at a broad stand of bushes rising like a fortress out of the dark and, raising the lamp, picked her way carefully through the thick branches. I looked ahead, beyond the wall of bushes, but there was no sign of the road, no sign of a waiting car. No light or movement at all. I kept after her, groping through the branches. Her lamp barely filtered back through the leaves. I moved as silently as I could, trying to hurry, afraid of losing her, afraid of making a sound. Then abruptly, the bushes gave way to another clearing.

Emily had stopped. She stood less than twenty feet away gazing around into the night. I crouched, breathing silently, not daring to move. A scratch on my cheek stung like crazy. The sweat felt slick on my face. Beyond the narrow reach of warm light the darkness was solid. She lowered the lantern to the ground and set her parcel down beside it. Then she straightened up, bathed in the glow. I thought at first she was waiting for something, some signal from the darkness, some sound. But after a moment she reached up for the straps of her overalls.

I was so sure she was on her way to a crime, so prepared to see her step out of her overalls into a burglar's night-black disguise, that it was only when she slipped off the straps and let the overalls fall that I realized she was wearing nothing beneath them. The dark fabric fell away like a curtain from the pale silhouette of slender hips and legs. Then she reached down for the hem of her t-shirt and drew it up over her head in one long, smooth motion that left, like an afterimage on my retina, the single frozen glimpse of her, pale as a statue. Smooth stomach, the bent curve of arms reaching up, and her heavy breasts rising to the gesture.

I should have left immediately, I know. I should have crept back through the bushes into the darkness and driven home. But I didn't. I didn't want to risk the noise. Now, especially, I didn't want to be discovered, at the moment when my motives, which had seemed so pure, became anything but. I could no longer pretend to be a guardian angel waiting to jump out and save her from herself. In that instant I lost even the pretense of disinterest.

At the center of the broad, invading darkness, she stood wrapped in light. The glow painted her dark-tipped breasts, the smooth curve of her hips. She stood, pale as the moon, bleached of all color but the blur of her nipples and the soft V of pale copper hair. Then she turned and, without fuss or flurry, waded into the stillness of the pond that emerged from the darkness at her feet.

There was a technique for stage magic popular in the late nineteenth century. It offered the most startling effects of levitation and vanishing, of transmutation and sudden, breath-taking appearance. The technique was simple: the entire stage was cloaked in black velvet. Every surface, every wall. A row of lights along the base of the stage was tilted toward the audience, casting the fabric darkness into even deeper shade. The magician wore white. In the course of his show he would make a series of pale, beautiful objects appear out of nothing, float across the stage, transform themselves into other beautiful white objects, and finally wink out into nothing, right there before your eyes. The audience would not have been aware of the magician's assistant, cloaked in velvet like the walls, whisking black coverings off objects, carrying them across the stage, then cloaking them again.

It was a simple trick, barely a trick at all, but the effect was a marvel. It had to be seen to be believed. You couldn't imagine the wonder of something so luminous appearing suddenly out of the empty darkness.

The climax of the act was inevitably the appearance and then sudden vanishing of a beautiful woman, as if all that went before was just preparation. The woman would stand on the stage wrapped in black. Then, with a word, the magician would sweep aside the darkness to reveal her, shining and pale. She was always there; that was the secret. She was there all the time, just as solid and real and magical as could be, but you never really saw her until she stood revealed, pale as light. Then, just as your eyes were opened, she vanished. That was always the final trick of the evening. The magician draped his own white cloak over the woman, from head to toe, and slowly, very slowly, peeled it back, starting at the feet for maximum effect. And as he peeled back the white cloak, leaving a second night-black layer in place, the lovely assistant would disappear. And the audience could do nothing but watch as the woman vanished into darkness as though slowly submerging into water black as the night.

Love is a Box

What is love? After so much has been said and written about it, so much spent in describing its every ramification and element, what are you left with in the end? The philosopher George Berkeley was prepared to argue that sensation was no evidence of existence. That the physical world existed only in our minds, and that a coffee table was no more real just because you might bump your shin against it. But in his ironic and fiercely contrarian approach, Berkeley revealed not just a kind of determined wrong-headedness, but the unruly depths of his own optimism. Because if the world were all in our heads, then there might eventually be some fevered, desperate chance of changing our minds.

But, one demented Irish bishop to the contrary, the only evidence you have of the world is that sharp bump of the table on the shins. You can't trust what you see; ask any magician. Only what you feel. And in such a case, what is love but a heightened awareness of your own vulnerability? An increased sense of danger. A raising of the stakes in everything you do so that even the smallest of things becomes suddenly saturated with the threat of disaster. You slip into it unwittingly, without warning, without realizing that you're feeling anything out of the ordinary, anything more than a perfectly normal reaction to the day. But it sneaks up on you. So you can be standing there, feeling worried and fretful, lost in the grip of adrenaline, like a wild animal caught between fright and flight, and then suddenly realize that the only thing that's in danger is your heart. And there's so little you can do about that.

I arrived the next night at the playhouse just after five. As I set up my equipment and ran slowly through the more difficult moments, brushing up my technique, getting my timing back, I watched Emily as she led her troop of child thespians through the last of the day's rehearsal. They sang and danced their way to the end of "Somewhere Over the Rainbow," and then with the last lingering note they stood frozen for a moment before dissolving into the strident confusion of a school playground. Laughing and bickering, replaying their roles as they walked, ignoring Emily's shouted reminders and last-minute instructions, the children gathered up their clothes and wandered away, leaving us alone.

There's a sense of potential on an empty stage when the show is over and the audience is gone, a sense of being on the verge. The dust and silence, the emptiness in the air where the shapes and sounds had been. It takes a moment for it all to become ordinary again. I stood at my magic table and watched Emily drift around tidying up, straightening away the extra costumes and abandoned props. She wore a pale leotard and nylon sweatpants despite the heat, and she moved with a distracted grace, as if there were something on her mind.

And as she puttered I ran through my routine. Standing there in a pair of gym shorts and my tuxedo jacket, with all its carefully placed pockets and vents, I might have been back on the road again, out on the sidewalk before a show, trying to spark a little interest, trying to catch the eye of a pretty girl. Except that everything had changed. I tried to recapture that old, careless feeling, but it was now beyond my grasp.

On the road there weren't any real people—almost by definition. Audiences came to seem as much a part of my imagination as the tricks I was performing, and since they weren't real, I didn't have to worry. But among magicians, where deception is everything, there's an easy rule of thumb: if it makes a difference when it disappears, then it's real.

As simply as that, Emily had become real.

I did a pass over the deck and fumbled it. Tried it again, and again. I'd done it ten thousand times, so often it seemed impossible it could ever go wrong. A simple act, a movement: it was just one of the things I did now as naturally as breathing. Though it's possible, I suppose, to forget to breathe.

Emily bent and scooped up the last of the costumes. Her shoulders were pale. Her back curved like a wave breaking. She hesitated, then turned as if about to reveal something striking, but held only the bundle of clothes in her arms. I suppose it's a mistake to look for answers in every motion, but it's something you can get in the habit of. Every movement serves its purpose of disguise or deceit; every gesture moves the trick forward. Each motion is a telling one.

She smiled. "You look a little like your brother when you concentrate."

I frowned. Shuffling, cutting, "Does he ever come to watch you rehearse?"

"No. He keeps pretty busy."

I dealt out four cards, naming them before they appeared. "Ace of spades, ace of hearts, ace of diamonds, ace of clubs."

"Only four?"

I had her image in my mind, the paleness of her skin, the smooth, unencumbered curve of her breasts as she slipped into the dark water. After all the time on the road, with Kevin bulking so large in my imagination, it was odd that he could suddenly seem so insubstantial, and all my desire for revenge along with him. But with last night he had shifted from the weighted center of my preoccupations, to a thin and gravitational shadow behind the other brighter creatures of my thoughts.

"Did you really saw a woman in half?" she asked.

"More a girl than a woman. It didn't go very well."

"So I gathered."

"It was a long time ago."

She dropped the gathered clothes into a laundry hamper against the wall. "Do you ever think of doing it again?"

"I'm trying to learn from my mistakes."

"It sounds like a good trick."

"I don't think so."

She shrugged. "You're probably right. It's a little old fashioned anyway. We should stick to something more exciting."

I caught the teasing note in her voice and glanced up. "Oh," I said. "It's pretty exciting."

"Not for this crowd."

"I don't know," I said. "You'd be surprised how scary it could be. If you do it right."

"You don't know kids today."

"Maybe. But, sawing someone in half...? There's always the chance that something could go wrong."

Emily laughed. "You've been doing too many card tricks, Charles. This is the twenty-first century. Magic doesn't scare people anymore."

I smiled slowly and held up a single, prognosticatory finger. "Then I have just the thing." I returned the cards to my pocket and straightened my jacket, slipping into the smooth, quicksilver patter of a sideshow barker. "May I have a volunteer from the audience please? Anyone will do, anyone at all. Perhaps you, there. Yes, you. The one in the leotard. It shouldn't be too risky, but please make sure you sign the insurance waiver on file in the theater office before approaching the stage."

Emily closed the lid of the laundry hamper. "Golly," she said. "Me? Oh I couldn't possibly."

"Don't worry, little lady. You'll do fine. You're not a bleeder, are you?"

"I don't think so."

"Well. I guess we'll find out." I reached down and lifted the Chinese Hand Box out of the big trunk and set it on the table. "This is what I do instead of sawing ladies in half. It's a little more portable, and it's easier to get the blood stains out."

It was a small box, just big enough to fit a single, outstretched hand. I flipped up the top and opened the ends. Within the box were the palm and finger guides laid down on the bottom. "Now, you just place your hand in there, within those ridges. Thumb there. Each of the fingers in one of those slots. Good. Now I'll just close it up. There's no need to be nervous." I shut the top, and slipped the two hinged doors at the end around her wrist. Then, I closed the hasp on the cover and padlocked the box shut.

She glanced up at that, the first glint of surprise in her eye.

"I don't want you leaving until I'm through," I explained. "If you move suddenly it might break my concentration. Wiggle your fingers."

The box was arranged so that the tips of her spread fingers protruded out one end, the tip of her thumb stuck out the side. She wiggled them gamely. She was still smiling, but I could see a hint of uneasiness building on the surprise. It happens each time. It's the padlock that does it; the sense that your hand is spread open, exposed, and for the moment at least, beyond your control.

I drew from their case the three needles, each fifteen inches long and thick as a piece of string. They looked vicious as I laid them out on the table beside the box. With them was a small, folded sheet of instructions. I opened it and frowned over the directions for a moment.

She watched me for a moment uncertainly. "How many times have you done this, exactly?"

"Actually, this is the first. But don't worry. The directions are right here. It's a piece of cake." I glanced down again. "Oh, right." I shook my head sheepishly. "Wouldn't want to forget that." And I set the sheet aside. "I haven't used these needles in a while. But they stay pretty sharp." I tested one point against my fingertip. It drew a drop of blood.

She watched as I wiped the blood away. She was still smiling gamely, but her voice held that first thin thread of unease. "Are you sure you know what you're doing?"

"Pretty sure. It doesn't sound like that difficult a trick."

She was standing awkwardly, leaning forward to keep her hand in place. She was glancing warily now from the needles to the box to my hands. It was warm in the theatre. I could see the perspiration gleaming like flecks of mica at the edge of the hair just above her temple.

I picked up a needle, and fitted it into the first of the tiny guide holes. With one hand to steady the top of the box, I slowly pushed it in.

"Wait," she said.

"It's okay. It's magic."

"But I feel that."

"No you don't," I said soothingly. "You just think you do. It's a trick." I prodded the needle again.

"No, really."

"Really?"

"Stop."

"You feel that?"

"It's pricking my hand."

"It's just the power of suggestion," I said, then I frowned. "At least... I'm pretty sure I'm doing this right." I drew the needle out. It looked long and wickedly sharp. "Maybe it's broken." Slowly I pushed it back in.

"Ow!"

"Did that hurt?"

"No. No, it's all right," she said unsteadily. "I was just surprised." She grinned nervously. "I don't think I want to do this, Charles."

"Of course, you do. This is the twenty-first century. It's just magic. There's nothing frightening about it."

"I'm not frightened. Ow! Will you stop it!"

"It's nothing."

"I can feel it."

"No, you can't."

"I can!"

I frowned. "What's the matter? Don't you trust me?"

"It's not that. It's just.... Are you sure you know what you're doing?"

"Of course. Well... Pretty sure." I gave the needle another nudge, at the same time pressing the secret button on top of the box that pressed a hidden toothpick gently against her hand.

"Ow!" She frowned. "I think we'd better stop."

"Don't be silly. This almost never goes wrong."

"But what if--"

"The worst that can happen is that you'll need a few stitches. How bad is that?"

"Bad enough!"

"It almost never happens."

"But, I don't think--"

"You just have to trust me."

"But...Wait!"

She was standing so close. The little gleam of mica flowed into a tiny dribble down her cheek.

"There's nothing to it."

"I've got a bad feeling."

"Don't worry."

"Charles..." She gazed up at me, smiling weakly, her eyes warm and imploring—deep as a pool. "You wouldn't hurt me, would you, Charles?"

"Not in a million years," I said, and I shoved the needle hard into the box.

She yelped and jumped as the needle slid through its carefully angled hole, past her hand, through her spread fingers, until it jutted gruesomely out the other side. I released the secret button.

Emily stared for a long, startled moment at the box, at the needle so clearly going straight through her palm. Then her whole body sagged, all stiffness gone, and she burst out laughing. "I take it all back. Everything. You're scary. You're very scary. Magic is scary. Now, please, please, please, give me my hand back."

I drew the needle out and undid the padlock, then spread open the top. Emily lifted her hand out and flexed it, as if to prove it was really hers. "Do you use this trick much?"

"I save it for special occasions. It's good for hecklers."

"I guess it is." She stood, rubbing her hand gently, a ruminative smile warming her face. "You know, sawing a woman in half might go over pretty well, after all."

"You think?"

"Could be."

I shrugged. "And who am I supposed to saw? Some poor little kid from the audience? She'd start panicking, and I'd end up getting bloodstains all over everything."

Emily grinned. "I'm onto you now, Houdini. Here I am. Do your worst."

"It takes a lot of time."

"We've got time."

"And practice."

"Come on. It'll be fun. And the kids would love it. Think of the danger."

I smiled, but it didn't seem quite so funny. I was thinking about my previous experience with the trick, thinking that the dangers weren't all as obvious as the physical ones. And I was aware of that low tremor of anxiety which is undifferentiable from the early pangs of love. "I don't know," I said. "I'm not sure I want to go through all that again."

"All what?"

"Don't you remember? It didn't go all that smoothly the first time."

"Well then," she said. "This is your chance to do it right."

The Box is Burning

One day years ago, out of the blue, Rudy decided to add a new trick to our repertoire. It began with a standard escape cabinet, but there were two important modifications. Instead of walls that collapsed outward revealing the suddenly empty box, this cabinet had sides and a front that folded down like an accordion. This meant that, as the rear wall fell backwards, the rest of the cabinet toppled in on itself, collapsing like a building in an earthquake. It was a nice effect. But it would have been no more than ordinary without the second small improvement. The sides and front were fitted with horizontal grooves, tiny troughs actually, which were filled with naphtha. Not a lot of naphtha. Just enough so that, when sparked, the whole cabinet burst into flames.

Rudy didn't bother to mention this last bit to me, at least not until after the first performance. Perhaps he thought it would make me nervous, and I was already a little more than concerned.

"Come on," he said, "get in. Do you want to live forever?"

It was our first rehearsal. I looked at the box. It was made of seamless aluminum, about half the size of a telephone booth, and painted to look even smaller. "I'm not very good in small spaces."

"You don't have to be good. I'm good," Rudy said. "You just have to be quiet. And compact."

"I can be quiet. But this is as compact as I get."

"I don't know, Rudy," said the large man beside him. "He doesn't look like he's through growing." The man sounded like a salesman in the boy's department of a clothing store, but he looked like a former Hell's Angel: fat and bearded in a stained work shirt and a pair of thick red suspenders. His name was

Paul Sisco, and surprisingly in a line of work in which people seldom looked like what they were, he really was a former Hell's Angel, though nowadays he spent his time fabricating the finest magic props east of St. Louis. "You get this now," he said, "you just have to get another in a couple years."

"He's a big boy. How much more can he grow?"

"The numbers are tight on this one, Rudy. There's not much leeway. Now, if you want to try the floor-escape model he could use it for years."

"No. Not where I work. No trapdoors, no platforms. It's all closed box."

"Well, then, this is good as it gets. You used one before?"

"Years ago."

"Pressure latch. Half swing door--"

"I've used it."

The man shrugged. "Okay."

Rudy stepped up to the cabinet. "That's your cue, kid." He held it open for me, like a sinister doorman with dark schemes on his mind.

"But I don't know what to do."

"You'll figure it out," he said.

I stepped in, crouching low, and he closed the door.

That was my sixth summer in Saratoga Springs, and the time had come once again to expand the act.

Saratoga was the closest thing to a steady gig we had. We returned every summer for three months, rotating on and off through half a dozen venues during the bustling tourist season. The audiences kept changing, so we didn't have to, and the steadiness of it allowed us to use larger and more intricate props than we could have carried on the road. This meant that each year Rudy could add one or two new tricks to the act. He kept them, during the off season, in a U-Store-It bin in Sisco's warehouse, and that first moment each year, when he undid the padlock and opened the door, marked the start of the summer season. No more buses. No more nights on the road. We had the same motel room for three months straight and a swimming pool every bit as big as a ping pong table just outside the door. It was heaven on earth.

The cabinet closed behind me with an emphatic click, and I waited. As I've since learned, the first lesson in being made to disappear is simple: as soon as the door closes, get busy. There's a lot to do, and just barely enough time and space to do it. But the only disappearing I'd done up to that point was by bus, so I just stood there.

After a moment the door opened, and Rudy glared in. "Well?"

"Well what?" I said.

"Well, what the hell are you waiting for?"

"Instructions."

"What do you think, they come printed on the side?" But he was startled, even embarrassed, as if for a moment he really had forgotten that I might not know how it's done. I wondered where he thought I'd have learned it, or how. But more than that, I wondered who he thought I was.

In those last few years Rudy's memory had begun to play tricks on him, treacherous shifting games. He drifted backward and forward along the tracks of his past, and fit me in where he could. Sometimes he called me Lennox, sometimes Hammond, whoever that may be. Sometimes in a gentler voice he called me Harry and, talking all the while, explaining or encouraging or criticizing, he would gaze right at me, but I had no idea who he was actually seeing. That was before I knew much about his past; before I even knew he'd had a son.

"The back," he said impatiently, in a different voice, now. And though he was annoyed, at least I knew he was really talking to me. "You open the back."

Sisco eased him aside and leaned into the cabinet. He was much too large to fit, but he could reach to the back wall. It was smooth, featureless, and solid as the ground. He laid his palm on a point two-thirds of the way across and pressed. There was a click, and out of nowhere the seamless wall cracked, and a narrow section swung out.

"It's magic," I said.

"That's the idea." Sisco ran his fingers down the polished edge of the door. "There's a spring lock. You have to pull hard to close it, but gently. Like closing a Swiss watch. Remember, if it breaks, you're stuck in there."

He withdrew. Rudy stuck his head in. "Okay, take it from the top."

He closed the door again. There wasn't much room to move. I squirmed around and had begun to squeeze into the compartment behind the secret door when I realized there was no way in the world I would fit. The space was less than eight inches deep and the door opened no wider than a foot. I had to somehow jam my shoulder in, then twist around and force myself in. I had to bend my knees but keep them flat against the back wall, and bend my head sideways, and straighten my shoulders. I squirmed half way in, and then I got stuck.

I felt like a puppy with his head trapped in a box of dog food. It was absolutely dark and too cramped to get any leverage. I couldn't back out, I couldn't go forward. And suddenly, with three loud thumps on the side of the cabinet, I started to fall. Or rather, the cabinet began to fall, and I fell with it, leaning, tilting, toppling over backwards in the dark. I was about to cry out when I hit the ground, and any sound I might have made was knocked out of me along with my breath.

I lay there a moment, half in, half out. Then I felt a hand on my arm, and with a jerk, not at all like closing a Swiss watch, Paul Sisco yanked me free. "Get off," he said. "You'll bend it."

I scrambled to my feet and realized that the magic cabinet hadn't tipped over. It had come apart, the back wall falling away to lie flat on the ground.

"Bravo," Rudy said dryly.

"It's too small!"

"You just have to learn how."

So I did. We rehearsed in the mornings, and once Rudy finally realized that I hadn't simply forgotten how to do this but genuinely had no clue, he became a very good teacher. He demonstrated the dipping, twisting movement of the shoulders required to half-slide, half-wedge yourself into the tiny space and pull the door closed behind you. Once the door was closed there was a little more room, so that, when the cabinet collapsed, you could squirm out the top and slip behind the curtain backing the stage, to reappear at the dramatic finale.

It was a great trick, especially when we added the flames. A young boy, trapped in a burning box, is made to vanish out of harm's way, and reappears magically from beneath a pile of his empty clothes. It was a good story, and we worked on the plot and narrative much more than on the mechanics of the escape. Paul Sisco came and videotaped our rehearsals from every angle of the audience, then Rudy pored over the tapes, refining his movements and timing, though he never let me watch. Then we were ready for the first performance. It came at the end of the show, the grand finale.

The audience loved it.

Sisco taped it for his archives, and that night, in the empty theater after the performance, we sat, the three of us, and watched.

"Ladies and Gentlemen." On the screen Rudy spoke with a flourish, an elegant figure in white tie and tails dominating the center of the stage, as the actual Rudy, stripped down to his t-shirt in the heat, leaned forward to catch every nuance. "We have a young boy with us tonight. A young boy anxious to try his hand at magic."

I stepped onto the screen, without my usual formal attire, wearing instead the clothes of someone much younger. At the time, I didn't know why the clothes were important, why it had to be a young boy who escaped from the burning cabinet, but Rudy was adamant. More dramatic, he said. More compelling. Well, from a distance I could play young, and he was right, it was compelling.

"The cabinet, as you can see, is solid and safe." He rapped the side. "A fine place for a boy to hide. Though nothing is certain in the realm of magic."

As he spoke, I crept furtively up to the cabinet and slipped inside, closing the door behind me.

"Now we cloak the cabinet for secrecy," the magician on the screen announced, as Rudy, hunched forward on his chair, echoed the lines under his breath. On stage he gathered up a wide, gauzy sheet and draped it over the cabinet. It hung like a veil, thin and translucent. "And now we weave the magic spell." He turned to face the cabinet and with a movement of his hands there was a spark, a flash, a puff of smoke. Then he leapt back. "My God! What's happened?"

The gauzy veil, impregnated with alcohol, went up in a single, huge bloom of flame, burning away instantly, but setting the grooves alight. The cabinet burned like a small building, the flames licking eagerly up the sides. I could see now why Rudy didn't let me see the rehearsal tapes. Watching now, seeing Rudy's terrified face and the high flames, I couldn't believe anyone could survive that.

A voice floated over the audience, a voice we had recorded some weeks earlier. "For God's sake, help him! Do something!"

But on the stage, Rudy appeared to hesitate, cowed by the sudden fire. He didn't know what to do. He looked powerless before the flames. But then suddenly he straightened up, a bold, resolute figure, and spreading wide his arms, commanded in a booming voice: "Don't be afraid! By the powers at my command, I bid you: flee! Rise up! Escape! I bid you: Vanish into the air!"

And with a loud, echoing boom, the cabinet collapsed into the flames.

I had rehearsed the trick daily for three solid weeks, and now it still caught me by surprise. I stared as the flames died down to nothing, and some part of my mind was actually searching in the midst of the cabinet for an unconscious body or charred remains.

Rudy stepped over, and waved his hands through the empty

air, then bent and lifted from the middle of the cabinet a blackened shirt, which was all that remained. "He vanished," Rudy announced to the audience. "But did he vanish in time?"

Tossing away the charred shirt, he strode across the stage to a table and picked up a small satchel. From it he drew a new, clean shirt, new pants, socks, shoes, a sweater, and one by one tossed them down into a pile on the stage. Then he drew out a series of large, black cloaks and added them to the pile. Then, tossing aside the satchel, he stood over the clothes, and spoke. "With all my powers, I gather you from the thin air. I call you down, out of smoke, out of flames, out of nothing, and command you to take shape." As he spoke he bent and picked up the black cloaks from the pile one by one, swirling them up before him and tossing them away. And with the last black cloak, swirled up and cast aside, there I lay, curled up on the floor, dressed in all the new clothes. I climbed to my feet, and Rudy embraced me, and the audience went wild.

As the tape flickered to black, Rudy nodded to himself. Then without a word he reached out, pressed the controls, and rewound the tape to the beginning.

"That's enough, Rudy," said Sisco gently.

"I need to see it, again."

"You don't need to. It went perfect."

"I want to be sure."

"It's not a good idea."

"One more time," Rudy said firmly, and he started through it again, murmuring along with the tape.

Sisco watched him for a moment, then he turned and wandered away. I got up and followed him off the stage. "What's the matter?" I said. "Why not see it again? It was pretty damned great."

"I don't like it," Sisco said. "Any of it. I been against this all along."

"Why? You saw it. It was terrific. It went beautifully. For a moment I thought I'd gone up in flames, myself."

He lowered his voice. "Don't you think it's just a little eerie?" he demanded.

"The audience loved it."

"I mean for him."

"For Rudy?"

"Don't you think?" Sisco looked at me. Tall, broad, bearded, hard as a hammer, he shook his head like a man who has heard the worst. "Given what happened, I mean?" I must have looked blank. "To his son?" he finished.

"His son?"

"He died."

"What?"

"Years ago. He was twelve; almost twelve, not quite. He was in their hotel room, asleep. It caught fire. There was nothing anyone could do. Nothing Rudy could do. He tried to go in after him, but they stopped him. He had to stand there and watch it burn."

I glanced up at the stage, where Rudy sat, staring at the screen. The videotaped flames crackled and leapt, and then died down as though on command. Their light painted his face and then dimmed.

"It was a long time ago," Sisco said. "I thought he put it behind him."

I stared at him a moment longer, then shook my head. "Is it so bad? Doing the trick?"

He shrugged. "Why put yourself through it again?"

And I had no answer for that. Not then. Magic was only a series of tricks to me then. And this was a particularly good one.

So we kept it, and the audiences continued to love it. But I never forgot the expression on Rudy's face the one time I saw it on that television screen, appalled, terrified, then gathering himself up and taking command—pulling the boy back out of nothing, out of flame and thin air. Reaching across all the years to save him. And gradually I understood that Rudy was putting it all behind him, or at least trying, the only way he could.

He couldn't make it disappear. It was years past and out of his reach. But he could change it, at least for a moment. If he had nothing else, he had the power to do that.

And maybe it was a little eerie. But after all, what's the good of magic if not that? Isn't that ultimately the point: to make the world the way we want it? To reshape it? To take everything, even the past itself, and give it a new, more merciful form?

I thought about that, every evening in Saratoga, every time we did the trick. I thought about it when Rudy died. And later, months later, when I stopped by my parent's attic to pick up the plywood box I'd built to saw Gracie in half all those years ago, I thought of it again. I'd never expected to see that box again, never thought I'd want to resurrect it. I'd given up on so much when I'd put it away. But now I thought about taking it out again. Paul Sisco was right. In the end it was all just illusion; the past remained unchanged. But as I thought about setting up my own magic cabinet in the auditorium of Shortfellows Playhouse, I wondered if there might not be some sliver of truth to the illusion. And like Rudy, if I couldn't change the past, perhaps I could finally at least put it behind me.

The Last Thing We Want

I began to stop by the theater most afternoons, getting there about three and staying as long as Emily did, usually into the night. What I did the rest of the day I no longer remember. I must have shopped and done my little store of laundry and cared for the rabbits. I didn't work. I still had a little money left over from Rudy and I lived on that, looking forward all day to the evenings. At Shortfellows I practiced until I got my timing back, and then I spent the time on other things. The magic cabinet had suffered a bit in the last seven years. There were repairs to be made; a new coat of paint. And then there were the props and scenery for Emily's show. We spent hours stretching and painting canvas, the large room grown cozy in the light of two floor lamps, the smell of paint and sawdust giving the air a close and friendly feel. In some ways it wasn't all that different from past summers: rehearsing, planning in the close, dusty air of an auditorium. Though in other ways it was very different. Less difficult. Less serious. More like high school theatre: lolling around, joking, talking desultorily as we worked. I felt like a teenager again, as if somehow I'd slipped back in time, stripping away the last seven years like a bad coat of paint.

"How long has it been since you've performed?" she asked one night.

"Mid-June. A couple of months."

"Do you miss it?"

"Parts of it. Rudy used to like performing almost as much as he hated small towns. It got to be a sort of contest. We'd pull into a particularly seedy town, and I'd just wait and see whether he'd make it on stage or not."

"What if he didn't?"

"It got so I could read the signs. I was usually ready."

"And if you weren't?"

"We had to cancel the show. I used to hate that."

"Professional pride? The show must go on... that sort of thing?"

"Not exactly. It almost always meant we had to find some other way to make our money. Which usually meant playing poker."

She glanced up, smiling. "What's the matter? You don't like poker?"

"Not this kind. High-stakes. Serious money. Very serious players. There wasn't a lot of room for error."

"Don't tell me you got nervous."

"Are you kidding? It scared the living shit out of me."

Rudy had been making this particular circuit through these towns and states for years, and he always knew where to find a game. But the problem was we never had enough time to rehearse, and the first time we tried it the audience didn't look like very good losers. There were four other men at the table. I don't know what Rudy had told them, but they seemed to think he was some sort of traveling salesman. They kept making jokes about lonely housewives and being run out of town, at least until the game settled down. After that, they barely spoke. Holyoke, Massachusetts was not much of a town, and this weekly game might have been the most important thing in it, at least to these four. It was seven-card stud. The betting went around five times per hand, and the pots tended to top out at five or six hundred dollars. I hadn't played much poker before.

"Maybe you shouldn't have done it," Emily said cheerfully, "if you were so nervous."

"You got that right. But Rudy thought it'd be good for me. And we always needed the money."

Rudy believed very strongly that a magician should have a second line of work. Something to protect him against the vicissitudes of the road. And after all, having worked so hard to develop our skills, he said, it would be a shame to waste them.

Which actually helped. Once I stopped thinking of it as a game of skill and started seeing it as a large and intricate card trick I was all right.

They were watching Rudy, of course. He couldn't look clumsy if he tried, and when he handled the cards his long and crooked fingers came alive. They moved within their own small field of grace and potential as if finally doing what they were supposed to. When he gathered up his hole cards, when he spread them on the table, even when he threw them in, he always looked like a man who might be up to something. So they kept their eyes on him.

And that was just fine. Every magic trick needs a moment when the gaze is trapped, when your eyes, which could go any-where, are drawn to one particular place. And at the moment you're looking there, of course, you're not looking anywhere else. No one was paying any attention to me.

My job was to control the deck. I had to keep track of the high cards, track their position, shuffle them, hide them, and then produce them on demand. It was a bit like picking a dozen peo-ple out of a crowd of fifty-two and keeping track of them for an entire evening. It required concentration. But there was a certain amount of incentive. At least two of the four men were wearing guns.

"Guns?" Emily burst out laughing. "You were cheating at poker against men wearing guns?"

"Does the name Nicky the Tick mean anything to you?"

She held a paintbrush in one hand, poised over the half fin-ished canvas. "Nicky the Tick?"

"I didn't learn his name until later. That wasn't exactly how he introduced himself. Carbone was his last name. Nick Car-bone. Apparently Mount Holyoke is a sort of junior farm team for the Providence mob. I'm not sure exactly what this guy did. I didn't ask. But I gather he was there in his private capacity. Just another citizen arriving for a friendly game."

"And the other gun?"

"An off-duty policeman named Frank."

"Frank the Tick?" she asked.

"Frank Carbone. I think they were brothers."

She laughed so hard the brush scattered droplets of chocolate colored paint across the half-finished scenery. "You're making this up."

"It was a very strange town."

"And you cheated these people?"

"For what seemed like days."

"And they let you walk away?"

"We didn't take much. We developed a good rule of thumb. If you're in a crowd like that, you don't want to walk away the big winner."

"You just want to walk away."

"Exactly. We had a plan. What you do is choose the toughest guy there and make sure he wins a lot more than you do."

"Just like that?"

"It takes a little work, but if you're careful you can manage it."

"So who did you decide? Frank or the Tick."

"There was a man called Mr. Regius."

"You're kidding."

"Believe me, there was no question about it. He was a union representative. The Teamsters, I think. He won twelve hundred dollars that night, and nobody made a peep."

"And you?"

"I lost twenty-five." She looked startled, and I smiled. "Rudy won four hundred and sixty. We left town the next morning."

I rarely ran into Kevin in those days, and that was fine. I had slowly come to believe that somehow I was working my way free of him. He never came by the playhouse, and I never looked him up. I began to think we could just go about our business and leave each other alone. I saw him occasionally in the Municipal Building, or on the streets, but I began to be less aware of him. Or rather I was more frequently aware of how little I was thinking about him, which I suppose, in retrospect, was not quite the same thing. Whatever plans he was making for his own version of urban renewal, whatever struggles were seething between Kevin and Hugh, went on in the deep subterranean recesses of their lives, and I ignored them. I thought that was all I needed to do. Which was ridiculous, really, at least in retrospect: a magician thinking that just because something was out of sight, it could be ignored.

I didn't see much of Wendy, either. When I couldn't sleep, or when I had an unwelcome evening to myself, I stopped into a bar named Dagmar's that a handful of Dewey Reynolds' reporters frequented just around the corner from the paper. It was clean and quiet, if a little impersonal. I never stayed very long. One night I came home to find a message on my answering machine. "Charles? What the hell? Is this your number? This is Wendy. I tracked you down. At least I think I did. Um. Hell of party. Remember? Kind of a long time ago." I think she was trying to sound jaunty. I could heard the sound of the television in the background. "I haven't seen you in the bar for a while. Give me a call, why don't you. Uh, Kamisky." And she spelled it for me, slowly, at first, and then about halfway through, as she began to get embarrassed, rushing to the end. "I'll see you around. Bye."

Occasionally Emily and I would order pizza or I'd bring chinese and we'd eat it as we worked, or take a break and have a picnic on the dusty floor of the large and empty room, and we'd tell stories as the night hovered beyond the windows. Each time seemed somehow accidental, as if we both just happened to end up there night after night. Other evenings Emily would leave shortly after the children. She'd disappear up to her office in leotard and shorts, and return in street clothes. She would smile and wave from the door, tell me to lock up when I left, tell me not to work too late. I tried not to think about where she was going.

I told myself it was none of my business.

"Big date?" I asked one night, early on.

"I'm just a social butterfly."

I drew a white cardboard carton from the bag in my arms. "I have Kung Pao Chicken, extra hot sauce."

"I can't."

"I'd hate to have to throw it in the river. Who knows what it would do to the aquifer."

She laughed. "Not even threats can sway me. I've got an appointment."

"So where's Kevin taking you?" I asked.

"No such luck. I'm just meeting some friends for a drink."

"Which friends? Is this Richard and Tina again? Another club meeting?"

"Maybe."

"That Richard didn't look like much of a drinker. A little too concerned with the environment to pollute himself."

She was grinning. "Who knows? He might surprise you."

I hesitated, marveling at the warm, proprietary feeling that had crept up on me over the last few weeks. "You remember what I said? About telling me, before you do anything?"

"Is that what you're doing here, Charles. Babysitting?"

I opened the carton of chicken. The aroma of spicy peanut sauce rose. "I haven't seen much of Kevin. I mean, around here."

"That smells good."

I held it out to her. She reached in with her fingers for a long piece of green pepper. "He's busy. I'm busy." Emily smiled wryly. "I think we're having a little spat." Then she popped it into her mouth, licking the sauce from her thumb.

"Too bad."

"No big deal. I happens occasionally. He thinks I'm unreasonable, I think he's unreasonable. It works itself out. " She shrugged. "The price of being with a mover and shaker, I guess."

"Who usually apologizes first?"

She considered that for a moment, as if it were something

she'd spent some time ruminating on. "I think," she said finally, "I have a larger sense of my own unreasonableness than he
does."

"Well, if it's any comfort, I think you're much nicer."

"Well, that's always a comfort." She helped herself to a piece
of chicken.

"You know," I said, watching her chew with a wry, distracted
expression, "maybe we could have a drink some time."

"You and me?"

"It's just a thought."

She hesitated, frowning down at the second little nugget of
stir-fried chicken, slippery with peanut sauce, poised in her fingers. The longer she held it the less appetizing it looked.

"Or not," I said.

She dropped it back into the carton. "You know, Charles. That
doesn't sound like such a great idea."

"No. Right."

"I mean.... I just don't think--"

"That's fine. I understand. It was just a thought," I said. "Really."

And she gave a tight and rueful little shrug.

Each night after she left I never stayed very long. I'd leave
and go out to a movie, or I'd go home and feed the rabbits, or
read, or make whatever little repairs needed to be done on the
equipment. And when the apartment inevitably began to feel too
empty I'd go out for a drive.

At first I drove anywhere, down vague curving roads through
the darkness, driving just to pass the time. The scenery blurred
past the windows. I drove all over the county, and at the end of
each night, when I got tired, when I could finally imagine sleeping, I drove past Emily's house. That was always the final point
on the long, wandering loop; it was always the point where my
path, however erratic, finally turned back. I would drive past the
gravel driveway, catch a glimpse of the ramshackle white house

with its bright blue roof, standing in an island of light; I'd catch sight of the grey Pontiac station wagon, solitary as a boulder, and with that small reassurance like a little trinket in my pocket, I'd drive home.

It wasn't that I spied on her, or even followed her, not after that first night. I didn't need to know what she was doing or where she was. I just needed to be sure where she wasn't. I suppose I could have achieved the same thing by staking out Hugh's house or his factory, but the fact was I didn't care so much whether Hugh was burglarized; I only cared that Emily didn't do it. And, in fact, it began to seem as if my preoccupation was protecting her, as if my presence was keeping her from harm in the same way carrying an umbrella might keep the rain from falling.

But then, one evening, Richard, the ecoterrorist, stopped by the playhouse, and Emily spent a long time up in her office. It didn't sound like a happy meeting. There were sounds of a long, wrangling argument. I crept part way up the stairs, until I could just make out the voices. "This is no longer a group project," Richard announced.

"Of course it is."

"It's beyond policy."

"This is exactly what we do."

"I'm not going to put this group at risk for your personal business!"

There was the sudden scrape of a chair, and I hurried back down to the auditorium so that I was sitting on one of my trunks shuffling a deck of cards when I saw him stomp down the stairs and out. A moment later Emily appeared.

She looked angry. "I've got to go," she said. "Something's come up. Lock the door when you leave, would you?"

I stood up. "Is everything all right?"

"Everything's fine," she said stiffly.

"You sure?"

"Don't work too late."

"Maybe you should stick around."

"I can't." And we both hesitated.

I should have said something more. She seemed to be expecting it. 'I don't want you to do anything stupid,' I should have said. 'I don't want you to take any chances. I don't want to see you go to jail,' I should have said all that. But I just stood there.

After a moment she nodded. "I'll see you, Charles." And out she went.

It was late. The sky was already dark as asphalt. I stood at the front door and waited until I saw the grey Pontiac drive past, then I jogged to my car.

The road to her house had grown familiar. I checked off the half-noticed landmarks as I drove: the fast food strip, the country fire station, the abandoned buildings of an old chicken ranch sagging into decay. I anticipated the curves the road would take, hurrying through each bend. There was no sign of her tail lights, just darkness ahead, and I had time to wonder if I had miscalculated. She would have to go home first, I told myself, if only to change. She must need equipment, help, something. She wasn't going to be on her own, was she? And I realized, with that thought, that I could no longer imagine Emily Burke breaking in anywhere. That image had faded over the last few weeks, until I could no longer place her at the scene of any crime. When I tried to, I could only imagine her in a leotard, or a t-shirt and shorts, or in overalls peeling away the darkness from her pale and glowing skin.

I pulled off the road just before her driveway, and crept up through the woods. The station wagon was there, and the lights were on in the house, upstairs and down. I started forward, ready to walk right up and knock on the door. No sneaking around, no spying. But what was I going to tell her? That this wasn't the best way, anymore? That breaking into Hugh's house or his factory wasn't going to solve anything? That I'd help her? That she didn't need Richard? That she didn't need anyone but me?

But as I crossed the yard, the pink-curtained glow from Emily's bedroom went out. I stopped and stood, waiting for another sign. Then after a moment there was a little flare of light deep in the room as she lit a candle. The glow flickered through the thin fabric. Then a shadow crossed the window, and Emily spread open the curtains.

I had no trouble seeing her, even in the dim light. She struck another match and lit a candle that must have been right on the window ledge. The warm glow rose up, washing over her, splashing across her face, across her pale shoulders, across her bare breasts. She stood there, just for a moment, leaning forward to smell the night air, to gaze out into the darkness. I was now creeping through the shadows beneath the trees, beyond the reach of the porch light, but as she leaned forward I stopped, staring up at her. And though I couldn't see her eyes, could barely see her face, there was something in the perfect stillness of her body that stilled me as well.

We stood, silent, with all the darkness between us. Then I started forward. And in that instant there was a vague movement in the background of her room, and another shadow shifted against the deeper darkness as someone stepped up behind her. Two hands appeared on her shoulders, tracing their way down her sides, cupping her breasts as if to lift them out of the light.

I froze, like one of those little plastic walking toys that hurries to the edge of the table and then runs out of momentum, looking out over the precipice and wondering how it got there. Beyond the Pontiac in the corner of the yard, hidden by shadows, another car stood parked, dark and shiny, and my very first thought was that it wasn't at all what I would have expected from someone like Richard. But then the man bent to Emily's throat, kissing her, drawing her back into the room. And I thought, at least that explained such a large and shiny car. It wouldn't have been Richard's style at all. A little too showy and out of his price range. But the mayor is supposed to have an expensive car. After all, he's an important guy.

It may be that who we are is decided at a level below anything we can reach. That what we do is beyond our control, and we're destined to go through the same things over and over again. Perhaps it isn't fate. Maybe it's personality. Maybe some of us are just made to be stupid. I climbed back into my car, which was neither shiny nor expensive, and drove away as fast as I could. And all the time I was thinking of Gracie, wandering up to the attic with her mind on anything but magic or me, with her mind on Kevin, in fact. And I thought of the darkness by the river bank the night I found them there. It seemed so stupid now. Why follow them? What did I think I'd learn that I hadn't already known? What did I hope to find? Not proof, certainly. It turns out proof isn't really what we're after. Not at all. Not even when we think it is. In fact, more often than not it's the very last thing in the world we want.

The White Eagle

The first thing I noticed when I stepped into the bar was the noise—Jimmy Page, again, louder than usual—and that dense, red, submarine glow that made you feel, with the first step inside, that you had already gone too deep. The place was jammed, hot and steamy, and everybody was moving, though there was no place to go. I squeezed my way to the bar and stood, wedged so tightly I could have lifted my feet off the ground.

Wendy was keeping busy. She wore her cap again, the snap brim riding low over the nape of her neck, and a baggy white t-shirt with the sleeves torn off. She was pouring a row of shots while keeping half an eye on the beer pitcher slowly filling under the tap, and as she set out the glasses she was regaling the hunched row of customers with that brusque and aloof amiability which is the sole property of a bartender near the end of her shift. Then she turned, flipped off the beer tap, and saw me.

She regarded me for a long moment, then lifted the full pitcher and set it down in the middle of the shots. She muttered something to the men, but all I heard was Robert Plant singing something which was itself incomprehensible. The men laughed and one of them, a round-headed biker, hoisted the pitcher as if he were prepared to drink it right down. Smiling gamely Wendy picked up a few bills from the bar and rang them into the cash register. Placing the change on the bar she shook a cigarette out of her pack, lit it, and then finally, as if it were the last thing on her list, turned and wandered over.

"What can I do for you?"

"Well," I said, "a drink would be nice." But she wasn't having any. She waited, with a stiff, impersonal expression. "Scotch, please. No ice. Soda on the side."

"Any particular kind? We're pouring Old Shit-for-Brains."

"That sounds about right. Better give me a big glass of that."

She squinted through the rising smoke, then took a deep drag on the cigarette and laid it in the ashtray, exhaling out of the corner of her mouth. She poured a shot of Dewars and set it on the bar, then carefully filled a side glass with warm soda up to the very brim. Then, as if it were all part of the same rhythm, she reached over and upended it down the front of my pants.

"Shit!"

"Oh," she said grimly. "I'm so sorry. That was clumsy. Please let me get you another."

I was glancing around for a napkin, but they all seemed mysteriously to have vanished. "Thanks," I said. "But just the one is fine."

She shrugged and set the empty soda glass before me. "That'll be three bucks."

People were peering over, wondering what they'd missed. On either side of me the bodies edged away, glancing warily down at the darkening stain seeping into my crotch. I held out a five. "I don't suppose I could have a napkin."

"There must be one around here somewhere," she said, but when she returned she had apparently forgotten it. She laid the change on the counter. My pants were clinging stiffly to my legs, and my underwear felt slack and clammy. Wendy picked up her cigarette.

"Busy night," I said.

"It's been busy the last few weeks."

I hesitated at her tone, caught for an instant in that little slough of bitterness that is the flip side of a bar's manic charm, then I took a sip of my drink. I waited for that old, familiar burn, but it felt as if my throat had gone numb except for a hollow ache of sadness too deep to reach. I emptied the glass in one rasping swallow and felt it catch on the way down, but now it was less a burn than a kind of sudden shiver that grew and blossomed and found its final expression in a fit of rich, tubercular coughing that left me hunched and rasping. It took a moment to catch my breath

"Real smooth," said Wendy.

Still gasping I held up the empty glass. She regarded it for a moment undecided, and then filled it in the spirit of someone pouring gasoline on the flames. Then turning, she strode over to the sink where she began furiously to wash glasses and stack them on the drying rack before her.

I watched her for a moment, waiting for her to turn or glance over, but she was consumed with cleanliness, so I drained the rest of my scotch, tough as a cowboy, and tried not to cough again as it caught in my throat. Then, eyes watering, I held up the glass. "Could I have a little service down here?"

She ignored me. I waved the shot glass back and forth, but I couldn't have caught her eye with a flare gun. The thin, bearded guy next to me looked over with an expression of mounting concern. Hurriedly he drained the last of his beer and, tentatively at first, began signaling as well. "Did I miss it? Is it last call?"

"Only for me."

"Miss?" he said more urgently. "Bartender?" But she didn't bat an ear. I suppose in the noise of the jukebox she couldn't differentiate his voice from mine. Finally he stood up and, with a grave and offended look, picked up his empty glass. "Jesus Christ, man. Don't you know enough not to piss off the bartender?" Hurriedly he worked his way to the other end of the counter and squeezed in again. Without a word Wendy interrupted her dish-washing to draw a fresh beer and set it in front of him, then returned to her sink.

The scotch was letting me down. I could usually count on it for a smile at least. Even when the show used to go down the toilet, or when there were so few people that we just returned their tickets and spent the night getting drunk, we'd finish up the evening laughing—hurt and furious and laughing our asses off. But tonight I couldn't find a laugh to save my life. "I could use a drink down here," I called and banged the glass on the scuffed Formica with its look of real wood. "I'm dying down here. Bartender? Does anyone know CPR?"

And I suppose it was possible, given the volume of the juke box, that she really didn't hear me, but then she lifted her hands out of the water, dried them off, and picked up the remote control, raising the volume on the television so that the barking voice of the basketball announcer filled any remaining gaps in the general noise. The thin, bearded guy at the other end of the bar raised his nearly full beer in an ironic toast. I still had my glass in my hand. I threw it. Well, more of a toss really. A gentle, arcing shot from just beyond the three-point line that bounced once on the stainless steel edge of the ice-bin and chunked into the sinkful of water.

Wendy whirled around. "What the fuck was that?"

"Just trying to get some service here."

She stalked over, wiping her hands on her shorts, and leaned over the bar. "You throw that fucking shit one more time, I'm going to call the cops. You got it?"

"I got it."

She thumped a fresh glass down and jerked the scotch out of its rack.

"I'm sorry," I said.

"Fuck you!"

"I am. Really."

"What you are really is a fucking asshole!" she snapped.

I waited, but with that she seemed to have shot her bolt. She stared at me for a moment, shaking her head at all the things she might say to me with complete justification, and then calmly she set the bottle of scotch down and filled a glass with soda. "Maybe you should slow down," she said.

"I don't think so." The burning in my throat was slowly diffusing into a warm and foggy feeling in my chest that I was prepared to interpret as comfort, and I didn't want to risk stopping now.

"You look like shit," she said.

"Thanks."

"Were you planning on calling me sometime?"

"Here I am."

"You sure are. Where the hell have you been?"

"Driving around."

"Just driving?"

"That's it." I took a sip of soda and put it down. "I think I'm going to have to trouble you for another drink."

She was leaning forward, one elbow on the bar, glaring at me from beneath her thick black eyebrows and thick black cap. "Why don't you make one magically appear?"

"I've just said the magic words. It doesn't seem to be working."

"Maybe it's because you don't have your lovely assistant."

I shook my head. "I work alone."

"Well, there's something new!"

"No. It's an old policy. Never underestimate the value of old policies." I peered up at her. "How about that drink?"

She snatched the bottle out of its rack and poured a generous slug into my glass. Then, turning, she rang it up, slapped the ticket down beside it, and stalked off.

I sipped the scotch, but I'd been drinking too much too fast, and it was having no effect at all. I thought of Emily standing at her window with the candlelight washing over her breasts and Kevin's hands moving so surely over her. And I thought of Emily standing like a vision by the pond in the lamplight before disappearing in front of me eyes. And I was cursing myself. I should have known at the time it was just an illusion. After all those years on the road, I should have known the difference between what's real and what isn't.

Wendy was at the beer tap, filling a pitcher, but she was glancing back at me now, even as she kept an eye on the rising foam.

"How's your mother these days?" I asked.

She eyed me suspiciously. "She's okay."

"I wanted to apologize," I said. "To her. And to you."

"Is that right?"

"I shouldn't have just left like that."

"Gosh," she said, "do you think so?" But she seemed to have lost the sharpest edge of her anger. She slapped at the tap, shutting off the beer. "So, is that why you came in tonight? To apologize?"

"More or less."

"How much less?" she asked.

"Can I buy you a drink?"

"No." She turned and carried the pitcher to some more deserving soul at the other end of the bar. But when she returned she seemed hesitant, uncertain, without the organizing force of her anger. She picked up a rag and gave the counter a listless wipe. "You know, you could have stayed. The other night, I mean. It wouldn't have killed you."

"I know. I was a little freaked out."

She frowned. "I guess I didn't mention I lived with my mother, did I?"

"No. I don't think you did."

"It's just temporary. You know. She likes having me around."

"That's good. It's nice that you get along."

"Yeah. She's all right."

"I could never live with my mother," I said. "You've seen her. We'd gnaw each other to death like weasels. Or worse."

"What could be worse?"

I smiled weakly. "We wouldn't. And I'd grow up to be exactly like her. Like both of them."

"Oh, come on, Charles!," she said, suddenly angry again. "Why is that such a problem?"

"You've seen them."

"Yeah, I've seen them. Big house, nice furniture, nice clothes. Pretty shitty all around!"

"You said you hated their clothes."

"Hey. All I said was I wouldn't be caught dead in them."

"Well. Neither would I."

"So what was that all about then? That whole party?"

I hesitated. "Just a party. I was invited."

"So don't go. You're a big boy. Tell them to go fuck themselves. Or is that what I was doing there?"

"I thought you'd like it."

"Bullshit, Charles. Was I just the big fuck you, you couldn't say yourself?"

"No. I didn't want to go alone. Is that such a crime?"

"Listen, Charles. I'm nobody's fuck you but mine. You got it?"

"I got it."

She leaned forward. "So, fuck you." But she said it almost gently.

I peered up at her for a moment. "Come home with me," I said.

"Forget it."

"Please."

"Why should I?"

"Because," I said. But I could think of no other reason. She was staring at me. "Because I want you to. I really, really do."

Wendy gazed at me for a long moment as if the very foolishness of the third-grade diction gave the words their own earnest weight. "Who are you trying to fuck, Charles? Me or your family?"

I thought of Emily, leaning toward the open window, a perfect picture in the candlelight except that there were too many hands. "You," I whispered hoarsely. "Just you."

She seemed pleased by the flight of rickety steps leading up to the apartment. I don't know what she was expecting, but she smiled when she saw them and nudged one crooked riser. "Nice stairs. Sure they won't collapse?" And when she stepped into the kitchen she laughed. "Whoa! Do your parents know you're living like this?"

"What are you talking about? It's a perfectly nice place."

"You've got no fucking furniture."

"That's not true. There's a sink. A refrigerator. I've got a bathtub."

"That's not furniture. Those are appliances."

"A sink's not an appliance."

"Well, it sure as hell isn't furniture. Don't you have anything else?"

She spoke with the bright and exaggerated carelessness that always marks the nervous end of a late night, and I stood aimlessly in the middle of the kitchen. My mouth felt dry, even after all that scotch, and there was an uncertain, fluttery feeling in my stomach. "I've got a bed," I replied.

"Well," she said, "that's something."

She wandered out into the living room. "Jesus Christ. It's a fucking petting zoo."

"Keep your hands and feet away from their mouths," I called. "I haven't fed them yet today."

"Are you kidding? It's the middle of the night. They must be starving."

"How many are there?"

There was a moment's pause. "Six."

"Okay. Good. They haven't started eating each other yet."

I followed her out. She was standing at the low fence gazing down at the rabbits, with an expression of hesitant unease, looking suddenly awkward and off-balance. But who am I to criticize? She was standing in a strange living room in the middle of the night without any real place to sit down and with half a dozen sleepy rabbits shuffling over their newspapers. I suppose she was doing pretty well. But I was suddenly aware that Kevin would have no wildlife roaming around, and that Emily, when she invited someone up, would not have to worry about the faint, acidic odor of rabbit pee and wet newspaper.

"Do you ever let them out?" asked Wendy.

"We go to the park sometimes, but they don't do any more than they do here. They eat and sleep."

"Doesn't sound like much of a life."

"It's all what you get used to." But it made me wonder what it meant that the rabbits, given all the possibilities of a new setting and all the freedom of an open field, did nothing at all about it. As if even the hope for change was illusory.

Wendy turned and stepped up close. "You think your friends will mind if we move into the next room?"

"I think we're probably just keeping them awake anyway."

"Good." She took my hand.

The bedroom was blue. A gloomy blue. The walls were mottled and cold, and even in the hottest part of the summer the room never warmed up. There was a mattress on the floor and a thrift-store lamp in the shape of a gumball machine on a packing case beside it. Beyond that, the decorating urge had abandoned me. I clicked on the lamp, and Wendy glanced around. The lampshade was yellow, with red and blue gumballs, and the bulb glared brightly through the top. "I don't suppose you have any candles?"

"I haven't been entertaining all that much."

She stepped over to the lamp. Reaching down for the hem of her t-shirt, she snaked it up and over her head. It was a familiar movement, arms stretched high, body curved like a bow. I had seen it before. Wendy's t-shirt snagged a little on the brim of her cap, but she managed to get it off with the cap still in place. Then she bent and draped the shirt on the lamp. The glare dimmed to twilight. Her skin turned shadowy and pale, anchored by the black margin of her bra.

"That's better," she said.

"Won't it burn?"

She smiled, knowing better than to answer. Instead she sidled up to me, easing so close we stood all but touching. She smelled of cigarette smoke and sweat. Then, reaching up she started unbuttoning my shirt. Her fingertips, at odds with the warm scent of her body, were cool against my chest. She tugged the shirttails free.

"I bet you want to kiss me," she said.

"How did you know?"

I kissed her, running my hands up her arms, and as I did, I had the sudden image of other hands reaching out of the darkness into candlelight. Her skin was cool and smooth. If you closed your eyes, did all flesh feel the same, or could the fingertips, all by themselves, distinguish? She reached behind her back, elbows bent like a pair of wings, and the smooth satin of her bra collapsed, sliding forward off her shoulders and down her arms.

I whispered, "Your mother's not hiding in the kitchen, is she?"

"I guess you won't know for sure until you try to fuck me." She smiled puckishly, but the word jarred against the silence. And later, when she was hunched forward, straddling my hips, with her hands gripping the pillow on either side of my head, she bent low and whispered, "You're not going to make me sorry, Charles, are you?"

It caught me by surprise. "No," I said with a start. "I promise." But even as I said it I felt a vague foreboding, as if, even then, I should have known better. She pressed her face against my throat so that her voice rose to me, muffled and soft. "Tell me you like me, Charles," she said. "Tell me you do."

Breaking In (part two)

You're not going to make me sorry, are you?
What was I thinking? What could I say?
No. I promise.

I meant it, of course. In some ways I still mean it, long after the worst has happened and any possibility of keeping my word has long come and gone. I spoke with an ardent sincerity that grew as much from my own best intentions as from the silky, smooth compulsion of the moment, but still, I should have known better. You should never make a promise you can't keep. And after all, has there ever been anybody I loved who wasn't eventually sorry?

The sound of her voice followed me throughout the next day. When I thought of her it wasn't the slow, demanding heft of her body—hesitant at first, then growing both more pliant and more ardently peremptory—but the knowledge that, in the end, the only thing a promise gives voice to is what's most fragile and exposed in our lives. It was the promise more than anything else that left me uneasy and distracted like someone waiting for the moment when disaster comes due. It's like performing a trick when you know you haven't practiced enough. You walk through it, step by step, trying your best and just waiting for the botched and stuttered pass or the buzz of disappointment that marks the moment of discovery.

I stepped into the bar early the next evening, before the rush but just after what appeared to be an entire men's softball team, complete with jerseys, gloves, and white stretch pants, trooped in. They filled the place, laughing and waving their mitts and clamoring for beer. Wendy was working hard, setting out glasses, filling pitchers. She didn't see me come in. I eased past the boys of summer and slipped into a corner booth, turning to watch her work. She was joking with them, teasing and laughing, hefting the full pitchers and ringing up the tab. I tried to see if there was some new spring in her step, some new sense of lightness, but I couldn't tell. A whole forest of money appeared, fluttering from raised hands, and she plucked the bills like leaves. I was aware of the small and sudden urge to stand up and leave, to ease my way out under cover of all that activity. It wasn't anything sharp or definite. It was more an almost tangible sense of what it would be like to step out the door and walk away. It wasn't anything I wanted to do, exactly. It didn't even form a complete thought. But I was aware of a faint ribbon of unease unfurling in my chest when the team settled down, sitting on their stools, pouring their beers, and Wendy looked up and saw me.

She smiled, more to herself than to me, and came wandering over with an empty tray and a cloth to wipe the table. It was a warm night. She wore a pair of yellow and black Bermuda shorts hanging down to her knees and a baggy white tank top that focused all attention on the scarlet bra beneath. Her eyes still had that dark smudged look, but her lips were thinner than I'd expected. I remembered them feeling so full. That made me think I should probably stand and kiss her, but then I wasn't sure about workplace etiquette, and I couldn't tell from her smile if she expected it, or would even enjoy it. I felt awkward and uncertain. But just as I was deciding, she bent and kissed me lightly on the lips, and then stood, gazing down at me with a fond and patronizing look. "You're here early."

"Aren't you going to ask me what you can get for me?"

"What can I get for you?"

"I like that shirt."

She plucked at the baggy fabric and glanced down musingly at the brightly visible bra. "Is that right?"

"I thought this place'd be empty."

"And what if it was?"

"Has anyone ever told you you've got great lips?"

"Great shirt. Great lips. I must be really something," she said, but she was smiling still.

"You want to sit down?"

"I'm working." But she slid onto the bench across from me.

"I was thinking maybe on this side."

"Is that what you were thinking?" She gave the table top a quick wipe with her cloth, brisk and businesslike.

"I was thinking you've been working way too hard. Maybe you need to take some time off."

"Do you think?"

"Can I buy you a drink?"

"You can buy yourself one. Then I can get back to work."

"What about later?"

"What about it?" she said. She eased out of the booth and ran her cloth once more over the table.

"You do run a clean place," I said.

She leaned forward through the noise, her elbows on the bar. "And I've got a great shirt," she said. The loose, cotton neck gapped wide.

"Yes, you do."

"Tell me about my lips again."

"Great lips."

"That's right." She was smiling as she turned away. "Dewars straight up, soda on the side?"

"What makes you think so?"

"I get off at twelve," she called back over her shoulder. "I generally go straight home."

I stayed for as long as I could. But as the bar grew more crowded and the noise rose, the idea of sitting and drinking for five hours seemed unutterably grim. After the last few weeks of rehearsals at the theatre, the evening stretched out before me, long and dreary. I thought about all the magical props, spread out in that vast, empty room, ready and waiting, and I wondered what I was supposed to do. The prospect of performing with Emily had taken on its own bleak and sour aspect after the other night's revelations. But it seemed strange even to consider not working; and after all, I had promised. At the same time I wondered if this wasn't all some kind of a sign. Maybe this empty and ragged feeling was just another way of saying it was time to pack it in. Maybe it was time to admit that magic had never brought me anything in the end but unhappiness.

I waved at Wendy on the way out. She was in the middle of a crowd of needy drinkers, but she waved back and pointed to her watch. Twelve o'clock, she mouthed. I stepped out into the muted darkness and walked to my car. I drove towards home.

Hours later I was still driving, winding my way down the curving roads, past the Shop'n'Save, past the firehouse. I was just driving, I told myself. I didn't have any plans. And in fact that proved to be perfectly true. When I sailed round that last bend and coasted past the gravel gap in the trees, I saw nothing but a dark house and an empty driveway enclosed in the silent woods. I stopped, but for no good reason, and after a moment staring at the empty silence I drove on again with even less of a purpose. So that, when the pale lattice of my parents' old white fence appeared suddenly out of the darkness it looked so definite and familiar, so precisely a part of my life, that it seemed like the answer to something. I pulled off and cut the engine. It was late, and all the houses were dark. The whole street had long ago given up on the day. I opened the door, and the dome light came on, much too bright. I switched it off and sat there in the darkness with all the old sounds and scents drifting in through the open door alongside the faint, settling creak of the hot engine.

I thought about that morning long ago, wandering from the bus station to this house as if pulled by the long, uncoiling wire of the past. And now here I was again. I'd been in such a hurry to leave. What did it mean that I kept being drawn back? Reaching over I lifted the bottle of scotch from the seat beside me. It was unopened. I'd picked it up somewhere on my travels, and so far I'd just been carrying it around. I decided to carry it a little further, and climbed out of the car. Behind the fence the row of rhododendrons had spread into an almost solid wall, though the gap was still there if you knew where to find it.

When I was growing up we'd had three enormous elm trees, two and a half feet thick and taller than the house. They'd arched over the back yard, blocking out the sky, and on summer evenings I used to sit at the base of one in particular and gaze down the hill at all the plantings and rooftops of the neighborhood descending the shallow slope. In those days I could look down through the smaller trees and see one large white and brick house standing out from the others, and I could see the bedroom window where Gracie used to send Morse code messages by flashing her lights on and off. The messages weren't big on content. It's not as if we didn't talk every day, and by nightfall there wasn't much more to be said. But it was the attempt itself, all that effort to say something like 'good night' or 'brush your teeth' or 'over and out,' that made it worthwhile. The fact of the message rather than its content.

But the three old elms had died in the late eighties and, as if to take up this sudden extravagance of space, all the other trees in the neighborhood had grown together, hunching around the houses, obscuring them, so that now, when I sat on the grass and looked down the hillside, all I could see in the moonlight was the faint hint of a pale grey rooftop peering out from behind the encroaching leaves.

There was a rustle in the grass behind me. It could have been the breeze, or a raccoon; it could have been Wendy wondering what I was doing or Emily coming to tell me she was sorry for having let me down. I turned.

"That was always your favorite spot, wasn't it?"

Ambrose stood beside me, gazing over my head into the darkness. He sipped from a mug of coffee, steaming in the cool air.

Figure it out. It was an hour when all the world was drinking hot milk or cocoa or scotch, and Ambrose drank coffee. I'd forgotten that about him.

"I seem to keep coming back," I said.

"It's your home."

"I don't think that's why. Do you suppose it's just a rule of the universe? You keep trying to make a new start for yourself, but every step away just seems to bring you back to all your worst fears."

I thought he'd laugh or shake his head in angry impatience, but he stood, considering that for a moment. "I used to come out here sometimes," he said, "when you were gone. I'd come out and sit right here and wonder how you were."

"How I was?"

"What you were up to. You were always pretty independent, but sixteen isn't very old."

"I was seventeen."

"Sixteen, when you left. A week before your birthday."

"Oh. Right."

He glanced down at the bottle nestled in the grass beside me. "Having a drink?"

"Thinking about it. But it hasn't been doing all that much for me lately."

"I brought some coffee." And he held up his other hand with a second mug steaming gently. "Milk no sugar. Is that still right?"

"Thanks. Perfect."

"It's decaffeinated."

I took the mug. It was too hot to drink, so I just held it.

"I saw your car light," he said. "Thought I might take the opportunity...." From his pocket he drew a small package. It had been neatly gift wrapped once, a long time ago, but now it had the rumpled look of something put away in a drawer for a while.

There was a card, one of those little tags supplied by gift wrappers. I opened the paper carefully, prying up the old tape, pealing it back. There was a plastic box. I opened the top and there was a wrist watch: gold dial, gold band, gold numbers. It was no longer running. Seven years of waiting was more than it could stand. I looked at the card: So you'll be on time to all your classes, and not oversleep on that first day of Law School. I stared down at it.

"I wasn't sure what to get you," he said finally.

"This is nice."

"I know you've already got a watch."

I turned it over in my fingers. It felt cool and durable. As if it could wait seven years and still need only the tiniest help to start working again. I checked my own watch, that old Timex of Rudy's. So much time, so little to do. Eleven thirty. Where did the evening go?

"It might need a new battery," Ambrose said.

"That's probably it."

He stood there a moment longer.

"I like it," I said.

"I'm glad. Do you mind?" He settled a little awkwardly onto the grass beside me. "How is everything?"

And it seemed so like my father to use just that phrase. "Everything?" I said. "Actually everything's not all that great."

"Where have you been tonight?"

"Nowhere in particular. I didn't want to go out. Didn't want to stay home. I wasn't sure where that left me."

"Here, I guess." He sipped his coffee, looking out into the darkness.

"It's a pretty view," I said. "I mean, in the daytime. At least it used to be."

My father smiled. "I always wondered about that. I used to look out the bedroom window, all those years ago. See you sitting here in the evenings, just staring. I used to wonder what you were looking at, what you saw. After you left, I used to come down with my coffee, just to sit. I looked around at the trees and the houses that I'd been seeing more or less all my life. I realized I hadn't the slightest idea how it looked to you."

I glanced up at him, surprised and a little touched that he would even have given it any thought. "How about Kevin?" I asked. "Did you ever wonder how it looked to him?"

"No. I never did. I thought I had a pretty good idea about Kevin. But you..." He hesitated for a moment. "I watched you once, when you were a little kid, practicing some card trick."

"When?"

"A long time ago. I climbed up to the attic. It was lunch time. I was going to call you, but I just stopped at the top of the stairs and watched. You didn't see me."

"No."

"I must have stood there twenty minutes. You did the same thing over and over again. Something with a card. I couldn't see what, exactly. But I watched your face. You were twelve years old. Staring down at that card. Flipping it between your fingers. The same thing, the same movement, over and over again." He shrugged. "In the end I decided you'd get your own lunch when you wanted it."

"I was trying to make it disappear," I explained.

"All that effort."

"It's not easy."

My father shook his head, all those years of something almost like wonder sounding in his voice. "You were such a tough little kid, Charles. All that concentration. I used to admire it. I used to think you'd go far."

"I did. I went far."

"And was it worth it? All that work?"

I thought of all those years of practice. The same movement, over and over again, until it becomes second nature, until it's as if your hand can move only in that way and there's no possibility of a mistake. But then one day you find out you've been doing the wrong trick all along, and there's no way to change.

The silence stretched out. After a while my father stood up. He tossed the last of his coffee out onto the grass and reached down for my mug. "Well. Just wanted to say hello."

"Thanks for the coffee," I said. "And the watch."

"I'm trying to understand, Charles."

"I know. Me, too."

He stood there, looking out over the slope of the hillside dropping away into darkness. "I'm beginning to see what you like about this view. It is peaceful. You can't see all that much, but still. It kind of grows on you." He hesitated, and I thought he might be about to say something more, but with the faint, phantom touch of his fingers in my hair he turned and wandered back over the lawn.

I glanced down the hillside toward the roof of the Barker's house just barely visible, a lighter smudge in the darkness. My father was certainly right. You couldn't see much. Gracie's window was hidden now. Between the trees and the blackness it was gone. But neither the night nor all the time that had passed could ever make it peaceful. It was a view that grew on you, but not in the way he meant. Each time I looked, all I could see was a house poised beneath the shadow of disaster. Smoke signals gone awry. Cries for help no one could hear. It was a house where lives unraveled. And what did it say about me, that it kept drawing me back?

It's a five-minute run down the hill, ten minutes if you're no longer in any hurry. You take a path across the lower potion of the hillside, then through a gate into another back yard, around a rose garden and past a garage. Then you cross the street and follow the hedge along a curving driveway into the wide darkness and follow the last of the slope down to the house at the very bottom.

In Hugh's yard I settled onto the ground beneath a huge and crooked oak and gazed up at the house, which I could see very clearly now. But even up close, hunched in the darkness, I couldn't be sure whether I was looking into the past or the present. I thought of Emily. Without even closing my eyes I could picture her still, framed in her bedroom window. I wondered what she'd been thinking, what exactly had been going through her mind. Though what could be more stupid? I mean, what did it matter, what she was thinking, when what she was doing was so clear? I thought of Wendy, looking up at the clock over the bar, now, wondering where I was. I tried to imagine what she'd think if I didn't go back there, if I didn't go home at all, if I just got on the bus and left. If we're creatures of our mistakes, does that mean we have to make them over and over?

I was so lost in my thoughts I didn't notice the car at first, and even when I did, it took me a moment to make sense of it. There was nothing particularly remarkable, a black car gleaming in the moonlight, except that it seemed so solid: the one stark and determined idea in an otherwise hazy darkness. It drove past slowly and pulled off onto a stretch of grass beneath an enormous maple tree. Out of reach of the moonlight, the solid black became a shadow. There was the muffled thump of a door closing, and after a moment a smaller shadow detached itself from the larger: a single figure, dark as the night, wearing clothes I'd seen before, hanging on the back of a door. A black turtleneck, black jeans, a black cap gathering up her hair. She hesitated at the edge of the road, though there wouldn't be another car along till morning, then started across, slipping through the shadows toward the house.

I stood up. The car hadn't moved. The low idle of the engine blurred into the murmuring background. The grass under my feet felt spongy, and the night itself had turned suddenly vague and unstable, as if on the verge of almost anything. I wondered if any of this was really happening, if I wasn't just imagining this once again. But Emily was at the house now. She paused at the brick wall beneath the double windows of Hugh's second floor study. I thought of those windows all those years ago, opened wide to let the smoke out as Gracie huddled inside desperate to be saved. Emily stared up at them, a blur of darkness against the brick. She hesitated, and I wondered for a moment if she could see in them everything I could, if the weight of all that had already happened was slowing her to a stop.

But, of course, it wasn't memory that gave her pause. It was only the height of the wall. And after a moment, without a sound, she started to climb. The brick was rough and uneven, with plenty of finger- and toe-holds if that's what you were looking for, and as children we'd climbed it often. But never very high, and never at night, and never with the police just one mistake away. As she reached the second story I held my breath. I could have warned her. I could have rushed over, calling hoarsely through the silence, waving her away, but instead I stood there waiting for the siren or the bells or the flashing lights, for whatever would come when she set off the alarm. But she reached out for the screen—and nothing happened. Nothing at all. Before my astonished eyes, she slid the window open and after a difficult, unsteady moment, shifted her grip on the sill and climbed right in.

I stared. It was against all reason. Where were the sirens? Where were the lights? But then I remembered what Dewey had said: that Hugh tended to get up at night, that he never armed the alarm on the second floor for fear of accidents. I turned. There was Kevin, sitting in the comfort of his large black car. Inside the house Emily moved silently, everything going according to plan.

I was suddenly furious. Furious with Kevin for sitting there so calmly. Furious with Emily for so much more... for trying this again, for not leaving Hugh alone, for breaking the law, for none of those things. For risking so much once again for Kevin. I felt the fury like a bubble in my chest. I looked around. I was standing by a garden bed, neatly weeded and edged with stone. I reached down and wrested from it a chunk of granite the size of my fist. Then I ran stiffly and unsteadily down the sloping yard and threw it through the nearest first floor window.

That did the trick. The floodlights came on. A siren started wailing. I ducked back into the shadows, trying to catch my breath, trying not to be appalled by what I'd done. The yard was lit up. The air shivered with sound. Out of the corner of my eye

I saw the sleek black car come to life like a startled animal. The headlights came on, and Kevin accelerated smoothly, almost silently away, slipping beyond the reach of the noise and glare.

Inside the house, as well, the lights were coming on in the bedroom at the far end of the second floor, and at the same moment Emily squirmed halfway out of the study window. She hesitated for a moment. There wasn't much of a ledge, and it's always harder to climb down than up. The alarm was throbbing. The patio stood out clearly beneath a pair of floodlights. And in the middle of it all, Emily was alone: a hard, dark shadow moving much too slowly down the brick wall. I stood, staring. Other lights were coming on, room by room, moving toward her, but she had stopped, halfway down, hunched awkwardly against the wall, struggling for a foothold.

I sprinted across the yard to the patio. "They're coming!"

She looked down, too desperate to be surprised. "I'm stuck!"

"You're not stuck! There's a foot hold. Right there."

"Where?"

"Your left foot!"

"Where?"

"Forget it! Jump!"

"I can't!"

"There's no time!"

"No!"

"Jump!"

She didn't jump so much as slip, though at the last minute she pushed herself away from the wall. I was under her. I tried to catch her, to steady her as she landed, but she came down hard.

"Ah!" Her voice was sharp in my ear.

"Come on!"

I had my arm around her, turning her, but she caught her breath in a sudden hiss. "My ankle!"

Abruptly the alarm stopped, cut like a ribbon, and in the stark silence her breathing was loud and rough. She wrapped one arm around my neck and started forward, her voice catching with every step.

"Not the street," I said. "Up the yard."

"I've got a car."

"No, you don't."

And only then did she notice how empty the place beneath the tree had become. In that moment the faint, distant thread of a police siren began drifting toward us.

We started up the hill, wrapped in shadows, but with the siren winding closer. We were panting with the effort. "You're doing fine."

"They're coming."

"It's just a little further. Just up the hill."

We crossed by the curving driveway and staggered through the darkness of the next yard, then started up the long slope. It was so much longer than I remembered, and I couldn't imagine how the police could take so much time just to get to Hugh's house. The town wasn't that big. But we were all trapped in the same slow and desperate motion.

Emily and I reached the top of the hill clamped together tightly, struggling for breath. My parent's house stood, large and strange, in the darkness. "What now?" she said, gasping.

"My car."

The level ground was easier than the hill. We stumbled across the yard towards the road and squirmed out through the hedge and the old, familiar white fence. It was my childhood all over again, but a tighter fit, this time, and a police siren wailing through it.

The Audience Will Be Disappointed
If There Isn't a Certain Amount of Blood.

"What's the bravest thing you've ever done?" asked Emily.

We were sitting together, shoulder to shoulder, on the rough wooden porch of her house bathed in the harsh glare of a bare yellow bug light. Her ankle lay propped on a pillow before us, wrapped in a thick bundle of ice and bandages.

"Nothing," I said. "I've never done anything brave."

"Have you ever run away from anything?"

"Everything. Everything I could."

"Not tonight," she said.

"No."

We sat, staring straight ahead as if still in my car, still driving away through the darkness with the sirens weaving a distant knot behind us. She was sitting so stiffly, so hunched with tension, that I knew her mind was miles away, stalking over its own uneven terrain, and I was wondering what she was thinking. It could have been about anything, but I wanted it to be me.

"He had to leave like that," she said suddenly, her voice bright and unconvincing. "We made it part of the plan."

"Is that right?"

"It's no good both of us getting caught. And we decided it would be easier, if something happened, to try to get away on foot." She was working doggedly, spinning out all the excellent reasons. "There are lots of trees. Lots of places for one person to hide. But we couldn't risk that car being seen. It just made sense to split up…." Her voice faded away. The fact of how it had all turned out seemed to startle her, and she sat there, awkward and hanging on the silence.

"So you two thought it through?"

"That's right."

"What a great plan."

She stared down at her bandaged ankle and beyond it at the scuffed and patchy grass of the yard, imagining perhaps what Kevin was looking at now, or what the view would have been from a holding cell down at the police station. She had changed out of her basic black. She was wearing overalls and a t-shirt and the bandage on her leg.

"You sure you don't want to go to the emergency room?" I asked again.

She shook her head. "It's a little suspicious, don't you think?"

"Just one more ankle in a whole room full."

"Not tonight."

"Doesn't it hurt?"

"Not enough to go to jail for."

I hesitated. "I don't know all that much about sprained ankles. Do they get better by themselves?"

"I guess we'll find out." In the terrible yellow light her face was pinched, her hands were clenched in her lap. She was sitting up straight, gingerly balanced, as if the only thing holding her together was the binding force of those two clenched fists. "You should probably just get going," she said.

"There's no rush."

"I'm okay."

"I know. But I've got some time."

I wanted to reach out and slip my arms around her. I wanted to soothe that bleak look out of her eyes. But I leaned back, peering out into the vacant, deceptive calm of the night. Beyond the range of the bug light the woods were hidden in darkness, and anything at all could be happening. It was like an ocean of black possibility. And I wondered, with a little rush of perception, if it wasn't in the moments between our intentions, the moments squeezed out of events against our will and against all likelihood, that we found the true course of our lives. If it wasn't always the accidents that directed our steps, in the face of all good planning and intention. I felt a wild and rising weightlessness at the thought of just how much is out of our control, and how that alone can sometimes carry us along.

"You know," I said, "it could be this isn't such a bad thing. I mean, I know it hurts, but think what good training it is. After all, if I'm going to saw you in half, you need to learn how to handle a certain amount of pain. And of course, it's nice to know you don't bleed excessively."

She glanced over. "Is that right?" And after a long moment she smiled. Reluctantly, a little crookedly, but still....

"The audience is always disappointed if there isn't a certain amount of blood, but nobody wants to go overboard."

She regarded me hesitantly. "So, we're still on for that? I wasn't sure."

"The cabinet's just about ready. A few adjustments and we can start rehearsals. If you still feel like being sawn in half."

"Actually," she said wanly, "I feel like that right now."

The smile hadn't lasted very long. She was staring out into the clearing again, grim-faced and bleak, thinking about that jail cell, maybe, or thinking about Kevin. I just sat there with my hands half-raised in a helpless, unfinished gesture. "Are you going to be all right here? Up and down the stairs?"

"I'll be fine."

"I mean, I could stay, if you needed me. If there's anything I could do."

"I'll be fine."

"You should probably lie down. Get some sleep."

"I will."

"When?"

"Soon." She glanced up again. "Scout's honor."

I hesitated. "Don't worry," I said.

"About what?"

"About anything." And it sounded so much like something my father would say that it almost made me smile. Was this what it was like for him all those years? Standing by eager, heartfelt, and completely in the dark. Wanting to offer some kind of comfort or support, and having no idea how to manage it.

Emily nodded tiredly. She was looking out at the night, the driveway, the vague trees in the distance, as if daring the whole fixed scene to do something, as if waiting for it to change.

I followed her gaze, but I didn't see anything. Then, with a little start, I realized what she was waiting for, and I felt a sharp twist of disappointment. "Kevin's coming over, isn't he?"

She hesitated, shrugged. "I don't know. Yes. Probably."

Of course. What was I thinking? All those vague comforting thoughts seemed suddenly foolish and juvenile. What was I, in fourth grade? Was I planning to carry her books home, buy her a malted at the Soda Shoppe? Whatever it was that I could offer, it was clearly not what she was counting on, even now. Reluctantly I stood up. "Okay, then."

But as if to prove our thoughts and desires are never as clear-cut as we imagine, Emily laid a hand on my arm. "I'm sorry."

"About what?"

"I don't know...Things. I don't know."

"Forget it."

I started to draw away, but her grip tightened on my arm. "I have a question," she said. "You don't need to answer."

I smiled wanly. "It's probably yes."

"Don't be so sure."

"I'm pretty sure."

"Would you have driven away like that?"

I gazed down at the hand clenched around my wrist. She'd scraped a knuckle in falling, and though she'd washed it, the blood was seeping back over the pale, shredded skin. "I'm not a good person to ask," I said. "I tend to run away at the drop of a hat."

"Just answer yes or no."

"I thought I didn't have to answer at all."

Her fingers tightened. "He couldn't take a chance on being caught," she said pleadingly. "It would have ruined everything. And he knew, even at the worst, nothing really terrible would happen to me."

She had a strong grip. The blood was pulsing in my wrist. "Then what are you asking for?" I said.

"Yes or no."

"It doesn't matter. You said so yourself: when you love him, you love him. When you hate him, you still love him."

"Just tell me."

"What? Would I have driven away? Would I have gone off and left you hanging there all by yourself?"

"Yes."

"No," I said. "Not on your life. Not in a million years."

She let go of my wrist. "Okay, then," she said. "Okay."

I drove home through the darkness, listening for any hint of trouble, any sound of alarm, but everything was quiet. There was no one out on the street at that hour. No sign of movement. Everybody was asleep. Turning onto Stack Street past the school on the corner, the only lights I saw were my own. The windows of my apartment glowed like a lantern above the sidewalk, and though I didn't remember leaving a lamp on, I was grateful for it now. Fatigue was like a blanket over my head, and there was a sharpening ache in my shoulder from when Emily had fallen out of the sky on top of me. I tried to picture her now. Hobbling up the stairs, easing the overalls down over her iced and bandaged foot, stretching out on the bed, waiting. I could imagine the ache in her ankle, but try as I might I couldn't be sure what else she was feeling.

The porch stairs were in darkness, and I climbed slowly, carrying the still-unopened bottle of scotch like an anchor in my arms, feeling for each uneven step. I marveled at the quiet. After all the uproar earlier in the evening, the silence itself seemed remarkable. But at the landing I turned and, reaching for the doorknob, felt rather than heard a hard, gravelly crunch under my shoes. I stopped, looked up, focusing for the first time. And I began to wonder if the rest of my life was destined to be defined by repeated acts of breaking and entering, because although the kitchen door was closed and locked, I could see, in the dim light glowing through the curtains, that one of the small panes in the door just above the knob was edged in a spidery pattern of broken glass.

I glanced down at the street. It was lined with parked cars, but none looked familiar. This was not a particularly prosperous part of town, and my first thought was that Kevin's black and gleaming sedan should have stood out sharply. But it wasn't there. And in its absence the whole street took on an expectant air as if, with that one possibility gone, anyone at all might be lying in wait. But what was there to do?

I opened the screen and unlocked the door, ready for the crunch of glass again under foot, but when I stepped gingerly onto the bare linoleum there was only silence. Most of the room was in shadow, but in the faint wedge of light spilling in from the living room doorway I could see the floor was clear. More than that, it was clean. The whole kitchen was clean. The few dishes that had accumulated in the sink were nowhere to be seen, the counters were bare, and as if to highlight the room's new state of hygiene the broom and dustpan had been left leaning casually in one corner. Even given my limited experience of burglars this struck me as a sign, though of what, I couldn't say.

I eased into the living room. At my entrance a faint rustle of newspaper rose from the darkness to my right, then subsided into silence. The boys hadn't waited up for me. The only light was from the narrow band beneath the bedroom door, throwing a silver trail across the floor. I followed it and a little reluctantly pushed open the door.

Wendy was lying, propped up in bed, the covers drawn demurely to her shoulders, arms pale and bare. Her hair was a dark, ragged halo on the pillow. She held a wine glass balanced on the draped curve of her stomach, and beside her the gumball lamp glowed beneath the thick drapery of a dishtowel, filling the room with warm light and the hot smell of singeing cotton.

"Surprise," she said pettishly. She looked annoyed.

"How long have you been here?"

"Aren't you glad to see me?"

"The front door's broken."

"I brought some wine." She tilted the glass. A little pool of golden liquid swirled around the bottom. "Except it's gone. Where have you been?"

"I was out," I said, "driving."

"Driving where?"

"Just around."

"With who?"

"Alone," I said. "Just alone."

She looked at me for a moment, weighing my tone, as if even in those two words she could read the bent trajectory of a lie. "I thought you were coming back to the bar."

"I was," I said. "Something came up."

"I thought it'd be a nice surprise. Come home to find a naked woman in your bed."

"It is a nice surprise."

She glanced without comment at the bottle of scotch, still cradled in my hands. "So, what came up?"

"I was driving."

"So you said."

I hesitated for a moment, awkward and unsure. What was the problem? I hadn't done anything wrong. I mean, all of my deepest desires aside, what had I done except gone for a drive, stopped, and come home? But I could feel the thin, crinkled texture of guilt in my chest, and I suddenly found myself saying, "I got lost. Off on some back roads, and it took me a while to find my way back."

"Is that right?"

"I was wandering all over the place, trying all these roads at random. You know how they all look just a little unfamiliar at night? Then suddenly you don't have the slightest idea where you are? I just kept driving. And finally I had to stop and ask at a farm house. And as soon as I found my way back to a road I knew, the car just gave out. The engine stalled."

Wendy said nothing. She just stared up at me. And in the face of her thin and skeptical silence I just kept going. Listening with a kind of appalled fascination as my own voice wandered down its extravagant and widening path.

"It must have overheated. I don't know. It's an old car. It just started stalling. I'd start it again, and it would go for a while, and then die. I had to call for a tow truck and then finally it came... And here I am." I stood there wearing a ghastly smile, with the terrible lameness of the whole story draped across me like a banner.

"Who was it?" Wendy said after a moment.

"Nobody."

"Come here," she said. She set down her glass and climbed onto her knees. The sheet fell aside. Her pale breasts quivered, dark-tipped in the warm light. The thick smudge of her pubic hair a deeper shadow in the darkness. At the edge of the mattress she reached up and begin to unbutton my shirt, working her way down to my belt. Then, without a word, she unbuckled, unzipped, and dragged my shorts and underpants down to my ankles. I stood there, stirring in the breeze with the faint throbbing tickle of blood and excitement. She leaned into me, pressing her face against my belly, inhaling deeply the heavy tincture of sweat and nervousness, but no scent of wayward sex or the incriminating cleanliness of fresh soap and water. Her breath was warm. She dragged her fingernails lightly over my belly and thighs, but I didn't move. I just stood there. Even with the blood engorging my hapless flesh, I didn't know what to do. I felt anxious and distracted, even as her warm lips, humid as a jungle night, slide without pressure or friction over the head of my cock. "Wait," I gasped. "Stop."

She drew back angrily, confusion and embarrassment struggling on her face. "What is it, Charles?" she demanded. "What the fuck is going on?"

"I don't know. It's just..." I stood there, my cock at rapt attention, and my brain a flurried counterpoint of guilt and indecision.

"What do you want?" she said. "You want me to leave? Is that it? You want more space? You're feeling crowded? You want me to leave you alone? What's with you, Charles? What is going on? Do you want to be disappointed? Is that it? You only want women who don't want you? What's the matter? You don't want to risk actually getting what you want?"

She was gripping the stem of the wine glass, glaring up at me, and I couldn't think of what to say. Is that what it all came down to in the end? I thought of Gracie, Emily. The same thing over and over. I thought of how much time I'd spent waiting for women who weren't waiting for me. How much of a coincidence was that? At what point did it stop being just bad luck?

"Just tell me what you want," said Wendy, "and it's yours. I'm a fucking genie. Tell me your wish. And I'll grant it."

But what could I say? What did I want? The image of Emily was still alive in my mind. Her overalls, her bandaged ankle, her high-wire nerve and fierce determination. Risking everything, and for what? For Kevin? When you love 'em, you love 'em. And when you hate 'em? All that risk, all that danger.... And even after driving away, all Kevin had to do was knock on her door. Is that really what I wanted: someone who'd do anything in the world for somebody else?

Impatiently Wendy started to climb out of bed.

"Wait."

She gazed up at me, without expression.

"Don't go."

"So, tell me about tonight."

"It was nothing. "

She leaned back against the pillows and drew the sheet back over her. "So tell me. I'm always in the mood for a story."

"I left the bar and I just started driving. Nowhere in particular. Just around..."

"Wait," said Wendy. "Is this going to be a long story?" She held out her glass. "Why don't you pour me a drink."

I started to turn toward the kitchen.

"I don't need any ice," she said. "Just whatever you've got there."

I broke the seal on the scotch and poured some into her wine glass, then capped it again.

"You're not having any?"

I opened it again, took a swig from the bottle. I barely even noticed the burn. Wendy was sitting back, propped against the pillows. Her breasts were pale in the warm light, her sturdy legs pressed chastely together beneath the sheet. "So your car broke down?" she said.

"No. No, it didn't. I drove around. Out into the country, all over the place, and I ended up—I don't even know how exact-ly—at my parents house."

"Your parents?"

I nodded.

"That's it?" She shook her head. "That's not a very good story. And then you came home?"

I hesitated, listening to the long seconds of silence collecting between us. "No," I said finally. "I stopped on the way."

She took a sip of her scotch, bracing herself, burying her nose in the glass as if she were trying to hide. "Am I going to like the ending of this story, Charles?"

"I don't know. I don't think so."

She looked up, wide-eyed and uncertain. "I think I've changed my mind. I'm not really in the mood for a story after all. Why don't you just get into bed? We don't need to talk about this now. You could just fuck me. Okay? Please?" She swallowed. "Don't you want to?"

"I think I should probably tell you."

She peered up at me for a moment longer. Then in one sud-den, angry sweep she yanked the covers off the bed and onto the floor, and lay back again, propped up on the pillows. The sheets were white, and against them, pale as she was, her skin stood out like warm ivory in the lamplight. Breasts slouching over her soft, creased belly. The dark nest of hair blurring into indistinctness. "So, tell me," she said.

"I was over by a house on Arbutus Street." My voice sounded thin and uncertain, as if it might say anything at all. "I saw a burglary. I watched somebody climb up a sheer brick wall and into a second story window."

"Just like that?" she said blandly. "Just straight up a wall?"

"That's right."

"Imagine that."

"Apparently the house had an alarm, but only on the first floor. Not on the second. Apparently it was turned off."

"Apparently," she said. "Apparently it must have been." Her voice was low. She had put down her glass, and as she spoke her hands slid up over her body, feeling their way blindly, smoothing slow circles around her already smooth breasts. Beneath the circling fingertips the blurred smudges of her nipples tightened. She drew her knees up slowly, as if she were planning to read in bed and needed somewhere to rest the book. "But you know, that doesn't really make sense," she said. "Does it? I mean, if you're going to bother to have an alarm in the first place." She eased her knees apart so that the book, if it had been there, would have fallen right through. "Are you sure you're telling this story right?"

"That's what happened."

"If you say so."

"He walks in his sleep. He's afraid he might set it off."

"The burglar?"

"No."

The lamplight washed over her breasts and belly and the rising slope of her thighs, defining smooth regions of light and dark so that her fingers, drifting down now over the curve of her stomach, slipped into the shadows as if crossing from day into night. Her fingertips, indistinct in the darkness, seemed to be smoothing the ruffled black hair as if it might have gotten mussed by the covers. "So what did he steal?"

"Nothing."

"Nothing? Are you sure?" Her fingers slowed in their motion. Her face tightened into an expression of concentration as if she were reading in braille the indistinct folds and contours beneath her fingers. Her voice carried softly. "No money? No stocks and bonds?"

"No."

"Jewelry? Silverware?"

"No. Nothing."

Her words were slowing down, receding as her breathing grew deeper. "Doesn't sound like much of a burglar."

My own voice seemed to slow down with her, to come drifting from a long way away. "The alarm went off. It scared her away."

"Her?"

"Him."

"The burglar?"

"That's right."

"I thought you said it was turned off."

"It must have come back on."

She waited.

"I threw a rock through the window."

"To scare the burglar away?"

I nodded. My eyes were on her. On her hands, on the dark hint of moisture in the darkness between her fingers.

"Isn't that remarkable," she said. She reached further down into the soft and indistinct shadow, spreading out pale hands as if shielding herself, then slowly, parting them. She drew back her fingers, holding herself open, framing a humid and indistinct center between the pale blur of her fingertips. In the stillness the warm scent of her rose on the air.

"It's lucky you were there," she whispered.

"I was passing by," I said quickly. "I just happened to see it."

"I said it was lucky." Her fingers were moving in small slow circles, her breathing deep in the silence. Her voice didn't change, low and distant. "Can you tell how wet I am?"

"Yes," I whispered. My voice was tight.

"Touch me."

I knelt on the end of the bed and leaned forward. I reached out, and her fingers, stroking her own soft flesh, stroked my hand as well.

"Did you fuck her?"

"It was a burglar," I said.

"Did you?"

"It's just a story."

"You did, didn't you?"

"No."

"Did you want to?"

My fingers were wet now, tracing the path of her damp fingers over her slick and yielding flesh. "No," I said. But the word sounded thin and dry.

"And what about me?" Wendy whispered. "Tell me you don't want to fuck me."

Her voice was low and indistinct. It drew me in. But even in that moment as I eased forward, sneaking like a burglar between her parted thighs, burying myself in the rich and velvety warmth of her cunt, her voice snagged on my memory. There was something in it, some softness in the timbre, some murmur of breath. "Okay, then," she whispered. "Okay."

In any magic trick there's always the danger. You change things around, you turn one thing into another: a rabbit into a duck into a woman into nothing at all, and always you run the risk of losing your way. In the effort of sorting out the illusion from everything that's real, it's easy to become confused. You need to concentrate. You need to know where each element is and you need to have them all in order. Because the danger is that you'll miscount, that you'll forget what it is you have hidden beneath the trap door, behind the curtain, beneath your hand. That you'll turn with that final flourish and discover that what remains is not what you expected. That all your efforts, all your careful misdirection have gone awry and you've worked your way to the end of the trick only to find yourself holding the wrong card.

Debbie the Tick

The next morning I ate a late breakfast in a narrow, listless restaurant on Main Street and returned, queasy with eggs and bad coffee, to find a message waiting on my answering machine. I watched the blinking red light for a moment, weighing the possibilities. Wendy had left only an hour before, wandering out into the sunshine with the squinting, wary look of a groundhog about to see its shadow. She didn't seem like the sort of woman who'd call just to say she'd gotten home safely. But any other possibility seemed distant and unreal. The night before at Hugh's house had turned strange in my mind, and in the bright and ordinary daylight the chance of a phone call from that realm seemed as unlikely as a message from beyond the grave. Yet some part of my mind was unconstrained by common sense. I pressed the play button with a faint, unreasonable flicker of hope, and in that fraction of second between the mechanical click and the rasping start of the tape, I had just enough time to conjure up Emily, sore and alone on the porch of her house, sipping coffee and in need of a friend, before Kevin's voice filled the room.

"Charles." He sounded brisk, business-like. Unworried. "I imagine you've got some questions. Why don't you come by the house tonight. Alone. Say about seven o'clock. Oh. And bring two hundred dollars in cash."

I arrived that night more or less on time, and found the driveway full of cars. It was an elegant house, though too large for one person. It had belonged to a colleague of my father, an elderly man named Paul Duboise who specialized in securities and trade law and grew orchids in a small greenhouse in back. He used to give dinner parties at which he would present each woman with a beautiful corsage, home-grown, hand-tied. I could always tell when my parents had been over to his house because my mother saved her flower for me. When I came down to the breakfast table the morning after, it was always waiting, a pearl and pink blossom, tiny and intricate as a trout fly. They were perfect for my small hands; I used to practice making them disappear, draping them with handkerchiefs, hiding them under the hem of my jacket, drawing them out of thin air with a flick of the wrist. The goal was to make them last as long as possible, to make them appear and disappear so delicately that the blossoms wouldn't be damaged. But, sooner or later, despite my lightest touch, even the most beautiful flowers came apart in my fingers.

Kevin greeted me at the door with a cool smile and led the way past a large, deserted living room to the den, tucked away in the back of the house. There were four men and one woman standing around a small butler's cart crowded with hors d'oeuvres. The air was glazed with cigar smoke, and in the background a green baize-covered table waited with a rack of poker chips and two decks of cards.

It was one of those smoky back rooms that you hear about in politics—or at least in certain movies about politics—but can go your whole life without seeing. Kevin must have been so pleased to have put it together. He gave me a moment to appreciate the scene, then steered me lightly by the elbow. "Gentlemen, my brother Charles. This is Victor, Pete, Roger, and you know Dewey. We're on a first name basis, here. And Emily, of course."

They all nodded. Victor, a handsome, silver-haired man who had something to do with an industrial park just on the edge of town, shook my hand. "This is a private party. Nothing we say leaves this room. Is that understood?"

I glanced at Dewey Reynolds, who was just managing to restrain a smile. I said, "Cross my heart and hope to die."

Emily stood in a dress the colors of autumn leaves, leaning on a wooden cane. She smiled thinly and raised her glass in greeting. She wasn't looking her best. Pale and tired, with a grim set to her mouth, she didn't look as if she'd slept much lately.

Kevin clapped me on the shoulder. "Help yourself to a drink. We usually start around seven-thirty."

I had heard about these games from Dewey. Kevin had organized them when he was first contemplating a run for mayor. Just a series of friendly games where the powerful and influential could get together and bask in cigar smoke and scotch, and talk about whatever was on their minds.

"But it would be a mistake," Dewey had said, in the comfort of his office, "to think of it only as backroom politics."

"You're going to tell me it's really about philanthropy and concern for the public good?"

He'd smiled and pointed the smoking stub of his Lucky at me. "I'm telling you it's all about money. Don't think of it as a game. Think of it as a weekly pissing contest."

"What could be more fun?"

"And, on top of it, you maybe get to drive home with a hundred dollars of someone else's money. It's what we live for."

"So, how do you do?"

"I kick in my money every week just to keep my hand in. I tell my accountant it's a business expense."

"And how about Kevin?"

"He chose the game. He's not a bad poker player, and he does like to win."

Now I poured myself a drink and turned to find Emily holding out her empty glass. "If you wouldn't mind. I'm sort of short-handed today."

"Can you believe it?" Kevin said. "Em twisted her ankle in rehearsal yesterday."

"Is that a fact?" I said.

Emily shrugged. "I got a little careless during a dance number."

"I imagine it's trickier than it looks." I held up the scotch bottle. "Something and soda?"

"Just something."

Kevin gave her a brief glance, but he kept his smile firmly in place. "Better go easy on that. You want to keep a clear head with this crowd. They'll take your money and won't even stop to thank you." But Emily didn't seem to hear, and after a moment he turned away to see to his other guests.

"Is this what the doctor prescribed?" I asked.

"It's a home remedy."

"How's it feeling?"

"It hurts like crazy. What are you doing here?"

"If it's just a dancing accident," I said, "maybe you should take it to the emergency room."

"Charles?"

"He invited me. Honest. He left a message on my machine."

Emily took a thoughtful sip of her drink, and it occurred to me to wonder if she wasn't just a little disappointed that I hadn't come swaggering in here on my own to find her. "He stopped by last night," she said.

"What a surprise."

"He said he was very concerned about me."

I glanced around at the den. It was cozy and comfortable, dark paneled walls and bookcases, lamplight on the dark green carpet. It looked calm and well-appointed; the room of a man who, on the surface at least, clearly had his act together. "Did you ask him where he went in such a hurry?"

She smiled dryly. "He told me I was very resourceful. I suppose he wants to thank you, as well."

"Do you think?"

She took a long sip of her drink. "He said you threw a rock through the downstairs window. That's what set off the alarm."

I hesitated for a moment, before the sudden yawning pit of my own bad judgment. "It may not have been a good idea," I admitted, "but I was a little angry."

"Does that mean I'm still supposed to thank you?"

"Yes."

"He explained to me exactly why he had to run away. It was all very reasonable. It made perfect sense."

"I'll bet."

She stared down into her drink, watching the ice cubes shift slightly as they melted in the scotch. "On the whole, I think throwing a rock is more honest."

I digested that for a moment. "How did you do after I left? Did you make it up the stairs?"

"Eventually. But I didn't sleep all that well. And you?"

I thought of Wendy and felt the faint heat of a blush warming my cheeks. "No," I said. "Not all that well."

Kevin strolled over to the table. "Have a seat, gentlemen. Emily, you're there; then Charles. Victor, Pete, me, Roger, and Dewey. Victor, why don't you be the bank. Charles? Give me a hand in the kitchen, will you?"

I held the chair for Emily as she eased herself down and hung her cane on the edge of the table. Then I followed Kevin out the door.

The kitchen was modern and shiny: all the latest appliances looking as if they'd never been used. On the counter, trays of hors d'oeuvres from Silver Spoon Catering were laid out, wrapped in cellophane with a typed sheet of instructions stuck to the top. Kevin switched on the oven, then turned and began unwrapping one of the trays.

"You know, Charles," he said, "I think you may have the wrong idea about something."

I was peeling back the cover of another tray. Mushroom caps, stuffed with sausage and breadcrumbs, beautifully garnished with parsley and red pimentos. They were lined up like little troops on parade. "What makes you think that?"

"I think you may have misinterpreted what you think you saw."

I looked up at him. His voice was cool and instructional. There was no suggestion that he might have been caught in a crime, that he was, albeit in a rather vulgar and perhaps strictly technical way, accessory to a burglary. There was only a small misunderstanding which he was now prepared to correct.

"What I think I saw was you helping someone break into Hugh's house. I just can't figure out why."

"See?" He smiled. "That's exactly what I meant." Then he glanced down at the mushroom caps. "Those have to be heated up, too. What temperature does it say?"

I untangled the bundle of cellophane to look at the instructions. "Ten minutes at three-twenty-five."

"These caterers are very good. Everything's designed to go into one oven. And it's all delicious."

"Good to know. I understand that's what they say about prison food."

He slid the two trays into the oven and straightened up. "Have you told anybody what you saw?"

"Not yet."

"I know what you're thinking." He smiled. "I know how friendly you are with Dewey Reynolds. And I know how important you think this is. But don't get any ideas about moral responsibility or public duty. Hugh won't thank you, if you do. I guarantee it." I started to speak, but he held up his hand. "Let me just have my say, and then you can make your own decision."

He opened a cupboard and took down a couple of white dinner plates, and drew from a drawer a new package of cocktail napkins. "Open these, will you?" He checked the timer on the stove, then turned back again, smiling with a look of calm and patient encouragement, and I had the feeling of being coaxed off a ledge I hadn't even known I was standing on. "The point is, Charles, you have to consider the larger benefits. This is about something more than Hugh Barker being woken up in the middle of the night."

"Is it?"

"It's about progress. For everyone. And justice, too, for that matter."

"See? You're right. I just didn't understand. I thought it was about that little urban oasis you wanted to build where Hugh's factory should be."

He looked a little pained at that, and I was aware of the thin ribbon of petty pleasure I took in his slightest wince. "There's more to it," he said. "Emily told you about Hugh? About the creosote?"

"She mentioned it. She also mentioned the fact that he had permission to dump it."

"Well," said Kevin. "Not permission, exactly. No one said, 'Okay, Hugh, please feel free to poison the ground water so you can make a few more dollars building ships nobody needs.'"

"The point is," I said, "he hasn't actually broken the law."

"Actually, he has." Kevin glanced over at the timer on the stove. The mushrooms were already starting to sizzle in their pan. He leaned down to peer in through the stove window, then straightened up. "These'll be good, I think."

I waited. Kevin glanced over, and when he saw I wasn't going to ask, he shrugged. He was the older brother, again, wise and patronizing, and it didn't matter what he was talking about. The old dynamic had slipped firmly into place, and there was no outrunning it, no smiling it down. That's the thing about family. Everything you do is about the past. Every little argument, every little struggle and contest, carries you back to childhood.

"He took out a loan," said Kevin. "About fifteen years ago. From the Community Savings Bank, in fact."

"For the renovation. I know."

"He used the factory as collateral."

"So?"

"So, banks tend not to lend money to factories that have a potential multi-million dollar clean-up on their hands. I'm sure Hugh wouldn't, if he were president. Anyway, the law says you have to 'identify any existing phenomena deleterious to the environment.' In fact, the law says you have to swear to it. So, Hugh did. Fifteen years ago he swore the land was pure as rainwater."

"So?"

"So, he lied."

The buzzer on the stove went off, and Kevin bent, with a pot holder in each hand, and slid the trays out, onto the counter. "We want a mixture, I think." He began arranging the hors d'oeuvres on each plate: mushrooms, little quiches, a few tiny egg rolls. He seemed delighted with them.

"But why do you care?" I said. "I don't get it. What are you suddenly? The moral avenger? You're breaking into his factory. You're breaking into his house, for God's sake! Just because he lied?"

"Actually," said Kevin, "that's just about right. I need to see a copy of that loan application. That's all. It's really as simple as that. Everything is always simple, Charles, at heart. Never as complicated as you like to make it. Sometimes I think you just enjoy complication."

I ignored that, knowing as I did that nothing, particularly nothing to do with Kevin, had ever been simple. "If that's all it is, I assume the bank's got a copy."

"You'd think so, wouldn't you? But they had a little trouble with their data storage, moving into this new building. A shortage of space. They got rid of all the less important papers. They might have it on microfilm somewhere, hidden away and forgotten. But I couldn't very well ask about it."

"You're the mayor. I'd have thought that was exactly what you could do."

"No. You see, that's likely to make things more complicated, rather than less."

"Why?"

He had picked up a spatula and was arranging hors d'oeuvres on a plate. "Because as soon as the bank digs it out of its files and takes a look, they're going to wonder if they can't think of a better choice for their future president."

"But I thought that was the whole point."

"The point," said Kevin, wiping his fingers on a dish towel, "is to get that factory into city hands. And to clean up the mess.

And to get Hugh off the hook."

I stopped and stared. "It is?"

"Of course."

"You're not being very clear."

"It's simple. I like Hugh. You like Hugh. Emily likes Hugh. We don't want to ruin his future. We just want him to give the factory away so we can clean it up."

"Give it away?"

Kevin glanced over at the empty doorway, then lowered his voice. "The point is, whether or not the dumping was legal, Hugh's the one left holding the bag. He's responsible. And he can never sell it, because no one's going to buy a factory that comes complete with a ten million dollar clean-up bill. And any attempt to sell it is going to require a site inspection that will turn up everything. But it's possible, if he donates it to the city for a public project, we can get aid from the federal Superfund. To help clean it up."

"Just like that?"

"With any luck."

"And Hugh's out from under it?"

"That's the general idea."

"So, you're doing him a favor?"

"And trying to build something the town needs."

"Then, what's the problem?" I asked.

"The problem is, Hugh won't give up the damned factory." Kevin glanced again toward the doorway, his voice lowered still further. "We're into a little grey area, here, Charles. Theoretically, if anyone knowingly acquires an environmental liability, he assumes responsibility for the clean-up."

"Even the city?"

"Theoretically."

"So, no federal aid?"

"As I said, it's a grey area. There's room to argue. But it would definitely be better for us if Hugh donated the factory without any public mention of the dumping. Then we could all just sort of play dumb."

"You're asking him to lie?"

"I'm asking him to be discrete. There's no crime in that. Listen. If he doesn't unload that factory, he's going to be ruined. It's as simple as that. All I'm trying to do here is just look for a way to encourage him."

"To force him, you mean."

"To convince him." Kevin picked up one of the plates. "It's for his own good. He doesn't lose by it."

"And neither do you."

"Everybody wins. Is that so bad? Hugh gets to be bank president. The town gets a new urban center and federal aid to clean it up. Tell me what's wrong with that."

I looked down at the mushrooms, laid out in perfectly straight and ordered rows on the plates. The only thing wrong with it, as far as I could see, was that Kevin would be getting exactly what he wanted.

"Think about it, Charles. He's going to be ruined otherwise. Is that what you want?"

"Does Hugh understand all this?"

Kevin shrugged. "He's being difficult. He feels guilty and he wants to punish himself. Now, the point is, should we let his guilt stand in the way of our chance to clean up the mess? And give the town something it needs?"

"How can you be sure about all this?"

"You can see for yourself, once we get our hands on that application."

"And you think Hugh has a copy?"

"Somewhere. In the factory, at his home. Listen. We only want him to do what's best. For himself as well as for the town." He handed me a plate of hors d'oeuvres. "Tell me that's so bad."

But even as I took the plate I remembered something, a time when I was young, six or seven and Kevin was a wise and worldly fourteen. He had a paper route, sixty two houses that he needed to visit every morning about five am. On day he told me he had a treat for me and the next morning woke me up with a treasure map in his hand. He told me I had to leave messages for each of these secret agents without being noticed. I was six years old, and he didn't usually pay any attention to me at all. I was aflame with excitement. I went to wake up Gracie, and together we snuck around the neighborhood every morning for a week, laughing, hiding from the occasional early morning pedestrian, carefully delivering the rolled and wrapped messages of newsprint. And it was only gradually, as it dawned on me that Kevin had ceased to wake me up, had ceased to give me my instructions, and had, in fact, taken to sleeping late, that I realized just how much I'd been taken advantage of. I stopped. But what has stayed with me all these years, and will until my grave, I imagine, is not just the anger I felt at being used. I remember the excitement of sneaking around the neighborhood in the blue light of dawn with Gracie, delivering messages whose entire meaning, as far as I was concerned, lay in the drape of mystery they spread over the visible world. And somehow I still harbor a kind of bitter and grudging wonder at the self-serving scope of Kevin's imagination.

He led the way back to the den. He smiled and sat down, as if nothing had happened, and I slid into my seat next to Emily, laying the plate on the table. I glanced at her, but she seemed oblivious, wrapped in scotch fumes and her own thoughts.

Kevin leaned back, relaxed as could be. "So how about it, gentlemen? Shall we play some cards? I'm feeling lucky."

"You're always feeling lucky," Victor said.

Kevin laughed. "It's a gift."

I glanced over at Emily, lost in her stony thoughts, and decided maybe I was feeling a little lucky myself.

It's said you can't cheat an honest man, but in fact all it takes is a little concentration. It had been a while since I'd played poker, certainly a while since that first game in Holyoke with Rudy, but it's a knack you don't lose. It took me a while to get the deal, but once I got it, I kept it. The trick is to identify useful combinations of cards and then to control them. Often the easiest way is to shuffle them to the bottom of the deck, then deal them out as needed. You have to be careful about choosing your cards: nothing too flashy, nothing people will remember. And, of course, you have to keep changing the cards, spotting the useful ones, saving them, rearranging them. It takes a fair amount of concentration, but working with a smaller audience made it easier. Poker, like magic, is fundamentally an emotional enterprise, and with five people in the audience, plus Emily, it was easier to keep tabs on how they were all doing.

From the beginning it was clear Victor and Kevin were the potential hot spots; the others, Dewey in particular, seemed likely to be better losers. So I took care to drop a little plum onto Victor's plate every now and then to keep his spirits up, and I let Kevin just simmer.

Emily was a cautious player. She bet low and folded easily. She paid too much attention to her cards, and not enough to the other players. But she was thoughtful and consistent, and fun to watch. I chose seven-card stud: three cards down, three up, and a hole card. The first time she got three kings on the deal her eyes widened ever-so-slightly and she glanced up hurriedly as if someone else might have spotted them, too. But when she got the fourth king face-up in the third round of betting she barely blinked. She bet a little too lightly on the hand, but she was delighted with the pot, and raked it in with a half-surprised laugh.

Kevin smiled a little tightly. By this time he hadn't won a hand in some time. "Not bad, Em. It's great to get the cards, isn't it?"

"I thought poker was a game of skill," she said.

"Well, it certainly doesn't hurt to be lucky." But by then Kevin had had all the luck he was going to get.

In the next hand I gave Victor a pair of eights, which was enough to win it; then came back to Emily with two spades down, two up, and the fifth in the hole. She bet the flush beautifully, holding tight at first, then raising through the roof with the last card. Kevin hung on till the end, and went down with three sevens to the tune of forty-five dollars.

"Oh, the poker gods are angry, now," observed Dewey wryly.

I glanced around. "I think I may be a little out of my league."

"Don't even think about leaving," Kevin said grimly. "We're just getting started."

I gave Roger an obvious full house that only netted him twenty dollars before people folded out, then I came back to Emily with three queens, all in a row, straight off the bottom. She looked at them thoughtfully for a long moment, then glanced over at me.

"You know," she said, "this reminds me of a game I once played with a friend of mine in college. She was a hell of a card player. We used to call her Debbie the Tick."

"Debbie the Tick?" said Roger.

Emily shrugged, smiling. "I don't know where she got the name. Maybe because she used to suck up all our money. But, boy, she used to get some great cards."

"It looks as if you've got a little Debbie the Tick in you tonight," Kevin muttered.

"Not at all," Emily replied, with a sunny smile. "She was a great player. I'm just very lucky."

The three queens turned into a full house, and Emily's good luck held. It was a pleasure to see. I don't think Kevin had ever lost so steadily before in his life. He stared down at his cards, marveling at the hands he got, as though unable to believe the universe could so conspire against him. There was a particular muscle I watched along the edge of his jaw. By the end of the evening it was standing out like a knot, and he was saying almost nothing.

The game ended at midnight. A clock chimed somewhere in the house, and as if on cue the game just melted away. Victor and Dewey pushed back their chairs, Pete and Roger stretched and began counting their chips. Emily glanced around at the combined movement and started gathering up her winnings. Kevin sat, staring down at the cards spread out before him, exhausted by the prospect: four kings and a queen, and nobody had bet a dime against him.

"What's the damage?" Victor asked. He held the thick wad of small bills that included everyone's stake. He counted it out, buying back the chips. Most of it went to Emily, four hundred and twelve dollars. He counted it out, and she picked it up a little gingerly. "Make sure you bring it all back next time," he said cheerfully.

"I'm not sure I'll be invited back."

Kevin smiled grimly. "Come back when your luck changes."

She gazed at him thoughtfully, perhaps wondering if it already had. But he didn't notice. He was just shaking his head as if he still couldn't believe those four kings.

She handed me the money. "Would you carry this for me? I don't have any pockets." Then she rose, careful of her ankle, and lifted the cane down from the table edge. "Thanks for the evening, Kevin. It was very educational."

He looked startled. "You're leaving?"

"I'm tired."

"You could stay."

"I don't think so."

He shrugged irritably. "Suit yourself. Let me get my coat. I'll give you a ride home."

"Don't bother," said Emily. "I'm sure I can get a lift with somebody."

Breaking Even

Outside, the air was warm and still. A huge stand of honeysuckle hovered in patchy bloom in one corner of Kevin's yard, lasting late into the summer, offering a faint sweet scent. Emily eased into the passenger seat and leaned back closing her eyes, resting the cane against the door.

I climbed in beside her. "Tired?"

"What the hell were you doing back there?"

"Don't look at me. I lost thirty dollars." I drew out the thick wad of bills and handed it to her. "I believe this is yours."

"Keep it," she said.

"You won it."

She fanned the money out in her hand and smiled reluctantly. "How could you do that?"

"It was hard work. Why? Didn't you enjoy it?"

"I feel like Nicky the Tick."

"Debbie the Tick."

"You've turned me into a criminal."

"How did it feel?"

She grinned. "Are you kidding? It was the best party I've ever been to in that house." She looked down at the four hundred and twelve dollars in ones, fives, and tens and shook her head. "But what am I supposed to do with it now?"

"Spend it. Give it away. Give it back to Kevin."

"Not on your life."

"Well, then. Real estate's always a good investment."

She laughed. Then, peeling off three tens, she held them out. "At least you should break even."

"Keep it. I don't mind paying for my fun."

"He didn't look pleased."

"There was a little muscle twitching in his cheek," I said.

"Was there? I didn't notice."

"Right there." I reached out and traced one finger down the smooth line of her jaw.

"Oh. That one," she said quietly. My finger slipped under her jaw and followed the graceful line of her throat down. In the faint, shifting light of the other cars, pulling out and driving off, her face looked smooth and cool, sculpted with shadows. The slim muscles of her throat shifted as she swallowed. "I think I'd better go home," she said.

"How about a drive instead?"

"I can't."

"But do you want to?"

She sat silently for a moment, as if weighing everything about the evening: the air, the stillness, the scent of honeysuckle, until the silence itself became its own kind of answer. "Please," she said finally. "Just take me home."

I started up the car and drove, following the curving roads down to Main Street then out of town, past the bright strip of restaurants and the vastness of the Shop'n'Save, then out into the darkness of the country. We drove in silence, Emily leaning back, her hands folded loosely around the roll of bills in her lap. The scent of her perfume drifted on the air. It was a long time since I'd first noticed it back in Hugh's office, and it seemed like an entirely different scent to me now: warmer, tinged with the hint of sweat and a whisper of tropical longing still lingering in the faint coconut grace notes of her shampoo.

"You played some good hands tonight," I said.

"I had some help."

"You still played well."

"Thanks."

The darkness was soft and protective. As I drove, guiding the car along the now familiar curves, I kept glancing sidelong at her face, at the gentle rise and fall of her breathing.

"Tell me again what you love about Kevin," I said.

"Don't ask me that now."

"I'd like to stop, anywhere along here, and spend the rest of the night just sitting in the dark with you. We wouldn't have to say a word. We wouldn't have to touch."

"Please don't. Just keep driving."

Eventually the trees parted at the mouth of her driveway. I thought, just for an instant, of driving past, but at the last moment I turned. Drawing up beyond the van I switched off the engine, and in the sudden stillness, the whole night held its breath. Then gradually the cicadas picked up again and the frogs down by the pond. Emily sat for a long moment, staring down at her fingers, curled in her lap. "I could invite you in for a drink," she said hesitantly. "If you thought that was a good idea."

"I could use a drink."

"I'm pretty sure I've got some scotch."

"That would be nice."

She gave a tiny nod, more to herself than to me, then climbed out of the car, fumbling a little with the cane. She led me into the house, through a small, crowded living room to the kitchen. The walls and shelves and cupboards were thick with uniform layers of old pink paint, that gave the narrow kitchen the air of an ancient powder room. "Don't blame me. It was this color when I moved in," she said.

"I didn't say anything."

"They say pink is soothing."

"Do they?"

She took a couple of glasses and a nearly empty bottle of scotch from the cupboard. "I thought there was more."

"I don't need much."

She hesitated, gesturing vaguely with the bottle. "How about the Front porch?" I said. Then I followed her out into the yellow glare of the bug light and the enormous darkness beyond. "You don't get nervous out here, on your own?"

"I enjoy it. It's quiet. I like the privacy." She sank onto a wooden bench, and lay the cane on the floor. Then with a little frown she leaned forward to adjust the bandage on her ankle.

"Does it hurt?"

"Not much. It aches a little."

It was when she sat up that I kissed her. Just like that, under the sickly yellow glare of that unshaded bulb. I slipped an arm around her shoulders, drawing her back on the bench, and kissed her as if she were a fountain of water and I had just come out of a year in the desert. Her lips were lush, softer than I could have imagined, blossoming under my mouth. I was startled by the fragile feel of her: the delicate ribs beneath the thin fabric, the soft, yielding weight of her breast. It was the feeling a blind man must have, reading a favorite book for the first time in braille: all the familiar emotions and longings, but sharpened through a new set of senses.

After a long while she pulled away. "I can't breathe."

"Emily?"

"Please."

"What?"

She shook her head helplessly. "Please."

"You keep saying that. Please, what?" But she just shook her head.

It was a hot night. There were glintings of moisture at her hairline; a droplet of sweat in the shape of a tear trickled down her temple. I had an arm around her still. "You should go home," she whispered.

My chest felt hollow. I couldn't get enough air in my lungs. "I didn't realize you'd feel so good."

"Charles."

"Have you always looked this way?"

"What way?"

"You look so beautiful."

She shook her head helplessly. "Don't say that. You don't need to say that."

"Yes, I do."

"You can't stay."

"Why?"

"Because you can't."

"Would it be so awful?"

"And then what would we do?"

I was grasping wildly at straws. "I could make you breakfast. Coffee, French toast, orange juice. Do you have orange juice...?"

"Charles." Hurriedly she freed herself and stood up, but as her weight hit the ankle she winced. "Ah!"

"Don't stand on it."

"Well, what am I supposed to do?"

"Keep your weight off it."

"Easy for you to say! Ow! Where's my cane?"

"I've got it."

She slipped a hand onto my shoulder, steadying herself. "Now what do I do?"

"I don't know. Aren't you supposed to elevate it or something?"

"So you're a doctor now?"

"Well, how does it feel?"

"It hurts, God damn it!" After a long moment she said in a soft, half-reluctant voice. "Maybe I should lie down."

We eased our way through the living room to the stairs. They were old farmhouse stairs, narrow and steep. I held her tightly and edged my way up almost sideways, half-carrying her. She could probably have made it more easily on her own, a hand on each railing, but she didn't suggest it and neither did I. Her bedroom was dark and low ceilinged, crowded in under the steep roof. She turned on a lamp on the bedside table, but it made the space seem even smaller, all sloping walls and shadows, and full pink curtains on the window.

"I'm beginning to suspect you like this color."

She turned in my arm, standing by the bedside. Her face looked golden in the lamplight. The room smelled of old wood, like a hunting cabin. She was standing so close. "You'd better go," she whispered.

"All right."

Then she reached up, her fingers light on my cheek, and she kissed me.

My hands were at her waist, half caressing, half-supporting, some part of my mind still on her sprained ankle, and all the rest on the feel of her body and the hungry pressure of her lips. Her hands were on my neck, my scalp. With two fists in my hair she dragged my head back. "This doesn't mean you can stay," she gasped.

"I know."

"You've got to leave."

"I know."

She leaned into me. I couldn't get enough of her mouth. She tasted of scotch and lipstick, and she felt like something fierce. We were short of air, both of us, as if we'd just raced together over long, rough country and pulled up at the same moment. Her hands were on my chest, fumbling with the buttons, slipping beneath my shirt. "God," she murmured. "Your skin."

"Emily?"

"Yes."

"Are you sure?"

"No."

"I should go."

"Yes," she said. "Wait."

From my very first sight of her, in clown's makeup in her office all those weeks ago, she had seemed somehow mutable, changing shape and substance every time we met: slender then broad, solid then insubstantial, as if never quite real. That night, too, she seemed to change from moment to moment. My hands glided over her body without friction, smooth and cool. The shallow slope of her back dipped at the waist, then rounded into the curve of her hip. Below me in the darkness she was as warm and weightless as the rough sound of her breathing in my ear, all substance compressed into that sound and the soft, silken pressure of her skin. But rolling, turning, she knelt above me, the smooth, reassuring weight of her anchoring me in the darkness, keeping me from drifting away, as with cool, firm fingers she guided me in to the sudden, velvety shock of her cunt. And straddling my hips, posting to her own slow rhythm, with her face nodding and her breasts a silky pressure against my chest, she was the center of the night, firm and substantial, the only thing around that was solid enough to hold onto.

We fell asleep, wrapped tightly together despite the heat, and I drifted, dreamlessly until a sharp knock woke me to the less perfect darkness of three a.m.

"Emily?" a voice called. "Let me in. I just want to talk." It was Kevin, his voice carrying clearly up through the open window. The knocking came again, sharp and insistent. "I know you're in there Em. It's important. We need to talk."

I lay stiff and unmoving, trying to keep everything, even my breathing, silent. Emily lay perfectly still under my arm, though I knew she was awake. The glow of headlights shone in through the window and, looking down, I could see a faint answering glint in the corner of her open eye.

Kevin knocked again, but less confidently this time. "Please, Emily. I want to apologize."

She didn't move. I could feel the rise and fall of her breast, but there was no sound, not the faintest rustle of breathing.

"I can wait all night," Kevin called warningly, but already his tone was weakening. I heard footsteps on the gravel, then the click of a car door and the sudden, loud blare of a horn. Three long blasts. Then silence. I wondered if Kevin could possibly miss my car, pulled forward into the shadows behind the station wagon, but I heard nothing more for a while. The silence stretched out. Then there was the slam of a car door and the sound of the engine, and I heard the crunch and skid of gravel as he turned and roared away.

We lay still for a long time, barely breathing, unwilling to move. After a while I slipped my hand lightly into her's, and gently she pressed it. Eventually, with the faint beating of her heart against my fingers, I fell asleep.

In the morning light I awoke. Emily was lying perfectly still, eyes tightly closed, as if concentrating hard in her sleep. I leaned over, whispered, "Em?" but she didn't stir. I gave her a little shake, but she kept her eyes resolutely shut. After a while I slipped out of bed and climbed into my clothes as slowly as I could, making no attempt to be quiet, hoping she'd open her eyes, but though she shifted once, she kept her eyes shut, and in the end I left without speaking to her, leaving only a brief note that couldn't begin to say what I felt.

I ate breakfast sitting on my living room floor: coffee and a day-old muffin that I'd found in the fridge. I sat and sipped the bitter coffee and read the morning's paper. My eye caught on the police blotter. There were a few drunk driving tickets, a couple of public intoxications, an indecent exposure, and two burglaries from the night before, but for the first time in a long time I was confident that Emily had had nothing to do with either.

Sawing a Woman In Half

I called her a dozen times in the course of the day, but the line was busy. After the fourth try I just got in the car and drove. The station wagon was parked where it had been. The house was quiet. I knocked on the door, but there was no answer. I was about to call up to her, but then I remembered Kevin last night, calling and calling fruitlessly, and I was suddenly afraid that, if I called, Emily might not answer, and all the delicate filaments of hope and happiness that had been spun out last night would be torn to pieces. So I climbed into my car and drove away.

In the afternoon I strolled casually over to the Playhouse. My heart was pounding. I was rehearsing opening lines like a boy on his first date and trying to imagine how she'd respond, but in the end it did me no good. As I climbed the front steps the broad door opened, and Kevin stepped out.

I froze. He looked at me and, after the slightest hesitation managed a smile, but his eyes were dark and preoccupied, and I could read anything I wanted in them.

"Afternoon, your honor," I said.

"Charles. Imagine running into you here."

His voice was dry. I wondered if he'd spotted my car last night, after all, or if, after a night of stewing, he'd come up with a reason for his worst game of poker ever. I was suddenly aware of Emily's scent, very faint, on my skin, or perhaps just lingering in my imagination. In that moment, I thought he could peer right into my mind and see everything. "I'm rehearsing," I said. "For the show."

"Of course you are. Say, Charles? Did you take Emily home last night?"

Someone had reached into my chest and grasped my lungs in a tight fist. I swallowed. "Yes."

"What time did you drop her off?"

"What time?"

"I'm just curious."

I shrugged. "It's about a half hour drive, so I'd say about half an hour after the game broke up. Why?"

"Did she seem all right?"

"I don't know. I guess. A little preoccupied."

"Hm." Kevin half nodded to himself. "Thanks." He started to turn away, then stopped. "By the way, how'd you do last night?"

It took me a moment to answer. "I lost about thirty."

"Too bad."

"Not my best night," I said, "but I've done worse."

"Well, we'll have to try it again sometime. Maybe we'll both do better." And with another nod, his mind already elsewhere, he turned and strolled away.

I pulled open the heavy door and hurried up to the auditorium. Emily was there, but she had sent the children home early. She was sitting on the floor leaning against one of my trunks sipping a mug of tea. Even now, in the middle of summer, the room felt cool as a vault. I could see the steam rising, and as I got closer I caught the scent of licorice, warm on the air. She looked up at my approach, but she said nothing. She just watched as I approached and stood awkwardly before her. "I tried calling you today."

"I took the phone off the hook."

"I stopped by."

She nodded, smiling sadly. "Sorry about that."

"I was getting a little worried."

Emily bowed her head and blew at the tea, setting the steam swirling. "I'm okay," she said finally. "How about you?"

"I guess that depends."

I didn't know quite what to expect; I'd never found myself in this situation before. But a smile would have been nice, a gesture, a kiss, something to tell me I hadn't made it all up.

Instead she gazed soberly up at me with the steam drifting

past her cheeks and I realized that the room must have been even colder than I thought because now, with that look, the chill was stealing all the way into my chest, wrapping thin fingers of dread around my heart.

"That tea looks good," I said.

Without a word she offered me the mug, raising it up, and I wrapped both hands around it. "What did Kevin have to say?"

"He came to apologize. He said he behaved like a jerk last night."

I sipped the tea. How did it stay so hot, when the air itself seemed to be sucking the warmth out of everything? "What did you say?"

She sat hunched. "Why is it so cold in here? It's ninety degrees outside."

I handed her back the mug, and then cautiously eased down beside her and after a moment's hesitation slipped an arm around her shoulders. "Are you all right?"

"I didn't tell him," she said. She sat stiffly in the curve of my arm. "I should have. I should have just told him."

"Do you think he knew?"

She shrugged, then slowly relaxed, leaning against me. In profile her face was smooth and distant, as if meditating on something far away. "I told him he was right. He was a jerk." The curve of her lips quirked into the barest hint of a smile. "I asked him how he did last night."

"What did he say?"

"He lost a hundred and eighty-five dollars."

"I don't suppose you offered to return the money."

"No." The smile vanished. "I should have, shouldn't I?"

"No. He can afford it."

But she didn't reply. She was shaking her head, reaching over to brush at a pale smear of dust on the knee of my pants.

"Emily...?"

"I'm not good at this."

"What exactly is this?" I asked, and then suddenly felt anxious at what she might reply. "I love you," I said.

There was a short, loose thread dangling from the seam of my pocket. She had found it and was working at it, rolling it between her fingers, tugging it, worrying at it. "I'm engaged," she said, "to be married." As if there were some other kind of engaged. "In case you've forgotten."

"I haven't." I reached down, stilling her hand. "But you don't love him. Anyone can see that. I can see that. Oh, sure. He has nice hair..."

"Stop it."

"Well, do you?"

She shook her head. "Just because someone makes you angry, is that enough reason to stop loving them?"

"Is that an answer?"

"I don't know."

"He doesn't deserve you."

"It's not about 'deserves.'"

"Then what's it about?"

"And anyway," she said, "what about you?"

"Me?"

She sighed. "Why can't I remember her name, do you suppose?"

"Wendy."

"Right."

I waited, but she said nothing more. The room was vast and silent. "What are we going to do?" I asked.

"Nothing. Nothing more. We can't do it again."

"Does that mean you don't want to?"

"It means I can't. I hate this, Charles! I hate this so much."

My heart felt cold again. "But you like me, right? Come on. You have to say it."

Without a word her head sank slowly onto my shoulder. Our fingers had gotten tangled together, and she made no effort to untangle them. "How did things get so complicated all of a sudden?"

"They're always complicated. It's just that sometimes you don't notice."

We sat there, listening to the faint sounds of traffic that filtered through the thick walls and windows, all the hurry and noise of the cars muted to little more than a thickening of the background silence.

"It'll be all right," I said hopefully.

"Really?"

"Absolutely."

She shook her head. "I don't know what makes you think so."

Sawing a Woman in Half (part two)

On the road I'd always marveled at people so at home in their lives they didn't need a second chance, because I had come to depend so completely on the ongoing possibility of starting over. I lived within the conviction that the earth was larger than anyone could know, and that all possibility was tied to place. If luck ran out in one locale, you need only move on to some new vein of chance. So that life on the road, with so little to support it and a future that took shape only a week at a time, could feel strangely safe, operating above a safety net of inconsequentiality.

But, standing in the auditorium of Shortfellows Playhouse all that week, I realized that the only comfort of a strange place was that you were always about to leave. And the knowledge that this town suddenly included something I could never give up terrified me. All your life you hold out hope for love, you wait for it, strive for it. You imagine that it's the answer to something unimaginable, that it will provide the last, certain solution to the problem of your life. But then you find it, and love turns out to be nothing more than its own series of questions.

"Now, you have to lie still," I said. "I'd hate to make any mistakes."

"I know, I know. You're worried about bloodstains." Emily squirmed around. "It's a tight fit."

"It's a little small, but I think it'll work. I can make some adjustments later."

The cabinet was a long, rectangular box that rested on a black-painted cart so it could be wheeled out on stage. There were holes at either end for the head, hands, and feet, and a lid that padlocked shut. It wasn't quite long enough—Gracie had been three or four inches shorter than Emily—but I could adjust for that. At the midpoint there was a pre-cut groove which would be filled with plastic wood before the performance so the saw could be seen to cut through something without wandering from its course.

As Emily lay in the open box, I slid the long blade of a cross-cut saw into place. It slipped down and balanced lightly on her taut stomach. She was wearing a maroon leotard, with bare legs and feet, and a thick ace bandage still wrapped around her ankle. Leaning over I measured the angle of the saw and lifted it out. Then, after a moment's hesitation, I reached out and traced the line it had made with my finger tip, following the smooth, almost frictionless fabric over the curve of her belly and hip.

"Is that part of the trick?" she asked.

"Yes." I started to swing the lid closed.

"You don't really have to lock it, do you?"

"You need something to push against," I said. "If it isn't locked you end up lifting it up, instead of pushing yourself down."

She smiled wryly. "Will this make sense eventually?"

"It's very simple. The box has a false bottom. We wheel it out and tilt it up, so the audience can see there's nothing fishy going on. We tap the bottom," I held up my magic wand, "run the wand around it..." I tapped the sides. "Then, as you climb into the box--"

"I'm already in the box."

"Bear with me, please."

"Should I get out?"

"No. I'm explaining. As you climb in, I release the catch hidden on the side here. Then the bottom divides in the center and drops down."

She looked wary. "What do you mean, drops?"

"Gradually. It's on springs."

"I don't see any springs."

"They're built into the sides of the box."

She rapped one side. It made a hard, solid sound, and she smiled appreciatively. "Aren't you full of surprises."

It was a rough job by professional standards—all plywood instead of aluminum and fiberglass—but I was still proud of it, and it pleased me out of all proportion that she noticed. All the secrecy, all the care to guard the tricks makes it all the more important that you have at least one person to share them with.

"So you pull the pin and I sink down."

"Ideally. If the springs are calibrated. What's more likely is you use the leverage of your feet and hands to push the whole middle portion of your body down out of harm's way."

"Just like that?"

"Couldn't be easier."

I closed the lid and locked it. The expression on her face was mildly bemused. She shifted slightly, settling herself, and stretched out her fingers to brush a tickling lock of hair from her face, but her hand was tight in its hole, and she couldn't quite reach it. She blew at it, a couple of quick puffs, then looked up at me. "Do you mind?"

I smoothed her hair back, then bent and kissed her. Her lips were startled at first, cool in that large, cool room, but they warmed under my mouth. I drew back.

"So that's what this trick is all about," she said softly.

"That's what makes it magic." I straightened up. "Ready?"

"Fire away."

I pulled the hidden catch. Nothing happened.

Emily waited expectantly. "Is that it?"

"Not all of it. Try pressing down. Gently."

She braced herself and pushed down on the false bottom, frowning with the effort, but it didn't budge. "Are you sure you unlocked it?"

I pulled the release again. "Yep. It's the springs. They've been sitting around for seven years. They probably just need a little loosening. Give it a little more oomph."

"Gently, you said."

"A little gentle oomph."

She braced her hands more firmly in their slots and pushed,

gradually increasing the pressure. "I don't know," she muttered. "I don't think it's--Oof!"

The springs broke with a muffled snap, and the bottom dropped. With a look of sudden shock, Emily's face remained exactly where it was, held in the opening at the end of the box, as the rest of her dropped sixteen inches into the upper compartment of the cart.

She lay there for an instant, dazed, and then burst out laughing.

"No, no," I said. "Gradually."

"You said oomph."

"A little oomph. I said, a little"

"That was a little."

"That was a lot more than a little."

She shook her head, trying to catch her breath. "Would you get me out of this death machine?"

I rattled the padlock. "Uh-oh. It's stuck. You'll have to burst your way out."

"No, stop it! Let me out. I have an itch."

I held up the saw. "Just tell me where it is. I'll see if I can reach it."

"Charles. I'm warning you..."

"Well," said a dry voice from the doorway. "Isn't this a little raucous for a magic show?"

Kevin strolled in, elegantly tailored, calm and collected.

I wondered how long he'd been there. I tried to remember what we'd been saying. He was glancing around at the painted scenery and props, looking cheerful and cool and just a little above it all. I wondered whether his expression had always been so impenetrable, or whether it was just my guilty conscience.

He stopped before the magic cabinet. "That looks familiar. Did you build another?"

"It's the same one."

"I was going to say, I don't know where you find the time."

Emily was fidgeting in the box, her face serious now, a little embarrassed. "Charles. Would you mind?"

"Oh, don't get up," said Kevin, and leaning down before she could move he kissed her lightly on the lips.

Hurriedly I undid the padlock and swung the lid open. Emily sat up. "Thank you." Her voice was drawn tight. I reached out to help, but Kevin stepped up from the other side and took hold of her arm. He helped her down, and with his hand still lightly on her arm turned to me. "I wonder if we could have a word in private."

For an instant, under the prick of my guilt and irritation, I wasn't sure just which of us he wanted to talk to, but Emily glanced at him and nodded. "We can go upstairs."

I shrugged. "I've got a few repairs to make here anyway."

"It might take a while," said Kevin coolly. "You may not want to wait."

Emily considered that for a moment, then glanced back. "Maybe I'll just see you tomorrow."

Kevin stood back, letting her lead the way out the door. Her bare feet made no sound at all, but I could trace their progress by the crisp sound of his footsteps fading up the stairs.

I turned back to the magic cabinet. The perfect, solid-looking bottom had utterly collapsed, falling down like two halves of a highway overpass in a bad quake. All four springs had given way, sheered off by the sudden, unexpected force. I lifted the bottom up and locked it into place, then started gathering props, straightening my equipment, wandering around the room in larger and larger circles toward the door. Another moment, and I had eased out into the hall and stood at the bottom of the stairs. There was no sound, but the stillness only gave reign to my imagination. As the time stretched on I began to wonder what they were doing so silently, alone in the privacy of that cozy office. I tried to shut off the wilder thoughts, but images kept revolving through my mind: Kevin, shrugging out of that expensive suit, and Emily, her body now vivid in my memory.

I left. It seemed pointless to stay. I walked down Main Street toward the parking lot. It was early still, not yet six. I was hungry. I thought about dinner. Wine and candlelight. I thought about a picnic we might never take on the edge of Emily's pond. Fresh from a swim, eating bread and cheese by lantern light, wine poured from my mouth to hers. And at that, I thought of Wendy, and stopped. She might be at the bar still, or at my apartment, or at home, wondering what in the world was going on. I looked around. Main Street was still busy with the last of the day's traffic, everybody finishing up, with nothing to do but head home. I felt like the only one with nowhere to go. The cars and pedestrians moving about their business formed such a reasonable, uncomplicated picture.... I wondered how I had slipped so far out of it.

Across the street stood the ancient storefront of Van Buren's Hardware, just closing for the night, and on impulse I crossed. It was a dark and crowded little place that carried none of the utensils and appliances of a modern store, but in the back there were bins full of small bits and pieces, as if everything that might have been sold elsewhere in the store had been disassembled into its component parts. I found the springs I needed: exactly the right size, brand new, waiting in their own particular spot as if expecting me. I lingered for a while in the back all by myself, just looking around, soaking up the atmosphere. I wondered if they'd let me stay the night. They could lock the door, just leave me in, camped out among the unbroken bits and pieces. I could cook my dinner over a butane torch and spend the night reassembling all these pieces into one giant jigsaw puzzle.

When I finally stepped out onto the sidewalk again I hesitated, thinking about my apartment, thinking about Wendy's bar. Then I turned and headed back toward the Playhouse. I climbed the stairs slowly, listening for the sound of voices, but there was nothing. A thin bar of light was leaking out from beneath the auditorium door. I stopped and eased it open. Emily was there, standing over the broken cabinet as if she had misplaced something somewhere else and half-expected to find it there. She looked up as I came in. "I thought you'd left."

I held up the small brown paper bag. "New springs."

She was no longer wearing the leotard. She had changed into a t-shirt and jeans, though her feet were still bare, and the ace bandage peeped out from under one cuff. Without really wanting to I searched her face, looking for some telltale flush, some bruised softness of the lips, but there was no clue to whatever had gone on upstairs, except perhaps a faint, reserved shadow in her eyes.

"Kevin?" I said.

"He left."

"I thought I might as well fix this thing tonight. Just put the new springs in."

"Okay," she said. "Do you want some help?"

"Don't you have other plans?"

"Not for a while."

"Have you and Kevin made up?"

"Not exactly." And she shrugged, as if there were no reason to expect more certainty in that realm of her life than in any other.

Together we lifted the box onto the floor and turned it on its side. Emily held a flashlight as I reached into the hollow sides and unscrewed the clips holding the old springs. It was a narrow space, narrower than I remembered, or perhaps my hands had grown in the last seven years. I managed to remove all the old hardware, but I couldn't install the new clips. They kept slipping out of my fingers and tumbling onto the floor.

"Let me," she said.

Her hands slipped in easily. I knelt beside her, aiming the flashlight into the cavity, though she was operating mostly by touch. She was gazing up into the middle distance, and her mind could have been on anything. I would have liked to know what. She attached the springs, tightened the screws. It had taken me forever to put them in originally. Now it was done long before I wanted.

"We should test it," I said.

We set the box back onto its cart and I picked up my wand, though I felt much less than magical. "Ladies and gentlemen, we have here a perfectly ordinary box." I tilted up the cabinet and rapped the bottom and sides, showing an imaginary audience how hard and solid it appeared. Then I helped her in.

"Now, the tricky part is the timing. As soon as you climb in, I'll unlock the bottom. When you stretch out, you press down as well, but it has to look as if you're just lying flat." I released the catch.

Emily sank gracefully down below the rim of the box. "Not bad," she said and lay there for a moment, eyes closed. "Can we enlarge the foot holes?" she asked.

"No problem."

"They're a little snug."

"You won't always be wearing that bandage."

"No, the other one too."

"Okay. How's the rest of it?"

"Fine. Good." She lay there a moment longer, still and silent. Then she sat up. Drawing her feet in, she wrapped her arms around her knees. She sat hunched as if about to perform a different trick altogether: hiding in a small place, perhaps, or disappearing completely.

It gave me a sudden, panicky feeling. "What is it?"

"There's something I have to do."

"I'd rather you didn't."

"It's for Kevin."

"I know who it's for."

"He told you about the loan application? That Hugh has?"

"Yes."

"I said I'd get it for him."

I stared at her. That one little piece of paper, it seemed absurd. The whole business with the factory, with Hugh and Kevin, it had nothing to do with us. It was their problem, some minor battle in Kevin's great master plan that seemed no more substantial than any other trick or game. A small distraction from the main show. But somehow had become the single, thin fault line running under the complex terrain of my heart. At first glance so tiny, so easily ignored, it had come to assume all it's terrible importance as a kind of ultimate test—the one, thin and hairline trigger of my happiness.

"No," I said. "Not you. Not now. You don't need to now."

"Yes, I do. Especially now."

"Let him do it himself."

"This is something he needs me to do."

"But I need you not to."

She sat there, hunched and silent.

I reached out, smoothing the tensed curve of her back. "Emily? Please? For me?"

"What am I supposed to do, Charles? Sleep with his brother and then not do this for him?"

"Does he know?"

"I know."

"It doesn't mean you have to steal for him."

"It does to me."

"Doesn't it matter that I love you?"

"Yes," she said. "Of course it does. That's part of the problem."

I waited for what seemed a very long time. "Does that mean you love me?" I asked.

She sighed and rested her chin on her upbent knees. "I said it was a problem."

Night Work

At the age of ten, when I first broke into Hugh's factory as a prank and an adventure, it felt more like a test of Kevin's nerve than mine. I don't remember everything about it, but I remember a feeling of unreality, as if I weren't actually doing anything wrong, as if, at bottom, I wasn't at risk because it was all Kevin's idea. I could follow along, creeping through the darkness up the drainpipe in back, across the roof, through the narrow window that never quite closed, and the worst that could happen was that we wouldn't get in, or Kevin would be disappointed, or we'd have to run away. It felt dangerous, but at the same time I was somehow protected. It was Kevin who was doing it, and his determination and nerve was like a cloak around us all.

Now, in some strange way, that hadn't changed. After all these years it was still Kevin's determination that was leading me back through the deeper darkness at the base of the factory, but I no longer felt protected by it. Everything that had happened, everything I'd been through, and here I was, all but ten years old again. Standing at the base of the back wall, staring at the drainpipe that crept up one corner to the roof, I wondered how in the world I could have done it all those years ago.

"It's not as bad as it looks," said Emily.

She was dressed entirely in black, except for the bandage on her ankle. Her face looked pale and drawn against the darkness of her turtleneck, though I couldn't tell whether that was nerves or the pain in her ankle.

"I have done this before."

"Then there's nothing to it."

"I know. I know." My throat was dry. It made my voice sound thin and unconvincing. I reached up and grabbed the pipe. That first step is always the hardest—a leap of imagination from the horizontal to the vertical. My sneakers scrabbled against the brick, struggling for purchase. I leaned back, hanging on to the standing pipe, forcing my feet hard against the wall, and with that first step I hung there, startled, as if having put something over on all the laws of physics. Then, half-crouching, half-dragging myself, I began to inch my way up.

"Don't look down," she whispered from the darkness below, but my lungs was clenched like a pair of fists, and I didn't have the breath to reply.

It seemed to take forever. And as it happened, Emily was wrong: it was every bit as hard as it looked, and it got even harder at the top, since once I got that high, the last thing I wanted to do was let go of the pipe, even to grab hold of the roof. I dangled there a moment, just beneath the gutter, aware of all the darkness and empty air beneath me. Aware, too, of Emily, watching from below. I tried to plan it out ahead of time, to figure out how to ease smoothly up over the edge, but in the end I just lunged up with one arm, grabbing the low parapet, and with a wild and panicky flailing of feet, pulled myself up and over, onto the rough gravel of the roof. I rolled onto my back, and lay there, staring up at the clear sky, gasping like a fish on the shore.

"Charles!" came a hoarse whisper. "Charles! Are you all right?"

"Just a sec!"

I waited for the excitement of it to kick in, for that sense of adventure that should have been left over from my childhood. And I wondered if I had simply used it up. I lay there hunched and awkward, breathing hard, and only gradually did I realize I was grinning like a fool. Hurriedly I unwound one end of the rope from my waist. "Coming down," I called, and with a short toss, threw it over the side. Then, swiveling around, I braced my feet against the parapet and waited for the two sharp tugs on the line. Then I started to pull. At first it felt as if the rope were tied to the basement of the building. It strained and tightened, but didn't budge. Then, as I leaned back, feet braced hard against the parapet, it started to move. Emily climbed as best she could with one good leg, but it seemed to take forever. A couple of times she paused, braced against the drainpipe, while I caught my breath, then I pulled some more, and eventually she eased up over the low wall and rolled gracefully onto the gravel.

"Not bad," she said.

"I think I need to start lifting weights."

"Don't bother. We won't be doing this again."

We crept carefully across the flat roof, the gravel scrunching under our feet. For one nasty moment I thought that Hugh, after all these years, had finally gotten around to fixing the window latch. It was closed tight. But when I eased the tip of the screwdriver under the edge, it popped right out, and the window eased open as if it had been greased especially for us. It wasn't a large space; barely big enough for a ten-year-old; but Emily had done it before. She tied one end of the rope under her arms, and turned, squeezing through.

"Easy on the ankle," I whispered.

She nodded, frowning at the tight fit. "You got me?"

"Go ahead." I gripped the rope. "You know, this is kind of fun."

She smiled, tightly. "See you soon."

She slipped down out of sight. I sat in the dark like an ice fisherman, straining at the line as it vanished into the dark hole of the window. Her weight on the rope was the only real thing I felt. My arms were jumping with the effort, but soon the weight eased and vanished, and then, after a moment, came two sharp tugs. The rope pulled up easily, the bare end dangling. I moved quickly now, not giving myself time to think. I gathered up the rope and hurried back to the drainpipe. Throwing it out into the darkness, I eased over the edge, feeling for the pipe with my feet. It was only twenty feet, I told myself. Only twenty. I could jump that far in a pinch.

With a deep breath I reached down for the pipe. Okay, I thought. Nothing to it. But my hand was sweaty. It was like holding onto glass. I slipped, started to fall, and made a grab with the other hand, kicking at the walls for traction, then caught myself, clutching the pipe desperately as if someone might try to separate us, whispering little curses like endearments to the brick wall against my cheek. It was a long moment before I caught my breath, before I could start to inch my way down, feeling for each of the braces, snagging my hands against the rough seams in the metal. I might as well have closed my eyes for all I could see: dark brick, rusting metal inches from my eyes. The ground, when I finally reached it, was steadier and more wonderful than I would ever be able to say.

I crept around the corner, and there was Emily leaning out into the darkness from the low office window. "Okay?"

"Nothing to it." I reached up and tried to climb in, but whatever strength I'd had was gone, and my arms were like rubber.

"Come on," she hissed. She grabbed the back of my shirt and hauled up. The collar dug into my windpipe, and with a sound that was meant to be a growl of determination but ended up closer to a sob I dragged myself up and slithered in over the sill.

Emily knelt by my head. "You're doing great," she whispered.

By the beam of a tiny flashlight she guided us over to the wall where the Wyeth painting hung just as it always had for as long as I could remember. I swung it back on its hinges. There was the brand new safe, shiny silver and black, the one that Hugh had installed all those months before, when he'd realized what Kevin was after. In the narrow circle of light I tried the old combination, for no reason except that it had worked once so long ago and was so much a part of my childhood that I couldn't resist.

"I tried that one," Emily said impatiently.

"Just playing," I said. "Let me check the desk."

She held the light as I drew open the drawer, pushing aside a scattering of paper clips, pencils, and old rubber bands. There it was, faded and blurry with age: the old, familiar numbers, arranged in a long string just waiting to be decoded. And beneath it, in the same blocky hand, there was a second more recent number.

Part of me knew it couldn't be this easy. As I hurried to the safe, muttering the numbers under my breath, I was already wondering what we would do when it didn't work. But I dialed them in, and pulled down the handle, and the lock clicked open as smoothly as if I were still ten years old and all the intervening years had passed without any change at all.

"It worked?" Emily murmured.

"Shine the light in here."

There were stacks of documents: insurance policies, stock certificates, the deed to his house, and at the bottom of the pile an old manila envelope with an old, out-of-date Community Savings Bank logo in the left-hand corner. The glue on the flap was dry and dusty. The paper itself seemed fragile. I opened the envelope and slid out a single sheet, densely printed, with spaces filled in by typewriter and by hand, and a bold block heading across the top: Certificate of Lending.

It was anticlimactic. Even in the glare of the flashlight at the center of the dark room it looked too ordinary and insubstantial to be worth all this trouble. Though at that moment I should have remembered that very first trick of Rudy's and how the most innocent card, appearing out of nowhere, could bury itself between your ribs.

We drove through the night with the wind in our ears. After the silence of Hugh's factory, where the loudest sound had been the pounding of my heart, the rush of air and the whine of the rough road were like a chance to breathe again.

Emily leaned back, staring out at the dim shapes of the countryside as if they were all brand new. "What a beautiful night," she said. "Do you remember it being so beautiful?" The wind was catching her hair, turning it wild.

I reached over and found her hand, lacing my fingers through hers. "I wasn't sure we'd do it. I wasn't sure we could."

She gripped my hand, still looking around. The shrouded

trees and buildings slipped past. The roadside was a blur. "The air's so clear," she said, marveling. "It smells so good. Do you notice?" She took a deep, deep breath.

"What are we going to do?" I said.

She hesitated. In her other hand, the one that wasn't holding mine, the worn manila envelope looked stiff and out of place. "About this?"

"All right," I said. "Yes. What about that? How did you leave it?" In that private darkness I didn't even want to bring in Kevin's name.

"Up in the air."

The wind was tugging at the envelope, trying to snatch it away. We rolled up the windows, and the pressure of the air died to nothing. I felt too light in the sudden stillness, as if even the pounding of my heart could unbalance me. The road curved ahead through the woods, unrolling in the headlights, and beyond the trees, just for a moment, was the gleam of dark water, a river, a pond. I thought of Emily, pale and naked, slipping into the water out of the light. And as I recalled that image, I suddenly wished I had waited that night by the pond so I could have seen her climb out again, because everything now seemed like an omen to me, and I would have liked, in the fleeting uncertainty of this rushing night, to have the memory of her emerging instead of disappearing.

"Would you go swimming with me?" I said.

"Now?

"Tonight. When we get there. In the pond."

She still held my hand, tight in her lap. "Aren't you afraid of making things more complicated?"

"What I'm afraid is that I'll never see you naked again."

"Charles." And her voice was so soft in the darkness that I almost pulled over. "No," she said hurriedly. "Don't stop the car."

"No."

"We can't."

"I know."

She held my hand, and we drove, without looking at one another, staring ahead at the unfolding road, and in that moment I wanted it to go on forever, steadily unrolling before the warm reach of our headlights, so we could just drive and drive. After a moment I felt her shift in her seat. I heard the rustle of fabric, and the low sound of a zipper. Still I drove, looking only ahead, afraid to turn and look. She drew my hand closer and slipped it beneath the cotton of her shirt, pressing it warmly against the smooth curve of her belly. "Don't stop the car," she whispered.

"I won't."

My mouth was too dry for anything but a whisper. My heart was pounding. I might have been climbing that pipe again to the factory roof, suspended again high over the ground, with nothing beneath me but air and only the barest possibility that I might not fall.

Emily slipped down in her seat, easing her thighs, then gently guided my hand down over the slope of her belly beneath the thin waistband of elastic and cotton. My fingers brushed the soft whisper of hair and my hand molded itself to a perfect curve of flesh that softening beneath my touch, splitting like a ripe peach. She reached down and pressed my hand against her. "Talk to me," she murmured, leaning back, eyes closed. Her voice in the darkness was a rustle against the muffled rush of the car. "Tell me a story."

I sat barely moving, balanced in place, as the dark countryside slipped past.

"Once upon a time," I whispered, "I saw a town. Years ago. Somewhere in New York state. We went through it on a bus, Rudy and I. I don't know where we were going. So often we weren't going anywhere at all."

She moved ever so slightly beneath my hand. "Your voice, Charles. I love your voice."

"I was sleeping, dozing in the early morning, as we drove through beautiful hills. Trees. Narrow roads rising up, then curving away into valleys that I knew I'd never see again. They looked untouched by anything. By time. By sorrow."

"Your touch," she whispered.

My voice barely rose above the distant wind, the low whisper of her breathing. "I was dozing, leaning against the glass of the bus window, and it appeared there. This town. Out of my imagination, maybe. A perfect town of white buildings and narrow streets. A beautiful town, only as big as the tiny valley that held it. Like a coin lying in somebody's palm."

"Did it have a name?"

"I don't know. We were through there in a minute. I saw it, and it was gone. It was so beautiful."

"Charles."

"But it stayed in my mind. Frozen in my mind. There was a hotel, a large, white hotel on the main street. With a balcony, a long, perfect balcony. It was white clapboard, green shutters, and this perfect balcony across the front, where you could stand and look out over the street and the houses. Where you could stand and hold the entire town at once. The sun was rising just over the hill. The light was golden red. As if someone had just poured it over the town. Glowing on the buildings, through the trees. The trees were on fire with the light."

Now the night mattered less than the sound of her breathing, the way the story wrapped around us and that remembered view lifted us out of time altogether.

"I'd like to see it," she said. Her low voice made it more like a breath than a word. Her hand was light on my wrist. She was wet against my fingers. "On that balcony," she whispered. "Looking out."

"Yes," I said. "A corner room. We'd wake up with that light coming in through our window."

"Yes."

"We'd open our eyes and step out onto the balcony. Before the town was awake. We'd step out into the soft air, the scent of dew and the hills. Into that light."

"Yes. Just like that. Like that. Oh, Charles." Her voice caught on something, on the sound itself, and she drew my name out into a low, soft sigh as the hot, wet touch of her, moving gently in the darkness, scalded my fingers.

We drove the last few miles in silence, neither one of us moving; my hand in both her hands now, and her scent on the air. I slowed the car. I wanted never to arrive.

Emily looked over. "I feel like a swim, Charles," she said. "Would you swim with me?"

I turned into the driveway, and Kevin's car was there, waiting for us.

Kevin

I drove in and parked, as Emily hurriedly rearranged her clothes. He was sitting on the porch as if he'd been waiting for a while, and as we climbed reluctantly out of the car he stood and came walking toward us. He was carrying her cane.

"You're right on time."

"What are you doing here?" Emily demanded.

"I thought it would be nice if there were someone to greet you after your daring escapade. In case you wanted to celebrate." He gave us both a long look that reminded me of the way he watched a magic trick, without illusion or amusement, determined not to be fooled. "Or have you celebrated already?"

Emily's shirt was rumpled and a small edge of the hem puckered out over her belt. Without a word she smoothed the fabric, tucked it back into her jeans.

"We drove straight home," I said.

"Of course you did. And how did it go?"

"We got it."

He nodded with a smile that seemed to include us all in the warm glow of his self-congratulation. "You were made for a life of crime, Charles." He held out his hand. "Let's take a look."

"Not just yet."

He hesitated, the smile dimming a little, as he cast a cool and ruminative glance between us. "Of course. What am I thinking? What kind of a host am I? I'll bet you could both use a drink. God knows, I could. How's the ankle, Em?"

"It's been worse."

"Allow me." He crooked his arm toward her, a little show of gallantry that stopped just short of the ironic.

But she reached out and took the cane instead. "Thanks."

He continued, all unfazed good cheer. "Nothing a comfortable chair and a drink won't cure. Come inside. Make yourselves at home." He led the way to the house.

Emily stood, watching him without a word.

"Are you all right?" I asked softly, but she just watched as if still marveling at his sudden appearance.

Kevin was waiting on the porch, holding the screen door open. After a moment Emily stepped up to unlock the house, and without another glance at me, walked in. I followed. Kevin closed the doors quietly behind us. No slamming, this time; no long blasts of the car horn; no shouting. He was smiling and hospitable, as if he happened to be up anyway, and we had just dropped by for a visit.

"Come into the kitchen," he said. "I think there's some scotch somewhere."

"This is my home, Kevin," Emily said.

"Of course. But there is some scotch, isn't there?" She watched him stroll to the liquor cupboard and take down the bottle. "Sorry. I thought we had more, but it seems to have vanished without a trace. Is this one of your tricks, Charles?"

When I didn't reply he just shrugged and busied himself with the glasses. "Everybody wants one, I assume. God knows, we've earned it. Charles?"

"No thanks."

"Suit yourself. Em?" He held out a glass.

She was standing stiffly, fist clenched around the head of the cane. Behind her I had to resist the urge to stroke the tension from her back. Her scent still clung faintly to my fingers, but the small, remembered town bathed in light seemed a distant figment of my memory.

Kevin shrugged. "Well, you don't mind if I do." He poured himself a large one and gestured toward the living room. "Finally. We can make ourselves comfortable, and you can tell me all about it."

We walked in. Kevin sat down at one end of the sofa and gestured invitingly, but Emily walked past him and took one of the two easy chairs. I sank into the other.

"So, let's take a look," said Kevin.

He was holding out his hand expectantly, but she passed me the envelope, and I drew out the single sheet and held it close under the low light.

"It all went smoothly? No complications?"

"No," she said. "No complications."

"The ankle didn't cause any problems?"

"We managed."

I read the loan application carefully, got to the end and read it through again.

"Everything all right?" Emily asked.

I glanced up. "There's nothing at all about the ground water here."

Kevin smiled patiently. "It's there. Read it again."

"I've read it again."

"Well," he said. "You just have to know where to look. Try section E, down near the bottom."

I looked down. List all liens, encumbrances, disqualifications and liabilities upon the property. In the white space below Hugh had typed the word 'none'.

Kevin shrugged. "I would have thought a ten million dollar clean up would constitute at least a small encumbrance."

"That's it?" I said. "That's your proof?" I stared down at it, feeling deflated, that this is what it had come to. As if Emily and I together had labored all night to make something marvelous appear, and had managed in the end only a trace of grey smoke.

"Let me see," she said.

I carried the sheet to her and, perching on the arm of her chair, we read it through again.

"It doesn't say anything at all about dumping," I said. "Nothing about the condition of the land. Not a work about creosote. Nothing illegal. Nothing criminal."

"Not specifically," Kevin said. "After all. How could the bank know when Hugh didn't tell them?"

Emily stared at him, a faint light of startled disbelief in her eyes, as if even now she had been prepared to believe him. "There's nothing here, is there?"

He was smiling.

It shouldn't have surprised me. I had spent so much of my life performing on that fine line between appearance and reality. But now I felt somehow undone, because this was supposed to be my expertise. This was supposed to be what I had mastered all those years. I thought if there was anything that I could do better than Kevin it was exactly this sort of sleight of hand. But I realized even in this I couldn't match him.

"Of course there is," said Kevin. "You just have to read between the lines. Applying for money under false pretenses. That constituted fraud last time I checked."

I waved the loan application. "It was fifteen years ago. He may not even have known about it then. The wells didn't go bad until after the work."

"Actually, that's just a technicality," Kevin said. "Fraud is as fraud does. And in this case, fraud did."

"That's what you say."

"No, Charles. It doesn't matter what I say. What's important is what other people say. What will the courts say? Or, more importantly, what will the board of directors of the Community Savings Bank say? This has got to be embarrassing, at the very least."

"What makes you think they'll say anything?"

"I imagine they'll be obliged to. Once they see that."

The paper felt thin and flimsy in my hand. Barely there at all. I folded it twice. "See what?"

Kevin's face darkened. "Don't be stupid, Charles."

"Why should I change now?"

"But it's not yours to decide."

"Mine as much as anybody's."

"You weren't the only one to take some chances for this." He glanced urgently at Emily. "You know what we're trying to do here, Em. We've both gone out on a limb. But we've got it now. We have to use it. It doesn't do any good, if we don't. All that risk just wasted."

"You lied to me, Kevin."

He frowned. "No, I didn't. I didn't at all. I told you it was what we needed, the last piece in the puzzle. And it is."

"It's blackmail. Nothing more."

"Listen, Em. It's a good cause. You know that. We get that mess cleaned up. The right people held responsible. That's what you want."

"How do you know what I want? I'm not ever sure myself anymore."

Kevin shook his head impatiently as if they'd been over this before. "You want what's best for us, what's best for everyone. I know that. You know that, too. You're just tired, now. And over-wrought. You want to make a difference. You always have. And that's what we're doing. Cleaning up the town. Making it an example of what can be done."

"Kevin," she said quietly. "That's what you want."

"It's what we both want. Don't pretend it's not. It's what you've been working your whole life toward, too. We're in this together, remember?" He glanced at me, perched awkwardly on the arm of her chair, and then back. "I don't care what's happened here," he said. "It doesn't make any difference. A little slip. That's fine. We're bigger than that. This is what's important. And it's just the beginning."

"It is?"

"It can be."

I hated the sound of his voice. There was something so implacable in his tone. He sounded like a reasonable man with the truth on his side, and it made me want to hit him. It made me want to shout something, anything, something compelling, something powerful. But all I could do was whisper, "Things have changed, Kevin."

I reached out and laid a comforting hand on Emily's back, but she stiffened a little under my touch and after a moment I let it drop.

Kevin leaned forward. "Is that right, Em? Have things changed?"

"It's gotten complicated."

"Of course it's complicated. But what's changed? I haven't. The important things haven't. What about what's right, Em? Has that changed? This is important. You know it is. This is our future we're talking about."

"Maybe it's your future," I said. But there was a knot of dread in my stomach.

Kevin leaned forward. "Em. I'm not always easy. I know that. I can be a jerk. But think about this. About what we've done. It's a good cause. And we make a good team. There are things we can do, Em. Things we need to do. Emily, I love you. I can't do this alone."

"Stop it," she whispered.

"It's true," he said urgently. "Of course it's true. I love you. And more. That's what love is for us. It isn't just talk, Em. It's about doing things. Making a difference. Two people, working together. Isn't that more important than some little slip, some little fling? Think about it, Em. Think about how far we've come. You want to do something with your life, Em. You know you do. And I can help. We can make a difference here. And we can go on making a difference. More and more. How many people can say that? How many?" And he glanced at me, as if daring me to speak.

Still she wouldn't look up. She wouldn't look at me. I realized how little I had to offer; how slight a grasp I had on her. I thought about what Rudy had said all those years ago, about knowing something completely only when it was about to disappear. And I felt in that instance that if I knew Emily any better, if I wanted her any more, she would already have vanished.

"Emily," I whispered.

But that was all. What else could I say? Somehow, somewhere

in the back of my mind I had expected this night to settle it, to prove the matter beyond a doubt. Because in some way I had believed that love was risk, that danger was the one undeniable proof, that everything else was just talk. But talk was Kevin's element; it was like daylight to him. And in retrospect the burglary, the adrenalin-sharp clarity of the long ride home, were just strange, short-lived dreams, cloaked in darkness. They couldn't survive the light of an ordinary living room. And what if he was right? What if love was more than danger, more than just two people fleeing through the night? Then what did I have to offer? A few tricks in my pocket? A little town in New York state I didn't even know the name of?

Kevin leaned back again on the sofa. "I think we all need time to sleep on it. It's late. We're all exhausted."

He stood up, and for a moment I thought he was just going to leave. I thought maybe he'd just stand up and walk away, but no. Of course not. He stood, waiting.

Reluctantly I got up, and we all stood for a moment, in a silent, unacknowledged contest. Kevin's calm infuriated me; his air of certainty. At that moment I was prepared to stand all night.

But Emily turned to me. She looked miserable, exhausted. "Charles?" she said. "Please?"

I must have been more tired than I thought. Her voice took it all out of me. Perhaps I had hoped, even up to that point, that this was just a sort of nightmare. But a nightmare was what happened out in the darkness. Once in the light, you had to recognize it was nothing you were going to wake up from. I hesitated, struggling through that long moment, then I leaned in and brushed my lips against her forehead. It wasn't much of a kiss. But I couldn't bear to leave just like that, without touching her. "Take care of that ankle," I said. And without a glance at Kevin I turned toward the door.

And Emily turned with me. "Goodnight, Kevin," she said.

He looked startled. "I think we still need to talk about this, Em."

"Not tonight."

"I think so."

"No, Kevin."

He hesitated, then shrugged. "All right. It's been a busy day. We'll talk about it tomorrow." And we walked out together.

Just once on the way to my car I turned back. For one last word, perhaps, one last sign. But Emily was gazing out with an expression of such bleakness that I couldn't find a thing to say.

Nothing Up My Sleeve (part two)

I stepped into the bar as if into someone else's past. It was all familiar, the noise, the hot red light, the crowd, but now it seemed to be unwinding at a distance like a long loop of film I had shot too long ago to remember. I hesitated just past the doorway. It was late, long after midnight. In the far corner Driscoll and his colleagues were so advanced in the process of working the kinks from their muscles that they were barely upright, but no one showed any signs of wanting to go home. It was hard to remember how I could have enjoyed such a place, or what I might have been looking for all that time ago.

Despite the noise, the tall, skinny kid with the pony tail and the wispy mustache seemed to be dozing. He looked as if his part in the evening's entertainment was just about over, and when he spotted me he approached unenthusiastically as if I were intruding on some private moment.

"What'll you have?"

"Is Wendy here?"

He shook his head. "It's her early night."

"Where did she go?"

"Beats me. Maybe she went home to do her nails."

He started to turn back toward the other end of the bar, then stopped. "Hey. Is your name Charles?"

"That's right."

"Then I've got a message for you. If you came in she wanted me to ask you where the fuck you think you've been?"

He regarded me for a moment. Maybe he was waiting for a reply. Then he turned and took his place again beside the beer taps gazing indifferently out over the crowd.

When I got to my car I sat there, staring past the steering wheel out into the darkness. I couldn't see much. In the distance the lights of Front Street, trailing along the river bank, defined the invisible edge of the water. Beyond them the dark current showed only by the occasional, cryptic glint that it was in motion. The night was so empty I could imagine anything I wanted in it, but all I could see was Emily's face, looking so sad it couldn't mean anything but goodbye. I looked for some hint in the constellation of streetlights that might offer hope for the future, but they hung fixed in their curving path, as if all the decisions had already been made. I started the engine and turned the car and drove home.

My apartment was dark as the river. The windows gave not the slightest thing away. I climbed the stairs. The door, patched with cardboard, was the only sign that things were not as they had always been, and even that damage had the worn look of old news. As I stepped into the kitchen the tang of neglected rabbits was sharp on the air. I had lost track of them lately, fallen a little behind. Without bothering to turn on the lights I dug a scoopful of rabbit chow from under the sink and carried it into the living room. Everyone took an interest in that. I poured it into their bowl and six pale blurs made their separate ways over to it and began to munch away in the dark. Somebody needed me, at least. I sat down on the floor beside the low fence. If anyone wanted anything more than food, I thought, they knew where to find me. After a moment Rex hopped over and I lifted him out and onto my lap. He couldn't have had a chance to eat enough, but even among rabbits there are always some for whom love is more important than food.

After a while we stood up, Rex and I, and together wandered into the bedroom. There was no sign of Wendy. If she was doing her nails, she wasn't doing them here. The lamp was without its t-shirt drape. There was no wine glass, no wine bottle, no cigarette butts in the ashtray. The covers were no more rumpled than I had left them. In the darkness the bed floated pale and empty like an abandoned raft.

Rex was unmoved by the sight. I settled down onto the end of the mattress. In the next room I could hear the crunching of little rabbit teeth. A tiny sound, but it filled the apartment, gnawing away at the silence. I thought of Emily's expression, so bleak, so torn, and at the end of such a long evening, so empty. Ladies and gentlemen. As you can see, there is nothing up my sleeve. What more could she want? I had offered all I had. Once again. Every trick. And once again Kevin was there to turn it all into nothing. It was becoming a habit, no question. And after everything, all I had proved once again was that you don't actually have to possess something in order to make it disappear.

Rudy was right. This was the moment of knowledge, disappearance, and revelation all rolled into one. And I realized how much sense it made. After all, how can you expect to know how much you want something until it's just out of your grasp? But the problem is, once you know, then what do you do? Rudy never mentioned that part. He never explained what exactly it is that empty hands are good for.

I carried Rex back into the living room and set him down near the food dish. After a moment he hopped over and began to eat. It wasn't what he wanted most in the world, but since it was in the neighborhood he wasn't going to pass it up.

I slipped out the door and down the rickety stairs, moving quietly for no very good reason since there was no one else around to be disturbed. But I felt precariously balanced in the silence, and the slightest noise might have overtipped me. The car started up right away. I drove out of town over the bridge, stark and empty under the fluorescent lights, and headed south. This time I was expecting them, all the different landmarks. I looked for them, clicked them off in my mind: the miniature golf course, dark and deserted, the row of identical apartment buildings. Each intersection, spread-eagle beneath the too-bright lights, passed like a kind of warning: too empty, too bleak, as if I had already driven too far. After a while I began to wonder if I'd missed the turn off, if I had gone past it or simply forgotten my way, and I couldn't tell whether I felt more disappointed or relieved. But I kept driving and within a mile I came to the corner with the muffler shop and the Seven-Eleven.

From there on it was guesswork, turning left and right through the darkness of the back streets, each corner looking the same, all the houses and yards interchangeable. I might have been traveling in circles, the dark roads a kind of Mobius strip carrying me on a single long curve that ended where it began, except that all of a sudden the house appeared, low and unremarkable, and I stopped the car.

For a long time I sat there across the street, headlights doused, engine idling as if for a getaway. The upstairs looked blind and dark, but on the ground floor a faint vein of light showed in one window.

In the middle of the night, judgment comes unmoored. As if in keeping with the indeterminate darkness, desire follows its own course without regard to what is smart or good or true. If in the bright light of day you're constrained by the visible knowledge of what is right and proper, in the dark you do only what you have to. I pulled into the driveway, blind without headlights, and cut the engine. The sudden silence gradually filled in with the background hum of air conditioners. Reluctantly I climbed out and approached the door.

I knocked. Within the house there was the muffled sound of voices and then silence. I knocked again, and after a moment I heard footsteps, and the porch light came on over my head. The door opened, and there, standing behind the lattice of the screen door, was Mrs. Kamisky in her pink chenille bathrobe, though without the curlers in her hair. She looked pale and nervous, and she clutched at the lapels of her robe.

"Hello, Mrs. Kamisky. I know it's very late."

"What is it?" she said anxiously. "What do you want?"

"We've met before? My name is Charles? I'm a friend of Wendy's?"

She looked so worried and uncertain, everything I said came out as a question. But gradually her face cleared. "Oh, yes. Of course. Did you say...?"

"Charles. That's right."

"Well, Charles." She seemed to settle herself more comfortably, falling back into a more familiar role. "Wendy's home. Would you like to come in?"

And from inside came her voice. "Who is it, mom?"

"It's your friend Charles."

There was a long silence as Mrs. Kamisky stood there, holding the door, peering back into the kitchen. "Well," she said doubtfully. "Aren't you going to come say hello?"

I stepped past her into the kitchen, and there was Wendy, standing by the far counter in the light of the hallway beyond, hunched in a plaid flannel bathrobe, cradling a mug in both hands.

"We were just having some cocoa, Charles," her mother said. "Would you like to join us?"

"He doesn't want cocoa, mom."

"He might."

"Thank you," I said. "I don't think so."

"It's no trouble," her mother said. "Or," she glanced back at her daughter, "something else? A drink? What do we have, dear?"

"Thank you," I said. "If it's not too much trouble, maybe some cocoa."

"I thought so," Mrs. Kamisky said with satisfaction and turned busily to the cupboard, pleased to have something to do. I stood there.

"What's the matter, Charles?" said Wendy. "Don't you have any cocoa at home?"

"I came to talk."

"You're kidding. After all this time? Isn't that nice. Don't you think, mom? Pretty flattering. Coming all this way to talk."

Her mother looked a little disconcerted, but she continued to prepare the cocoa, lifting a mug down from the cupboard, spooning in the chocolate, glancing nervously at the tea kettle as if willing it to boil. "I think we have some cookies somewhere," she said, "If you think he'd like them, dear."

"Thank you," I said. "That isn't necessary."

"What do you mean?" said Wendy. "Of course we'll have cookies. A whole fucking plateful. Just dump 'em on there, mom. Let's eat a whole lot of cookies."

Her mother was just staring at her, an open package from Pepperidge Farm in her hands.

"Wendy...," I said.

"What, Charles? What? What is it? What did you come to talk about?"

"I thought we might talk alone."

"Why bother? I've got no secrets. Anything you can say to me, you can say to my mom. Right, mom?"

But her mother was setting the package of cookies back on the counter. "I think I'll just go upstairs," she said. She was kneading her fingers, glancing from Wendy to me. "I'll let you young people alone." And she smiled painfully. "I've got a wonderful mystery I'm right in the middle of. I can't wait to finish it." And she hurried from the room, vanishing up the stairs.

The kettle was boiling. We both stared at it for a moment. Then I walked over and turned it off.

Wendy watched as it gradually subsided. "Shit," she said softly.

"Wendy."

"Don't do this, Charles."

"I have to."

"You're going to hurt my feelings, aren't you, Charles?"

I said nothing. There was nothing I could think of to say.

"You asshole," she said softly. "You fucking asshole. After all this. And you make a special trip just to break my heart."

"Something's happened."

"Hell, yes," she sneered. "Something."

"I didn't plan it."

"Yeah, Charles. Isn't that swell?"

"She's engaged to my brother."

"Jesus Christ!" She stared as of she'd been expecting it, and still couldn't believe it. "That is so fucked up. Do you know how fucked up that is, Charles? You're a fucking mess."

"I know."

"Are you trying to be an asshole? Is that it? Are you looking for ways to fuck up?"

"I wasn't looking for it at all."

She leaned back against the counter, her shoulders drooping. She was shaking her head in disgust, in disbelief. "Well, fuck you, Charles," she said softly. "You know? God damn fuck you. Is it true love? Is that it? Is it true fucking love?"

"I don't know."

"And what about me? You can't just do this to people, Charles. You can't just wander in, fuck 'em when you want to, and wander off. What do you think? That's all right? You think that's what people do?"

"You know it's not like that."

"I know it? Fuck you, Charles. You don't even know it. How am I supposed to know?"

"Listen, Wendy. Please. I don't..."

"No. You listen. You're the one who came after me. I didn't come after you. You wanted me. I didn't give a shit about you. You were just another asshole in the bar." Her voice was rising. "Just another prick trying to stick your hand up my shorts and your tongue in my mouth. God, Charles. Maybe you spent a little too much time living out of dumpsters. Maybe you forgot what real people are like."

"No," I said. "I remember."

"And you think this bitch with the stick up her ass is going to see anything but a waste of time when she looks at you? A waste of time, Charles. That's what you are. You know? And, what? She's going to give up Mr. Politics for you? She's going to decide she doesn't want to marry some big shit motherfucking mayor just because she wants you instead?"

"No," I said. And that cold fist was in my chest again. "I don't think she is."

"Aw, Charles," said Wendy bitterly. "What's the matter? Doesn't she love you? Isn't she crazy about you? Isn't she going to give up everything just to have you?"

"I think she's going back to him."

She stared. "Shit," she whispered. "You shit. She's going back, and you're still doing this?"

"I have to."

"Well, fuck you twice, Charles. You know what? I liked you, you stupid prick. I thought you were nice. And you liked me."

"Yes."

"Tell me you did. How much? A little? A lot? Tell me."

"A lot. I liked you a lot."

"A whole lot, Charles?"

"I did."

"Well, it wasn't fucking enough, was it?"

She clutched the lapels of her bathrobe, hugging them tight around her, leaning back against the counter. She looked up at me tired and hurt and disgusted. "What is this, Charles. Is it some game with you? Another piece-of-shit magic trick? You think you can just come in, mess around, and then wave your magic wand? Are you going to make us all disappear?"

"That's not what I'm doing."

"Bullshit! But I'll tell you, Charles. It doesn't work. I'm still here. And so are you. You can't make all your mistakes just disappear. You can't just wave your fucking magic wand and make someone fall in love with you."

"I know. I'm sorry."

"Sorry? That's it? You're sorry? Well, fuck you. I'm sorry, too. I'm sorry I ever met you." And she waited, as if I might have something to add to that, but in the end all she could do was shake her head grimly. "Aw, come on, Charles. Don't look so sad. Have a cookie. What did you think? It was going to be easy? Did you think it was going to make you happy?"

But no. I didn't think that. I didn't think it would make me happy. In fact, I'm not sure what I was thinking. But what I needed wasn't happiness now. It was more desperate than that. I needed to strip away everything I had, every possibility of love or pleasure or happiness. I needed to peel away everything. Because Wendy was right. I needed something to hold up against that bleak look in Emily's eyes, and what else did I have? Against all that sadness and doubt and uncertainty, against all of Kevin's accomplishments and smooth, reasoning voice and promising future I had nothing except my loss to balance the ledger. What was I thinking? I'm still not sure. I must have thought unhappiness alone was a force to be reckoned with. Love and unhappiness against all that Kevin stood for. I must have thought somehow it could make the difference. Or maybe it was just the hope, the knowledge of any magician that, if you want to make the magic card appear, your hand first has to be absolutely empty.

Without a Trace

The next evening I arrived early at the Playhouse, but there was no sign of a rehearsal. The auditorium was empty and silent. I climbed all the way up the stairs, but the office, too, was deserted. So I set up the magic cabinet, arranged my props, laid out everything. Still Emily didn't arrive. I was pacing around the auditorium, turning over the painted scenery, picking up and putting down props and costumes, when finally I heard the sound of the heavy front door. Footsteps shuffled up the stairs, and after a long moment the auditorium door opened and in she walked. She was barely limping on her bad ankle, but she looked so bleak it made my heart sink.

I was speaking before she was halfway across the room, talking quickly. "I've got a great idea for the timing of this trick. It sounds like a little thing, but it'll be terrific. As you climb in you sort of shift around and look as if you're really stretching out, as if the box is just a little too long for you. We want to give the impression you're lying completely stretched out, so there's no hint you're sinking down into the compartment. It's not a big deal, but we've really got to practice it to make sure we've got it right. You've got to look perfectly natural as you climb in and stretch. All in one movement. It's going to take a lot of practice...." I sounded ridiculous. I was racing through, not even clear in my own mind what I meant to say, just aware that I needed to keep talking, that I couldn't give her a chance to speak.

She looked stunned by the avalanche of words. Pale and uncertain, she reached up tentatively to grasp the rim of the magic cabinet, as if bracing herself. "Charles?"

I shook my head. "It's not a big deal. It won't be a big change. We're already doing it more or less that way. But it's those little refinements that can really make the difference."

"Charles...," she said again, more faintly than before, and I thought maybe there was still hope.

"But what's crucial is that we keep rehearsing. We've got to keep practicing, got to really nail it down--"

"Charles."

In the end it was her expression, not her voice, that stopped me. My voice died away. I stood on the other side of the box, looking at her across the narrow wooden trough as if it were miles to the other side.

She closed her eyes, too tired even to look.

"Don't say anything, Emily. You don't have to say anything." And even as I heard myself I thought of Wendy and the fierceness that comes only with desperation.

"Yes, I do," she said. Her voice curled its cold fingers around my heart. If every mood had a tone, if every event had its own sound, then this was the voice in which things ended.

"I can't do this," she said.

"Good," I said. "Good. You don't have to."

"No. That's not what I meant. This." And she tightened her grip on the box as if, of all the things between us, that were the only one that mattered. "All of this. Us. I'm not good at it, Charles. It's cheating."

"Emily." I could barely hear my own voice.

"I know. It sounds stupid. I know. But I--"

"Don't!" I said sharply.

"What?"

"Don't tell me you love him."

She shook her head. "He loves me," she said.

"He left you. He left you hanging. He drove away, don't you remember?"

"He came back."

"But he left," I said.

"He was afraid. How can I blame him for that? Haven't you ever been afraid?"

I didn't tell her that I was afraid right now. "He doesn't deserve you."

"It isn't about deserving. How can it be? If we only got what we deserved...."

But I knew she was wrong there. I knew that, sometimes, at least, we got exactly what we deserved. Every bad choice, every bad decision, slipped back and twined around our throats.

"What would it take?" I said.

"Please...."

"I'll give him the paper. Hugh's paper... the loan application." I was rushing again, bargaining, trying to make a deal. "I'll give him Hugh. He'll get his factory. He'll get his fucking urban oasis. None of that matters. He can have what he wants. Don't you see...?" I slowed down, petered out, exhausted by the bleak look on her face. "I just want you," I whispered.

"Charles..."

"Don't you love me?"

"What does it matter? Don't you see? I'd hate myself."

"No. Say it."

"What good would it do?"

"Just tell me. Yes or no," I said. "No tricks."

She opened her eyes wide and looked up at me, and I suddenly thought of sleeping beauty awakening. It's such a good story, such a great fairy tale. How could it not have a happy ending? "It can't make a difference," she said.

"It makes all the difference."

"I can't do this to him."

"Why not? He would. You think he wouldn't? He'd do it in a minute."

"No." She shook her head sadly. "I can't. This isn't some trick we're doing. He's counting on me."

"I'm counting on you."

"Don't. Please."

"Emily. You're all that matters to me." But she was already turning away. "What are you doing?"

"I've got to go," she said.

"But what about the rehearsal?" It sounded stupid, even to me, but what else could I say? "We can't stop now. What about the show? At least we can still do that."

But she shook her head. "No. It wouldn't be fair."

"To who?"

"To you."

"I don't mind!"

"To Kevin, then."

"He doesn't care. He knows you're doing it."

All this time I thought I'd have given anything to see her smile, but now she did, and it was the saddest thing I'd ever seen. She smiled and shook her head. "But, he doesn't know how much fun it is."

And she turned away again, brushing her hand lightly along the side of the magic cabinet, though by this time, of course, it was no longer magic. For the second time in my life, after all the work and the practice and the rehearsals, it had become just an ordinary box, built more or less in the shape of a coffin.

Everything Burns

The Mayor's Office is the grandest room in town, out of all proportion to the rest. It was said to have been designed inadvertently by Robert Adam in 1768 on a trip to the Colonies during a brief stopover between New Haven and Boston. Supposedly the already famous architect was welcomed by the then-mayor, my great-great-great-great-grandfather Charles, to the existing office, a large but rather shabby room, where, over lunch, he expounded at length about the necessary accoutrements of public office. As he spoke he took out a pencil and began sketching a design on the linen tablecloth. It was just a quick rendering meant to elaborate all the many ways this room fell short: more a detailed and beautifully drawn insult than a design. But he hadn't counted on the determination of his host. The mayor kept smiling and nodding and topping up his guest's glass, and then, when the officious visitor had finally staggered out to his carriage, he preserved the tablecloth and turned it over to a skilled and resourceful architect who, despite all his skills and resourcefulness, was destined to remain anonymous. The office, when completed, was referred to as the Bentchley room. It was large and grand and formal, and over the years there came to be a general separation of mayors into two groups: those who felt overwhelmed by it, and those who didn't. Kevin, of course, felt perfectly at home.

He was sitting behind his desk when I walked in. And Emily was there. She was standing at the corner of the desk, hovering, as if she couldn't quite bring herself either to leave or sit down. I stared at her for a moment.

"I knew you wouldn't mind," said Kevin smoothly. "I asked Emily to be here. Anything you can say to me, you can say to her." Then, as if it were part of the same thought, he picked up the old intercom phone. "Lucy? Why don't you take an early lunch? No, that's all right. Take your time. You can go do some shopping or something. Thanks." In the anteroom I heard the secretary gather up her purse, put on her coat, and leave.

"Why don't you sit down?" Kevin waved at a heavy leather wing chair parked across from the desk.

I ignored him, my eyes on Emily. "I've called you. Over and over. I've left messages."

She nodded, wrapping herself in the sad, grey cloak of her smile. "I know. I just couldn't. I'm sorry."

I turned to Kevin. "How do you do it?"

"Do what?"

"You know Emily quit the magic show."

"Charles." He smiled sympathetically. "You must have known she would. It wasn't really her kind of thing."

"You told her to."

"I never did. Did I, Em?"

But she was silent as one of Robert Adam's frescoes lining the walls: Charity, Courage, Beauty. Graceful and watching, as if from outside it all.

"I love her," I said. "More that you ever will."

Kevin frowned, leaning back in his chair. "You know, Charles. You really don't get it. You never have. You think it's always about love."

"Not always."

"Always," he said. "You think people let you down. You think they disappoint you. You think they don't love you. And maybe they don't. But it's never just that."

"Never?"

"You know what your problem is? It's always been the same. A failure of nerve. You settle for pretending. For make believe. You pretend to make things change. But the world isn't about make believe. It's about doing things, Charles. Not just appearing to. It's about reality. And you've never been all that good at dealing with that."

"This isn't about me," I said hotly.

"Of course it is. That's what it's always been about. You... and me."

"And what about Emily?"

"What about her?"

"Do you love her?"

He glanced over at her, smiling, as if to say, What did I tell you? then back to me. "See, Charles? We're back to love again."

"Tell me."

"I do. Yes. Of course I do. And you know what? Emily loves me."

"No."

He smiled. "What, Charles? We're going to argue about the nature of love now? Does she, doesn't she? Well here's a quick test. Who are you going to be sawing in half for the magic show on Friday?"

I stared at him, feeling his brisk and certain voice open a hollow in my chest. I said, "You don't really think you can make her happy, do you?"

"I wouldn't dream of it. It's not up to me. It's not some little trick, Charles. Wave your magic wand and happiness appears. Emily's a strong and determined woman. She can make herself happy. It's in her hands. Not mine. And, you know what, Charles? That's why she loves me. Oh, maybe she loves you, too. Maybe a little bit. Or thinks she does. But that doesn't matter. Because she's a doer, Charles. Like me. She wants to accomplish something. She wants to make a difference. And I help her. That's what love is, Charles. I give her that chance."

"Because you're so selfless."

He shrugged carelessly. "What do you want me to say? It isn't selfish to see things the way they are. You can't control what other people feel, Charles. You can't make them happy or sad. And it's just egotistical to think you can. Why does she do it? Take all those risks? All those protests? Chaining herself to gates? Standing on ledges? For me? No. She does it for herself. That's why we do everything. Emily, me, and you, too. "

"So it's every man for himself?"

"Is that such a bad thing? Counting on people to look out for themselves?"

"And when they get hurt?"

"Then they get hurt. What can you do about it, really? In the end, it isn't your strength that hurts somebody, Charles. It's their own weakness. You can't blame me for everybody's weakness."

"And what about Gracie?" I said.

"What about her?"

"Everything."

He frowned impatiently. "Not everything is my fault, Charles."

But I didn't reply.

"That was years ago. An accident. That's all. No one could have saved her."

"You could have."

"I wasn't even there."

"You should have been."

"No, Charles."

"And so should I."

He shook his head. "What's the good of thinking like that? We did nothing wrong. Nothing that killed her. And there's nothing to be done but accept it. And forget it."

"Just like that?"

"It was a long time ago."

"Not so long," I said. "You know, she came to see me."

He glanced over at Emily in surprise. "When?"

"Gracie," I said. "That afternoon."

"Which afternoon?"

But I could see he knew.

"She knocked on our door. She was shaking. Crying. She stood there, in our doorway, and I wouldn't let her in."

Kevin peered over at me. He wasn't smiling anymore.

"I thought she'd come for you," I said. "I told her she couldn't come in. That you didn't want to see her. You'd been gone for hours by that time, but I was so angry. Can you have any idea how angry I was?"

"At me?" He seemed genuinely surprised.

"She was sobbing. Gracie. Sobbing in the doorway, and I didn't even let her in."

Kevin was staring wordlessly, trying to imagine it, perhaps, and failing to. But I could see it so clearly, could see her, standing there, face blotchy with tears, blonde hair mussed past caring. She looked terrible. She was wearing her usual tee-shirt and shorts, but she was transformed—face clenched with a love as strong as fever and a feeling of calamity that had nothing to do with me. Maybe that's what hurt most of all: that she could have felt all that for Kevin. It turned her ugly in my eyes.

"He's leaving me, Charles. He's going away," she said. She was fifteen, but she sounded like a grown woman, lost and forlorn. "What am I supposed to do?"

And I sneered. "Don't ask me. Why don't you ask your boyfriend?"

I could barely see her then, I was so angry. I could barely hear her voice. I might have been reading her lips. She might have been just mouthing the words. "He said he loved me." She begged, "Help me, Charles."

And what did I say? How did I respond? I said, "Help you? I don't even want to talk to you."

"Please." She swallowed hard, her whole body tightening around the word.

I stopped, and glanced up at Kevin. "You knew she was pregnant?"

"No. Of course not."

But he answered too quickly.

"She came to me for help," I said. "And I slammed the door in her face. She came to me because she had nowhere else to go." And more, I thought. Because she had always come to me, because we'd been children together all our lives. But she wasn't a child anymore, and I still was —though, for the last time.

She said, "Pregnant," and at first I didn't know what she meant. It was like an anagram that took time to decipher. I just stared, feeling my chest preparing to burst. "I hate you," I said. Just like that. I said it quietly, I remember, because I had a little trouble breathing. But even to my own ears it sounded unimaginably hard. I still hear it, sometimes, late at night. "I don't care if I never see you again."

I stepped back, and the door swung past and shut.

She stayed there, pounding at the door, crying. Her voice was muffled, but I could still hear it. I turned and left. I slipped out the back, walked for hours. I heard the sirens in the distance, but I didn't pay any attention. At the time I didn't imagine they could have anything to do with me. When I got home, most of the smoke had already blown away.

"Why tell me this?" Kevin demanded.

"Because you're so good with reality. And because, after all these years, I wanted to make sure you knew. "

He leaned forward, suddenly icy and angry. "Look. I'm sorry for Gracie. But I didn't kill her."

"You broke her heart."

"No one dies of a broken heart."

"But that's not all. I turned her away. Don't you see? I did. And after all these years. After all the time I've spent hating you. It turns out I'm no better than you are."

He looked at me without a word.

"I used to envy you," I said. "Oh, nothing you might imagine. It wasn't this." I gestured at the room. "It wasn't all the things you did. It was that you never felt bad about people. You never worried about them. You never felt responsible. There was always that difference between us. I used to think it was an advantage I'd never have. A sort of head start I'd never be able to make up for."

He smiled crookedly. "Charles, I--"

"No." I waved him to silence. "I used to think it made you

stronger."

"I haven't done anything wrong," he said.

"You know, all these years…. I always thought I was the magician. But look at you. A little twist of the wrist, a magic word, and Poof. The past is gone. Forgotten. But the thing is, Kevin, there's something you don't really get. You never have. It doesn't disappear. Not really. Whatever you make disappear…? It's always right there. Always. Just not where you think it is."

"You're upset."

I pulled Hugh Barker's loan application out of my pocket. I'd almost forgotten it, but now I held it up. "I have a little trick. You can try to guess how it's done."

I pulled out a cigarette lighter.

"Wait!"

"Don't be silly," I said, flicking the lighter. "In a trick like this, timing is everything."

"You can't."

"Of course I can. Without this you've got nothing."

"Think about it."

"I have. I've thought about it a lot."

"Have you thought about going to jail?" he said.

I almost laughed. "You're going to arrest me? For what? Arson?"

"Breaking and entering."

"I don't think so."

"Burglary. Theft. Harboring stolen property. Take your pick."

"What stolen property?"

"You're holding it."

"Not for long."

"Wait!" He was standing, now, leaning over his desk. "You broke into Hugh's factory. In case you didn't know it, that's against the law."

I smiled. "I see a problem here, don't you? If you blow the whistle on me, I'm sure as hell going to blow the whistle on you."

"And what are you going to say? That I came along? That

I thought it up? Can you even say I asked you to do it? You wouldn't want to lie, Charles."

"Some people will believe me."

"You'd be surprised how few. And you might find yourself in jail pretty fast."

I stood, marveling at him. The lighter was still burning. "You'd send me to jail?"

"If I had to."

"And then what? After all that, do you think there'd be anyone, anywhere, who would ever even think about voting for you again? For anything? You'd be the youngest and briefest mayor in the history of Connecticut."

Kevin stared at me, stony-faced. It reminded me of that poker game, how he'd sat there, looking so fierce and determined, when I knew he had nothing in his hand but a pair of twos. "You'd be in jail," he said.

"I've been in jail."

"But this isn't play-time. This isn't off in some anonymous little town. Real jail in real life."

"You know, Kevin," I said. "I think it might be worth it." I raised the lighter and held it to the corner of the paper.

"Then, what about Emily?" he said.

I watched the flame, just licking at the very edge of the paper, but I was listening now. "What about her?"

"How is she going to like jail?"

I stared up at him.

"You're not going to put her in jail," I said.

"It won't be up to me. Listen, kid. I'm out on a limb here."

"Then maybe you should climb down."

"Understand this," Kevin said grimly. "If I don't pull this off with Hugh, I'm dead in the water. Washed up at thirty-one."

"And that's supposed to matter?"

"And this town is washed up with me. No federal money. No new commercial interest. Just the tail end of two hundred and fifty years of nothing. Understand, this is something I've got to do. I've got no leeway. Emily understands that. I can't be seen to break the law. If this comes out I'll have no choice. This is something Emily and I have both been working toward. She knew it would be risky. She accepts the risks, and so do I. But you, Charles. You're the one with the choice here. It's all up to you. You can stop it, or you can send her to jail."

Emily said not a word. She was gazing at Kevin with a calm inscrutable expression. Then she turned to me to see what I would do.

"You know, Kevin. You're an asshole, but even you wouldn't throw your own fiancé in jail."

"Of course not," he said. "I won't have to." He was watching me closely, and as I stared at his face I could see the very beginnings of a smile. "Careful," he said. "It's burning."

Now You See It...

The factory looked familiar in the afternoon sun, with a worn and patient air as if the recent indignities of our nighttime incursion were only the least of what it had endured over the years, as if in the bright sunshine it was just waiting for me to return to the scene of the crime.

Hugh was in his office. He opened the door, and when he saw me he smiled. A little tiredly, perhaps, but still, a smile's a smile. "Charles. Come in. But watch your step. I'm drowning in paper."

The office looked as if it hadn't been touched since that first night all those weeks ago. It was cluttered past believing. Drawers hung open, files scattered on every surface.

"Have a seat," he said. He glanced distractedly around at the mess, then bent and removed a pile of folders from a chair. "Here."

"I think I'll stand. I'll just be a moment."

"You don't mind if I sit. I've been on my feet all day."

He settled into his chair and gazed up at me, old and familiar as the building. Years ago his was the last friendly face I saw before I left. It seemed only right to see him now.

"I'm thinking about leaving," I said.

"Leaving what? Town? Now?"

"Soon."

"But you just got back." He looked startled, sad even. I was touched. But I thought of Emily. What does it matter that people are sad if, in the end, it still just means good-bye?

"Why?" he said.

I shrugged. "I'm running out of reasons to stay. When I came back I wanted to prove this was more than just the place where I kept losing things."

"But it is," he said. "Isn't it?"

"I think some places are just unlucky."

"This is your home."

"Even worse luck."

He was peering up at me uncertainly, searching for something, as if the words weren't enough to make sense of. "It can't all be about losing, Charles. Not the whole town. You must have found something here."

"I found this." I drew the loan application out of my pocket, unfolded it, and laid it without a word on the desk before him. It was singed and fragile and ready to tear.

Hugh regarded it wordlessly for a moment. "I've been looking for that," he said softly.

"I thought about trying to sneak it back, but decided you deserved better."

"How did you get it?"

I nodded at the Wyeth painting, hanging ajar over the new safe. "You wrote the combination on the desk drawer."

He shook his head. "My memory's been playing tricks on me off and on." Gingerly he picked it up. "It doesn't look very important, does it?"

"It's been through a lot."

He stared at it. He'd been holding onto it for so long, keeping it as a reminder that all your best intentions can come to nothing; that nothing you do is every forgotten; that the consequences of every action remain, lurking, waiting for the moment to make themselves felt. Now he reached out delicately and brushed a fingertip against the crumbling blackened edge. "I thought about burning it myself a few times," he said. "I even tried once, at home. But the damned alarm went off, and I lost my nerve. I ended up just ruining the ceiling."

"You can burn it now."

He glanced up at me. "It's funny, but I was expecting someone else to come. Why you, Charles? "

"It's complicated."

"Did you wonder what I'd done? Just how bad it was? Well,

it's all right here." He said, lifting the document.

"No, it's not," I said. "That's exactly the point."

He raised his hand and touched his temple. "Then, it's all right here. In the end there's no difference."

"It was nothing illegal."

"But I knew, Charles. That's the problem. Oh, at the time I told myself there was room for doubt. There was no real evidence of any harm. The ground water was fine. The river was fine. And I told myself the earth was big enough to forgive a lot of mistakes. Even mine."

"It's possible," I said. "You could have been right."

He flicked a finger at the singed edge. "It's funny. I was almost pleased to find it gone."

"You were?"

He smiled bitterly. "I've been sitting on it for fifteen years. Too honest to burn it. But not quite honest enough to want it made public. When it was stolen, things were out of my hands. It was up to your brother, then. What could I have done? I couldn't let Mary suffer for my mistakes. I would have had to give in. The best of both worlds. Then he would simply have buried my guilt. Or better yet, cleaned it up. He would have taken all the responsibility off my shoulders. Just like that. My fairy godfather."

"Is that so bad?"

"After everything he's done? After Gracie? Just like that?" He shook his head, smiling tiredly. "I couldn't just give it to him. But for a while there I actually thought, deep down in some dark corner, that I just might get to have it both ways. I could let myself off the hook, and lay all the blame on Kevin for being the lying, blackmailing, unprincipled son of a bitch he is. And no one would have to know what I'd done. Except me, of course."

He sat staring down at the paper, still balanced lightly between his hands. I looked around at the office, that old, familiar room, wondering how long we have to carry things before we can let them go. Papers, files that hadn't seen the light of day for years were spread out now, open to the sun like all our oldest faults.

"Gracie came to me, that last day," I said.

Hugh looked up unsurprised, as if of all the things that had happened, this was the only one he'd expected. "She loved you, Charles."

"She came to me. She asked me to forgive her, and I said no." I paused bleakly. "Who does that to a person?"

Hugh said nothing. What answer could he give?

For years I'd hated Kevin, all those years on the road, because he took her away, because he stole her from me. But most of all because in that last gasp of that last afternoon, after everything he'd done, I was the one who let her down. You spend so much of your life trying to hide from yourself, trying to make up for things when there's nothing that can be done. You fool yourself into thinking the past is there to be changed. If you can just concentrate, if you can find the key, the proper words or moment, you can somehow make right what you had long ago made wrong.

But in the end nothing works... all the rehearsals, all the performances. The Boy in the Burning Building. The Young Girl Sawn in Half. You do them over and over, but they move you not one step closer to the past. I thought of Rudy, of all he'd done, all he'd taught me. And I thought, What was the good of magic if it couldn't alter the one thing we would give everything to change?

"She wouldn't want you to hate anybody, Charles. Least of all yourself."

"You think?"

"She'd forgive you, if she were here."

"But that's just the problem. She isn't."

"No."

"What will you do?" I asked.

He laid the fragile paper down on the desk and smoothed out the creases. "I don't know."

"You could give it to him. To the city, I mean. Let him have the factory."

"After all this, just let him have his way? After all he's done, give him exactly what he wants? Where's the justice in that?"

"He'll clean it up. He'll have to. Who knows? Maybe the town really does need a new urban oasis."

"And what about me? A bank president, living happily ever after?" He smiled bleakly. "Where's the justice in that?"

"Nobody's keeping track but you. Are you going to spend your whole life paying for your mistakes?"

"But how can you know when you've paid enough, when nothing can ever change what you did?"

I gazed down at him. He looked weary and lost, and I thought how strange it was to hear my thoughts on his lips. But it's always easier to forgive someone else.

I nodded at the document in his hands. "I lit it on fire right in front of Kevin."

"Then why didn't you just let it burn. Why bring it back here?"

Gently I lifted it out of his hands and smiled.

On the road Rudy and I performed for anybody. It didn't matter who was watching. It was the tricks, the sleight of hand, that mattered. But now, in this old place, surrounded by all the ghosts that every life produces, I realized that the most important thing about magic wasn't what you did. It was who you did it for. On some level, everything I'd done, every trick I'd performed, had been for Kevin. All those years, over and over again. And to no avail. Kevin didn't care. And magic's only magic if you believe. But Hugh had always been a good audience. "I want to show you a new trick," I said.

I held up that single sheet of paper. "Watch carefully." I tore it once across, then turned it and tore it again. Then again. I pulled out my handkerchief and draped it across my palm and placed the fragments of the loan application squarely in the center. Then I folded the fabric over it and held it out. "Blow."

He looked up at me for a moment, startled, amazed, with a look of what might almost have been hope, then hesitantly he leaned forward and lightly blew. I lifted the handkerchief and flicked it open. And with a snap and a flutter it spread out, bright and empty as the air.

Nothing Disappears

The houselights in the auditorium dimmed and the stage brightened as Kevin, immaculate in a black tuxedo, stepped out into the gathering applause. He stood there smiling and bowing, as if he had actually done something to earn that warm welcome, as if he had worked for it, rehearsed and prepared, instead of simply showing up ten minutes before and strolling out into the limelight.

He held up his hands for quiet. "Ladies and Gentlemen. I'd like to welcome you all to tonight's performance and congratulate you on your good taste in supporting such an important part of our community. I've been doing my own part, of course. But love and affection only go so far. The time has come to give money. So I'd like to thank you all for opening your checkbooks and for coming to our little fund raiser."

The audience laughed and clapped, cheerfully applauding themselves and him. My hands were clenched tight. I searched the auditorium. There was no sign of Emily.

"But before I introduce my long lost brother Charles, returning from distant lands to entertain us here tonight, I'd like to make an announcement of my own. Through the generosity of one of our leading citizens, Strawberry's Landing will be the site of one of the most innovative urban renewal efforts to make it from the drawing board to the city street. Many of you will have heard the rumors. Well, I'd like to be the first to tell you they're true. Thanks to Hugh Barker, and with a little help of my own, you won't be losing a factory; you'll be gaining a whole new downtown and an exciting new future."

They applauded once again, and this time he didn't try to restrain them. He stood there, basking for a long moment, and I watched with something that might actually have been wonder if he had been anybody else. Each time he spoke he twisted the world into some new form, and each time, somehow, it held its new shape.

"And now, ladies and gentlemen, for your viewing pleasure. My brother Charles."

His timing was perfect. As he bowed his way off the stage the clapping never really stopped, so even as the lights faded out for my entrance, the applause for my brother continued to fill the room.

The auditorium sank into deepest darkness, and I felt myself sinking with it even as I stepped forward into my act. I reached the center of the stage and threw down the smoke pellets just as the spotlight hit. The white cloud billowed up like a wall, glowing in the light, and I stepped through. But it felt all wrong.

In the past, that moment had always marked the transition from nervousness to excitement, from darkness through that thick, milky cloud into the bright light and the roar of applause. But tonight I stepped through into nothing but emptiness. I heard the applause, I raised my hands, waiting for that flow of energy and excitement, and I felt nothing at all.

But seven years of practice had anchored the performance. I had the first bouquet of flowers ready even as I began to speak. "Ladies and gentlemen, boys and girls, have you noticed a certain disturbance in the air? I think there are forces at work tonight about which we can only wonder...." I listened to my voice. It seemed to be coming from a long way off.

Emily stood out in the audience, I could see her now, off to one side. I could just make out her familiar silhouette, through the glare of the spotlights. I had watched her before the show, setting up chairs with a couple of the older kids, but I could think of nothing to say to her that I hadn't already said before. She'd been working busily and hadn't met my eyes.

There are limits beyond which even magic won't go. Even Rudy used to admit that, though not very often. It wasn't something he liked to stress, though sometimes he clearly had it on his mind. That final summer in Saratoga especially.

He was moving more slowly, more hesitantly then, but at the time I thought he was just tired. It had been a long year, and we'd both been working hard.

"We've got to take it easy," I said.

"We've got to think ahead."

"Why? You'll never get old. You'll just get meaner and more cranky."

"I want to have something to pass on."

"We don't need to talk about that now."

"Sooner or later," he said.

"Later, then. When you retire. We'll become alchemists. We'll spend all our time making gold."

We were sitting at a table out by the pool at our motel. We'd only been in town a week; just enough time to get the bookings arranged, get our schedule organized. It was always a great time of year: the beginning of the summer season, before the real work began. We had time to take it easy, to get the last of the lingering winter cold out of our bones. At least, that's what I told myself, though even then I must have suspected.

"Hey," I said, jumping up. "Here's something I've been working on. It uses the Langdon Change, but from underneath. You'd have to have eyes in your feet to spot this one."

I shuffled and cut, spread the cards. He pulled one, glanced at it. I cut the cards again, held out the bottom half. He was moving very slowly, taking deep breaths, like a deep sea diver working against all that pressure. And I started to speed up, talking faster and faster as if I could somehow compensate for him.

"Okay. Back it goes. That little card back into the center. Disappearing forever. Hope you remember it. Then we do a little shuffle, a little cut. A little shuffle."

"You're talking too much," Rudy said quietly. "Don't talk. Just do it. They'll figure out what you're doing." But he was moving so slowly, talking so slowly. My fingers felt light and nimble, my hands felt fast; how could he be slowing down? The thought was like a sliver in my chest.

I straightened the deck, palming the top card. "Now, I'll take a handkerchief, any handkerchief."

"Less talk. Smoother," said Rudy.

"This one, for instance." I drew the bandanna from my pocket and held it out. "If you'll please check it to make sure there are no rips or holes or secret pockets."

He held it in his hand, but he didn't really look at it. His eyes were focused on some middle distance. He was breathing was the fastest thing about him. Too fast. Much too fast.

"Where are your pills?"

"It's okay."

"Where are they?"

"I've got them."

"Well, take one!"

"It'll pass."

And after a moment, it did. His breathing eased. "See?" he said finally. "It's magic." He licked his lips, but they were the only thing dry about his face. His forehead gleamed with sweat. His face was chalky. He handed back the bandanna. "No rips," he said tiredly. "No secret pockets."

I folded it and, reaching out, blotted his forehead dry. "Why don't you take your pills?"

"They don't always work." He took a sip of water. The color was seeping back into his cheeks. "Besides, their expensive. We don't want to waste them."

"We've got money."

"Not enough to waste. I'm saving for the future."

"This is the future."

But he just smiled. I didn't realize what he meant then; that he was saving for my future. At that point I still thought of the future as ours.

We were booked into the Adelphi Theatre for the first half of June. Every year we tried to start and end the summer there. It was a great old building with a rococo stage and ceilings of carved plaster and ormolu. I loved that theatre. I loved the feel of it. The whole atmosphere gave itself over to our show. For that hour on stage we might have been performing back in the golden nineteenth century, the era of Thurston and Kellar and the Great Hermann. We were one more link in that long chain of marvels and magic, and that theater was our home. At least, it was as close to a home as we had. It was the one place we returned to.

So, I suppose, in retrospect, it was somehow fitting that it happened there. What better place could there be? To stand on a wide stage, before a full house—all our performances were sold out that June—at a theater which, for that hour at least, might have been built for us. I like to think he was pleased, at least with the effect.

We were doing "Rescue From The Burning Building". I suggested trying something else. I suggested leaving it out. It was hard work; I thought he might conserve his strength. But that was the heart of our act, the climax, and you can't ask a showman to leave out the best part.

The cabinet was wheeled out. The smell of naphtha hung like a halo around it. I stepped out from the wings, in the clothes of someone much younger, and Rudy began the story. "We have a young boy with us tonight. A young boy anxious to try his hand at something marvelous. And he discovers the cabinet, a fine place for a boy to hide. Though nothing is certain in the realm of magic."

I stepped in, and he closed the door. I slipped easily into the escape compartment, counting off the rhythm of the trick in my head. His voice came to me, muffled by the aluminum. "Now we cloak the cabinet for secrecy. And now we weave the magic spell." I couldn't hear the gauze veil being draped, but I heard the tiny puff of ignition and the whoosh as the cloth went up, setting the trick ablaze.

I braced myself for the collapse of the cabinet, and waited for the next line: My God. What's happened? But all I heard was silence and the faint breath of the flames. We had rehearsed so often, we had set the rhythm of this trick so seamlessly, that it was a shock to hear the silence. It stood out like a gaping hole in a sheet of fabric. Then, much more softly, in a tone I never want to hear again, "Sweet Jesus. What's happening?"

I hit the emergency release, and felt the cabinet come apart, falling back in that narrow, claustrophobic darkness. I braced myself, and crawled out. Then, from behind the back curtain I peered out. The cabinet lay open and empty. The audience was applauding. Rudy was kneeling on the floor clutching his chest, looking back at me with an expression of such surprise...

I clawed at the curtain, searching frantically for the opening, and finally found it. Rushing over I knelt beside him, my arms around his shoulders. The audience was still applauding. The tape that we used in the trick had slowed or stalled, the timing was all off, but now the voice, recorded long ago, floated out over the audience. "For God's sake, help him! Do something!"

But there was nothing I could do.

"Your pills," I said.

But he didn't hear me. He was struggling for breath. His face was grey. He was clutching me, clutching my arms that were doing so little good circled around him. "Thank God," he gasped. "You made it."

But I didn't know where he thought I'd made it from. I still don't know. What was he thinking? That I'd had to travel a long way to get there, or that maybe I might not have come?

"Somebody call a doctor!" I shouted. And though the audience had finally stopped applauding, they just sat their now, buzzing with confusion and the first hint of worry. A stage hand hurried off to telephone. I just knelt there. I had loosened Rudy's collar. Now I was going through his pockets, patting his coat. "Where are those God damned pills?" But he never carried them on stage. He worried they might get mixed up with the other props and distract him.

"Easy," I said. "Take it easy. The doctor's coming."

"I was afraid I wouldn't be able to get you out," he whispered.

"You did," I said. "I'm out."

"All that fire."

"I'm safe."

"I couldn't have forgiven myself."

"You rescued me."

He was leaning heavily against my chest, in the circle of my arms. His grip relaxed. His eyes closed, as though, knowing I was safe, he could sleep. "Don't leave me, Charles," he murmured.

Charles, he called me. Not Lennox or Harry or kid. I was glad of that.

"I won't," I said. And I didn't.

We had a very small funeral. Me, Paul Sisco, a few others. I found a place for Rudy on a hillside on the outskirts of Saratoga. It had a beautiful view of the center of town, the blocky main street with the high, spiky roof of the Adelphi rising above. Rudy had always looked forward to the summers. He used to say the audiences were better, more reliable, and he loved the theater.

So I took the money, almost all the money he had saved over the years, all the money from a long life on the road, about six thousand dollars, and I rented the Adelphi for a week. I opened it up to anybody, anyone who wanted to come, and every night I performed Rudy's show. I worked through his entire collection of tricks, his whole life laid out cover to cover. And the audiences loved it. Packed audiences, crowded houses, they cheered and applauded. The noise rose like smoke, like canon fire.

But now as I worked my way through his show once again, one last time, I felt my hold on the magic loosening. Or rather, its hold on me. I felt unanchored, as if I'd lost my way. I missed Gracie, I missed Rudy. I looked out over the faces, but in the darkness there was no sign of anyone I knew. I was alone in the harsh light. And the magic, which I had counted on for so many years to hold me up, could no longer bear my weight. The audience laughed. They applauded. Parents and their children, my parents, Gracie's parents. It might have been the whole town there, everybody I had ever known. But I didn't recognize a soul.

I might have been anywhere. I might have been still on the road, without Rudy, now, but playing the same shows, the same small and shabby halls. Alone now, a bus ride away from the next night's performance, and playing to the empty air. And at that moment I stepped into the void that Rudy must have carried with him all those years before we stumbled onto each other. I was back where he had been, and his past was my future, yawning before me. I might never have come home, for all the good it had done. For all my attempts to come full circle, I could have stayed on the road forever. Because a circle doesn't stay a circle, not in this world. It's only a break and a twist away from an open spiral that leaves you endlessly tumbling, repeating your mistakes, your losses.

Grimly I unwound one trick after another, but I kept waiting for something to happen, for the cloak to lift, for the sides to fall away. I just continued: one trick flowing into the next, even as I heard Rudy's voice in the back of my mind: "By the powers at my command, I bid you: flee! Rise up! Escape! I bid you: Vanish into the air!" But his voice seemed too distant, now, too weak. He was too far away to help me.

Then I realized that the magic was actually flowing out of my hands. I was losing it. Every trick I did, I lost. Every card that vanished, vanished forever. Every scarf, every flower, every rabbit that disappeared, was gone beyond my reach. I continued the act, I couldn't stop, but I was losing it. With every movement it was giving itself up to the air. The show unfolded on schedule, like a silk flower in the hand, then it vanished, and there was nothing I could do.

I began the last trick. A deck of cards fanned out, then vanished in flame. A huge silk bouquet appeared in the air, then transformed into a rainbow of streamers. The streamers went into the empty hat, and a white rabbit appeared. The rabbit vanished beneath a cloth, and when I pulled the cloth away there was a flash of flame, a cloud of smoke, and the last of it, the last of it all, vanished with me, leaving only the thinning white cloud, that shivered and shook apart with the applause.

I stepped back onto the stage, bowing and smiling, but hollow as a mask. Kevin stepped forward smoothly from the opposite wing, genially clapping along with the audience. "That was wonderful, Charles. Just wonderful."

I felt disembodied, like the thin afterimage that remains on the retina without any substance of its own. Standing there, in the dying applause, I wondered what I would do, now that all I had been was gone.

"Please give him a big hand, ladies and gentlemen." Kevin gathered up the whole audience in his gesture, managing even now to appropriate all this as his own. There was nothing else for me to do. I turned to leave.

And there was Emily, dressed in a silver leotard and tights, wheeling my childhood—that rough, homemade box—out onto the stage.

Kevin glanced over, startled. "What are you doing?" he whispered.

"I changed my mind," she said.

"Since when?"

She gazed up at him coolly. "Since now."

Kevin was still smiling for the audience, but as he stepped closer his voice sounded hoarse. "I don't think we have time for this."

"We have time."

"I don't think it's such a good idea."

"What I can't understand," said Emily, "is why that ever could have mattered to me."

Kevin glanced back at the waiting crowd. "This really isn't the moment."

"You got your factory, Kevin."

"I got it for us."

"Well, take it and get off the stage," she said. "You're holding up the show."

For a moment it looked as if he might take even this in stride. After an instant's hesitation he started to turn back to the audience.

"Don't bother," said Emily. "We'll introduce ourselves."

He left the stage, but there was no applause this time.

Emily turned to me with a frail smile, thin and fragile, a smile that had been through a lot—but still...

"I can't do this," I whispered.

"Yes, you can."

"I've lost it. It's all gone."

"It's not gone."

"It's just leaking away."

I don't know how she could have understood what I meant, but she did. She smiled and stepped up to me. "It'll come back."

But I couldn't remember what to do. My body felt heavy. My fingers were numb. I stared at her, then helplessly turned to the audience, blank as a slate.

Emily laid her hands on the edge of the cabinet. "Ladies and Gentlemen. An ordinary wooden box." Her voice was clear and strong, a voice you could hold onto. She tilted up the box so they could see the bottom. She rapped it hard with her knuckles. The sound echoed. "Though," she said, "nothing is certain in the realm of magic." Ah, Rudy.

She turned and reached out to me. My hand was shaking. I helped her up onto a step stool then into the box. She stretched out.

I felt like a child again, stumbling through, step by step. I closed the lid and locked it. I released the catch. I felt as if all the years of practice had vanished, as if all the assurance of seven years on the road had evaporated. In its difficulty, the trick felt utterly real to me.

I picked up the saw. I had cut so many things out of my life, but now as I started sawing along the narrow, pre-cut groove, it felt as if some single, jagged wound was closing. I had no patter, no dialogue. The only sound was the rasp of the saw. The audience was quelled into silence.

I thought of the past seven years, of how I'd tried to flee from so much and had run instead right into the arms of all that had been waiting. You can only move forward, that's all you can do. You can take each step and hope it leads to the next. You can reach for the empty hat and hope that the rabbit is there, or a silk scarf, or a broad bouquet of flowers waiting to be found. You can light the fire and say the words, and hope that everything most precious to you slips safely from the flames. But nothing is certain. All the years of practice, all the preparation, don't make it certain. Every trick could go awry. In the end all you have is hope.

I cut through to the bottom of the grooves, and laid the saw aside. Then, hesitating, I took a thin square of plywood and pressed it into the groove. It slipped down smoothly to the bottom of the box and stood there, so clearly impossible that the audience sat stunned. In the utter silence all I heard was the sound of Emily's breathing, soft and sure.

"How do you feel?" I asked.

She smiled. A sad, sure smile. "Never better."

About the author

D. K. Smith is a graduate of Yale and the Iowa Writers' Workshop. He is the author of two additional novels: *Missing Persons,* and *Bunny, a romance.* He teaches Medieval and Renaissance literature at Kansas State University

Lightning Source UK Ltd.
Milton Keynes UK
UKOW04n0437261017

311650UK00001B/1/P